ALSO BY NANCY CLARK

The Hills at Home

A Way from Home

JULY

AND

AUGUST

JULY AND AUGUST

Nancy Clark

PANTHEON BOOKS, NEW YORK

This is a work of fiction. Names, characters, places, and incidents either are the product of the author's imagination or are used fictitiously. Any resemblance to actual persons, living or dead, events, or locales is entirely coincidental.

Grateful acknowledgment is made to Harvard University Press and the Trustees of Amherst College for permission to reprint "A soft sea washed around the house" and excerpts from "After a hundred years" from *The Collected Poems of Emily Dickinson,* edited by Thomas H. Johnson, copyright © 1951, 1955, 1979, 1983 by the President and Fellows of Harvard College (The Belknap Press of Harvard University Press, Cambridge, Massachusetts). Reprinted by permission of Harvard University Press and the Trustees of Amherst College.

Library of Congress Cataloging-in-Publication Data
Clark, Nancy, [1952–]
July and August / Nancy Clark.
p. cm.
ISBN 978-0-375-42329-1
1. WASPs (Persons)—Fiction. 2. Family reunions—Fiction.
3. Family—Fiction. 4. Intergenerational relations—Fiction.
5. New England—Fiction. 6. Domestic fiction. I. Title.
PS3603.L368J86 2008 813'.6—dc22 2007036896

www.pantheonbooks.com

Printed in the United States of America
First Edition
2 4 6 8 9 7 5 3 1

FOR TOM AND SARAH

A soft Sea washed around the House
A Sea of Summer Air
And rose and fell the magic Planks
That sailed without a care—
For Captain was the Butterfly
For Helmsman was the Bee
And an entire universe
For the delighted crew.

EMILY DICKINSON

CHARACTERS

LILY HILL—An elderly maiden aunt whose expansive home in Towne, Massachusetts is a magnet for assorted family members

HARVEY HILL—Lily's tough-nut brother, a retired gentleman

PENNY NICHOLLS HILL—A lively lady and Harvey's fourth wife

ALDEN LOWE—Lily and Harvey's nephew, a gentleman in retirement

BECKY LOWE HAPPENING—Alden's former wife, who has remarried and is living in Libya with the disgraced American diplomat, William Happening

GLOVER LOWE—Alden and Becky's oldest son, an Army officer

BROOKS AND ROLLINS LOWE—Alden and Becky's younger sons, who are twenty-something high-tech moguls

JULIE LOWE—The younger sister, formerly known as Little Becky, who shed that confining name and now lives in London

GINGER LOWE TUCKERMAN—Alden's sister, who lives in Kansas with her husband, Louis

BETSY TUCKERMAN HAPPENING—Ginger and Louis's daughter, who lives in California

ANDY HAPPENING—Betsy's husband, a university professor and William's nephew

SALLY HAPPENING—Betsy and Andy's little girl

HANNAH MAY—A very fine cook and owner of Hannah's—In A Hurry?, a line of frozen foods

DAVID MAY—Her son

JASON SCHMITT AND MATT CAVALIERI—Friends of David May

GINEVRA PLATT-WILLEY—A young woman who is looking after her parents' house for the summer

PETAL—A fashion model and a particular friend of Rollins

TARARA—A fashion model who doesn't stick around

CAM SAMRIN—The youngest daughter of a Cambodian immigrant family

HUN AND MUNG SAMRIN—Cam's parents, who own and operate the Casa di Napoli, a restaurant

OM AND TRU SAMRIN—Cam's older sisters

THANH SAMRIN—Cam's older brother

MR. DESOUZA—Lily's partner in her farming enterprise

DEAN CHURCHARD AND CECILIA RUIZ—Representatives of The Merit Group

TINA—The Marry-Me-Nomar Girl

CALLIOPE KARIOTIS—A young wife and mother, and a friend of the family

HARRIS DESMARIS—A lawyer

ANNA WEBSTER, ROSALIE CHUBB, MACK MACNALLY—Residents of Towne's Senior Village

DORIS—The Towne Taxi driver

THE REV. PENWORTHY—Rector of All Saints'

BABE PALMER—An unpleasant presence in Towne

NICHOLAS DAVENANT—The man Julie says she is going to marry

CONTENTS

JULY
AND
AUGUST

ONE *The Third*

LILY KNELT AMIDST THE strawberry vines reaching for the brightest fruit among the stiff crowns of leaves. The ripe ones wanted to be picked; their stems released from the runners and they subsided into her palm, several accumulating there coolly ajuggle before she dropped them into the waiting flat which she was shoving and dragging along as she moved down the lane of bushes (for there came the moment when she reached among the foliage and reached at nothing and so had to move on from the previously prime spot she had just made a nest of). Fixing on a promising new spot speckled with berries like a mother lode of rubies in the rock, she settled into the dusty dirt with a henlike declination, her shoulders rounded above a soft slump of torso and limbs, her head lowered and questing forward, nose first, into the foliage as she plucked. Her left hand operated independently of the right, and she was doubly productive. Sometimes a berry resisted as her fingers closed round its shoulders, and she tugged at it to no avail. Not yet, Lily would think, her easy rhythm broken, and she would pause to consider just how something knew when it was ready to be taken and how it knew, just as well, when it was not.

She swiped her brow, conveying the berries' rose-and-honey scent that infused the skin of her hands nearer to her nose, and overwhelmed as if by a fermented draught of summer, she toppled over, sitting down hard on her bottom. She recovered herself and looked up and about with the immediate desire of having been left unobserved. Her position was not a dignified one; then again, she felt more comfortable resting on her haunches in the soft dirt than braced upon her knees with all her weight reliant on her toes, which were no longer quite so reliable as they'd once been.

An entire field of strawberry bushes swelled to surround her, row upon row swerving with the contours of the land. At present, there was no moderating breeze, no intervening frill of clouds, and the full strength of the midmorning sun had sapped any early freshness from the air. The edge of the woods that bounded the field was melting away, half-obliterated by a haze of overheated ozone. The particulars of branches and trunks, so various in their shades and shapes, looked still-wet, as if the scene was still flowing from the brush of a watercolorist who lingered and retouched and would not be hurried along that sultry morning.

Lily turned toward her house as if to make certain that it, too, was not dissolving beneath the scorching day. The peaks and chimneys of the roofline were just visible from her present position, and she peered harder as if trying to determine whether her visiting niece, Ginger, was as yet awake and stirring within. Resolving to call her (having been debating when best to call and not being able to decide between catching her too soon or too late—for she felt there was no chance of getting Ginger at a good moment), Lily snapped open her cell phone and tapped a button.

"Ginger? It's ten o'clock. I want to remind you; it's time for your medicine." Lily listened. "You've taken it all?" Lily listened. "I'm delighted if you say you're feeling better, but don't overdo it because you'll want to be in good form this evening when Betsy and Sally get here. And tomorrow too, when the rest of them will be there at Alden's, and then there'll be the parade, and after the parade, remember, we have a picnic." Lily listened to Ginger's reassurances about her fitness to withstand the demands of the following day. Indeed, Ginger now wanted to know whether it was not too late to enter a float in the parade. She had just been lying in bed thinking of how amusing it would be to make a giant gypsy moth caterpillar out of a long tube of duct-taped black plastic garbage bags supported by a dozen pair of black-tights-covered legs (everyone in the family would get to take part in this). She would give the creature its characteristic bristle by securing scrub brushes along the spine and attach big yellow eyes made from balls of yarn (she had spotted skeins of just the right shade in Lily's knitting bag). Harvey, whom she could not quite picture being coaxed into wearing a pair of tights and consenting to huddle beneath a sheath of garbage bags, would walk in front of the caterpillar waving a big green leafy branch beneath its nose, which would be cleverly fashioned out of a paper towel tube, like a snout. Ginger was certain they would win some sort of prize if only all of this could be organized at the last minute.

"They've never given out parade prizes," Lily told Ginger. One could only imagine the hurt feelings.

"Perhaps we shall inspire them to create one," Ginger said.

Lily turned toward the woods, noting, above the shimmer of tree tops, the thrusting pinnacle of the very cell tower which was making this conversation with her niece possible. Lily wasn't quite sure how that business all worked, but she understood satellites were involved, and even as Ginger lay upon her bed just a few hundred feet away from the strawberry patch, the words passing between them were being sent bouncing off into the deepest reaches of outer space only to come bounding back again, or something like that. Last winter, when the argument had taken place over the optimum siting of a new cell tower in Towne (which subsequently had been erected in Lily's own High Field), opponents had spoken disparagingly of raising another Babel Tower, but in Lily's opinion, the structure radiated pure intelligibility. Since its appearance, at last bringing reliable cell service to the area, she had fallen into the habit of calling herself when she was out and about during these long summer days to leave messages and reminders on her own answering machine; *Lily, it's Lily* (she called herself Lily). *Order more wooden pint boxes; Lily, pick up the dry cleaning or they'll start charging you storage; Lily, ask Mr. DeSouza what he thinks of Silver Queen corn instead of Platinum Lady. I myself am conflicted in this matter.* Lily had discovered that she very much approved of any and all of these new methods of keeping in touch, whenever, with whomever, wherever, whether or not they were even there, and in recent years, almost everyone she cared about had been very much elsewhere. Words could be planted on a spool of tape or left embedded in pixels upon a screen in a way which struck Lily as being almost organic; they would sprout into speech or text in due time. Well, here she belabored the point but she knew what she meant in terms she could appreciate, and furthermore, the much-derided cell tower (which was going to be such an eyesore, its opponents charged) made her think of the Eiffel Tower; the local edifice seemed quite as intricately assembled and loftily ascendant as the original, if lacking a certain panache. But then again, the Eiffel Tower only served to let one know one's whereabouts in a tourist's Paris; if one kept that exclaiming silhouette always in sight above the rooftops, one could get back to one's hotel without having to ask a native (for even if successful at framing the question, one found oneself at a further loss after attempting to act upon the ungrasped answer). The High Field Tower performed multiple marvels of function and usefulness, and not only that, the communications company had to compensate Lily for the use of her land. Another check had arrived in the mail just the other day. She had torn open the envelope bearing GlobaLink's imprint, frowning with annoyance because she had sent them last month's phone bill, only to discover, written below a perforated line, Pay to the Order of Lily Hill. She and Ginger had had a conversation about whether there was any nicer surprise than that of money arriving out of the blue, and aside from the unexpected appearance of a loved one upon the doorstep, they gave a monetary windfall second place, although depending upon the particular loved one who had resurfaced, in certain instances, Ginger said she would rather have the cash.

"Besides, they don't allow last-minute parade entries," Lily told Ginger now. "You had to have applied and submitted your idea to the design committee, so don't run around collecting scrub brushes and balls of yarn and pairs of black tights. Besides, it's too hot for you to be exerting yourself. Find a shady spot on the terrace and just sit out there and read your library book." This suggestion was met without protest, and Lily rang off, reassured, or as reassured as one could ever be with Ginger, who would do as she pleased. Ginger had always done as she pleased.

Lily resumed her strawberry picking. She propped herself on her knees and toes and readdressed the thicket before her, methodically making her way down the long row, filling one flat and a second and a third, which she left where they were, too heavy and mounded with berries to be lifted by her; she could haul them along just so far and no farther before abandoning them below the tangle of vines. She snapped open her cell phone and tapped a button.

"Thanh? I'm finished up here. I need you to swing by with the tractor. What are Om and Tru up to? They're in the barn? Well, in that case, who's looking after the farm stand? Who? Oh. Oh dear. Whose idea was that? Yes, well I'm sure she wanted to. I'm sure she said she could manage. I'm sure it was her idea. I'm just not sure it was a very good idea."

THE FARM STAND was known to all as the Farm Stand. Lily had tried to come up with a better name but she had not succeeded, Vegetable Kingdom being the sort of thing she and her immediate circle had thought of; also Salad Days, Lettuce Berry U, and Faith in a Seed, which last suggestion her brother Harvey had said sounded just plain odd, but he was getting back at Lily for snorting at his Lettuce-Berry idea, which he had liked well enough to filch from his wife's list of possibilities, although Penny had only been amusing herself at Lily's expense—for Penny admitted that she had initially felt rather blindsided when Lily suddenly upped and announced her ambitious plans to start a new business. Penny would have said that she was supposed to be the lively and enterprising old lady in the family, whereas Lily had always been the reliable and constant presence by whom one set one's watch and moderated one's opinions and calculated one's contributions. Penny had more seriously proposed The Busy Bee as a name, saying she would be confident of any commercial establishment that chose to call itself that, and certainly bees were agricultural. Nothing could flourish in nature without the timely interference of a busy bee, although she'd read somewhere that *busy* was a corruption of *buzzy*, and wasn't it funny how words and the way we speak them could change even in the course of one's own lifetime; take a word like special, which used to signify something other than its current use. Nowadays, upon being notified something or someone was going to be special, one knew to brace oneself to be especially kind and patient and uncritical. Harvey would have to be reminded beforehand to be nice and again be spoken to about it, once they got there.

In the end, the length of barn board set aside to serve as the sign, and the size of the letter cutouts included in the commercial-grade stencil kit she had purchased, had decided matters for Lily. There was not even space for a *The* (The Farm Stand). However, she had regarded the venture as more of an *a* (a farm stand), for she had not been convinced that any of this was going to amount to anything anyway, and then, even when things had taken off, she continued to hold to that first modest line. She was, at the time, approaching her seventy-fifth year and had not felt the need to prove anything to anyone, although there were those who seemed set upon viewing her as an elderly prodigy. People did not mean to but nevertheless they managed to come across as being quite condescending, Lily thought. They had exclaimed over her as if she had just learned to tie her shoes and spell her name—or perhaps they had exclaimed because she could still reach down to tie her shoes and was, as yet, deemed capable of affixing her signature to binding legal documents. For she was now an "Inc." Harris Desmaris, her lawyer, seemed to believe that this Inc. status would stand between Lily and the rest of the world should she ever be sued, and he had described circumstances in which others in her position had lost everything. A person who slipped on a pea pod (say) could end up owning her house. Lily might once have objected that anyone who had a problem remaining upright in the vicinity of a fallen pea pod would find all the steep staircases and uneven floorboards in her house even more troublesome, but early on in the process of setting herself up in business, she had learned not to protest that human beings, when massed into that entity known as the general public, could possibly be so stupid or grasping or wicked as the law anticipated. Harris, whose business this was, knew better than Lily—or, perhaps in this matter, he could be said to have known worse.

The stand, located down on the River Road at the end of Lily's long driveway, was built of rough boards with an original gravel floor long since trampled away to hard-pack dirt eight years on, by this the 1999 season, which had commenced over the Memorial Day weekend, when early peas and bouquets of lilac were just ready for sale. A pair of big maples loomed over the roof, shading the shingles that had weathered silver and mossy and porous in places. The outside front-corner post of the structure bore splintery dents at rear-bumper height; parking could be a problem on the weekends, in part because everyone drove around Towne in those big, oblivious vans and Jeeps. There was a notice saying Please Do Not Block the Driveway, which was often ignored or reasoned away *(We'll only be a minute)*. This would make Harvey roar, should he be denied free passage driving in or out (for Lily had agreed to let them share her driveway when he and Penny, just lately wed nine years earlier, had built their new house up on the ridge behind her house). Whether or not he was in a hurry to get someplace, Harvey didn't think he needed to assess the urgency of his errands and appointments while some bounder lingered over a purchase. But the more considerate people stopped on the road when the parking lot was full and they walked the extra distance alongside the river, which ran darkly and fluently through this stretch of country, overhung by a line of moody hemlocks and larches.

The front of the stand was comprised of shutters that lifted up and were secured by hook-and-eye latches. The produce was arranged, or heaped in the case of peas and shell beans, on a single level of broad shelving set at the height of a tall person's waist. This shelf sloped forward in an offering manner, although the incline could also be treacherous. Rounded produce, the tomatoes and apples and acorn squashes, would tumble and roll when a balance was disturbed, and their further tumble was not necessarily contained by an edging lip of ogee molding. "That always happens," Lily would say, when this happened. There was space beneath the shelving for bushel baskets and crates that held more of whatever was presented above. Often, customers rooted through these reserve baskets and crates, motivated by some personal maggot of human nature that Lily did not fully understand. How had they come to believe something fresher and riper was being deliberately kept from them? She found their suspicions aggravating, and sad as well, although on the whole, she had to say she found these people more aggravating than sad.

Everything was clearly labeled as to specimen and price per pound or unit, written with a black marking pen on the backs of cedar roof shingles of which Lily possessed the lesser, and lessening, part of a bale, up in the barn. The shingles were affixed to the walls with banged-in nails. A claw hammer and the bag of nails were kept handy at the counter for this and other purposes; bits and pieces of the rough stand structure sometimes sprang loose and needed to be pounded back into place.

Lily had learned, after a while, to charge 20 percent more than they were asking for the same item in the Stop and Shop flier which arrived in her mailbox so conveniently for research purposes, week after week. She reckoned Stop and Shop knew better than she what things ought to cost and she figured what she sold must be that much fresher and better than anything they stocked. There was nothing at the supermarket comparable to her heirloom tomatoes, however, and she marked them as high as she liked and she could not meet the demand. A tomato orange flag was flown to indicate when there were Brandywines available, or German Johnsons, although not everyone had been clued in on what the orange flag signified. Harvey said the IRA used to communicate with its members in a similar manner, signs and symbols hidden in plain sight, although an orange flag would not have been used by them, of course, unless the Sinn Fein were being exceptionally wily, which he wouldn't have put past them.

After a few years, a new lift-top freezer unit took its place alongside the farm stand counter. This refrigerated unit was stocked with a line of fresh-frozen entrées locally produced but on the way to becoming a nationally known brand. Hannah May, herself the Hannah of Hannah's—In A Hurry? liked to try out new ideas on a small sampling of the general public, and everybody enjoyed being her guinea pigs, although certain never-to-be-repeated experiments were yearned after by those who had developed a taste for a dish too intricately composed ever to be assembled on the production line. Some customers eschewed these prototypes altogether, having concluded that it was better never to have loved them at all.

Shoppers picked up flat woven baskets with drop-away birch handles stacked availably by the door. Lily thought they were impractical; plastic baskets could be rinsed with a hose and would last forever, but the rickety wicker was more charming, and Penny, of all people, had said these quaint little touches added up. She'd been the one behind the pair of big stone urns filled with red geraniums set down on either side of the door. The geraniums flourished there despite having cigarettes stubbed out in their dirt and the dregs of Coca-Cola cans shaken over them (which confirmed what Lily had always suspected—that geraniums were very common plants). Penny had also said that Lily should braid the beet greens and tie up bundles of radishes with raffia and scrub the carrots with a rough brush to brighten up their color. But leave a little dirt on the potatoes, Penny said; people expected their potatoes to be earthy.

Customers lingered and customers hurried over their selections.

They scooped trustingly or they inspected with sniffs and the pressure of thumbs against vegetable flesh. They thumped and listened for known tones of interior ripeness. Every order piled in its wicker basket might have been a still life study worked in shades of green and red and yellow and purple and in shapes of spheres and cones and bulbs. This was a common observation and one which at present was being made by Calliope Kariotis as she picked up strawberries and peas for the Fourth of July, and a package of one of Hannah's latest inspiration, which she meant to serve as an easy dinner that night, on the eve of the holiday.

Cam Samrin presided at the counter. She set aside Calliope's two quarts of strawberries and then she stood upon the straight-backed chair on which she'd been sitting and keeping watch on her sole customer over the top of an upheld book. She steadied the hanging scales and dumped the peas from the basket into the scoop. Her eyes and Calliope's eyes watched the trembling arrow leap, as if alarmed, and scuttle back and forth in a panic of indecision before settling on a number etched into the dial. Cam, who had supplied herself with a flimsy plastic bag recycled from the Stop and Shop before she climbed onto the chair, tilted the weighed order into the bag. She knew all the prices by heart and could do sums in her head. She stepped down from the chair and wrote $32.12 on the ledger page where the record of the day's sales was accumulating and she shifted the ledger book so Calliope could see for herself the amount that was due.

"What grade are you in, Cam?" Calliope wondered, not unimpressed by the child's mental dexterity. She herself had been expecting to pay "around" $30.

Cam displayed two fingers.

"You're entering the second grade in the fall?" Calliope concluded.

Cam nodded.

"Mike is going into fourth grade, and Lindy will be starting first," Calliope informed Cam of her own children's standing. "I'm just on my way to pick them up at swimming lessons."

Which information was of no use or interest to Cam, a big boy and a big baby splashing about in the bathtub-warm water of the Towne Pond staying between the yellow safety lines and obeying the shriek of the lifeguard's arbitrary whistle. Cam swam in the river like an otter. She jumped in and caught the current and floated downstream until she bumped into an abutment of the old railroad bridge and then she hauled herself out and walked back along the road, wringing out the tail of her shirt and shaking her hair dry. The only annoying thing was forgetting where she'd left her shoes along the embankment, necessarily hidden from view. She'd been told a hundred times never to swim alone in the river, which she reckoned she had done successfully a hundred times, but the grown-ups got to say no and she got to swim, and everyone would remain satisfied unless she drowned. Then there'd be big trouble. Cam expelled a long sigh and because she'd been thinking so hard about being in the water, she was surprised that a column of swirling bubbles didn't erupt from her lips.

"Where is Miss Hill today?" Calliope asked.

With the point of a finger, Cam directed Calliope through the woods and around the house and up past the herb garden and into the strawberry patch, if one knew the lay of the land hereabouts, as Calliope did.

"So you're in charge," Calliope said.

This observation was answered with a shrug, accompanied by a general glance of proud possession.

"How are your parents? Good? The business is going good for them? They look busy, whenever I drive by. I always look, of course," Calliope said.

Cam nodded.

It occurred to Calliope that she ought not to have let Cam off the hook by supplying her with the query "good?" at which she might merely nod. Calliope always felt challenged to draw the child into speech. The child resented the customers who came and carried off all the pretty vegetables. Certain careful pyramid constructions of eggplants would be disturbed, and a wonderful spiraling string bean would be carried off, ultimately to be eaten. Once, Calliope and Lily had had a conversation about Cam and what Lily supposed to be the case with her. Lily had had to put a stop to the setting aside of every vegetable that resembled some forest creature or seemed to bear the face of a well-known person. All potatoes looked like the late Mrs. Nina Khrushchev one way or another, in Lily's opinion, but she had to ask herself whether there wasn't some inherently Buddhist impulse behind Cam's actions. Cam's parents, Hun and Mung Samrin, kept a cheerful shrine, shiny with bits of foil and beads and flowers, behind the cash register at their restaurant, the Casa di Napoli, which they owned and operated now, having bought his family's business from Calliope's husband, George, a few years earlier when George took a good job at Raytheon, with more reasonable hours, benefits, and a pension plan.

Calliope opened her purse and extracted a twenty-dollar bill and a ten and two ones from her wallet. She delved into the change compartment, which was empty but for two flat nickels.

"Tchah," she said.

Cam slid a fingertip across the countertop and nudged a china saucer full of pennies. She tapped a folded-over card standing beside the saucer which read, If You Haven't Any, Take a Penny. If You Have Too Many, Leave a Penny.

"Thank you. I'll take two cents this time," Calliope said.

Cam waved away her thanks, rather grandly. The penny saucer had been her doing and was proving successful beyond her expectations. More people tossed in their spare cent pieces, and unwanted nickels and dimes as well, than took them away, which was an excellent and unanticipated development. She opened the cash box and tucked the ten- and twenty-dollar bills away in the larger denomination envelope hidden beneath the till. She clattered the nickels and the pennies into their compartments and set about exchanging the dull pennies in the saucer for the bright pennies in the cash box as Calliope took her leave, toting a bag in either hand, her bundles evenly packed so she would not list to one side or the other, which was a particular courtesy of Cam's. She did not like to see the customers limp away as if they were the worse for wear from having visited the farm stand.

But Cam's will was about to be tried, Calliope noted. Babe Palmer had just turned into the farm stand lot, pulling up unnecessarily close beside Calliope's van as if to let her know that Calliope had not parked correctly (nosing in toward the stand slantwise instead of heading straight in—was that the officially preferred angle or Babe's own insisted-upon method?). Calliope would have to climb into her van through the passenger-side door and ease herself over the stick shift, splitting the seams of her shorts if she wasn't careful.

"Have you left me any peas?" Babe asked, her glance zeroing in on Calliope's laden plastic bags. Babe held a list in her fist which she shook in demonstration, the list and the fist.

"Oh yes, there is plenty," Calliope said, wishing then, of course, that she had been greedier. She had, however, wrenched the very last package of Hannah's Bucatini all'Amatriciana from the freezer ice, so at least she had that satisfaction.

"Oh good Lord above," Babe sighed, spying Cam inside behind the counter. "Must I deal with that strange little one? Where's Lily in all this?"

Calliope could almost hear Babe thinking a dismissive, *Foreigners*, but Babe caught herself just in time from uttering the word aloud, remembering who she was talking to. Calliope, who had come from Greece to marry George a dozen years earlier (and hadn't looked back since, as she was fond of saying), quelled a wish to begin acting Mediterranean over Babe's inconsiderate parking. A shouted denunciation, a stamping foot, torn and rent garments—would that sufficiently rattle Babe?

"Miss Hill is up in the strawberries, picking more," Calliope said.

"Well then," Babe said. She supposed there was nothing wrong with that. Then again, a further thought struck her. She advanced and addressed Cam. "What about all these *old* strawberries you have out? Are they still good? When did you pick *these*? But why am I asking *you* anything?" She ought to have called the house first, before venturing out, to ascertain Lily's picking schedule. But what if Ginger answered the phone? Babe had no wish to engage in casual chitchat with Ginger, for one knew now, less than ever, quite what to say to Ginger.

Cam moved several water-filled jars containing cosmos and coreopsis bouquets across the countertop to make a frondy and morassy screen from behind which she could keep a weather eye on Mrs. Palmer, who was a known rearranger of the contents of pint boxes, which was very much against the rules. (Please Do Not Repack the Boxes, Or We'll Feed You to the Foxes—that was Mr. Harvey's poem, which he had written on a shingle and posted above the strawberries.) Every pint box had been very fairly filled, and the berries on the bottom were as beautiful as the berries on the top. The pity was that all strawberries could not be on top, Cam had once said to Lily, who pointed out that that would only be possible if they used very wide and flat boxes, and then they would have to build a larger farm stand to contain them, which she was not about to do. Cam had been so disappointed to learn that. Among her papers back home in the apartment above her family's restaurant was a drawing of her future vision for the farm stand. The building would sprawl along the River Road all the way to the railroad bridge, gleaming with plate glass windows and alive with automatic doors and a revolving neon sign on the roof which would proclaim The Farm Stand Starring Auntie Lily and Cam Samrin! There would be spaces for one thousand cars in the black-top parking lot. So far, Cam had ruled in the lines to indicate half that number, and very elegantly angled lines they were.

AROUND MIDDAY, Lily rode down the driveway steering a motorized golf cart between the ruts and hauling a trailer load of strawberries. She left a wake of jounced-off berries that the birds had already found, and they fluttered and flurried along behind her. The barn (and house) cat had wedged itself onto Lily's lap, hitching a ride down to the riverside, where, with any luck, there would be something drowned and dead to roll in. Several customers approached the golf cart, alerted by the drone of the electric engine, and they reached for the freshest strawberries before Lily pulled to a complete stop. Cam, in full scowl, emerged from the stand to herd them off, but Lily shook her head as their *Aren't people awful?* look passed between them, which gratified Cam, who only cared what Lily thought and liked to know they were thinking the same thing. No one attempted to make a pet of Agnes, as the cat was called. Agnes rose from Lily's lap and leaped off with a painful tensing of her claws. Everyone stepped out of the cat's way, wondering whether the animal had lost the tip of her ragged ear to violence or to disease. Cam returned to the stand to deal with a woman who was rummaging through a big basket of basil set aside to wait for one of Hannah's staff to come pick it up. Lily entered and ran her eye down the ledger page to assess what sort of morning they had had.

"Go to the house now, Cam," she said. "Your lunch is on the table." Lily had just stopped by the kitchen where Cam's elder sisters, Tru and Om, and brother, Thanh, were sitting at the table eating ham sandwiches and potato chips and vinegar cucumbers, on a break from their work in the fields. "But remember to be very quiet," Lily warned Cam. "Auntie Ginger is resting, and we mustn't disturb her. Afterward, go see Auntie Penny. She called me to say she needs you up at her house to help her with something."

That something was soap-opera watching, Lily suspected. She had overheard Penny and Cam discussing individuals and situations that could not possibly exist here in Towne, however much Towne had changed in recent years. Lily was sure she would have heard had the crown prince of Richtenstein moved into a mysterious mansion on the outskirts of Towne, especially since the only large and remote local dwelling to fit that description would be her own house, and the last time Lily had looked she was certainly minus one prince.

Cam collected her belongings; her knapsack, her favorite book of the moment, *The Lion, the Witch and the Wardrobe,* and a fat, fused-double strawberry, which was to be a surprise for Auntie Penny, or possibly for Auntie Ginger, whom Cam understood to be in need of cheering up. If only there had been two of the fused-double strawberries, but, after all, they were not that rare, and most likely there would be another one found tomorrow to give to the Auntie who was to go without today. Off Cam ran.

As she weighed peas on the scale, giving the scoop a shake to settle the pods, which seemed to weigh up more truly when the air was knocked out of them, Lily noticed how grimy her fingernails were, and her knuckles, as well; gnarled and hard and dirt-stained, they sat like a row of snails across her fingers. Her knees, beneath the hem of her divided skirt, were brown from crouching between the strawberry rows. She had a kneeler mat, but the kneeler mat got just as dirty as the dirt. In the evenings, after her bath water emptied from the tub, there would be a drift of silt left behind, accumulated around the drain hole, and by that evidence Lily had never felt so clean as she did on these summer evenings after her bath and before bed, sitting on the terrace reviewing the events of the day just gone and making plans for the one to come.

So she did not mind the scratch of grit beneath her fingertips or even the rather furlike sensation of mud and vegetation that had settled inside her sneakers between the canvas and her Peds. She had never felt so well occupied as she did, these days. An idea came to her that her love of gardening was at long last reciprocated, and she ought to have guessed that love would be like this, its embrace all-enveloping and really quite messy.

She tilted the peas into a plastic bag recycled from the local Market Basket and she cinched the handles into a loose knot and then she called up to the barn on her cell phone to ask Thanh to come down to help out. The Saturday-afternoon rush was about to begin. The van from Senior Village had just pulled up by the door to discharge its half-dozen passengers, and a side hatch had swung open as a hydraulic lift lowered one and then another wheelchair to the ground.

"When are you going to put in handicapped parking? When are you going to get a handicapped ramp? You're in violation of the Americans with Disabilities Act, you know," Rosalie Chubb informed Lily. Rosalie worried her chair, rolling forward and backward, stubbing the wheels against the threshold of the farm stand.

"That's only the slightest sill. Surely someone can hump you over," Lily said.

"Hump me over?" Rosalie objected to that. Talk of humping wasn't very nice. She was surprised at Lily.

"Mack," Lily said. "Would you please *bump* Rosalie over the sill?"

"With pleasure," Mack MacNally said, tipping his tartan cap and then swiftly replacing it, remembering the post-biopsy bandage plastered over his bald spot.

"And don't forget my handicapped discount," Rosalie called over her shoulder.

"Five percent," Lily promised. Mack grinned. The senior discount was ten percent.

Anna Webster occupied the other wheelchair, although she was only temporarily disabled (Rosalie suffered from some sort of progressive geriatric scoliosis). Anna had fallen from a ladder while dusting the upper architrave of a door frame and broken her foot and ankle and knee and wrist and elbow and a rib but not (she was very lucky, everyone said) her hip.

"Decrepitude is not good for one's character," Anna confided to Lily as they shook their heads over Rosalie. "I snapped at my home help this morning when she pushed me into a wall. I said to her, I said, 'Marietta, that wall has always been there, hasn't it?' And then she looked at me oddly. I think she's been told to monitor my mental state."

"She sounds like she's the one who needs monitoring," Lily said.

"Oh, but it can't be much fun for her. She's young. I've noticed the aides from the hospice service are much better trained and very respectful, but you have to be in a really bad way to qualify for one of them, who're tactful at deathbeds. So I suppose it's really quite a good sign if your home help is surly and unhelpful and propels you into walls," Anna said.

"Huh," said Lily, who had no wish to argue Anna out of her accommodating mental arrangements. It would be neither useful nor kind. "Thanh, please look after Mrs. Webster," she said, and behind Anna's back, she opened and closed her hand four times, her five earth-streaked fingers splayed—20 percent discount for Mrs. Webster. Then she took off to shoo Rosalie away from the set-aside order of herbs waiting for the runner from Hannah's to fetch them, Rosalie having become one of those people who believed something fresher and riper was being kept from her, just out of reach.

OF COURSE LILY HAD HELP. That first spring eight years earlier when she requested a hundred pounds of silver white corn seed, consulting a slip of paper on which she had worked out all the numbers twice, Barry, the dean of the Co-Op clerks, had asked her just what she thought she was doing. Lily, who had walked into the Co-Op very determined, had at once become less certain. Her figures, which rang so true at the kitchen table, sounded a different note in the cold and cavernous warehouse where the seeds and grain were stored in bulk to be shoveled from bins into rough-edged burlap bags. One of the boys would heft the filled sacks into the back of her car (for Lily also required quantities of pea and bean and pumpkin seeds), but she had realized that she would not be able to lift them out on her own once she got home and she was sure it would not be good for the tires to drive around Towne with several hundred shifting pounds of agricultural supplies sprawled in her trunk until the ground thawed (this being early in March but she'd been keen to get started, or perhaps she'd just hurried out to make her purchases before her nerve failed). Barry, upon being advised of Lily's plans, had thought at once of Bill DeSouza, who had sold his farm over in Essex, just that week passing papers with a group that planned to develop the property into a thirty-six-hole golf course with a clubhouse and restaurant housed in the barn, or a replica of the barn (for the preservation of the barn became less of a certainty after the signing, despite verbal assurances which of course meant nothing). Mr. DeSouza had been reluctant to sell the farm which had been in his family for seventy-five years, and the family before them had held on to the place for a solid century; however, Allora, Mr. DeSouza's wife, said the money was too good to turn down, and now they would have the time and the funds to do some traveling. In the end, though, it was Allora and her sister who went to Spain (and China and Amish country and Peru) while Mr. DeSouza drove his two tractors no farther than Lily's place, where he installed them in her barn with a complement of iron and adamantine attachments; a deep ripper, disc plow, rotary tiller, dual-axle trailer, lift disc, and a toothy cultimulcher, which Harvey, hanging about on moving day to offer free advice and issue fair warnings, promptly dubbed the *multiculcher*. Ever after Lily herself could not not call it that even though Mr. DeSouza's forehead creased beneath the visor of his John Deere cap whenever she did so.

She and Mr. DeSouza formed a partnership in which Lily assumed the more equal part; he possessed the greater knowledge and muscle, but she had held on to her land. Mr. DeSouza came and went from his condominium at the over-fifty-five community a few miles distant in Newbury, which Allora had had her heart set on (everyone aspired to get into that place; you'd think it was Harvard, as Penny said). Sometimes Mr. DeSouza showed up with a crew, his former workers rounded up from their known haunts (most of them evidently having landed not on their feet so much as upon a barstool). Sometimes, between times, Mr. DeSouza showed up on his own to pace the fields, vigilant of the crops at every stage from sprouting to spurting and flowering and fruiting and on through to the swelling and sweetening on the vine or stem or stalk. He maintained an office in a corner of the barn equipped with a desk and a telephone and a file cabinet. Over time, he amassed a collection of articles turned up by his plow—corroded horseshoes and ancient nails and bits of broken, busted iron implements abandoned where they fell until Mr. DeSouza picked them up and arranged them across the top of his file cabinet.

Lily and Mr. DeSouza enjoyed many good chats in the barn. They found they could disagree without rancor and collaborate without ego. Over the years, they had installed a system of irrigation which only they understood; it was a very sweet design, gravity fed by waters that rose from springs deep in the woods which, thus far, had proved to be never failing. The farm stand had gained a certain renown for supplying unusual and challenging hot pepper varieties, and Lily and her partner had been featured in several newspaper and magazine articles: "Hot Enough for You?," "New England Sizzlers," "Unlikely Pair Produces Unlikely Habañeros." These pieces had been clipped and framed and suspended from a wall of the farm stand below a fringe of blue ribbons awarded at area agricultural fairs, some since faded to gray, strung along a beam. There were so many ribbons Lily could not have said which had been awarded for what event, but they attested to a history of achievement and acknowledged excellence.

AT FIVE O'CLOCK, Harvey rolled down the driveway in his big broad Buick. Cam sat fuming in the back. She was too small and slight to ride in the front seat; in the event of an airbag deploying, she would be crushed. Harvey resisted her arguments that he need only drive down the road at one mile per hour and honk his horn at the approach of any other vehicle and then she'd be safe from any accident; Harvey told her he may be old but he wasn't that old. Om and Tru sat on either side of their little sister, preferring the backseat and the proximity of the fuming, flouncing Cam who was all elbows and ire to being obliged to carry on a front-seat conversation with Mr. Harvey. He would make such unanswerable assertions. The summers used to be summerier, he was fond of telling them, which Om and Tru very much doubted; nevertheless, they wondered whether this land had not once, long ago, been a warmer, sunnier place before they ever came here, which was not so long ago. But they seldom thought about the past; they recalled almost nothing about their earliest years in Cambodia beyond a memory of their parents pulling them from their beds one night. They had all run through the dark and, when they stopped running, after many days of darkness, they had clung to one another amidst a chaos of strangers. Then, after a long blank spell of existence in the camps, they had boarded a plane and been met at an airport in America by more strangers (but kinder ones) who gave each girl a baby doll that looked just like themselves and whose tending had turned into a graceful means of teaching the little girls how to live in America. (Show your baby how to hold a knife and fork like *this.* Tell your baby the English word for *jor* is *doggie.*) Thanh had been given a GI Joe and a baseball mitt. At home (the home they had now) their parents still continued to lead them away from the darkness and point them toward a brighter future which would be achievable by means of much polishing (of restaurant cutlery and windowpanes and countertops) and the further enlightenment gained from studying hard at school. That their children worked on a farm like peasants, turning brown skinned and thick soled over the summer, would have displeased the elder Samrins had Miss Hill herself not labored as long and as hard alongside them in the fields, and Lily, they knew, was considered to be a particularly fine lady in the community.

Cam just ignored Mr. Harvey's assertions, as he ignored hers. Besides, today she was busy keeping the cake she and Penny had baked upright on her lap. It was a very fine Fourth of July sheet cake, frosted with white butter cream and adorned with strawberry stripes and blueberry stars, although on the real flag, the stars stood out white against a blue field, but neither Cam nor Penny could quite figure out how to manage to make that happen on a cake. Penny could tint the butter cream blue (Cam receiving a lesson in how green and yellow became blue, with a further demonstration thrown in to show how blue and red combined to create purple), but neither of them could come up with a white fruit, pale green grapes coming closest, but grape flavor didn't go very well with the flavor of cake, and besides, Penny said green stars would bother her. She was pretty sure green stars were Islamic and she had no wish to be controversial. As Om and Tru passed a tube of lipstick back and forth over her head, Cam's finger lifted an edge of the Saran Wrap covering and she scooped up a dot of icing from where no one would miss it. She had laid the stuff on thick in one corner for this very contingency.

Harvey came to a stop beside the farm stand. He lowered his window and announced, "Shanghai Express, chop-chop."

Several customers looked up alertly—were people supposed to shout things like *Shanghai Express* and say *chop-chop*? Harvey waved at them and called out "Hi-ho" on the off chance he was supposed to know those people who were regarding him as if they smelled something funny.

Thanh slid into the front seat and grandly ordered Harvey, "Home, Jeeves, and don't spare the horses." Harvey cracked up as he always did when Thanh said this.

"Will you be all right running the stand by yourself, Auntie Lily?" Om asked, leaning through her own open window as Lily came over to thank them for a good day's work. Cam raised the cake for Lily to see what she had accomplished with her afternoon. Lily expressed her admiration, being a fan of any well-executed Fourth of July flag sheet-cake, and then she passed four envelopes containing four paychecks to Om, the eldest.

"I'm getting ready to close. I'm just waiting down here for my grandniece, Betsy Happening, and her little girl, Sally, whom we're expecting at any time, in case Betsy doesn't remember the way," Lily said. She meant to flag them down should they drive obliviously by.

"Of course Betsy knows the way," Harvey said. Lily could worry the warts off a toad with her useless fretting.

"It's been nine years since she was last here," Lily reminded him—when Ginger had run away from home, dragging her then-teenage daughter, Betsy, with her to spend an entire year at Lily's while she sorted things out, as Ginger would later characterize that time. One need not go into all of that now. Besides, no one's version of the year's events would agree with that of anyone else's, although Lily supposed each individual take would be more revelatory of the truth than any attempt on her part to come to a more general understanding of, and explanation for, her family's late misadventures.

"Nine years? It can't be nine years since Betsy was here. Time certainly runs faster than it ever used to do," Harvey said. He shook his head.

"How can that be?" Thanh asked. "Time is time. It is measured out, and we have all agreed what a minute is, and a day, and a year. So we can know when to show up for work and when to go to school and when to get to the cineplex to see a movie from the very beginning." Then again, Mr. Harvey didn't have to worry about getting himself to work or school at an appointed hour, and he had nothing positive to say about any movie Thanh ever mentioned having enjoyed, maintaining he didn't need to see one of Thanh's chosen movies to know it was no good.

"Take this watch of mine." Harvey tapped his wrist. "It runs a fifty-five-second minute; that's so I always get a head start. That way, I get where I'm going before I get there so I can have a look around first."

Om and Tru stirred. Mr. Harvey's snowy white head and the upturned collar of his acid green polo shirt did seem to crackle and blur a bit from some inner energeticness. Cam laughed and rustled beneath the Saran Wrap, under the cover of her laugh. She daubed up more frosting and let the melting sugar trickle down her tongue as she pondered the problem. She said, "That is seven thousand and two hundred seconds every day, which is fifty thousand and four hundred seconds every week that Mr. Harvey doesn't use up."

Om and Tru exchanged a look over their baby sister's head. She could be a spooky-smart little kid sometimes.

"No, that means I get to keep all those seconds of time extra," Harvey said. "I've been saving them up for the end."

"For the end of what?" Cam wanted to know. "For the end of the summer? What do you need extra time saved up for the end of what?"

Harvey grizzled back at Cam that her question made no sense, and Cam had no will to frame her query more clearly.

BETSY AND SALLY MUST HAVE just passed Harvey on the River Road. They would have waved at one another had either recognized the other's car. Harvey might have spotted the California license plate and leaned on his horn to cause a commotion which would, at the very least, have gratified Cam. Betsy, for her part, encountering the large American-made car bearing down upon her and taking up more than its share of the River Road's pavement, would have descried her elderly uncle but for the ball of late-afternoon sun ablaze across the windshield which made it seem that the car was being driven by an Aztec deity whose hogging of the road no doubt befitted such a being, as Betsy had been prepared to concede at the time. She had just driven cross country and witnessed too many fantastic sights in blurred, blink-eyed passing to be other than calm about this latest and last manifestation. All across America dogs had been driving ten-wheel trucks, and hitchhikers had metamorphosed into fence posts, and forests had opened and then abruptly closed upon scenes of people about to murder one another.

As once-familiar place names began to appear upon the highway signposts, those hometown names ending in the steadfast syllables of *-ford* and *-field* and *-borough* instead of beginning with *Santo* and *Palo* and *El,* which over time she had become used to, Betsy found herself becoming unaccountably heartened. That is, she felt a faster beating and experienced a sensation of fullness beneath her breastbone and she realized then that she was ready to get there after all, for her stated reasons for choosing to drive all that way from California to Massachusetts had been contrived to delay this moment of arrival: having the use of her own car for the summer; taking a detour en route to visit her father, detained in Wichita with work; seizing the opportunity for a brief wedding anniversary reunion with her husband for whom flights and scheduling had worked out to get him from Helena to St. Louis, midweek; giving Sally the chance to see the "real America" before its total Walmartization occurred. But other arrangements had been available: she could have rented a car in Massachusetts; she would be seeing her father in August, when he was coming to join Ginger; Andy could be more easily rendezvoused with on another day, in Boston; and really, was it entirely kind to instill in Sally a love for an American landscape which was, presumably, so soon to vanish? The child expressed a deep affection for tepee-shaped motels and roadside reptile museums and she had longed to stop at every café or hamburger joint that was representationally not what it appeared to be—a windmill or a top hat or a spaceship, all of them flying past the car window (first appearing as such intriguing daubs on the horizon and then growing in immensity and allure only to be beheld in full for a futile flash before they reeled away from her, dwindling into nothingness, much like her hopes that maybe this time they would pause and partake). Betsy had been in too much of a hurry to stop even as she deferred arrival at her destination, as if she was attempting to outrun a pursuer even as she knew she was racing straight into her pursuer's very trap.

She could not recall whether she had vowed never to return to Towne. She thought she might have proclaimed something of the sort with adolescent adamant even though she had met and married Andy there when he had been installed at Lily's house as a graduate student who was writing his dissertation on people like them, so of course Betsy had to say that only good had come of the experience. Nevertheless, she felt that a switch had been pulled and she had been shifted onto another track entirely and while she did not mind where she had ended up, she was very much aware that another path could have been followed just as easily. It was the randomness of the assignment that tugged at her, as if someone had just flipped a coin or forgotten to submit the correct form to some final, deliberative authority.

Sally had borne the journey well enough. She had carried along as much stuff from home as the backseat could contain, books and board games and a cassette player and cassettes, and a bagful of healthy snacks which she had been told must last and were lasting the trip, the husbanding of raisins being more interesting than the eating of them. She had with her, unopened, a beadwork kit, a pot-holder weaving kit, and a Play-Doh modeling clay kit equipped with a lightbulb-powered kiln, deferred amusements for long afternoons in the strange place where (the subject had already arisen) she must remember to play gently and quietly. Included among her stores was a further inventory of indispensable everyday items declared to be her own: a deep-sided Lion King cereal bowl and a soft pillow and a light blanket and a pink parasol, which she raised against the sun as it shone in at her through one car window and then another, for the sun would never let her take her car-naps (although she objected when informed it was car-nap time). To be thwarted in her attainment of the unwished for—Sally, cinched into the backseat, fiercely stared up at the abiding view of the back of Betsy's head, at that same swirl of pale hair caught up and secured with a silvered clasp, the post of her earring spearing through the tiny hole in the ear lobe, the crescent curve of face which presented only a set line of jaw and a triangle tip of nose telling Sally nothing. Her mother seemed as remote as the moon in a withdrawing phase.

Betsy, who exploited all opportunities to educate her daughter, undertook to explain how the sun and the earth worked together. At breakfast in Albuquerque, she had demonstrated the passage of a blueberry earth as it rotated round the fixed position of a grapefruit sun, showing how and why there was night and day and, sometimes, the sun in one's eyes. Afterward, Sally had made sure to grab the blueberry planet and swallow it at a gulp.

This lesson had inspired a series of backseat drawings of the universe. Sally wore her sun yellow crayon down to the nub, and the blue one was rubbed away to just a stub because of all of the surrounding sky that needed to be filled in. The clouds were never very successfully rendered, the white crayon not leaving much of an impression across the waxy spread of darker colors however hard Sally pressed down with the tip of the crayon, which grew hot and soft and almost burned when she tested how hot the wax had become against the skin of her forehead. These pictures had been wafted over the front seat to land in Betsy's lap, like dispatches sent from a far-off land.

"WE ARE TRAVELING EAST because the sun is behind us now," Sally said. "Setting. In the west. Because it is later," she added. She had been drowsing over a *Highlights for Children* magazine, ineffectively trying to solve a maze puzzle (find the lost stupid puppy), but the thunder-rumble of car tires across the treads of an old wooden bridge, trembling against her cheek and inside her ear, had roused her. Recalled to consciousness, she worked an impatient pencil, laying down a thick black line between the en-mazed little dog and the edge of the puzzle page. "Follow *this,*" she instructed the stupid puppy.

"Correct," Betsy said. "We are traveling east."

"North is that way," Sally pronounced. She stretched toward the front seat as far as her tethering seat belt would permit and thrust a directing finger beneath her mother's nose.

"Correct," Betsy said. "But please remove your hand from in front of my face when I am driving or I shall have an accident." She spoke the word *accident* with something like satisfaction, as if a smashed fender and a spewing radiator would attest to the high degree of annoyance and agitation one suffered when driving so long and so far in the company of a child.

"I will never get lost in the woods," Sally declared as she withdrew her hand and settled back in her seat. She noted the thick trees crowding both sides of the narrow road. They were no longer on the highway. At last, they were driving someplace more eventful, where there were houses and yards and lawn sprinklers and people, although not so many of them, and she stared out the window as if viewing rare specimens of a certain kind. They were older and paler people than she was used to seeing at home but some of them waved as if they knew her, which Sally thought was presumptuous of them; if they believed she was their friend, they had the wrong little girl.

"Lucky you," Betsy said, slowing and searching for landmarks along the River Road. She remembered the flag-painted mailbox and the barn that sat too close to the side of the road and the historic marker erected on the site of the first sawmill in Towne at the place where a brook narrowed and tumbled over a cataract of granite boulders and a broken dam.

"If I was Hansel and Gretel and you were the poor woodcutter and his wife," said Sally, who'd been pondering further.

"Okay," Betsy said.

"Who so cruelly abandoned me in the woods," Sally continued.

"Oh dear," Betsy said.

"I would still be all right," Sally assured her mother and herself.

BETSY PULLED TO A STOP in front of the farm stand and she jumped out calling, "Aunt Lily, Aunt Lily," even though Lily was standing right there looking relieved and a bit vexed, for she had begun to worry about them. She had been telling herself all day where Betsy and Sally now must be upon the last leg of their long journey, but the travelers had not kept pace with her imaginings.

They clasped hands and did not let go, each drawing the other's hand nearer to a cheek, to a heart, as Betsy spoke and Lily listened. Sally freed herself from the car unnoticed, which suited her even as she chafed a bit at not being instantly exclaimed over by her newly encountered relative. She was drawn to the farm stand; she understood she was connected to this vegetable store by a family affiliation, so she was sure that exploring it would be all right and she slipped inside.

"I drove through the village just to see whether anything had changed," Betsy was saying. "Everything seems so small and I don't know, kind of mossy looking, although not so much in color as that there seems to be a film over everything. And that funny little house on the green? Is that the one Uncle Alden bought when he came back from Prague? That odd little house is his now? I drove round the green twice, just to look, but I didn't stop."

"You'll see Alden tomorrow," Lily said. "And Brooks and Rollins will be there, and Julie is flying in from London, and Glover is going to meet her at the airport. He's driving up from Washington. Which will be lovely for Alden, having the children there." Betsy blinked a bit at

Lily's assessment that any gathering of her cousins under his peaked and rough-shingled roof might be "lovely" for Alden; she'd have thought the word for that circumstance would be *lively*.

"So everyone will be home," Betsy said. "Or almost everyone," she added. She understood one broached the subject of Alden's former wife with oblique references and significantly raised eyebrows and small shrugs to indicate one's bafflement and disapproval and resigned acceptance of the situation, so she essayed this bit of prescribed mummery, but Lily only shook her head and tightened her lips with her own display of having nothing to say about the errant Becky who had broken poor Alden's heart.

"Oh, but where is Mummy?" Betsy asked noticing that her own mother was missing. "I'd have thought she'd be presiding at the farm stand, selecting everyone's salad greens for them. I figured she'd have some sort of little pastoral salon going on, entertaining green thoughts in a green shade, if I know Mummy. After all, it's so fashionable to be green, these days."

"Ginger is resting at the moment. She wanted to be able to keep up with Sally this evening," Lily said.

"Sally," Betsy declared then. "Sally, where are you?" she called. "Sally, what have you done? What's that all over your face?" she asked as the child presented herself, wearing a composedly bland expression. Sally snatched up the tail of her shirt and scrubbed at her mouth.

"It's strawberry sap," Lily identified the agent that had reddened and stickied the child's lips.

"You'd better not have spoiled your supper," Betsy said.

"We'll just say she had her dessert first tonight," Lily said.

Sally grew thoughtful and sidled next to her mother, who stuck a hand on top of her head and propelled her toward Lily. "So, what do you think of Sally?" Betsy asked. Sally half turned toward her mother; something in the way Betsy had put that question seemed to leave open the possibility that this newly met aunt might decide to be less than enchanted with her newly met niece.

"Can the child weed?" Lily asked, after she studied Betsy's little girl.

"Yes," Sally said, decisively. "I have been reading since I was five."

This statement made her mother and Aunt Lily start to laugh at her, and they had to catch their breath before they could explain what was so funny.

But then Lily offered to drive Sally up to the house in the golf cart, and Betsy had given surprising permission for there were no seat belts, and as Sally uncertainly reached forward and grasped the dashboard, she wondered whether she ought not to be wearing a helmet for this. However, once she got over her nervousness, Sally enjoyed the ride through the woods and up a bumpy dirt driveway that jounced her bottom and whooped her stomach at the worst places. They rounded a bend and were surrounded by a meadow filled with yellow flowers and a phalanx of swooping starlings alighting and arising with a single mind. The yellow flowers nodded on their stems as if seeing the golf cart off and away from the liveliness of the meadow and onto the calmer contours of a broad lawn that sloped (rather than rushed) upwards toward a big white house. At first, Sally had thought that Aunt Lily's house must be an apartment building because it rose so tall and had so many windows ranged across its front, but Lily said she lived in the entire place all by herself except, of course, when she had company.

The golf cart sputtered round to the side yard, and Lily steered right up the ramp of a great red-painted barn. Sally gasped as the cart drove on through the doorway; the doors were open, but the opening was so dark it seemed solid. But then the interior loomed all around her, even warmer than the outside and expelling a fug of itch-inducing smells that made her sneeze three times (then she was over it). The space seemed fully occupied with vehicles and implements and shadows, and Sally could not begin to imagine how interesting all of this was going to be, now that she was here at last.

"WELL, YOU'VE HAD YOURSELF AN AMERICAN ADVENTURE," Penny said to Betsy. She and Harvey had been invited down from the Ridge House for supper at Lily's. Penny carried a fresh batch of popovers wrapped inside an electric bread warmer, which she took the liberty of plugging into the kitchen counter's sole double outlet after she yanked out the cord of the coffeepot, being mindful to leave the radio on. Lily was waiting for the weather report as she sat at the table filling out a bank deposit slip. She required evening rain for her tomatoes and a sunny day for tomorrow's parade, and somehow it seemed more likely that she'd get her wish if she kept an eye on things.

"Yes, the road trip was very interesting, and I'm glad we did it. But parts of it seemed endless," Betsy said. "I mean, take New Mexico, for example."

"New Mexico," Harvey objected. He was rattling through Lily's spare hardware drawer on the off chance she had a two-inch washer which would save him the trouble of hunting one down along the Home Depot's miles of aisles, the local TruValue having closed within a year of the new Home Depot's opening. In Harvey's opinion, the downfall of the Towne TruValue had been the way that Chick or one of the boys asked you what you wanted the minute you stepped through the door and then they hustled and fetched it for you. They ought to have made the customers search the shelves in pursuit of the tin of window putty they'd come in for. Along the way, they would remember they also needed a perforated garden soaker hose and a new pack of sandpaper and perhaps acquire an impulsive can of red Rust-oleum paint to touch up the seat of the glider swing and so drop thirty dollars for a basketful of items instead of spending ninety-eight cents on just the putty. Harvey had sent an e-mail to the surviving TruValues in the area advising them not to accommodate themselves out of business, and the place in Danvers had sent him a coupon for a five-gallon vat of driveway sealer, which didn't do Harvey any good. His driveway was gravel where it was anything at all, and he took offense at the place in Danvers's assumption that he was the hot-top type.

Penny raised eyebrows at Harvey for snorting at the entire state of New Mexico, where he'd never even been as far as she knew, although admittedly there was a great deal of background that could never be filled in when one has contracted a late-in-life marriage; one forgot things either tactfully or actually. Lily made a note of some final figure upon her deposit slip and she rose and lifted the corner of the bread warmer's cloth covering to check whether Penny's popovers had inflated. Penny's recipe was not reliable or perhaps her oven was to blame or possibly she forgot to let the eggs sit out until they achieved room temperature, which was always a good idea. At any rate, Lily would have thought that producing buoyant, even exuberant, popovers would have been more in keeping with Penny's character, so there had to be an explanation for her frequent failures to do so.

"And funnily enough," Betsy was saying, "there seemed to be no end to Pennsylvania, I suppose because I thought I'd driven far enough east so the really big states were over with. Aunt Lily, you wouldn't by any chance have walnut oil?"

"No, dear," Lily said. She didn't need to rummage through her pantry to know that for a fact.

"Walnut oil," Penny marveled. "Walnut oil, Harvey," she said, nudging him with an elbow.

"Eh?" Harvey asked, rubbing the spot where she had nudged him. He rattled deeper in the drawer, as if to get away from her.

"Betsy asked for walnut oil, but Lily says she doesn't have any," Penny said.

"Why should she? We're not Italian," Harvey said.

"Well, walnut oil is a very nice thing to have, although I believe you have to not be French to not have walnut oil," Penny said. "It's very expensive," she added.

"Eh," Harvey said, mollified by the mention of the expense to which it had been smart of Lily not to have risen.

Betsy had offered to make a California-style salad to accompany a Hannah's Spinach and Aubergine Casserole Lily had brought up to the house from the farm-stand freezer. She had provided Betsy with a lettuce, tender and pale and ruffle-edged, and Betsy had asked for balsamic vinegar and cornichons and capers, none of which Lily possessed. Betsy did her best to emulsify cider vinegar and Wesson Oil at the bottom of the smallest of the nesting stainless steel bowls, using a whisk from which several loops of wire had detached and now whipped in the air as if seeking to put an eye out. She was recalling that most implements here in Lily's kitchen were not so much broken as could be said to work in their own ways, and Lily had already mentioned that Betsy should add one hundred to any oven degree called for by a recipe. Also, the mixer would "walk away" on its own if left unattended, when in use, and the refrigerator door had to be closed twice before it would stay shut.

"Well," said Penny. "We ought to go and introduce ourselves to young Sally." Penny peered eagerly beneath the sink, having just opened the cupboard door in search of paper towels. She had noticed a spot of spilled and trod-on flour on the floor linoleum.

"I sent Sally to help Mummy set the dining room table," Betsy said.

"No trays in front of the TV set tonight," Penny noted. "It's a special occasion." She hoped Betsy hadn't forgotten to add a pinch of sugar to her salad dressing to cut the acidity of the vinegar. She may well have neglected to do so after that long drive of hers, and with so much on her mind, poor girl.

Lily frowned at Penny for mentioning (or perhaps for having noticed) the habit she and Ginger had slipped into over the past weeks of eating in the little parlor with the TV turned on. They always tried to catch the end segment of the *The NewsHour with Jim Lehrer.* More often than not, a correspondent would be discussing a noteworthy book, going into the work so thoroughly one need not read the book oneself but would receive most of the benefit, nevertheless, from merely having tuned in. Or perhaps Jim Lehrer would be appreciating the life and legacy of someone who had died that day whom the world was sorry to lose, although often Lily and Ginger professed themselves surprised that the person hadn't died long ago. It was so easy to lose track of someone who had withdrawn from public life due to age or illness or the public's indifference, effecting a graceful early exit, Ginger said, which was much nicer than moldering and decaying and outstaying one's welcome in the spotlight's glare.

"Harvey, let's go have a look at Sally," Penny said.

"Sally?" Harvey asked. He pocketed a washer and he helped himself to a picture hook fitted with a slender nail. Penny had a daughter-in-law who had been bitten by the Georgia O'Keeffe bug and was off-loading her skull and petunia studies on anyone who let an eye stray toward a canvas. You had to sit in Rosa's living room resolutely looking nowhere like a blind detective, like one of those blind TV detectives, which made you appreciate their acting skills all the more so because once you allowed your mind to wander, your eyes inevitably followed suit, and here he was, reduced to filching the hardware so he could slap Rosa's latest daub onto the furnace room wall.

"Sally. She's Betsy's little girl. You know perfectly well who she is," Penny said. "We've been looking forward to her arrival all week. We have thought and spoken of nothing else."

"I've been regrouting the master bathroom shower tiles all week," Harvey reminded her.

They grumbled off. Betsy, who had assembled all the ingredients she could muster, began to slice the radishes Lily had provided from the kitchen garden. The radishes were so fresh that they leaped and hissed at each incision of the knife blade, expelling from their bright-white and exposed flesh a sharp mist which stung her fingertips and then cooled them, like a splash of menthol. Lily, having made sure that her niece was all right, turned her attention toward the radio. The *Business Minute* was on, a roundup of the past week's news in stocks and bonds, and she listened to that for Alden's sake. Weather would be next.

GINGER HAD DRAWN THE dining room curtains early and set candles and candlesticks upon the table and along the sideboard and across the mantelpiece. She had cleared the table of Lily's clutter of empty strawberry pint boxes, which she stacked behind a drawn curtain, and she added two extension leaves, although Lily had told her to wait for Harvey to arrive to do any heavy lifting. The extra leafs weren't necessary for just the six of them who would be dining that evening, but Ginger was going all out for Sally's first dinner at the house. A snowy tablecloth had been unfurled and flung and tugged and adjusted to flow and fall evenly from end to end and side to side. The doors of the china cupboard creaked open repeatedly, followed by the scrape and clink of china being removed. The stemware chimed in, too, as if made nervous by being touched after sitting, unrequired, for so long a while.

The candles had been lit in expectation; tall tapers, half-consumed tapers, and stubby emergency candles retrieved from the kitchen drawer when the supply of tapers ran out were all aglow. The waning light of the day had been imperfectly shut out, seeping in from the hallway and between the gap in the curtain raised by the transferred clutter of wooden boxes. The candle flames flickered wanly at first, pale in that grayness, but they would brighten and advance into the gathering darkness. The room was seen at its best by firelight, which forgave the faded threadbareness of the curtains and the red Chinese rug and was kind to the tarnished silver and undusted vases and scarred paneling surrounding a fireplace whose great opening was crossed with summer's cobwebs. As the gloom deepened, objects would emerge and be caught and presented on prongs of light; half-moon globes of silver bowls, the diamond facets of a crystal vase, the shimmer of webs, a deeply red round pool of rug. They would float forward as discrete images that Sally would carry away from this evening and they would survive in long memory like treasures from another century when Sally looked back upon the occasion of her first supper, here at Lily's.

NOW SALLY WAS WALKING the length of the dining room table. She had removed her sneakers for this but kept on her white socks, which somehow seemed more correct than treading there with entirely bare feet. She had hitched the ribbing up her calves, furthering formality. She moved mindfully around salt cellars and a cruet and the butter dish, already set out. The flame just singed her leg as she skirted a candle. Sharing the table with lighted candles was like wandering among a race of strange, anchored beasts who could be teased but could not give chase. She hopped a few steps of a candle-provoking dance which she cut short as the smooth tablecloth slid and skidded underfoot along the as-smooth tabletop, slippery like ice, and a flame lurched toward her.

She clutched a posy of spoons round their handles as she passed from place setting to place setting. She dropped to her knees above a plate and plucked an oval-bowled and a round-bowled spoon from the bunch. Ginger had shown Sally where to position the spoons as they stood facing the table, when Sally had had to rise on her toes and peer between the slats of a high-backed chair in order to see. Her arms would never reach round the chairs, Sally knew, but Ginger failed to notice this difficulty. She had turned her back, occupied at the sideboard as she counted out the other cutlery, and it was then Sally had shed her shoes and scrambled onto the tabletop prepared, were she to be criticized, to place the blame where it lay, which was squarely on her Granna's plate.

At present, Sally was puzzling over which was the right side and not the left side of the plate, which was the wrong side for spoons; everything had turned opposite on her when she climbed onto the table.

Nevertheless, she arrived at a decision about the spoons which chanced to be the correct one. Sally possessed a strong instinct for order. She rose from her knees and resumed her careful stroll down the table, sighing because she had so many place settings to visit and so many more spoons yet to arrange. She sighed more tragically and glanced at Ginger, who was paying no attention. Sally did not know what was wrong with her grandmother; she could always be counted on to notice what you wanted her to notice and to overlook everything else, and she could even do both at the same time because she was wonderful.

Ginger had sought out a side chair, where she sat with her eyes shut, so very still that Sally held her own breath and stood, as motionless, watching. Ginger slumped in her chair like a Granna-doll as Sally stood on the table like a statue-girl, although this wasn't much of a game, if game it was, and Sally sighed again, for that matter. Ginger opened her eyes and asked, "Should you be up on the table like that?"

"Yes," Sally said. "Because there are so many spoons." She had muddled her prepared argument, however, the fact of there being so many spoons rankled as well as the difficulty of positioning them.

"Ah," said Ginger, quellingly. If Sally wished to spin a line of complaint, Ginger had no will to pick up the thread.

"I'm taller than you are, Granna," Sally said, pressing her advantage.

"I am sitting down," Ginger reminded her.

"I'm still tallest when you stand up." Sally strutted on tiptoes and she reached and lifted her pigtail as high as her arms could hold it.

"Mind the chandelier," Ginger's voice said, as if from far away.

Sally ducked just in time. Crystal prisms trembled and rang with the abruptness of her bob and swerve. Sally bobbed and swerved to make this happen again. Her shadow, cast upon the wall, switched and scuttled, erratic as a spider chased from a corner.

Just behind her something moved, then, and thumped onto the tabletop. Sally spun on her toes, spiraling the fabric of the tablecloth into a pinwheel beneath her feet. A pepper grinder toppled and the candlelight staggered and all the room seemed to totter for an instant as Agnes, on the prowl, her head lowered and her tail raised and twitching, made her way toward the butter dish. Sally marked her progress with a narrowed eye.

"Granna," she reported. "The cat is lapping all the butter."

"What? You sound as if you are mistranslating from the French," Ginger said. She sat back, turning her head and pressing a cheek against the cool plaster wall.

"But look at the cat, Granna. She's eating the people-butter," Sally said. She could not believe Ginger was not interested in this. "You—shoo," Sally said, waving the clustered spoons at the cat not very meaningfully and keeping as broad a distance as could be achieved, given the dimensions of the tabletop.

"Prevent her," Ginger said, quite unalarmed.

"But she is dangerous." Anyone could see that. "She'll scratch me. You do it," Sally said. "You shoo her." Sally demonstrated how that might be done by waving the spoons again.

"I don't want to be scratched either," Ginger said, reasonably.

"Well," said Sally. She would much prefer that her grandmother be the one to take the risk, but she could not think of a very nice way to say so, and really, she had expected Ginger to *offer.* "Oh, bad cat," Sally cried.

"We shall just get more butter," Ginger said, although she did nothing about that, either. She just sat there with her head resting on the wall.

"We'll get different butter," Sally agreed.

As she turned to get on with her chore, Sally noticed the two new old people who had entered the dining room. She observed them with an aslant glance as she knelt behind the next place setting and very importantly positioned two more spoons beside the plate. She rose with a curtsying motion which felt quite satisfying to perform, like punctuating a featured solo fling in a dance class recital. She peered from behind lowered lashes to see how these people were taking her.

"Look at that naughty kitty mincing down the table in her white socks," Penny said. She advanced and lifted Agnes, who stiffened her whitewashed paws, refusing to form a malleable shape that could be stuffed into a basket. (For that was what Penny preferred to do with any cat, stuff it into a basket.) "Wicked Agnes," Penny said, for good measure, releasing her upon the floor.

Sally watched without regret this expulsion of Wicked Agnes, who slunk away and was eclipsed by the shadow of a large shuttered cupboard. Sally fanned the remaining spoons to let them catch the candlelight and glitter in victory.

"Sally?" Penny turned the full force of her attention upon the child, who had not taken the hint about the inadvisability of parading along Lily's dining room tabletop in one's white socks. "Sally, dear, hello," she said. "I'm your great-great-aunt Penny and this is your great-great-uncle Harvey. Aren't you pretty? Well, we knew that from the photos your mummy and daddy have sent from California. There's always one or another of those California pictures stuck to our refrigerator door."

Sally tilted her head to indicate she was prepared to listen to further estimations of herself, but Penny was content to leave it at that: the little miss had a sweet-enough face on her, if a tad rabbity, but those sorts of features were so often grown out of, especially if the parents believed in orthodontia, as Penny was sure Betsy and Andy did, and certainly the money was there to pay for good dentists. She turned then to Ginger, with something to say, whether or not it was her place to say so, although she supposed she had a right insofar as Harvey was hers to dispatch down to Lily's on thoughtful errands this particular summer.

"You weren't supposed to put in the extra table leaves on your own. Harvey would have done that for you," she scolded.

"I managed perfectly well on my own," Ginger said, reflecting that Penny ought to be commending her for having been able to pull apart the ends of the massive table and lift the heavy planks, which felt as if they were still weighted down by the press of all the platters and elbows that had ever rested on them. She was aware that her propped posture belied her assertion that she was perfectly all right and she rose from her chair. "Forks," she remembered and she leaned over the cutlery chest as she counted out enough. Penny stood by to receive the forks (salad, entrée, dessert, serving) lest Sally get hold of them and keep them there waiting forever for dinner to be served as she danced across the tablecloth figuring out where each utensil went. Penny decided that, bowed before the casket of silver, Ginger looked like one of those serene women in one of those indefectible old Dutch paintings; she appeared so pale and finely wrought by the candle glow. Certainly, Ginger seemed very far removed from this century, Penny thought, as if she had quietly slipped away and become resident in the past.

"I'm taller than you are, Uncle Harvey," Sally announced from the tabletop. Harvey gave her a glance as his hand stole toward his shirt pocket, the maneuver disguised as an adjusting pluck of the placket as he nudged the volume switch of his hearing aid console down and down some more.

Lily entered carrying the spinach and aubergine casserole, which she hoped was going to be large enough to feed six people. The box said the contents would serve four, but Lily meant to ask Hannah sometime which sanctioned entity in what official bureau got to pronounce how much everybody was supposed to eat. Tonight, Lily was catering to a variety of appetites, none robust and some nonexistent, so she would be all right, but she anticipated some other evening when Alden's boys would all be here, reaching across the dining room table helping themselves. Betsy followed with the salad bowl and the popover basket, which was trailing its cord.

"Plug that in, please. You'll find an outlet beneath the little table," Lily told Sally, who was standing upon the raffia mat (kneading her toes in the softly giving surface), which was where Lily wanted to place the very hot dish she was carrying. Her pot holders were beginning to fail her at certain flimsy points within the weave. "Please," she told Sally once again, and Betsy lifted her up and off the table. She set her down on the rug and handed her the basket cord.

"But Mummy," Sally insisted and she dropped the cord. She was not allowed to have anything to do with electricity. She had been taught to fear and to respect the powerful force that lurked behind every wall and was known to call irresistibly to all the little children, urging them to insert a finger or a knife blade into one of those snakebite-looking punctures cut into the mop board.

"It's all right. Do as Aunt Lily said," Betsy told her, as if she'd completely forgotten that she was always saying how dangerous sockets and plugs were for small children.

"Granna?" Sally asked, and Ginger motioned her toward the outlet with a wave which was at once sympathetic and impatient, an attitude Sally had not encountered before; if Granna understood, then she did not really care.

She picked up the cord, holding it caught between her thumb and forefinger and borne at all possible remove from her person. She scraped unwilling feet across the carpet, which felt just like skating on a velveteen pond, she decided, and she began to glide and flutter, lifting her arms above her head like a ballerina on ice.

"Now, please," Betsy said. "Do as Aunt Lily said."

So Sally flopped to her knees and inserted herself beneath the little table. Her shoulders wedged between the narrow legs, which caused a very old Chinese vase, long resident on the table's top, to slide about upon a pulled-thread doily. Betsy rescued the vase and prodded Sally on the bottom with an impatient toe.

"Ow," Sally objected but she ceased fidgeting, and with a tremendous sigh for how cruel her mother (and everyone else) was being, she touched the prongs to the socket.

"Ow, ow, ow, ow," she cried, springing backward. The cord flailed free and leaped up as if alive, and then dropped to the floor as if killed.

"I just knew that was going to happen," Penny said, calmly.

"Ow," said Sally. "Ow," she said again and she examined her hand closely as if believing she'd find spangles of pain embedded there that could be picked from the flesh like bits of glass. She sat down on the rug, so she could see better.

"You set yourself up for an electric shock by dragging your feet over Aunt Lily's carpet instead of doing as you were told," Betsy informed her.

"Tomorrow at the parade I'll show you how to make a balloon stick to your head," Harvey promised. (He'd been following the action as part of a dumb show.) "Same principle, static electricity."

"Well, maybe Sally doesn't want to be a balloon head," Penny said, because the child's lips were quivering and her eyes were beginning to swarm with tears.

"Sally, come take your seat," Ginger said. "I want you beside me to keep me company. What a beautifully set table," she added. Sally rose and came forward, having neglected to admire her handiwork thoroughly enough, upon its completion. She did so now.

But Ginger was the only one who noticed what a good job Sally had done with the spoons and Sally hissed as the rest of them shook out their napkins and picked up their soup spoons (Lily had had last minute doubts about the menu and opened a can of corn chowder), undoing all of her hard work without bothering to compliment her effort.

Over dinner, she listened to her mother give an account of their cross-country drive, which made that endless undertaking sound a great deal more fun than any of it had seemed at the time. The hot air balloons racing across the Arizona sky, the wedding party they had somehow become all mixed up with at the hotel in Oklahoma, a baby bear loping along the side of the New York Thruway—those few bright spots illuminated the entire journey, and having suffered so extravagantly throughout the experience, Sally was relieved to learn that the journey would hereafter be revisited as a romp, in the remembering.

But she didn't very much like the food here. Her hand hovered over her plate selecting tendrils of spinach, which she trailed back and forth to shake off the sauce. The rolls in the electric basket were excellent, however, and if no one paid attention to how little she was eating of the main course, they also failed to notice the inroads she was making on the contents of the honey pot Lily had carried in from the kitchen and set upon the table as another afterthought; the large table with its extra leaves had continued to look a trifle bare to her even after the addition of soup bowls and the soup tureen. When broken in half, the rolls proved to be hollow shells Sally could fill to the brim with lagoons of honey which could be sipped with pursed lips. She wished she had a straw, although she supposed it would be going too far to ask for one. She was sorry about the contaminated butter. She had shuddered with fastidious horror when Penny slathered a big knifeful onto her popover and taken a big, oblivious bite. Pats of butter would have made lovely islands, afloat in the sweet lagoons of the several popovers she consumed.

The grown-ups were far too busy talking to one another over her head to mind her. Harvey (who had restored his hearing for this) criticized the route Betsy had taken to get here, advising her she ought to have followed the shoreline of Lake Erie along Interstate 90 and then she wouldn't have had all of her problems with Pennsylvania. Penny wanted to know whether the fad for spelling out messages with tennis balls stuck between the interstices of the chain-link fencing of overpasses (such as Will You Be My Wife Angela? and Welcome Home Steve) had taken off all across the country, or was it just a local phenomenon. No, they're everywhere, Betsy reported. Lily remarked upon the potential for misunderstandings that could arise from these signs. Suppose the Angela who spotted the message as she was driving to work and excitedly got on her cell phone and said yes, yes, of *course* she would marry him, to her particular young man, who turned out not to have been the one behind the overpass proposal after all. Ginger pointed out that any mistakes arising from the mix-up might well prove to be happy ones; perhaps many unions that would never have been had been facilitated by the near-celestial mandate of such handwriting appearing on the wall, so to speak, just like *Mene, mene, tekel, upharsin,* Ginger said, only with a better outcome. But Lily said she still thought the practice verged on vandalism, or if not vandalism, then certainly it became a littering offense when all those tennis balls popped out as they surely must do, at some point. Harvey said he wondered where you got your hands on a couple of hundred tennis balls to do the deed. Penny said tennis clubs gave dudded-out tennis balls away for free. The Towne Tennis Center had a Help Yourself barrel full of them outside the pro shop. Yes, Harvey had noticed that but since old tennis balls were of no use to him he had forgotten, although now that he knew what they were there for, he might post his own message on a local overpass—Penny and Lily and Ginger braced themselves as he paused to come up with a possible subject, but he surprised them all when he charmingly said he would spell out, I "heart" Penny, that is, he would fashion one of those ubiquitous heart shapes that he was always seeing on T-shirts and that he assumed would require fewer balls than writing out the actual word, *love.*

There was nothing for dessert, as such. Penny was to have provided a Fourth of July cake, however Cam (Penny said) had been so taken with it she could not pry the pan from her fingers, and Penny was sure no one would mind that she had sent the cake home with Cam. Sally, seldom allowed sweet stuff, accepted the loss with what passed for good grace. She smiled a honeyed smile. She was more interested in finding out just who this favored Cam person might be and just why she got to take the cake and how circumstances might be altered so that this would not happen again in the future.

"There are graham crackers," Lily said, trying to come up with something dessertlike.

"I haven't touched that box of chocolates I bought from that Save the Rain Forest activist who wandered up the drive," Ginger said. "They're supposed to be very good chocolates, at least insofar as they're good for the rain forest. Which of course begged the question, then do corporate chocolates contain bits of bark and twigs? But the earnest young man couldn't say when I asked him."

"I have a new roll of butterscotch Life Savers in my purse," Penny said. "Oh, but I left my purse at home. I wondered whether I'd need it and then I thought, no, I won't but now I see I did. I'm sorry."

Harvey felt in his pockets and produced a linty cough lozenge, not quite sure what game they were playing, but anyway, there was his token, which he flung across the tablecloth. Sally's hand snatched it up and popped it between her lips before Betsy could prevent her. Sally's back teeth crunched the cough drop into shards and pieces which migrated to all corners of her mouth, facilitated by a wave of saliva which rose from her gorge, so that she had a very complicated time spitting out every last horrible fragment into her snowy white napkin.

THE LITTLE BEDROOM WHICH WAS TO BE HERS had been saving up heat behind a heavy door as an oven will, although the smell that surged out when the bedroom door swung open was not that of a just-baked pie; rather, the air held a savor of very clean soap and generously applied furniture polish. Sally saw that the door must be very heavy, for Lily had to secure it open by sliding a large rock across the floor which she nudged into position against the lower panel with her foot, saying, "There, Sally, now it can't slam itself shut on your fingers." The door's wood was dented and its white paint was scaled and flaking away in places as if it had been bruised while engaging in roughhousing, a word Sally had heard used before but not understood until that moment. She sidled into the room, unwilling to turn her back on such an unreliable door, and once within, she wondered how she would screw her courage up to venture out again. She supposed she would have to call someone to come help her: her mother, Granna, or even Aunt Lily.

Her luggage had gotten there before her. The suitcase perched on the desk chair with upright impatience and someone had already arranged her dolls, sitting them from biggest to smallest upon a shelf, completely ignoring (or ignorant of) the delicate balance of friendships and dependencies and enmities that existed among them. Forgetting her other trepidations at the sight of this more immediate concern, Sally crossed the room and sat about remedying the most urgent mismatches, separating Holly Hobbie from Furby and restoring the

Beanie Babies to the custody of Maria von Trapp, arraying them across her broad, aproned lap. The rest could wait until the following day. She informed them of this telepathically, for she seldom spoke to her dolls, having learned she could boss them around in her thoughts (and thus they could all play Save the Princess together, bemoaning her incarceration and conferring on a rescue plan and secretly having fun, whenever Sally was sent to the time-out chair to sit and meditate upon some incident of misbehavior).

Lily, who had placed the dolls on the shelf because they looked so uncomfortable jam-stuffed into the canvas-sided satchel that had conveyed them here, approved of Sally's fussiness over their disposition. Lily had always found doll squalor distressing and she was relieved she would not be compelled to spend the weeks to come rescuing upside-down and suffocating and indecently exposed little persons. "This was your mother's bedroom when she stayed here with me," Lily said in a welcoming way, warming to the child for the first time. She had been looking for something to like about Sally, although only time would tell whether she was someone to be loved for herself. Of course she would always be loved on the strength of whose child she was.

But Sally was not keen to pursue the subject of her mother's prior occupancy of this room. Everything she had heard from her mother's accounts (which she would not necessarily have credited but for Ginger's corroborating testimony) told her that her mother had been an impossibly perfect little girl with whom she could never hope to compete, and Sally didn't want to give Lily a chance to recall how neatly her mother had made that narrow little bed in the corner every morning and how neatly she had kept her T-shirts and shorts folded in the bureau drawers lest all of that exemplary tidiness turn into a blueprint for what was expected of her own behavior while resident here. She turned to a bookcase stuck full of volumes, every size and with colorful spines and obviously meant for kids. She eased a book from the shelf (they were tightly packed because there were so many) and sat down upon a square of rag rug to read, which in her experience always counted as a praiseworthy activity and one she didn't mind engaging in anyway. She sounded out the title of the randomly selected book, *Goops and How to Be Them,* and turning a page, began to laugh immoderately at an illustration of round-headed babies who were making a happy mess of their supper table. She felt sorry for the person who had been charged with setting that table, but not very.

Betsy had been out at the car searching for Sally's pillow, which had gone missing. She was starting to think they had lost it at the last motel; she recalled placing the pillow out of the way on the roof of the car as she stowed the suitcases that morning but she could not remember retrieving it before driving away. She had been distracted by a posse of motorcyclists who roared into the parking lot, all of them, leather clad and bandanaed and shaggy haired, sprawled astride those shuddering machines whose interior workings spilled out like the intestines and rib cages of those who had been wounded in battle. Convinced that a brawl was about to break out as several bikers banged on the door of the adjacent motel unit, shouting, *"Hey, Rudy,"* she had bundled Sally into the backseat and taken off, bucking over the parking lot's speed bumps and darting into the morning rush-hour traffic stream. Although at the present moment, Betsy was wondering whether Rudy, whoever Rudy was, hadn't just overslept and his friends had stopped by to rouse him. One of them had been carrying a cup of coffee and, upon reflection, her best guess told her he had also brought an extra Danish pastry left over from breakfast wrapped in a napkin which was stained with raspberry jelly and not, as had been her impression, blood. In retrospect, Betsy saw this much more clearly than she had as the scene was playing out in front of her and she told herself the incident was a useful reminder to her not always to assume the worst; the worst seldom happened. Things were rarely as bad as they seemed, she reminded herself.

She found Lily sitting next to Sally on the floor of the little bedroom, reading aloud. " *'The Goops are very hard to kill, So they hang out the Window-sill; Down the Banisters they slide—I could do it if I tried'.*" Lily paused and frowned and shook her head at Sally, who matched the frown and the head shaking. She was an adroit little mimic and had been encouraged, at home, whenever she essayed an eerily on point imitation of the little girl in the cereal commercial who asked for "More Coco Puffs, please." (Not that they ever let her eat Cocoa Puffs).

"But when Mother tells me 'don't,' Then, of course I really won't!' " Lily concluded, and Sally reached out to flatten the page for a better view of Goops flopping and falling down the stairs.

"Are *you* a Goop?" Lily asked her. The official text did not inquire, as such, but this query and reply method was a traditional family embellishment when reading the book. One needed to make certain that children understood that the featured behaviors were not attractive, however amusingly the offenses were described.

"No," Sally answered. She thought Lily was rather rude to ask her that, and she wondered what would happen if she said yes, she was a Goop. Her mother, who seemed to have read her thoughts, hovered and caught her eye.

Betsy unlatched the suitcase and rummaged for night clothes as Sally contrived to pay no attention to her. She indicated to Lily she wished to hear more by tapping the binding with a coaxing fingertip, and Lily began to read, " '*When 't is time to go to church Do you ever have a chill? When 't is time to go to school, Do you fancy you are ill? Oh, be very cautious, please, I can tell by signs like these You have got the Goop Disease!*' "

After Lily asked Sally whether she was a Goop and Sally rather wearily answered "No, of course I'm not a Goop," a pair of hands hoisted her up and tugged her shirt over her head, the neck band lifting her chin and swiping her nose and raising her eyebrows into a startled mask. The downward tug of pajama top left Sally's features lowered into a scowl. She would not cooperate, and so the bottoms went on backward, which was not comfortable because these were the pair of pajamas that had feet. She complained about this, and Betsy answered, "Well, you should have thought of that."

Betsy drew back the pink chenille coverlet and folded down the blanket and sheets and Sally climbed into the bed. She stretched out upon the mattress shrugging her shoulders and drumming her heels (as those empty feet things flapped), assessing how comfortable she was going to be. This bed was quite wonderful, so soft and sagging all down her back that she thought of clouds. There was something odd about the pillow, however, which was stuffed full at one end and fell flat at the other. She rolled her head back and forth between these extremes.

"But where is my pillow?" she asked, just as Betsy had begun to hope she wouldn't miss it.

"Your pillow has been misplaced," she said.

"What? What?" Sally asked. "My pillow? My pillow?'

"That's enough," Betsy said, leaning over to deliver a distracted kiss and to prod the provided pillow, not sure herself about this feather pillow, which was a sack of germs and allergens, in her opinion, and fifty years old if it was a day.

Lily slipped the pillow from beneath Sally's head and she held the case by its scruff and gave it a shake and a few hard punches and returned it to Sally, who was impressed by the beating Lily had administered on her behalf, and she settled back, satisfied.

"But where's Granna?" she asked, just as Betsy had begun to hope she wouldn't miss Ginger.

"Granna has gone to bed," Betsy said.

"So soon? Before me?" Sally asked.

"It's not soon. It's very late," Betsy said.

"How late? Is this the latest I've ever stayed up?" Sally wanted to know.

"Yes," Betsy said.

"Is this the latest you've ever stayed up?" Sally asked.

"No," Betsy said.

"Aunt Lily, is this the latest you've ever stayed up?" Sally asked.

"Hush, not another word. Don't quiz Aunt Lily," Betsy said.

"Why can't I ask Aunt Lily if this is the latest she's ever stayed up?" Sally asked, but her lamp was switched off in answer, and she heard the rock scrape across the floor and the heavy door was pulled shut. Silence and darkness befell her, and she lay there willing herself to be conscious of what she *could* sense; the soap and polish smells swirled throughout her nose and a feathery tickle insisted irksomely behind her neck. Her hand crept up and out from beneath the blankets and reached to scratch there, scrubbing at the itch with a reassuring rhythm.

The utter stillness and surrounding blackness lifted slowly, as if stealing away behind her mother's back when they were sure she wasn't going to return. Rustling, hooing, chirrups, a snap sounded, as suspended activity resumed just beyond the open window through which some sort of light from somewhere (the porch lamp, the moon?) faded the blackness like milk tipped into coffee. Visible now were the pair of white curtains which puffed and subsided with the breath of the breeze. They were long and loose curtains, silkily fringed and tied back with bows. As they flowed like veils and swept across the floor, Sally's last thoughts were of them while she waited to fall asleep. So, she could play brides and weddings here. They must all have played brides and weddings here, clad in gowns of long white curtains, her mother and Granna and Aunt Lily and Aunt Penny and maybe even Julie, whom she did not know, but they said she was nice and she'd be arriving tomorrow. Granna's Granna too, she must have played weddings and brides, and who else? Who else had there been; who else had there been who played brides here?

BETSY PADDED AFTER LILY, accompanying her on a final turn of assurance round the house. Perhaps Betsy meant to speak now that she was alone with her aunt and Lily might have things to say which she had not wished to bring up in front of other people, but the hour was late to begin any real conversation, and each apprehended the other's reluctance to begin, or misapprehended the cause, perhaps, and this was the moment when the habit of silence on the subject of Ginger became fixed between them.

Lily measured out beans and programmed the coffeemaker, down in the kitchen. She draped damp dish towels over the backs of ajar cupboard doors to dry and she filled Agnes's bowl with Meow Mix, adding the slice of boiled ham that had fallen onto the linoleum and which she had saved from earlier in the day. Then the clock in the big parlor needed to be wound with three turns of a key, and a plastic cover had to be dropped over the computer console installed in a corner of the little parlor. An empty vase in which some roses had died was restored to the dining room china cupboard. They passed through the hallway, where Lily straightened the corner of the rug caught beneath a leg of the deacon's bench and she retrieved that morning's cardigan from the hat rack; the day had ended warmer than it began. They turned to climb the elegantly spiraling staircase, Lily at last betraying her tiredness by leaning an arm on the strong, carved banister. She came to a stop on the first landing to gather her strength, and Betsy paused too, just behind her on the step below, until Lily told her to go on ahead and to go to bed.

BETSY CALLED ANDY AS she called him every night since he'd been stuck in Montana. The leader of a group of survivalists who had been the subject of a book he had written early in his university career was about to go on trial for bank robbery, and Andy had been asked to join the defense team to provide expert testimony and give context to the matter at hand, which he had agreed to do, intending to get another book out of the experience. At present, the prosecution was mired in procedural delays, but the case, deemed colorful midsummer fare involving mountain men and a long tunnel dug beneath a busy street and gold stolen from a bank vault, was going to be featured on The Justice Channel when the proceedings finally got under way in earnest.

"Oh, you know, Mummy. She's carrying on as usual," Betsy said in answer to Andy's first question. "She's lolling about in her bedroom and wandering through the house in flowing robes and setting glamorous supper tables using all of Lily's porcelain and crystal and silver and candlesticks."

She told him about the farm stand (really quite impressively stocked and professionally run) and she reported how the whys and wherefores of those tennis ball messages on highway overpasses had been thoroughly gone into at dinner. She predicted that this summer was going to be good for Sally, who had weathered several disappointments (a missing cake and a missing pillow), with not too much of a fuss; Betsy had been pleased with her, and she seemed to be making a good impression on Lily. "I think they bonded over the Goops," Betsy said.

"And Lily has put me in the third-best bedroom," Betsy went on. She was propped up in the high bed, admiring the bouquet of bearded iris placed upon the bureau top. Blooms crowded and sprung from the top of a tall cut-glass vase in a profusion that could only be described as lavish. "Although maybe it's been promoted to second-best bedroom because Lily had an en suite bathroom installed where the closet used to be, underneath the attic stairs, remember? It also connects to your old room if you can picture how it used to be."

"Tight quarters, that closet," said Andy, who remembered.

"Yes. They had to fit the bathtub in beneath the rise of the attic stairs, and the thing of it is, I just had a bath, and I have to say, they must have installed it backward because the faucets are at the only end you can sit in without banging your head on the ceiling," Betsy said. "Maybe it's to discourage loitering. Well, you'll find out when you get here and try to take a bath."

"Whenever that will be," Andy said. "Sooner rather than later, I hope, if I have anything to do with it."

"Well, you could sit at the other end of the tub where the ceiling dips, but you'd have to sink down really low, with your nose practically underwater, if you don't want to hit your head," Betsy supposed. "Unless you only fill the tub halfway. Maybe that's what you're supposed to do, and then you can sit at the more comfortable end and safely slump."

"Are you on your cell? I can hear you so clearly tonight," Andy said. "You sound so close," he said. His voice betrayed his wistfulness.

"Oh yes," Betsy said. "It's very exciting. Lily let them build a new cell tower up in the High Field right above the house, so the local service is excellent now. They're all chattering away like magpies. (Is it magpies that chatter? I think I meant macaws—or maybe monkeys?) Anyway, Penny told this very funny story about the tower, after supper, when we were having coffee on the terrace. She said she was out walking in the woods one day when her cell phone rang and when she answered it, this voice boomed at her wanting to know whether she was prepared to face disaster or dismemberment or death, and she answered, 'Oh Lord, I'll do my best with whatever tribulations you may heap upon me,' but it turned out just to be a salesman from Mutual of Omaha, or some place trying to sell her an extended-care policy. Well, I don't really believe she thought it was God talking, at the time. I'm pretty sure the Voice in the Wilderness angle just occurred to her afterward."

"It always makes a much better story, to say what you ought to have said," Andy agreed. "Here's a thought. Maybe Brooks and Rollins can invent some kind of real-life replay button we can push and keep on pushing until we get everything right. If not in the first place then maybe after two or three attempts. Ask them tomorrow, when you see them. And we'll tell them we also want a fast forward function, to shoot us over the rough patches and back into the clear again."

TWO Staying with Family

SEVERAL YEARS HAD PASSED since Alden Lowe returned alone from Prague and bought the last of the unimproved houses facing the Towne green. He had paid top dollar for a place which was admittedly a bit of a wreck, with shortcomings that went beyond the merely cosmetic concerns of sagging shutters and the sheet of plastic tarp left stapled over the front-door frame all year round as proof not only against the winter but which served to ward off the onslaughts of spring and summer and fall as well. The foundation stones tilted in on themselves, signifying serious sill trouble, and roof shingles blew off in high winds, landing on neighborhood lawns and lodging in shrubbery and cluttering the gutters. Several thick chimneys variously tilted, and sections of clapboard buckled and waved, creating the optically illusionary vision that the house sat there throbbing. A Historic District plaque affixed to the facade read PHARAOH DOUGLASS HOUSE 1712, which gave passersby some idea of just how long this had been going on.

Nevertheless, Alden had faced competition in acquiring the house. Any of the old dwellings that sat facing the green were considered to be highly desirable properties, and several sets of arrangements had been made by several sets of potentially interested parties to be notified the moment interior lights were observed burning late at night in an upper window and the ambulance came to take old Mr. Drake (the then owner) away in something less than any previous hurry. But having lately had his share of vain bargaining and unrequited negotiations—with attorneys, with God, with the universe, with whomever was supposed to be in charge—over the return to order and the restoration of his former wife to his life (for Becky remained locked in North Africa with her paramour), Alden had offered 10 percent above the price being asked by Mr. Drake's surviving niece. Perhaps Alden wished to explore the upper limits of just how much money could fail to buy him happiness. In this case the amount was established to be $825,000, a figure which, when published in the real estate transactions column of the *Towne Crier*, variously elicited gasps and smart remarks. At least the locals were enjoying themselves, and the niece, who lived in Quincy, was said to be laughing all the way to the Fleet Bank.

On his initial tour of ownership through the emptied house (there had been that condition appended to the purchase agreement by Harris Desmaris after he'd acquired the key on his own initiative one lunchtime and walked over from his office for a look), Alden allowed things might have been worse than he'd thought. He had blamed the late Mr. Drake's brown drugget carpets for the spongy give of the floors underfoot, but that sensation had not been bundled off with the rugs, and it was obvious that Mr. Drake's many pictures had been hung to mask water-damaged walls. Alden had noticed Mr. Drake's apparent fondness for framed genre scenes (*Oops*—boys, baseball bats, a broken window: *Open Wide*—a pretty girl, her dentist) and he had wasted a wince of pity for a sentimental old man who, it was now evident, had been in the habit of buying odd lots of framed pictures to nail over stains and cracks rather than hire a roofer and a plumber and a plasterer. Tommy, Alden's dog (who had attached himself to Alden in Prague and whom Alden had refused to leave behind), was beside himself, inhaling all the deep dank smells extant in this, his new home, of which humankind caught only a fugitive whiff.

Even Lily, who accompanied Alden at his request, all the while protesting she was the last person to ask about home improvements—she who was entirely too tolerant of rackety radiators and windows that had to be propped open with sticks—even Lily had said "Good Lord" when she set eyes upon Alden's newly acquired staircase, which, crammed against a central chimney mass, rose up at a pitch more suitable to the companionway on the *HMS Bounty* than a flight of household stairs. The risers lifted to uneven heights and the treads projected too narrowly to contain the straight-on length of any normal adult person's foot. At the top there was no landing; one came nose to brick against the chimney mass and stepped to the left or to the right, scaling one last unequal riser height into one or the other of the two small bedrooms lurking up there, below the roof.

They had made their way up and then down again. Alden said he supposed he would become accustomed to the stairs, but Lily told him the only way to survive stairs like that was never to become complacent about them. She had noticed next that the floor of the small hallway at the foot of the stairs lifted up; it served as a trapdoor entrance to the cellar. Leaving Tommy abandoned and anxious above, she and Alden had descended a leaning ladder into a dirt-floored and ancient space. Alden wandered over to a post and examined a fuse box suspended there, its circuits unlabeled and reliant upon copper-penny fixes. He tinkered with the pennies' uncertain balances and lost a few when they dropped into the dirt, as Lily, who had known enough to equip herself with a flashlight for this, probed hidden corners with a questing yellow beam that lit upon the remains of an old dug well rimmed with a low edge of stones. The water seethed, deep and infernal, when Alden, called over to see for himself, tossed in a loose stone selected from a rubble of fallen-free foundation stones.

"Alden," Lily had said. "This is what I picture happening. Some night the lights will go out in a thunderstorm and you will get up to investigate and you will take a misstep from your bedroom and plunge down the stairs, and in the meanwhile, the trap will have somehow been left mistakenly open so you will continue to drop all the way down into the cellar. You will pick yourself up, dazed and wandering in the complete blackness, and you will stumble and fall into the well and drown. And I don't know who would ever think to look for you there until you rise to the surface, and that won't be very pleasant for the person who has to find you." Alden had assured her he would bear all of that in mind.

Later, during that first prowl of possession, they paused in the parlor, where Lily at last found something positive to say about the wide pine floorboards and a corner cupboard which she believed to be original, for the hand-forged hinges looked right for the age of the house.

Alden said, "That fireplace mantel either *is* black, or it's been painted black."

Lily, who knew what he meant because they had already inspected the kitchen, bent for a closer look and she switched on her flashlight for added clarity. "That's paint," she said. "You know, some people painted their mantelpieces black to mourn the death of Lincoln, so perhaps that explains it."

"Ah," said Alden and he gathered himself into a respectful posture as if he were in the presence of a fresh grief.

"Though whoever they were, I should think they've gotten over it by now," Lily told him briskly. "She was finding his moon-faced mournfulness rather tiresome."

"But it's a significant historic feature," Alden said. "I shall keep all of this as it was," he declared, and his gesturing hand took in the black mantel and the rasping cupboard hinges and a network of plaster cracks covering all the walls and the ceiling.

"A black mantel will be very awkward to decorate around," Lily said. Then again, she supposed Alden would just retrieve the furniture and boxes that had been left in storage when he and Becky had taken off for Prague. He would arrange the chairs and tables and rugs just as they'd been placed in their last home, as best as he could recall. But perhaps that would make it safer for him to wander around his house in the dark, blindly able to avoid familiar hazards, if, in some sense, everything, or almost everything, was once again where it was supposed to be.

ALDEN AWOKE ON THE MORNING of Independence Day at Tommy's first stirrings. The soft brush of limbs across a cushion, the tip-tap of claws encountering floor, an anatomizing snuffle to take in whatever drifted afloat upon the air of early morning, and Tommy's own respondent release of odors of his own, of breath and dander and gases, caused Alden to open his eyes and raise his head to see what time it was and to mutter an inarticulate objection. Now that Tommy had Alden's attention, his tail swished, thumping the side of his master's mattress. Alden's awakening moan rang ripe with happy associations in Tommy's ears, which crimped to receive more messages.

"All right, all right," Alden said. He got up and got dressed in yesterday's shirt and khakis that he had draped over the back of a chair the previous evening.

Tommy scrambled to the door and stood there tense with joy, his nose shoved against the jamb to snuffle deeply as if he meant to breathe the very door down into his lungs and out of his way. He had such mixed feelings about doors; they kept him apart from many delights but nevertheless had a way of opening onto wondrous and new territories.

"Okay," Alden said. He shoved his moccasins on his feet, the final step. Tommy backed away from the door, his eyes staring at the latch, which Alden's hand, assisted by Tommy's levitating look, lifted and released. Tommy, first, shot down the stairs, sliding on his stomach and reaching forward to break the near tumble of his descent.

"Careful, boy," Alden said as he made his own way down, angling his feet to fit the shallow treads. There was no railing (he'd thought of installing a railing but hadn't gotten round to it), and he stuck a palm against either wall to steady and to catch himself, smudges on the plaster serving to map where other hands had always grasped.

Tommy pressed passionately at the front door as Alden slipped a leash from its peg and slung it over his shoulder. He pulled at the door, which always stuck until Tommy's sharp bark acted as the extra impulse to unstop it.

"Good boy," Alden said.

Tommy shot across the stone threshold and then, restraining himself, he nosed his way across the front yard, suddenly casual as if he thought a girl he liked might be watching him. (Having raised three sons, Alden imputed a range of boy emotions to Tommy.) At the gate, which sagged always-open between two listing posts, the dog paused and together, he and Alden strolled across the road to the green. Alden threw a tennis ball as far as his shoulder would let him. The ball soared and arced and squarely hit the trunk of an oak tree, spiking up and ricocheting back the way it had come. Tommy, giving chase, nearly knotted his legs as he changed direction on the fly, but he was too intent upon recovering the ball to shoot Alden the look of disgust he deserved. Not for the first time had Alden failed not to hit a tree, which surely was not all that hard not to do on such an expansive and open green.

The bandstand had been bedecked with flags and bunting and half a dozen hanging pots of Easy Wave petunias and variegated ivy on loan from The Garden Stop (acknowledged by a small sign). The lectern had been wrestled over from Town Hall and left there overnight beneath the roof of the bandstand beside a huddle of speakers and audio equipment, all roped together as if having to undo a few half-hearted half hitches would discourage thieves, although Alden reckoned anyone who wanted to steal the stuff would be doing everyone a favor; people talked the most awful drivel when they got hold of the Town Hall microphone and they always sounded as tinnily prissy as archival audio of Woodrow Wilson.

Alden saw no reason not to complete his usual morning circuit of the green. Today he would note what was different, just as tomorrow he would satisfy himself that everything was once again the same. No Parking on the Parade Route placards had been attached to lampposts, and a Dodge Caravan, parked in front of the Bendas' house, bore a ticket on its windshield, which didn't seem fair, those No Parking signs having sprung up overnight like mushrooms. The Bendas' house, a large and serene Greek Revival dwelling, had been decorated with a flag and bunting display of its own, although Merra Benda had managed to make her decor look tasteful and reserved, unlike the more raffishly arrayed bandstand. Merra had chosen a less harsh shade of red and a more subdued blue, and the white was ivory toned. Three cheers for the rose, teal, and ivory, Alden thought. Next door to the Bendas, the Wrights had raised the flag they flew on their flag pole every day of the year in front of their brick-end Federal, and apparently they didn't feel the need to do anything more than that. There was a Peace Now poster propped in the bow window of the Congregational parsonage, next door to the Congregational Church, and Alden wasn't clear just what the fellow meant (an interim minister, pleasant, divorced, not overly holy, a good golfer). Did the Reverend mean to say he thought we were now more or less at peace with the world, or was he demanding that peace be realized at once, with an exhortatory construction? Peace was a tricky concept, Alden thought, and he was inclined to believe one seldom recognized peace for what it was, whether one had it or not.

Tommy returned to Alden's side and walked with him for a few patient paces before spitting out the tennis ball at his feet. Alden retrieved it and threw, this time not hitting anything, although he came close to dinging the Civil War cannon that guarded a memorial roll call of Towne's Union dead.

He passed the library, which was housed in an old granite edifice with a modern wing tucked behind it, almost out of sight. Next door, the former Grange Hall had been gutted and transformed into a residence said to be quite something, now, on the inside, although the new people (from the midwest) had left the old Grange Hall sign in place, nailed beneath the roof peak, having been advised that it was a fine example of naive folk art. However, the new people were said to be very annoyed when anyone showed up at their door with a question about home canning or cutworm control, and Lily, in an unguarded moment, had said those people from Chicago ought to put quotation marks around the words "Grange Hall," and they ought to do the same on their Welcome mat, either that or get one of those kinds that merely read Wipe Your Feet. Harvey mentioned you could also get door mats that said Go Away—he'd have one of those on his own doorstep only Penny wouldn't let him.

At what seemed to be the head of the green (for how could anything circular, or oval, really, be said to have a beginning and an end?), the Unitarian Church and its manse stood, shuttered and apart. The Unitarians took the summer off from services and their lively coffee hours afterward, and Alden entertained the fancy that this was so God Himself could move onto the vacated premises for the months of July and August to be left on His own to read and think in peace (peaceful now) and to eat whatever He liked and to go to bed and to get up when He felt like it. One could do worse than take up a bachelor existence in a place like Towne, where all the gracious homes and civilized neighbors and the almost organic availability of every creature comfort had the effect of muting and dulling the din of any troubling news from far away. Over time, you learned that the world got on fairly well without you, just as you yourself managed to get on perfectly well without it.

Alden whistled for Tommy then. A panel truck had driven onto the grass and pulled to a stop. Men, men organized into a Pavilion Committee, hopped out and began to pull the components of an open-sided tent from the back of the truck. They fitted the ends of poles into the existing holes in the ground that had not filled in since the tent had last been raised, on Memorial Day. They unfurled the rolled-up canvas, kicking the diminishing roll before them as they trod upon and flattened the material. With that accomplished, they undertook to lift the canvas, which weighed down upon their heads and upraised arms as they careered across the green like a Chinese dragon. Tommy regarded this apparition and then turned away with a show of indifference as he did whenever something very large and very odd proved to be beyond his comprehension.

Alden returned to his house, following Tommy through the listing gate. He had not yet seen to his own arrangements for the day and he had a crowd coming over. His U.S. flag remained spun around its pole in the back hall closet where it fell onto his shoulder, the eagle finial catching a corner of his ear with a wing tip, whenever he rooted round the closet for his golf clubs or a yardstick or the stepladder. On the previous afternoon, he had only gotten as far as pushing the lawn mower from the barn to stand in the driveway beside a can of gasoline, creating a tableau of his good intentions, before he remembered the more urgent need to make the first of many successive batches of ice cubes in his refrigerator freezer's sole ice cube tray. People were going to want ice in their drinks, and Alden was always on top of that situation, although he himself no longer drank; he'd given that up as well, around the same time he'd decided he could do without a subscription to *The New Yorker.* He'd also given away any of his dress shirts outfitted with French cuffs, making a bundle of them for Goodwill. On that occasion, Penny had warned him he'd turn into a hermit if he didn't watch out.

He stooped and plucked a blade of grass from the lawn, which, when viewed up close pinched between two fingers, looked even taller than it had when left standing in the ground. Tommy, instantly interested, had approached to lick the blade of grass from Alden's hand. He wandered off, as suddenly disengaged, which Alden took as a sign he did not have to bother about the grass. Tommy was right; it was just grass. Besides, by whose authority could the landscaping be said to have passed from lush Eden to howling wilderness if, indeed, a slightly seedy suburban milieu could be said to aspire to either, or indeed to any other, extreme? Furthermore, an added benefit of cultivating an overgrowth was the invisibility it provided. Alden could sit unobserved beneath his untended grape arbor; occasionally he and an alighting bird startled each other, and even Babe Palmer, on the warpath and intent upon collecting a donation or his signature to facilitate the suppression of something, would come and go away unsatisfied if he kept to the arbor and remained motionless and silent. Well, he hoped Babe would leave them all alone today. He particularly did not want Ginger to be bothered by the likes of her.

This thought of Ginger reminded him that first, before he hauled out the U.S. flag, he needed to set up the lawn chairs. He headed round the side of the house, back to the barn, and dragged a chaise lounge to the front yard, where he hesitated. Would Ginger rather be placed in the sun or in the shade? Whichever he chose, she would acquiesce, although in the past he would have braced himself for a thorough repositioning of all of his arrangements. Ginger had once narrowed her fine eyes and remarked that the siting of a woodland pond was not quite right relative to her placement of the picnic basket.

He stood there, reviewing the incompleteness of his preparations: the flagless front door, his ragged lawn, a patch of unstaked phlox flopping forward onto the garden path which he'd meant to deal with, but a single chair as yet provided for the rest of the parade watchers, no ice bucket, no glasses, no small table upon which to set the ice bucket and the glasses. He checked his watch, which told him nothing. He'd forgotten what time he'd been advised to expect them all, although the hour of the parade must be approaching; on the edge of the green, a vendor was feeding helium into balloons, which rounded and rose skyward on strings. He rubbed his chin. He had not yet shaved nor had he showered, and yesterday's crumpled shirt and khakis would not pass muster. He would have to change. Would it make better sense, he wondered, to shower and shave and dress first, or last? If he saw to everything else beforehand, people could arrive and look after themselves. He would call to them through his bathroom window to let them know there was ice in the silver bucket and advise them that they could sit anywhere they liked upon the chairs that he had dragged round from the barn and dusted off—although what those chairs really needed was a power-hosing.

Alden was mulling this over and scratching Tommy, who had wandered over to sit quietly beside his silent master when a Winnebago motor home turned into the driveway. The rumbling vehicle rose and fell over the rough ruts, its deep-treaded tires picking up and spitting out gravel, until it rolled to a stop with a hiss of air brakes and a shudder of subsiding engine power. For a moment, nothing happened, as in old sci-fi movies when the spaceship lands in the park and earthlings unwisely gather to speculate, eyes trained upon the outlines of a portal etched onto a shiny silver flank. Alden approached, a frown of deep interest replacing the smile of welcome he intended for his sons as Brooks hopped out through a commodious door while Rollins remained in the driver's seat flipping off switches and shutting down systems.

"There's plenty of room for you to stay in the house," Alden told Brooks. "I don't know why you think you need this thing. I'm glad to have you."

"We can't stay with you," said Brooks. "We'd fry your electric system, or, more likely, your electric system would fry us. Nothing's grounded and there's not enough juice anyway. Plus the dust. There's far too much dust in your house, and computers hate dust. And heat. The Winnebago has air-conditioning. This way we can stay here all summer and still run our company from our shiny new mobile headquarters."

All summer? wondered Alden. Had he been told that they would be here for the entire summer?

"Hey, Dad," Rollins said, joining his father and brother. "Don't we have a lot of people coming over? Like real soon? Didn't Julie tell us that? We'd better get the lawn mowed and haul out the chairs and stuff. And start the charcoal."

"No, no, don't bother with the grill. We're not having a cook-out. Hannah's bringing a cold poached salmon," Alden said. For some reason, he was now able to remember that, perhaps because he'd been looking forward to Hannah's salmon, served with a chilled dill sauce and thinly sliced cucumbers and a loaf of good rye bread.

GINGER WAS SETTLED ON the chaise beneath the shade of a great old maple, a summer-weight blanket folded over her feet, a cube of plastic table provided to support a pair of sunglasses and a glass of ice water and her camera into which she had just dropped a fresh disc of film. Tommy had been drawn to her side by the sound of paper wrappings crackling open, and Ginger had snapped his picture, saying, "Good boy." Sally wobbled past, riding back and forth across the lawn on an old three-speed bike the big boys (Brooks and Rollins, whom her mother had been so happy to see that she hugged them both) had wheeled out from the barn for her. She had to stand to pump the pedals, peering between the oxbow handlebars to which she clung. She swerved onto the driveway, skidding in the gravel. Righting herself, she made an investigative circuit around the big driving house parked there (she knew what it was from the cross-country drive). She pretended that she and the Winnebago were racing along the highway and when she looked back in triumph as she whizzed by (for she had won), she noticed a face afloat in a window there, watching her. She did not stop to wonder who that might be. She could not stop; the bike's brakes were broken.

"Boys, don't move," Ginger told Brooks and Rollins. She trained her camera upon them now. The camera was a recent purchase. She'd been persuaded to buy the most up-to-date automatic model and she could not get used to the idea that everything was being done for her, although that had been the as-advertised aspect of this particular model which had decided her in its favor. She sparred with the light and the range sensors in an effort to get them to conform to a more desired standard she held of brighter and sharper images. Brooks and Rollins were obedient subjects, very much disinclined to move after all their exertions of cutting grass and shifting furniture. They made an interesting study in their enduring sameness. (No one had ever been quite sure which brother was which.) One might almost accuse the estimable camera of seeing double when she aimed the lens at her nephews.

Her finger hovered above the shutter button, indecisively tapping at air, and then it rose as if in exclamation as two other figures entered the picture. Brooks and Rollins scrambled to their feet to greet Penny and Harvey who had hooted when he saw the boys. Ginger snapped down firmly to achieve the documentary, if not the artistic, shot of Harvey happily thumping his great-nephews on their backs.

"Harvey's that excited to see them," Penny explained to Ginger. She set a covered basket down on the cube of table; she needed both her hands free to grip the arms of the chaise as she leaned over to brush dry lips across Ginger's pale cheek even though she had seen her the previous evening. She'd had a bad dream about Ginger in the interim and the kiss served to make up for the odd and confusing travails her subliminal consciousness had subjected Ginger to.

"Never have I been more wrong," Harvey was telling Brooks and Rollins. "Never have I been so mistaken. I thought you two were the sorriest specimens it had ever been my bad luck to know. I pitied your parents. I pitied your teachers. I pitied the nation, on your behalf. I was convinced you were headed straight for—" He didn't know just where he had thought they'd been headed, but he gestured down to the ground, low and hard. "I look for you every day in the paper, to see how GLowe Systems stock is doing; first thing, I take my magnifying glass and look for GLS, sitting between General Electric and Goldman Sachs, just like it belongs there. You closed the week up six points. That financial fella on the TV gave your stock a thumbs up—no, that's the movie fella. The financial fella gave you a golden bullet, no, wait, I mean a golden bull."

"Well, thanks," said Brooks.

"Which one are you?" Harvey asked.

"I'm Brooks," said Brooks.

"Why, Harvey, haven't you noticed? He has a tattoo on his arm, and Rollins doesn't, so now you can tell them apart," Penny said.

"A tattoo?" asked Harvey peering at Brooks's arms. "Now why did you go and get yourself tattooed? You're not a sailor. Are you trying to impress a girl? What sort of girl is impressed by a tattoo? Watch out for her, boy. What's the picture supposed to be? It looks Oriental."

Brooks tensed his bicep to raise and plump the inked lines. "It's the symbol for the word for *science* in the ancient Sanskrit. Or the tattoo guy said that's what it meant when I asked him for something appropriate."

Harvey snorted. " 'Appropriate' and 'tattoo' are two words that don't go together, sonny. But why didn't you get one too, Rollins?" he asked. "Weren't you there on that presumably lively evening in—where exactly were you boys sparking about?"

"We were in Vegas," Rollins said. "I accompanied Brooks to the tattoo place, but then I saw how it was going to look on me on Brooks, not to mention he was crying with the pain, so I said sayonara and hit the casinos, instead."

"Did the ancient Sanskrittians even know what science is?" Harvey asked. "I'm inclined to say they didn't. I suspect it was all mumbo jumbo and sleight of hand with them, their temple priests and what not."

"What do you think of my tattoo, Aunt Ginger?" Brooks asked.

"I don't know. I understand that body art is very popular these days, but call me old-fashioned. I've only ever been able to sanction something small and Ivy League on a buttock," Ginger said. "A male buttock," she added, as Brooks's eyes wandered.

"Ginger," Penny said, recalling that Louis had gone to Northwestern, so whose tiger-bottom was she referring to? "Where's Lily?" she asked. Ginger wouldn't have been talking so fresh were Lily present. "Is she up at the house? With Betsy? I've brought my date-nut muffins and cream cheese too, for those who'll want it."

"Of course, you still won't be able to tell Brooks from Rollins if they're wearing suit coats, if they ever do wear suits," Harvey was saying. "You certainly don't dress like moguls. Look at what you're wearing today, droopy drawers and flip-flops and T-shirts with writing on them. What's yours say, Rollins? Why's it all in pink, for God's sake?" He read his nephew's chest. " 'GLowe Systems 5K Run for the Cure.' Cure for what? What can you cure by running after it?" he wanted to know. "What dread disease picks up and runs the other way when a pack of beet red technocrats comes pounding along the pavement? Not any reputable disease I can think of."

"Oh, shut up, Harvey," Penny said, casting a concerned look at Ginger. "That's enough out of you. Come see Lily with me. Help me carry these muffins."

"We raised a whole ton of money for the NIH," Rollins told Ginger, and Ginger said that was very thoughtful of him.

GLOVER AND JULIE ARRIVED ON FOOT, walking the last mile or so. The organizers had almost pulled the parade together, a missing congressman having phoned to say he was on the way (they'd have started without him except the paper had reported he was going to be there and a Silent Vigil for Life had been organized against him on the St. Rose of Lima lawn—they'd gone to a lot of trouble erecting a thousand small white crosses in the parking lot, standing them up in coffee cans filled with sand). The downtown roads adjacent to the green were just being closed to traffic, and Glover had had to park in the lot behind the Casa di Napoli, where he and Julie bought themselves cups of coffee and sugary beignets when they stopped inside to let Mung Samrin know that the little cloth-top BMW with the Virginia license plates was Glover's and he'd move it as soon as he could.

Carrying their coffee cups (they'd wolfed down the beignets), they threaded among the other parade goers, Glover and Julie's progress perhaps a bit more urgent than other people's, for they were heading home or as near to a home as either possessed at the moment.

"All these little ones," Julie said, holding her coffee cup higher above the heads of all the children surging round them.

"Betsy has a little one. She's supposed to be there today," Glover recalled.

"Oh flip, I forgot Dad told me that. I was going to get a present for Sally," Julie said.

"Why? I'm sure there's nothing she doesn't have. You know how Aunt Ginger loves to shop," Glover said.

"I just wanted to be nice to Sally. She officially makes me no longer the youngest person in this family. I'm passing the torch to the next generation. Let her be the one to be teased and left out of things and never get to choose what movie to watch," Julie said.

"But Julie, be reasonable, the movie you always wanted to see was the very aptly named *The Neverending Story,*" Glover said. Besides, however matters had been arranged in the past, they all deferred to Julie now, and he wondered whether Julie herself realized how much of their mother's part he and Brooks and Rollins had ceded to her over the last seven years. They let Julie pepper them with instructive, hectoring e-mails and, by and large, they obeyed her commands. She reminded them to call their father. She had notified them: *Send Aunt Ginger a get-well card; she's back in the hospital again; here's the address.* And she had sent this message to Brooks or Rollins, which they had forwarded to Glover, either amused or piqued by its demand: *I know it's your big deal IPO, but give Glover ten thousand shares (at least!) for his birthday. He needs more than just his* Army pay, *so cough up guys.* Then, this past spring, when William, their mother's new husband, had had his accident and Becky had been so frantic, it was Julie who said she would fly to Tripoli, muttering (somehow, Julie could mutter via e-mail) that she'd have to "lose" her U.S. passport with its Libyan entrance and exit stamps and apply for a new one before she could return to the States. Otherwise, she would be taken aside and placed in a cubicle to be interrogated as her luggage wobbled round and round, unclaimed, on the terminal carousel. She always felt sorry for whomever those bags belonged to, but she would be even sorrier were they her own.

No doubt Julie was right not to want to greet Betsy's little girl empty-handed. The child had probably inherited the family propensity for making unsentimental assessments of her relatives, and she would be in a position to pass the true story of the Lowe siblings' parsimonious ways *(Yes, those Lowes, the genius ones, or at least the two younger brothers)* on to the next several generations. Glover foresaw being discussed and abused well into the twenty-second century, a thought which rather arrested him. Like Julie, he still thought of himself as being the youngest, generationally speaking.

"We can buy Sally a balloon," he said. Several had already bobbled past them, dragged through the air by children.

"That'll just be so obvious we forgot," Julie said.

"Too bad the Ben Franklin is closed," Glover said. They were just walking past its windows, which were plastered with patriotic pinwheels wobbling round on the ends of dowels as a fan blew air over them.

"No, the BF only sells those cheap dolls whose arms snap off when you change their clothes," Julie said.

(. . . and they gave me a maimed doll, which was their idea of a suitable gift for a six-year-old. Naturally, I howled.)

"Maybe she doesn't even care for dolls," Glover said.

"Are you kidding? Aunt Lily told me once that Sally's the sort of little girl who draws pictures of robins with eyelashes," Julie said.

Glover didn't know what to make of that other than to observe that perhaps the child was in need of a reliable ornithological field guide, and as they came to the far side of the green (for across the green sat their father's house), he and Julie noticed the tables set out on the library lawn heaped with used books, discards and donations, offered for sale. The midday sun shone upon old bindings making the books appear to be repositories of long-neglected wisdom just lately restored to the light, at least at first glance. Many hands were reaching among the many offered volumes and riffling, rewedging, then reaching again.

Glover and Julie joined the browsers. Julie, who by then had several objects in mind, searched with method. Glover soon found what he was after, for someone had labeled the tables well and he withdrew to stand beneath the library oak, his own posture as straight as that of the tree, as he turned to random pages and studied them, gazing up into the canopy of leaves from time to time as if to consult further among the foliage.

Julie, who had taken her time, appeared at his elbow, declaring that they were now in a hurry. "There you are," she said. She carried a stack of books and she tilted back the book in her brother's hand to read the cover. "Roger Tory Peterson. Oh, you can't. Put it back. You seriously can't give Sally a bird guide."

"I'll save it for myself, then. I need some kind of hobby to keep me occupied while I'm here on leave," Glover said. "It'll keep me out of mischief."

"Anyway, I found a very nice copy of *The Lion, The Witch and the Wardrobe* for Sally. We all loved it when we were kids, remember? You guys were always locking me in the front hall closet. Plus, I found *Good-bye to All That* for Dad; it sounds just like him, and here's something by some French person about the Empress Josephine with a lot of nice pictures in it, for Aunt Ginger. That's all; nobody else gets a present today. Where's the pay place? Oh flip, there's that awful Mrs. Palmer at the cash box. I don't want to have to talk to her. Here, you pay. It's a buck a book. Here's a five, but don't wait for change. Don't give her a chance. Just hand her the money and walk away, don't look her in the eye . . ."

Glover closed Julie's fingers around the five-dollar bill and gently lowered her hand to her side. He relieved her of her books. He felt equal to Mrs. Palmer, whom he doubted would recognize him anyway, and he resolved to make her use up one of her begrudged smiles on him. He would call her ma'am and compliment her on what a well-run book sale she was overseeing. He would vanquish her by means of a charm offensive for, lately, he had learned the benefits of maintaining the peace.

JULIE KNELT IN THE GRASS facing Sally as she inspected the child very thoroughly. She rubbed a thumb over a fresh, deep scratch on Sally's shin to stop the bleeding (Sally having brought her brakeless bike to a halt by riding it into the midst of a clump of lilacs which had hidden its spiky knot of branches behind pretty heart-shaped leaves). Sally watched, rather fascinated, as Julie's pressing thumb seemed to push the red beads of blood back into her veins, where they belonged. Then Julie posed several statistical questions about Sally's height and weight and the exact length of her long, fair braid and she inquired after her reading level in school. Sally answered that last query with an enigmatic "Blue." She studied Julie in turn. Julie had those small freckles scattered all over her nose and cheeks, those little flecks of the sort her mother made her wear sunscreen for so she wouldn't get them, and Sally supposed Julie's mother didn't care whether her daughter was speckled and so must not love her very much (because mothers subjected their children to unpleasant applications and practices and constraints for their own health and safety and well-being, which Sally knew for a fact because her mother said so). She met Julie's eyes, which were brown and fringed with very dark lashes; she would have liked to touch them (they looked so sharp and glossy), but she didn't quite dare to reach out. Julie's chopped-up hair was the color of a stoplight, and Sally would have liked to feel that as well. Julie's hair did not look real; it looked wonderful.

"So, you're a Blue reader," Julie said. She shrugged and, selected a book from among the several she'd plunked down in the grass, saying, "Here, this one's for you." Sally accepted her present prettily. Her mouth formed a rather exaggerated O of surprise and she wandered off to read quietly beneath the grape arbor, although a glance at the solid block of words comprising the first page of the story told her this book was obviously intended for a Yellow reader.

Julie rose and turned to face Ginger next. She scrubbed at the corners of either eye with the heels of her hands and quelled a sound of sniffling as she approached her aunt. "Hay fever," she explained, sitting gently at the end of the chaise and replacing the blanket, which had slipped from Ginger's feet. As she did this, the book about the Empress Josephine slithered from her lap, and Ginger, making a quick grab for the book, knocked an elbow against her glass of ice water, which teetered and rocked but was caught by Julie just in time before it could drench the expensive new camera, all of which had the effect of making the moment less awkward than Julie had feared it would be, Lily having warned her that she would find Ginger very much changed.

Harvey saluted when he saw Glover. He addressed him as Captain and drew his great-nephew aside to tell him what the army ought to be doing about the situation in the Balkans, his advice being that the army should just sit on its hands since no one had ever made those people see reason.

Lily and Betsy emerged from the house, each bearing a tray. They spotted the newcomers but before greeting them they had to set their trays down on the teapoy table that the boys had carried out to the lawn and then they had had to discuss the arrangement of what they had just set down. Betsy surprised herself by holding a different opinion from Lily's on the subject of deviled eggs, Lily advocating leaving them as halves while Betsy thought the halves should be fitted back together. Alden, seeing that his oldest son and only daughter had arrived safely, called out from his bathroom window to say he would be right down to join them.

"There's plenty of ice in the silver bucket," he added.

"Isn't it a bit early to start the cocktail hour, Dad?" Brooks called back.

"Dad's been on the wagon," Rollins reminded him.

"Then what ever must he think of us?" Brooks asked.

HANNAH ACQUIRED CAM AS HER COMPANION as she was loading the wagon she had used back when she was still in the catering business for transporting lofty and cumbersome wedding cakes from her van to banquet halls, pulled by one assistant and pushed by another as Hannah crept crabwise alongside with her sheltering arms outstretched. Today, with the downtown roads closed to traffic (she had not timed this very well) the old wagon, a rubber-wheeled and wooden six-passenger kiddie kart from Sweden, was once again earning its keep as a vehicle to convey to Alden's house all the food she had prepared for an alfresco luncheon.

She came and went from her commercial premises, an old woolen mill building downtown on Front Street, which she had purchased (and she and her son lived above the factory floor in a very nice loft apartment). She held a big copper fish poacher away from her body, so thrown off balance by the shifting and sloshing of the salmon inside that she had to look down to see where her feet were stepping as she walked. Her thumbs clamped the lid closed against the rise and the flop of the fish, which seemed to have come back to life, and indeed, Hannah wondered, as she had wondered before, whether she might not one day work some sort of reanimating magic by mistake. She used so many herbs and wild mushrooms and roots prised from the earth in her cooking and perhaps someday while tossing hoodooed produce into a pot she would accidentally recite something incantatory as well. There was always a lite-classic rock CD playing on the factory floor, the preferred listening of her staff (women, all), and lately, she'd caught herself singing certain infectious choruses under her breath as she chopped and stirred. Certainly the melodies and lyrics exerted a strange power over Hannah, refusing to vacate her head.

Cam was sitting on the curb. She had situated herself in proximity to the partially loaded wagon, keeping guard, although the passersby streaming toward the parade didn't give the cart or its contents a second glance. One could safely leave personal property unattended on the streets of Towne, although Hannah was less sure about the welfare of an unattended child, even in Towne, in this day and age.

"Cam, are you here on your own?" she asked.

Cam shook her head and pointed to the opposite corner where Om lingered with friends as she kept track of her little sister. Om's face brightened when she spied Hannah and she waved in a manner to indicate permission. Hannah understood that Cam had been transferred to her custody, an arrangement that suited both Samrins. Om and the other girls, who had wearied of child minding, took off for the green at a run, and Cam turned her attention to supervising the proper placement of the fish poacher among the rest of the foil-covered containers stacked in the cart. She favored a place of prominence balanced across two of the kiddie benches so everyone could see how brightly the copper top gleamed. Hannah, however, had kept clear a spot on the floor where the kettle could be safely wedged between ice packs, with another ice pack on top to secure the lid against the bump of the pavement and the flop of the fish. Cam then attempted to balance herself across the bench seats, but Hannah would not allow this, either.

"You're too big for me to pull," she said, and Cam, who wished to be big, or at any rate, bigger, received the remark with a gratified nod and her hand closed over Hannah's as they both reached for the wagon pull.

The distance to Alden's house was a half mile, a not insignificant trek under the circumstances. Hannah adjusted her stride to accommodate Cam's short steps and she stooped, her shoulder dropping lower and lower, as Cam irresistibly tugged the wagon pull down to her own level. Hannah's hand grew hot beneath Cam's clasp and her fingers began to lose feeling as Cam's grip tightened to secure her hold. But people made way for them as they rumbled along the sidewalk, and they were assisted over curbs and given a push when, taking a shortcut, they mired in the Congregational Church's lawn at the soft spot where the sump pipe gushed water through a cellar window. Cam's pace quickened as they approached the house, and Hannah wondered why the child was so determined to be included in this Hill family gathering. What did Cam want? What was Cam after? But the same thing could be asked of herself, as well, Hannah supposed.

THE FAMILY SAT IN THE FRONT YARD; their chairs had been pulled up behind the low stone wall that fronted Alden's property, aimed toward a view of the parade route and the green, which was thronging now with people. Harvey hoped, for Alden's sake, that they would all go home at the end of the day. Julie said there must have been a big sale, locally, on beige Bermuda shorts and lime green visor-shades. Penny asked Harvey why wouldn't people want to go home at the end of the day? Brooks leaned back and mused upon the possibility of someday making circuitry capable of moving as spontaneously as human beings negotiating a crowd of other human beings, adjusting and readjusting their paths at every obstacle, thus creating networks that could reinvent themselves infinitely. Betsy was worried that Ginger would not be able to see the parade; her chaise remained at a remove beneath the shade of the maple, but when questioned, Ginger raised herself on her elbows to demonstrate how she would manage when the time came. Lily thought about the farm stand, which was closed for the day, and she realized too late that it would have been a courtesy to leave a few dozen boxes of strawberries out on a table available for sale via the honor system for those who had forgotten to pick some up and were counting on the stand to be open after the parade. Rollins, to whom Brooks had mentioned his new idea about intelligent circuitry, said he had a notion how they might address the problem and he tapped a few thoughts into his BlackBerry. Harvey told Penny it wasn't for him to say why the crowd wouldn't disperse at the end of the day, but should the crowd elect to camp out overnight on the green, Alden had his sympathy.

"Here comes Hannah," Alden said, freshly shaved and showered and joining them at last. He had spied her from his bedroom window, pulling the cart past the bandstand, and when she came into view, Alden was given credit for having produced her, although he declined any responsibility. Hannah managed perfectly well on her own; he had always noticed that about her.

"This all needs to be refrigerated," Hannah said as the brothers and Julie swarmed, lifting containers from the cart and peeling back foil to divine the contents. Harvey expressed his relief that she had arrived at last with the legitimate grub and he drew her aside to confide in her.

"Penny *says* they're date-nut muffins," he said, indicating a basket on the teapoy table, "but she mostly used diced and dried unsulphured papaya chips because there weren't enough dates in the house, or enough molasses, for that matter. She manufactured some molasses from clear Karo syrup and soy sauce, but just because something looks like something else doesn't mean that's what it is," he asserted, and Hannah had to agree with him.

Cam quietly sought out Lily, catching hold of her skirt and tucking herself against Lily's side. Cam was where she wanted to be and she was determined not to be sent away until much later in the day after everything that was going to happen had happened and there would be nothing left for her to miss. Sally, for her part, had retreated to the grape arbor where she was laboriously reading aloud to Tommy from her new book. He lay there panting, but he lifted his head when Sally pronounced a strange new word she had just sounded out with exulting emphasis: "Lon-DON!" She had never commanded the attention of a more tolerant listener, but the commotion attending the arrival of the cart caused her to pluck a leaf from the arbor to mark her place and, setting the book upon the bench, she went to see what was going on.

Ginger called Sally over to her chair, and she crooked a finger at Cam, who was gazing out from behind Lily's skirt, yet another strange, watchful face regarding her here in this place. "Sally. Cam," Ginger said. "Cam. Sally," she clarified, which was news to neither child, for each had determined whom the other could only be.

"You will be great friends," Ginger told them. She seemed so certain of this that the girls took a step toward each other. Then they halted and turned to Ginger to make absolutely sure, and she tempered the power of her prophecy by saying, "Very likely, you will." Sally and Cam looked at each other blamefully, as if something had been offered and then snatched away.

"Granna," Sally said. She cupped her hands around Ginger's ear and leaned in to whisper, urgently. "Granna, is she wearing my shirt? She's wearing my shirt. And my shorts."

"Oh, no, I don't think so," Ginger said, pushing Sally away and frowning at her. She shook her head softly in such a way that Cam could not see.

"Yes. I recognize my red shorts with the star buttons and the blue and white shirt with the other star buttons. It's my Fourth of July outfit from last year," Sally insisted, as she turned to confront Cam.

"No. It's Cam's Fourth of July outfit," Ginger told her. "Let's hear no more about it."

"But Granna." Sally's face burned pink and she fended off the unfairness of it all, her fingers making passionate points in the air.

"Not another word. It's neither polite nor kind to Cam. I apologize, Cam, on behalf of my very rude granddaughter," Ginger said, and Sally fell into a heap upon the grass, unable to stand any more of this.

However, Cam, who seldom had anything new (not clothes or toys or a bicycle or books) was, if anything, pleased to meet the prior possessor of the shorts and shirt. She was never entirely satisfied with the condition of the garments that came her way; they were always afflicted with fade marks or an indelible stain or a deposit of lint in the pockets which had to be worried out and discarded. The shorts she wore today had arrived conspicuously lacking a star-shaped button on the left rear pocket and here at last was her chance to make an inquiry at the source.

"Where is it?" she asked Sally.

"Where is what, honey?" Ginger asked, and Cam twisted round and lifted her buttonless pocket tab and frowned down upon Sally who, at that moment far too clearly recalled how she had slipped the red shorts from the bundle of old and outgrown clothing set aside for the poor children who would be grateful to receive them—and who ought to be happy to get them in any condition; Sally had privately amended her mother's fine little speech on the subject of charity as she sawed at the stubborn thread with a nail file and bitten with her teeth until the star button dropped off. She had need of a starfish to drop into her dollhouse aquarium to join the macaroni shells and a silver lobster charm at the bottom of the sea. But to be confronted with the evidence of her misdeed, which had been committed so long ago and so far away, not to mention that she had been led to believe that all the poor children who would be running around in her old shirts and pants and jackets lived down in Chino, not *here*—

"Go look for it," Ginger suggested, believing the button's loss had just been noticed and thus must just have occurred. "Retrace your steps since you've arrived," she advised Cam. "Sally will help you, won't you, Sally?"

Sally scrambled to her feet, suffused with love for Ginger, who had not even begun to suspect the whole tangled story. "Sure," she said.

Cam did not explain that the button had been long lost, reasoning that it had to be somewhere and why not begin the search in the immediate vicinity, particularly since Sally had been enlisted to assist, which meant that Cam got to be the boss of the operation.

"Cute," Penny remarked to a passerby who had paused by Alden's wall to fix a sandal strap. "Aren't those two little ones cute together, just like a UNICEF poster reminding us how, red and yellow, black and white, we're all precious in His sight. We can all get along if only we act like children," she called after the passerby, who was hurrying away, sandal in hand.

For even though she knew the exercise was futile, Sally had crouched where Cam had told her to, and she earnestly hunted for any star shape, white and embossed with raised ridges and presumably—possibly—lost in the local grass. Because this single vision dominated her mind's eye, she missed the object that Cam suddenly reached for and seized right out from under her nose.

"I found a Barbie knife," Cam declared.

"Where? Let me see," Sally said, and Cam held up her open palm upon which balanced a single tine broken off from a pink plastic fork.

"Oh," said Sally, and she expelled a sigh which lifted the sliver of plastic and caused it to tremble toward her as if summoned. Cam's fist clamped shut, and she transferred her find to the back right pocket of her shorts, securing the flap with the remaining star button, which Sally now wished she had yanked off as well and then Cam would never have known that either button was missing.

After a further five minutes of not very serious searching, Cam noticed that Sally was walking like a duck and realizing that she, too, was squatting and moving with equal ungainliness, Cam straightened from her stooping posture so that she could turn and accuse Sally of waddling.

"No, I'm not," Sally said, jumping up.

"You were," Cam said.

"So were you," Sally said.

"So were you," Cam said, and she stuck her fingers in her ears so she would not hear Sally's retort, ending further debate.

But they had other fish to fry. They had crossed the lawn and come to the edge of the driveway; they had tended that way not without a purpose, for there sat the Winnebago. They approached a rear tire and inspected it, probing the deep treads with a picked-up stick. They moved on to demonstrate a further interest in a front tire by kicking it hard. Pausing to admire their reflections, mirrored by the bumper chrome and melted and stretched into sinuous figures of mystery, they slipped around to the far side of the vehicle to stare at the door whose handle was located high over their heads but which would be reachable if they stood upon something tall, which they could fetch from the barn, Cam said.

"There is an entire house in there," Cam said, standing back and gazing up at a shiny window.

"I know," Sally said.

"There's a kitchen and a living room and a bathtub and four bedrooms, one for each child," Cam said, dreamily.

"I know," Sally said.

"So all you have to do is stand up on something tall from the barn and reach," Cam concluded.

"I—no," Sally said.

When the door opened abruptly on its own, Cam began to shriek, and more startled by this than by the opening of the door, Sally screamed too. For she had just remembered the face she had seen at the window of the Winnebago and she supposed now that they need only to have knocked politely to gain entry. Two very pretty and very young women, alike in every way but their expressions, one displaying concern and the other radiating her annoyance, climbed down from the RV. Each, in turn, miscalculated the last step, which was a high one, and, nearly fallen upon by lunging ladies, Cam and Sally screamed even more shrilly. The sympathetic lady attempted to reassure them, saying, "Little girls, little girls, it's all right," while the annoyed one covered her ears and said, "Do not do this to me. Do not do this to me at this moment today."

Betsy and Julie and Glover and Tommy had come running at the first screams. Brooks and Rollins, rightly reckoning that this was all just a fuss and not a calamity, arrived a few beats behind.

"What? You had these women in there all this time?" Julie asked them. She regarded the newcomers with narrowed eyes, although she relaxed the arm that carried the suddenly seized garden rake with which she had meant to battle the forces that imperiled the little girls.

"Well, yes. All right with you?" Brooks asked.

"I don't know. The fact that you had unattributed women parked in Dad's driveway? It seems a bit, I don't know what," Julie said. She searched for the word.

"Downwardly mobile?" suggested Betsy.

"I'm Glover Lowe, how do you do," Glover said, reaching round Julie to extend a hand.

"I'm Petal. And she's Tarara," the more approachable one of the two young women responded. "I'm so sorry we startled the children."

"No. *They* startled *us*." Tarara set the record straight.

But Sally and Cam were keen to put all that behind them. Sally sidled toward Betsy and tugged at her skirt hem.

"What?" Betsy asked. "What now?"

"Can we go inside there?" Sally asked. Cam had already mounted the steps and was standing on the threshold of the Winnebago, gazing inside and mouthing to Sally, *It's wonderful.*

"Sure," Brooks said. "Go in and look around."

"Don't touch anything," Betsy said. "So's not to break it," she added, although that's not what she meant.

"Anyway, we picked up our friends Petal and Tarara in Newport on our way here. They had a shoot down there," Rollins explained.

"Furs," Tarara said, rolling her shoulders and basking in the memory.

"Huh? Furs? A shoot? You were hunting? In Newport? Help me out; I've got terminal jet lag; I'm confused," Julie said. "What's in season in Newport? I mean, aside from yachtsmen and tennis pros? Vanderbilts? Are there still Vanderbilts? You know, any snazzy ones?"

"I think Brooks and Rollins's friends must be fashion models. I mean, just look at them," Betsy said. "They're so attractive," she added, although that's not what she really meant.

"Oh yes, of course. That's all Brooks and Rollins date nowadays, fashion models, or so I read in *People* magazine, which is what I consult when I want to see what my brothers are up to. I howled at that graphic they had that showed what the kid would look like if Rollins married Claudia Schiffer," Julie said.

"Oh, I saw that. I thought it was so cruel," Betsy said. "I thought that was cruel," she told Rollins.

"Well, they were just demonstrating a function of a new feature we were introducing to our EnVision line," Rollins said. "It's all about the manipulation of images in order to explore potentialities. I quite understood why our child had my nose and Claudia's pout."

"Is the movie over?" Brooks asked the Tarara one.

"We were watching the DVD of *Titanic,* and I just had to know how it ended," Tarara explained.

"How it ended?" Julie asked. She nudged Betsy, and Betsy nudged her, and noticing all the nudging Petal spoke up, "Tarara wanted to find out specifically whether or not Leo drowned."

"Leo, is it?" Betsy asked.

"Although I personally think there was enough room on that floating plank or board or whatever it was for both Kate and Leo to have sat upon to survive until that other boat came along if only she'd stopped sprawling there being dramatic and hogging the whole thing," Petal said.

"Oh, that's just what I thought," Julie said. "There would have been room if they'd both sat up and, you know, hugged their knees and clenched their butts."

"Especially her," said Petal.

"Exactly," agreed Julie. "Especially her, and her butt."

"But then it wouldn't have turned out so nice and romantic and sad, I guess, if Leo lived," Petal said, and Julie and Betsy had to agree; sad was so much more satisfying, somehow. What more did the beautiful pair have to look forward to after their whirlwind romance on the high seas?

HARVEY WAS CHARMED, Alden seemed surprised, and Penny and Ginger found themselves a good deal less surprised when Petal and Tarara were presented to them. Presently, Hannah and Lily emerged from the house with a pitcher of Bloody Marys and a trayful of glasses (Alden's plain tomato juice identified by a wedge of lemon in lieu of a jaunty celery stick) and they too were introduced to the young women. They also said they were not surprised; they could both be said to be wondering a bit, but they were not surprised by the presence of Petal and Tarara.

"It's old around here, isn't it," Tarara observed, her eyes darting everywhere. Everything was small and cramped and crooked and made of wood. Nothing gleamed except for the silver ice bucket set upon a flimsy little table; the bucket was also obviously old, although it was a better kind of old than the other stuff, she would have said, for it shone out in a recognizably rich way.

"Are you interested in history?" Alden asked, making an effort.

"Not really. But sometimes I enjoy the hats," Tarara said.

Brooks and Rollins bore their girlfriends off to settle them before the parade started. The young women had consented to come all this way on the strength of the promise of a parade, or at least Petal had agreed while Tarara, who had not been paying attention back in Newport, now asked, "What parade?" Betsy and Julie and Glover tried to work out who went with whom; Rollins brushed a centipede from the arm of the Adirondack chair he offered to Petal, whereas Tarara seemed to expect Brooks to run interference for her over the matter of a yellowjacket that zoomed in tightening circles around her head, although here Brooks failed her; he flailed a slipped-off flip-flop to no effect. When the insect at last flitted away, it flitted away on its own terms.

"Their waists are like wands," Penny remarked to Ginger. "And look at the scowling one, how she sits. She can twist her calves twice around each other, her legs are so long."

"You make her sound like a snake," Ginger said and she closed her eyes, the better to listen to Betsy and Julie and Glover laughing together by the gate.

The fire whistle blew, signaling the official start of the day's events. So near to the fire station, here downtown, everyone felt flattened by the din, and Lily went around passing out Fourth of July–themed cocktail napkins to those who did not have them, liquid having sloshed from full glasses onto startled hands and wrists.

Sally and Cam had shot from the Winnebago at the clamor of the siren, Cam knowing what it signaled, Sally more generally alarmed. They ran onto the lawn and wheeled like starlings as they sought a place to alight: not by Brooks and Rollins and the strange ladies, who visibly contracted, drawing in their long arms and legs, as the little girls pounded past them, and not by Ginger beneath the shady tree (they would have hurled themselves onto the shady chaise and burrowed among the pillows and blanket, but Lily caught their eyes and shook her head no). They flew out of the gate, past Betsy and Julie and Glover. Betsy called, "*Sally*," and Sally froze, and Cam as well (for she understood that today she and Sally were in the same boat), and they sprang onto the wall, each settling upon a flat-topped stone. Cam's stone wobbled, and she rode it from side to side, amusing herself as they waited for something to happen (the parade had a half a mile to go before the first marchers passed Alden's house). Sally's stone remained stuck however hard she swayed, reaching down to hold on as she flung herself back and forth, until Betsy told her not to break Uncle Alden's nice old wall. Sally asked, "What about *Cam*?" several times until she accepted that no answer was to be her answer and she listened to the hollow grind of Cam's rocking rock as she regretted having been so gracious about letting Cam keep the Barbie knife; so far, Cam was winning at everything.

Drumbeats loudened and interest quickened and the parade finally arrived, the marchers debouching from Bridge Street to begin a final circuit around the green before assembling in front of the bandstand for a further prescribed ceremony. For such a short parade, it played itself out as rather a long one. There were sizable gaps between one component and the next, which was actually rather a plus, giving onlookers time to pick out the well-known faces and to figure out who the faintly familiar faces belonged to. Details of costume and decorations were noted as well, and it was generally argued, up and down the route, whether Betsy Ross had been a young and attractive blonde, as the Betsy Ross float was asking everyone to believe.

A boy rode by on a unicycle, and everyone agreed unicycling must be harder than it looked, and it looked pretty hard to begin with. Julie noticed that a television station had set up across the road from them and was filming the proceedings. Hannah began to explain that it was the new local access cable channel, which Julie would find tucked between the two Spanish language soap opera stations on the television dial, but Penny hushed her, glancing at Harvey; she didn't want to get him started on the Telemundo. The half-strength, hastily reassembled Towne High School band trooped past, and they all called out hellos to Thanh, who dipped and swooped the bell of his French horn in reply. Then, Revolutionary War reenactors, who had been pausing along the way to demonstrate a smart piece of drill, halted in front of Alden's house, where they were put through their paces saluting and presenting arms and obeying a series of seal-barked commands. The family all looked on as respectfully as if these really were embattled farmers about to go pick a fight with the British. Tarara remarked that their hats were excellent, and Petal wished she'd thought of liking hats before Tarara had declared an interest so that she too could comment knowledgeably about something. She was working on a remark about the soldiers' boots, but the company moved on before she could come up with anything. They were followed by the Hallelujah Campers, long a fixture in Towne in the summertime (the Baptists having gotten their hands on a hundred prime acres a hundred years earlier), who had entered a float which made a rather unclear point concerning the Gadarene swine, who were largely mistaken for a puzzling representation of pigs at the beach. Sally and Cam fell off the wall, they laughed so hard. Sally tried to nab Cam's rocking rock then, but Cam hopped back on when she realized what Sally was up to. A troupe of bagpipers strolled past, the Applied Pipers, a fixture at local festivals and funerals. Tommy sat up and whined as if singing along with them, although no one could make out the tune they were playing until Hannah identified it.

"It's 'Every Breath You Take,' " she said. " 'My fool heart aches, oh can't you see you belong to me?' " she recited. "That one."

"Ah," said Alden, nodding although he still had no idea what he'd just heard.

An open convertible was driving slowly down the road. A young woman sat upon the ledge above the backseat in the traditional and never-very-safe-seeming position of a featured beauty queen. Tarara bestirred herself to see just what was with this hometown girl who most likely had won one of those pageants where scholastic achievement counted for 50 percent of the score; that was often so obviously the case. However, the young woman perched there on view was unadorned by a crown or tiara. Instead, a spray of white tulle covered her head. Nor was she displaying an identifying sash over a lovely gown. Rather, she wore jeans and a T-shirt imprinted with the face of a hawk-nosed man and she was carrying a sign. She had turned the written-upon side toward the people lining the green, whose faces reflected their enlightenment as they read what it said.

"Quick, she's getting away. Who is she?" Julie asked. She whistled loudly between her fingers, and the veiled head swiveled toward her, the sign following suit.

"Oh dear, I was afraid of this. She's that poor Marry-Me-Nomar girl," Penny said. She clucked her tongue and sighed.

"Who?" several voices asked.

"She goes to every Red Sox home game she can manage, wearing her wedding veil and carrying her Marry-Me-Nomar sign, and then she sits in the bleachers, oh so hopefully. If you watch the games on TV, they always show her on camera," Penny said. "And then they show Nomar Garciaparra gazing into the lacings of his glove or tapping his bat, you know, with the way he has, always adjusting his wrist bands and fidgeting whenever he steps up to bat, which so annoys Harvey. But I had no idea the Marry-Me-Nomar girl was from around here."

"She catches the bus into Boston, from in front of Peddocks'. She lives here in Towne; she's the Houghton-Hortons' au pair," Hannah said. "The women who work on my line know all the local news," she explained. Most of her staff had to work extra jobs, cleaning the big, new houses. Hannah paid them what she could, but it was never enough; they all had kids and no husbands, and she knew how hard that could be.

"Well, you're much smarter off playing hard to get," Penny said. "Young ladies," she added, aiming a look at Tarara and Petal, who both started.

"I don't know, girls," Ginger spoke up. "Maybe throwing yourself at an all-star batter is the way to go." Julie glanced at Betsy, expecting her to roll her eyes and sigh or to speak a sharply warning *"Mummy"* and, indeed, Betsy did sigh and say, "Mummy," but she did so resignedly or perhaps even fondly. Julie could not quite discern her cousin's present relationship with her mother, whether rocky or reconciled or what.

The Boy Scouts were now tramping past, corralled behind a banner carried by the two most dependable Star Scouts, who were under orders not to let the fringe sweep the pavement. Over the course of the parade, matters had become rather hilarious in the ranks; an effort was being made to moonwalk in formation. David May, Hannah's son, gave the high sign to a pair of confederates when he spotted Brooks and Rollins in Alden's front yard, and with a subsiding motion, David and his pals allowed the oncoming rows of Scouts to part round and pass on without them. The three boys peeled off their tunics and badge sashes, tossing them in a heap atop the stone wall, and tugged their T-shirts free from the waistbands of their shorts to reveal the full texts and images imprinted upon them (GLowe Systems, VeeCube, Do You Dare?; 6th Annual Science Camp, July 7–14, 1997, Rensselaer Polytechnic Institute; I'm With Einstein—>). They crowded through the gate and made straight for Brooks and Rollins.

"Dude," Brooks greeted David easily. He'd met Hannah's kid on other occasions, and he was used to dealing with worshipful boys.

"Hey," said David, as Matt (Science Camp) and Jason (I'm With Einstein) gazed at Brooks and then turned to take in Rollins.

"Dudes," said Rollins, graciously.

Matt prodded Jason, and Jason elbowed Matt, and Matt spoke up. "The manual doesn't *tell* you," he said, "but isn't it true that the effect of the Mosaic Maneuver can be exponentially enhanced if the axial image is recessed by thirty degrees as, correspondingly, you increase the level of amplitude?"

"Oh, do not start with that electronics stuff. Do not even begin," objected Tarara. She rose with majesty from her Adirondack chair, attaining her full height and making sure that one camisole strap slipped errantly from her shoulder, but the boys failed to admire her. She glided off to chat with Julie and Betsy, whom she had decided at least seemed sensible even though they were poorly dressed, in shapeless and sleeveless cheesecloth summer frocks. She understood why they hadn't bothered to look good, the level of appreciation being so low around here. Not to mention the dust, or whatever the gritty substance was that had settled on every surface she touched and it would be murder to get the stains out of linen or silk, and she did not even want to think about suede.

Petal, as averse to technical discussions (although she kept meaning to ask Rollins just how a mirror worked because it was amazing that you never had to replace the batteries; mirrors just shone on and on), more politely removed herself, saying, "Don't mind me," as if permission not to notice her needed to be granted.

"David has gone AWOL from the Scouts," Hannah said to Alden.

"I think the parade is more or less over," Alden said. He stepped onto the sidewalk where Harvey had buttonholed a congressional candidate to whom he was explaining that he had done all he could during the last election to help the party; he'd kicked over a few opposition yard signs but he was only one man. The Towne ladder truck, polished and draped with flags, was slowly rumbling down the road, followed by all the people from further along the route, who were now streaming toward the green, where further ceremony was planned.

"Do *we* have to listen to the speeches?" Julie asked. She swallowed a yawn; for her it was now the evening of a very long day.

"We can catch most of the program from here. In fact, it can't be avoided," Alden said. At some point, Patch Hatch, head of the selectmen, would step up to the rostrum and lean on his elbows to read the Declaration of Independence. He always sounded peeved as if he'd written the document himself and was worn out by the effort required to defy a monarch and craft a nation. " 'He has plundered our seas, ravaged our Coasts *(sniff)*, burnt our towns, and destroyed the lives of our people *(sigh)*.' "

Cam caught the eye of the volunteer fireman driving the truck and she signaled, raising a hand and tugging at the air, to tell him she wanted to hear the siren. He obliged, and the blast dislodged her, and Sally too, from the wall. They fled to Ginger, who was holding her hands over her ears, but she widened her arms to receive the little girls, settling them on either side of herself in the chaise.

"I have to start seeing about lunch," Hannah said. "If someone would just help with the table and chairs, tote them down to the riverside," she reminded Alden.

"Boys," Alden said. "Do as Hannah says." Glover, Brooks, and Rollins moved to obey, and David, Matt, and Jason tagged along after them to lend a hand and to get underfoot.

"What can we do?" Julie asked, offering for Betsy and herself, but Tarara returned to the chair from which she had been routed in order to demonstrate, should there be any confusion, that her services had not been volunteered. Petal, however, looked wistful and willing all at once, as she lifted the muffin basket from the teapoy table and the plated slab of cream cheese and the platter of deviled eggs, which she balanced on the crook of her arm, prepared to convey them down to the river, or anywhere else, for that matter. "I used to waitress," she told Hannah, "before, you know, I found out I didn't have to be a waitress anymore." Hers had been one of those hometown success stories. "What are you doing here?" a customer had asked her one day while she was pouring his coffee, and as she was starting to explain about having had to leave school early and how she wasn't good with computers so that let out retail, he had handed her his business card and told her to come see him in New York.

Julie collected Bloody Mary glasses from all the places they had been left upon the lawn and wall. Tommy had licked most of them clean, a habit he'd acquired during his former life in Prague, where through no fault of his own, he'd fallen among a louche crowd of artists and politicians prior to throwing his lot in with Alden.

"Really," Ginger was saying to Lily. "I wish I'd had time to organize my gypsy moth caterpillar float. It would have been a hoot."

"What? What? What would have been a hoot, Granna?" Sally asked, and upon being told, she and Cam declared that they longed to wear black tights and walk down the road disguised beneath plastic garbage bags. But before they could extract a promise that they could all be gypsy caterpillars next year (Ginger was failing to say yes to that), Betsy stepped in to remind them that it was never safe to place anything plastic over one's head and she didn't wish to hear any more pleading on the subject.

Lily pictured, then, a long black worm slithering through the streets of Towne devouring everything that was green and growing and alive along the way, leaving nothing but barrenness and winter and death in its path. She wished Ginger would not go on so about such a creature; Ginger's idea was not nearly as amusing as she evidently thought it was.

HANNAH DID NOT FIND IT VERY EASY to operate in Alden's kitchen. He kept his coffee in the canister marked Flour, and the flour remained stored in the bag it had come in, which always acquired a small sifting leak from a secret puncture or an invisibly split seam. There was no counter space; one made do with an unanchored and rolling-about island unit topped with something that looked like butcher block but which was only a buckling and peeling veneered surface. Alden possessed a candy thermometer but did not have an egg beater; likewise, there was a pie chain but no slotted spoon. There was a lemon zester in the drawer but no decent paring knife. Hannah guessed that an important box had been lost, the one in which Becky had packed her everyday kitchen utensils.

Attached by magnets to the refrigerator door was an In Case of Emergency poster, handed out by the Red Cross years ago, which Alden seemed to think had "come" with the house and so must remain on display. It told, in text and pictures, what to do in the event of serious burns and deep arterial cuts and broken bones and choking fits and accidental drowning and the mistaken ingestion of a poisonous or a caustic substance, although Lily had stopped by one day and penciled in the now-current Poison Control 800 number. She had also blacked out the information on the old remedy for choking, replacing it with a brief description of the Heimlich maneuver, accompanied by a not very successful illustration of a gasping stick-figure sufferer and his would-be stick-figure savior engaging in the procedure. Hannah stood by the sink, studying the poster; a fainting victim, who had crumpled in a graceful swoon, was being lovingly tended, stretched out on a park bench with her feet elevated and some kind gentleman's suit jacket rolled into a bolster to support her neck. Everyone seemed to be enjoying themselves, and whatever the indisposition that had occasioned the collapse, it must have been a mild and decorous one, Hannah thought, as she held her hand beneath the tap, waiting for the fall of water to turn warm enough to facilitate the release of a vegetable aspic from its fancy mold. She was also engaged in a rather involved conversation with Petal, whom she had put in charge of the minted peas. Petal's job was to transfer them from their cooking pot to a serving bowl and sprinkle the top with more chopped mint and carry the dish to the riverside picnic table when the time came, and this struck Petal as being rather a lot to have to remember.

Julie and Betsy wandered into the kitchen to utter not very heartfelt offers of assistance. They were let off the hook by the presence of Petal, who was obviously set upon working hard and making a good impression. Betsy was interested in generally nosing about Alden's odd old dwelling, and Julie had already shown her the black-painted mantelpiece and the homicidal staircase and the place on the dining room pumpkin-pine paneling scarred with the zigzagging trail of a lightning bolt which was said to have come from a thunderstruck tree that had fallen on the head of an Indian sheltering from the storm beneath its boughs because not a single settler would allow him inside their houses. Betsy and Julie enjoyed being indignant on his behalf and thought making boards from the fatal tree was particularly cold-hearted.

"Are any two ceilings in this house the same height?" Betsy wondered. "Because sometimes I feel very small and sometimes I feel very big. It changes from room to room."

"Oh, there are various forces at work here to make *that* happen," Julie said.

They wandered out through the back door and onto a stone step and followed a trodden-on path to the driveway. They spied Tarara retreating to the Winnebago for some reason of her own; to attend to a makeup emergency, they speculated, or maybe it was time for her to take a purgative before she picked at her picnic lunch. Although they had to say they couldn't help liking Petal, and if she went with anyone, they were beginning to think she went with Rollins.

They wandered down to the river, steering clear of the table-and-chair arranging party. Having been carried and pulled into place, the chairs were now being sat upon and the tabletop was being leaned upon by all of the guys, who were arranged in argumentative or agitated or amused attitudes along its length.

LILY TOLD SALLY AND CAM to let Ginger be; they were squabbling over her camera, snatching it back and forth, each claiming to know how cameras worked. Sally tugged at the strap to make the shutter click, and Cam squeezed the casing with two hands as if she believed photographs could be wrung from the air. Ginger was letting them fumble, just to see how well they could do without her. "Figure it out for yourselves," she told them. "Learn to manage on your own." Sally didn't know what had come over her grandmother and she reached and tilted Ginger's dark glasses up onto her forehead to admit a little more daylight into her brain.

"I think you girls should participate in the games on the green," Lily said. She had clipped the schedule of events from the paper and now she read from her cutting. "There's an egg toss and a fifty-yard dash and a three-legged race for your age group," she said.

Sally had no idea what any of those things were supposed to be, but they all sounded suspicious to her. She turned to invite Cam to join in her reluctance, but Cam was surveying the activity over on the green, mulling over the list of contests and sizing up the competition and wondering what they'd be giving out for prizes this year.

"Hi, wait up. Here's a quarter. Buy yourselves something over there," Harvey said. "For a treat. No fun not to have money for a treat."

"You can't buy anything for just a quarter these days," Penny said. "Let me see what I have for quarters in my purse. Oh, I know where I keep a whole stack of them in the car for paying tolls." She bustled off to fetch them.

Sally edged up against Lily and stroked her skirt as Cam stood at the gate straining to be away, hopping in and out of the yard. Sally tugged at Lily's skirt until Lily was forced to take notice of her. "Yes?" she asked, and Sally explained that she was not allowed.

"Not allowed to what?" Lily asked.

"Not allowed to leave the yard alone," Sally said.

"You won't be alone; you'll be with Cam," Lily said.

"I'm not allowed to be alone without a grown-up," Sally said. "Granna?" she appealed. "Will you come?"

"No. You'll be perfectly all right with Cam," Ginger said. "Just don't leave the green and look both ways when you cross the street and come back in time for lunch. It will be good for you to be a little independent for a change."

"Perhaps we ought to ask Betsy," Lily said, but Ginger said she didn't think that would be useful since they already knew what Betsy's answer would be.

"I cleaned out the coin compartment," Penny reported upon her return from the car. "Pockets," she commanded Sally and Cam, who turned around and held up the flaps of their shorts pockets as Penny poured in quarters. To be in possession of so much money made Sally forget her certainty that none of this should be happening and willingly she went running after Cam, who had taken off like a shot once she found herself to be in funds.

Cam threaded through the crowd, exploiting openings between the massed flanks of strolling family groups, melting like a cat passing between barn boards. Sally, more dogged in pursuit, could only just keep the back of Cam's red shorts in view, the star-buttoned pocket now misshapen with money. The other, unsecurable pocket remained flat and empty.

They came out on the far side of the green. Sally blinked up at the foreshortened facades of the Congregational Church and the library building, struck by how much bigger things looked over here (as opposed to back there, at Uncle Alden's). Cam, for her part, was eyeing a lesser structure temporarily erected upon the church lawn. Here, one relinquished fifty cents for the opportunity to fling tennis balls at weighted tin cans covered in red, white, and blue crepe paper and set upon several tiered shelves, the object being to topple any three cans with the five balls supplied. Then they had to give you a prize.

Cam stepped up to the counter and plunked down her money. She pitched expertly, knocking over three cans with four throws. Choosing her reward required more effort; pinned to a black velvet display cloth were a representative four-leaf clover key ring and a pearl bracelet, and Cam had need of both. She pointed back and forth until the lady in charge told her to take the key chain; the four-leaf clover, embedded in Plexiglas, was real, whereas the pearls were not, she said.

Sally hung back, watching all this. Throwing things at things was something she had always been expressly told not to do because that was how all those people who had lost their eye had lost it.

"Your turn," Cam told Sally.

"My turn?" Sally asked.

"You can take your turn now. For fifty cents," Cam said.

"Fifty cents?" Sally asked. She was not entirely sure how to go about producing that. Fifty cents?

"It's two quarters," Cam said, low voiced. Sally was letting her down in front of the lady in the booth. Cam's quick fingers delved into Sally's back pocket, and two coins were pressed into her palms with ungentle emphasis and given a riveting spin to make sure they stuck. Cam turned her head and shielded her mouth from the booth lady. "Give them to *her*," she told Sally. "Haven't you ever *paid* before?"

"Yes, I so too have paid," Sally said. Or, at any rate, she had been present when she had been bought things. She had relinquished the things to be examined in some way by the store people and then her parents selected a shiny plastic square from their wallets, which was slid into a machine, and her parents wrote upon a piece of paper produced by that machine, and there was a tearing sound, and they were given a piece of torn-off paper as the things were collected in a bag or several bags. Then you could take the things home without being sent to jail for having stolen them.

"Then *pay*," Cam directed her. "Give the *money* to the *lady*." She indicated she could do no more and she retreated into contemplation of her key ring. She wondered just who she could now persuade to entrust her with the key to their front door. Her parents sure wouldn't, but Auntie Lily might be persuaded to let her have a key to the farmstand.

Sally stepped forward, her palm outstretched and open, revealing the coins. She selected one and lowered it onto the counter board and she placed the second coin beside it, aligning the two quarters so the picture of the man on the surface faced the lady, which Sally felt must be correct, and she was reassured when the lady swept the coins into her till, although Sally also suffered a touch of dismay at this; how swiftly and irretrievably had the money disappeared into the metal box. A lid chunked shut.

Five tennis balls, felted and furred and long since entered into retirement, were bowled across the counter. Sally flung herself upon them to keep any from flying over the edge and unconfinedly bouncing across the grass. (How Cam would despise that.) She slowly lifted herself up when she was sure the balls could be trusted to stay still.

The lady raised her own arm and indicated the arc of a throw, encouraging Sally, who, having watched Cam perform so successfully, figured there could not be all that much to the business of knocking over decorated tin cans, and her first throw was not so much tentative as trusting. Sally supposed that merely to launch it was enough, and the ball would propel and aim itself toward any one of the targets. But the ball failed even to arrive at the tier of shelves. It wobbled and plopped to the ground. A big boy, not noticed before, was crouched behind the shelves, charged with restoring the displaced cans between contestants' tries. He snickered at Sally's first feeble effort. She stood on her toes to have a look at him (he was one of those bumpy-faced boys) and then she snatched up another ball and lobbed it at the can she had identified as being the one most likely to fall onto his head.

"ARE YOU HERE FOR THE REST OF THE SUMMER?" Julie asked Betsy.

They had found the perfect spot on the bank of the slow green river beneath a bendy willow and upon a carpet of moss. The air was infused with a vaporous gloss; filmy insects hovered above the water, suspended there as if stuck to fresh varnish. A kayak rested, tilted on one side upon a sandy slice of beach. Kicking off their sandals, they could not decide which was better—to stand barefoot upon the moss or barefoot in the water. The moss was softer, the water was cooler, and they availed themselves of both, in turn.

"Yes, since Andy's stuck in Montana, and we really couldn't all be there together because the atmosphere surrounding the trial wouldn't have been very nice for Sally. I mean, I know Andy is on the defense team, but he says the guy is as guilty as sin," Betsy said. "So this seemed like a good chance to see my mother, and for my mother to see Sally."

"How is Aunt Ginger, really?" Julie asked. "I didn't want to ask her because she must be tired of people always wanting to know. Like there's only that one subject she can talk about, how she is."

"You can tell her you like the way her hair grew back in," Betsy said. "She's quite fascinated by how baby fine it is now. She and Sally use the same shampoo these days. Of course, Mummy's hair is really completely white, but she's pretending she's suddenly gone naturally platinum."

"Well, I was a bit shocked when I first saw her," Julie said. "I guess it must have been the hair; plus she's so thin and she didn't jump up and come running over when she saw me—but I guess she wanted me to make a little fuss over Sally first. So, she's doing well? Aunt Lily said she's finished with her treatments."

"Yes, that's why it was all right for her to go off on this big visit to Aunt Lily. Even Daddy was fine about her going away for a while," Betsy said, "and there's been quite the rapprochement on that front."

"Right, right, I remember how connubial they looked when Uncle Louis finally showed up for your wedding and they got back together again," Julie said. She considered. "Maybe there was something in the punch at the reception. Do you remember the recipe?"

"I believe it was Clicquot Club and strawberries, but you'll have to ask Aunt Lily. Oh," Betsy caught herself. "Sorry, but that's not what you meant."

"I'm thinking we'd need chloroform and straitjackets, where Ma's concerned," Julie said. "You know, to get anything going in the rapprochement department between my parents."

SALLY AND CAM HAD BEEN CAUGHT in the general roundup of six- to eight-year-olds. They were placed in a holding area defined by Department of Public Works sawhorses and told to wait until the five-year-olds finished their egg and spoon race. A teenager came and pinned numbers to the backs of their shirts, and they turned so each could read the other's designation (numbers 8 and 9), figuring they would be expected to know them. Sally worried about just how much she would have to pay to play these games. She jangled the quarters in her back pocket, attempting to line them up so she could count them between her fingers as she looked for a grown-up to ask, but the grown-up, when approached, told her that all Towne Athletic Association–sponsored events were free to any participant. Cam, who knew all about the magnanimous nature of the T.A.A., was very embarrassed by Sally's question and she regretted that she and Sally were consecutively numbered. Cam wished she was 30.

They lost the egg toss (not that they were ever going to win it) when Sally took her eyes off Cam in order to make sure that the new pearl bracelet she had twisted twice round her wrist for security purposes remained safe; Cam tossed, and Sally, admiring her elegant arm as she extended it to receive the egg, failed to catch it. For the three-legged race, Sally's right leg was tied (too tightly) to Cam's left leg with a band of cheesecloth. They were bidden to run to the bandstand, go once around, and come back again, and Sally and Cam were doing all right until two stupid kids blundered into their path, and they all crashed and fell down. Sally thought she would sit out the fifty-yard dash, but a lady with a megaphone addressed her in a loud, hollow voice, saying, "Number Eight, you're keeping the rest of us waiting." Sally approached the kids crouched at the ready behind the mark chalked in the grass, their fingertips clinging to the white line and bottoms thrust up to give them extra impetus at takeoff. She spotted a pair of red shorts with one starred and one starless pocket and she wedged herself in next to Cam. Cam muttered something that Sally failed to catch (much as she had failed to catch the well-tossed egg). A pistol popped and off they ran.

They pounded along, nearer the back of the pack than the front. An eight-year-old boy crossed the finish line before they were halfway there. Cheering informed them of this; however, the race that now engaged Sally and Cam was the race between themselves. Cam pulled ahead, then misstepped on a stone. Sally gained on her and maintained the lead until, looking back to ascertain the margin of her imminent victory, she decelerated, and Cam overtook her with a spurt. It was Sally who first crossed the official finish line, where the onlookers were still cheering the latecomers so that every participant would feel special. She halted and acknowledged this tribute but as she bent over to hack up the bug she had swallowed (she was one of those open-mouthed breathers), Cam went flying past her.

The contest resumed. Sally sprinted, pursuing Cam across the green, neither allowing the other to win; any advantage lost was seized again. People jumped out of the way; Sally knocked over a U.S. flag; Om, sitting with her friends in front of the tent pavilion, watched her little sister sprint by and chose not to wonder what was going on.

Their feet hit pavement as they left the green and crossed the road and veered down the library driveway and wove in and out among the parked cars to reach the Exit (Not Entrance) outlet onto Main Street. They swooped down a sidewalk; they pulled even, and Sally gasped at Cam to stop, and Cam agreed. She paused, and Sally paused, and Cam took off again, just a beat ahead of Sally, who had meant to play the same trick on Cam. They came to a stop only when a wall reared up in front of them, and they flung themselves at it, almost gratefully. They slouched there, supported and panting, only slowly coming to notice how uncomfortable the pebble-dash surface was, how rough and sharp and heated it was on this, the sunny side. Cam began to roll, face to wall, back to wall, face to wall; when she came to the end of the wall, she disappeared around the corner. Sally followed her, twirling toplike, and bouncing around the corner. She landed upon a cool, smooth panel of plate glass window, and she felt as if she had jumped into a very still and blue pool of water and discovered that the pool water not only looked like glass but was glass.

"Where are we?" she asked. She peered through the window, letting her eyes adjust to the interior darkness. She made out desks and telephones, computer terminals, stacks of files and drifts of paper. It was one of those office places.

Cam gazed through the window and recalled, "When Mr. Harvey's car fell into the swamp, the people here gave him money to buy his new one."

"They must be very kind," Sally said.

"Yes," supposed Cam.

Sally was about to ask how Uncle Harvey's car had ended up in the swamp (not that she was entirely sure what a swamp was, but it didn't sound good); however, Cam had taken off. She was walking purposefully down the deserted street in a direction that would take them even further away from the green, which Sally now remembered she had been told not to leave. She hesitated. The way back tugged at her as if a cord had been pulled taut and, pulling, broke along a frayed spot. She scuttled a few catching-up steps after Cam.

"Do you know where we are?" she asked.

"Yes," Cam said. She sighed. What a stupid question.

Sally would have liked to ask, In that case, where are we *going*? for Cam suddenly ducked down a dim passage that ran secretly between two structures. It was so narrow that Sally could stick out either hand and tap opposite brick walls, and what was interesting about this was that she got green smears on her fingers even though the bricks were red. But Cam was acting like a know-it-all. "Come *on,*" she ordered, as Sally called for her to turn around and share her amazement at the red-bricks, green-fingers phenomenon, and Sally resolved to ask her nothing more. She decided, further, that she would blame know-it-all Cam for whatever trouble they were going to find themselves in at the end of the day. Perhaps then Aunt Lily and Aunt Penny and everyone else would stop liking Cam so much and not give her Fourth of July cakes meant for themselves. Sally had just remembered the deprivation she had endured, last night at supper.

The alley ended where a dazzling expanse of pavement began. There was no sidewalk, and so Cam walked right down the center of the road, precisely treading upon the white-painted median line, imagining herself to be walking a tightrope. Sally remained in the weedy shoulder, trudging through soft and shifting grit as her socks subsided into her sneakers, weighed down by sifting-in sand. She very alertly watched up and down the road, each footstep in the yielding sand becoming a semirevolving one as she endeavored to catch sight of any approaching vehicle since Cam was oblivious to anything but performing her circus act. Cam stuck her arms out as she sought to maintain her balance, and several times she wobbled one-footed on the painted line as the other foot and her two arms clawed the air as if seeking something to hold onto.

They carried on like this for several minutes, which Sally kept track of, between keeping track of the occasional passing car, on a digital time and temperature display attached to the sign of a drive-in Bay Bank. Numbers scrambled and unscrambled, switching between the time and the temperature, reading 83°, then 1:06, then 83°, then 1:06. Sally had never known a longer or a slower 1:06. The sign flashed 84°, then flashed again, 1:06; even the hotness was clocking along faster than the minutes.

"Car," she cried. "Car, car, car," she insisted, and, as a station wagon drove by them, the man behind the wheel steering well clear of the two kids (one of whom was jumping about erratically as the other one darted across the road), the time became 1:07, which seemed like progress, but then 1:07 persisted, stuck there in minutes on the sign.

They continued on, trailing past the Bay Bank building, and Sally continued to watch the sign over her shoulder. At 1:11, inscribed in diminished figures upon the now retreating display panel, Cam bounded off the center line. "Come *on,*" she ordered Sally, and they marched across a small, almost empty parking lot toward a brightly painted building. Sally could smell tomato sauce in the surrounding air. She recognized that this was a pizza place and, as such, an excellent destination; she would give Cam credit for that.

They entered, pushing through a heavy door and the second door that came immediately after it. Sally held back, not sure what to do next. There was no one about, no one to tell her whether to sit at one of the tables or to climb onto one of the high stools that lined a long counter. A glass-fronted case displayed frosted and sugar-glazed baked goods. Sally rattled the quarters in her pocket and hoped she had enough for a doughnut thing (no hole) as well as a slice from the pizza that sat in a black metal pan. The cheese had congealed to the point where it could be most satisfyingly peeled off in a single piece. She glanced obliquely at Cam, prepared to follow her lead and even to anticipate where Cam was headed once Cam committed to a direction and so get to a table or a counter stool first. But, after stopping to jam all the selection points of a Coke machine on the off chance there was a can lodged in the chute, Cam approached the counter and, raising a hinged drawbridge with a practiced chop of her hand, passed through to the other side.

"No," Sally whispered urgently. Lawlessness had gone too far; that length of counter defined exactly the line that ought not to be crossed. "Come back," she insisted, too late, as a lady emerged from a further room.

This lady, however, only asked Cam a brief question which Cam as shortly answered. Sally, who hoped she would not catch the lady's eye if she stood completely still (she was like a cornered chipmunk in this respect), was noticed anyway and inquired about. Cam spoke and the lady nodded at Sally, saying, "Welcome, child." Cam then began to deliver a speech to which the lady only half listened as she busied herself with the task that had brought her to the front of the restaurant.

She filled off a trayful of salt shakers, unscrewing tops and inserting a funnel and tilting in salt from a cylindrical box, one shaker after the other, replenished. They all received a swipe with a rag as well; she cradled each shaker in the cloth and simultaneously tightened the top and polished the clear glass sides of the shakers, which many hands had smudged, with a single twist and turn.

As often happened at home in California when she knew what was being said without really understanding the words, when people talked in Mexican, Sally now followed the conversation that Cam was conducting in some other sort of non-American speech. That this lady was Cam's mother was evident from the way in which she ignored Cam as Cam kept on speaking in an attempt to convince her mother of something of which she had no intention of being convinced. Cam kept pointing to the pastry case and protesting, but her mother refused to be drawn into the matter.

With a further nod at Sally, Mrs. Samrin retreated to the back room. Cam passed through the drawbridge and she picked up the tray of salt shakers, at first attempting to balance it single-handedly over her head, but the shakers trembled, and one end of the tray dipped and had to be caught by Cam's other hand. She carried the tray from table to table, setting the salt shakers beside the pepper shakers, the pair of them standing between a saucer of sugar packets and a large container of red pepper flakes dispensed through a perforated top. Sally, after watching how Cam proceeded, began to help, plucking shakers from the tray and placing them upon the lesser tables, the ones in the corners. Cam failed to comment upon her table-setting skills, but Sally could tell she was impressed because she looked very hard to find something to criticize about Sally's effort and had not been able to come up with anything.

They sat, then, at the counter. They twirled on the stools in a quiet manner, taking meditative spins (and not furious racing spins). The slightest nudge of heel against the supporting stalk set the stools in motion. They had been well oiled at some vital spot. Sally spun ever so slightly and hitched herself up higher so she could see through the doorway behind the counter, which opened onto what she now realized was a kitchen. However, just to the left of the stove was a raised shelf that carried the very interesting statue of the figure of a man who sat there cross-legged. He was all-gold in color, and he wore such an untroubled smile upon his face that he made Sally smile, as well. Her chin dropped and her eyes softened, half-closed like his with a kindred contentment. After further reflection, she caught up her long yellow braid and coiled it round and round (twice) on top of her head, contriving to make its bristly end spike upward to simulate (she believed) the statue-man's very nice pointed hat. She admired the shiny rainbow swirl of colors painted on the board that framed him. A candle burned in a red cup set down upon the shelf, and there was smoke rising from the end of a stick which was stuck at an angle in front of the smiling, golden man.

"Who is that?" Sally asked. "In the kitchen?"—where people were supposed to hang calendars on the walls and pictures of fruit, and suspend plates that were too pretty to eat from and could only be looked at.

"He is Buddha," Cam said. Which reminded her of something she meant to do. She slid down from her stool.

"Who is Buddha?" Sally asked, as Cam raised the drawbridge and popped behind the counter.

"Buddha is like God; he's like Jesus; he's very nice," Cam said. She was used to explaining him and she had learned that this was what people seemed to like to hear.

"And he lives in your restaurant instead of in a church?" Sally wondered.

"Yes. He is ours," Cam said. She had positioned herself before the shrine. She bowed her head above tented hands and then reached up to jiggle the smoldering stick, redirecting the flow of smoke upward and away from the draw of the oven hood so that the smoke would not become stuck in the black trap, which was Thanh's job to clean out on Sunday mornings. She unbuttoned the back flap of her pocket and jangled around among the quarters. Sally watched Cam's exploring fingers trace beneath the fabric until she extracted, pinched between her fingertips, the Barbie knife. This she held up for Buddha to see before she placed it upon the shelf, just beside his knee. She bowed her head and whispered briefly above prayerfully rearranged hands.

That the Barbie knife had been offered to Buddha and had been accepted (a thickening of the smoke fuming from the end of the stick expressed his satisfaction at the gift), Sally understood. The Barbie knife was lost forever; it was his. No wonder Buddha smiled, if everyone gave him things. Sally reckoned she would smile too if all the people wanted to give her stuff, and yet, she realized, she was still smiling anyway; she and Buddha continued to smile back and forth at each other even though she was annoyed with him. He must be very forgiving, she thought, and she decided she liked him better than Jesus. Jesus was always so sad and He asked so much of you too. He required good behavior and extra effort for you to win a benefit from Him, demanding a sustained campaign of prayer and strict obedience, or so she had been led to understand. But this system which evidently only involved the actual exchange of a small treasured object for a desired favor was so much simpler (for though she had no idea what Cam had whispered, she knew in her bones that Cam was after something). Sally remembered that the earth was full of beautiful rocks and shells at the beach and feathers that had fallen from the sky and, indeed, there was even a surfeit of pink forks with plastic tines that could be snapped off to make as many Barbie knives as one could wish for, enough to give to Buddha, enough to keep for oneself—for she had spotted a box full of pink plastic forks sitting on a service trolley wheeled behind the counter. But now she was in no hurry to avail herself of a fork or of anything else. She nudged her stool, slowly circling, thinking how nice it was to know that there was more than enough of everything to go around and she had all the time in the world to help herself or, at any rate, she had the rest of the summer.

"LOOK. IS THAT SOME KIND OF HERON?" Betsy asked Julie.

"Don't ask me," Julie said. "It's some kind of something," she allowed. They watched the creature angle down through the tree cover and land with a long-legged skid and agitation of wing beats. It stood in the water above its reflection, which it consulted like a looking glass as it composed itself, wings tucked in and a head crest sleekened, like a spit-slicked pompadour. But no sooner had it settled than the bird took off again like a wind-blown umbrella, startled by the swish of a dipped oar and the approach of a canoe occupied by a single figure topped by a broad-brimmed straw hat.

Julie and Betsy waved in the usual way. Hereabouts, the single figure in an otherwise empty landscape required acknowledgment; it was more than likely that anyone encountered upon the byways and backwaters of Towne could be presumed to be all right. They would say hello nicely and move along beyond eye- and earshot. In fact, the true purpose of the welcoming wave could be said to define territory; the waving at also served as a waving on, in the nicest possible way.

But this canoe veered toward them with a purpose, and the identity of the paddler beneath the hat became an interesting mystery. Whoever they were, they had been to the parade; a bright balloon was tethered to a thwart of the canoe. Julie and Betsy waded out to see. Tea-colored water swamped their knees, and they bundled up their dresses as the hems melted into the river. The hat was flung off, its broad brim interfering with the higher lift of the paddler's arm as she pushed the paddle more deeply into the river.

"Why, that's Ginevra," Betsy told Julie. "Do you remember Ginevra? We were friends, that year I lived at Lily's."

Ginevra pulled her craft alongside the cousins, and they all caught up on the past ten years' worth of news, which could be summed up briefly for all the digressions and disappointments and successes and complications that had occurred along the way: Betsy was still married to Andy, still living in California, and they had a little girl now; Julie was based in London and working for a company that moved traveling and on-loan museum exhibits all over the world; Ginevra was teaching music at a middle school while she pursued a performance career; she lived outside of Worcester but she was looking after her parents' house for the summer while they were on retreat at an ashram outside of Sedona.

"Glover," Julie declared then, for she seemed to remember something about Glover and Ginevra having known each other once. "Hi. Glover," she called over to the picnic table. "Come here."

Ginevra sat up straighter. She swiped her hair out of her eyes and tugged at the fringed hems of her cutoff jeans and scuffed an empty Ring Ding wrapper beneath a flotation cushion with her foot even though the wrapper wasn't hers; she always fished litter from the river.

Glover came loping over to see what all the fuss was about, and he kept on loping into the water and up to the canoe where he leaned against the gunwale, catching and holding on to Ginevra when the boat skidded away from his weight. He clambered into the front seat and picked up the paddle propped there. Almost without saying, he and Ginevra glided off, leaving a cross-stitch-patterned wake and a series of small whirlpools to mark the paddles' plunges. Julie and Betsy, watching, similarly sighed.

"Wasn't that romantic?" asked Betsy. "The way he just saw her and claimed her and sailed off with her?"

"Only they won't get very far," Julie predicted. "They'll hit the dam and the spillway behind Peddocks and they'll have to turn around and come back unless they portage across Front Street." She and Betsy wandered out of the water and plopped down upon the mossy bank.

"How is your mother these days?" Betsy asked Julie then. The subject of romance had been raised, and Betsy couldn't help herself; there were aspects of her aunt's story, of Becky's reversal and flight (or her inexplicable change of heart, as Lily had called it, the one time she mentioned the matter in a letter), which she found intriguing. Besides, since coming here, Betsy had been aware of a pressing absence, of someone no longer being there where they were supposed to be. The empty air contained a shape and a voice and even a characteristic scent, fresh and light and floral like the powder Becky used to wear. A dozen times, at least, Betsy had looked up and expected to see Becky at Alden's side or Becky in the kitchen by the sink or Becky advancing across the lawn to greet her. All day, she had felt that she just kept missing her aunt.

"If you don't mind my asking," Betsy said.

"No, it's all right. Most people just don't want to talk about Ma. I mean, everyone goes all pale and tense if I mention her," Julie said. "And since we're all so exceedingly pale and tense to begin with, it feels unkind, you know, to exacerbate that condition."

Betsy couldn't remember, then, whether she had sprayed sunscreen on Sally, but she figured she must have spritzed her so automatically as they were going out the door that the act hadn't registered. Still, she wondered where Sally was at the moment so she could rub a thumb over her arm to confirm that it was slightly slippery with Sol-Safe #75. She must be with Mummy, or Lily, or possibly even pestering Tarara in the Winnebago; someone among them had to be keeping track of Sally, Betsy told herself, which left her free (and she was seldom free from Sally) to talk family scandal with Julie.

"I've been in touch with Ma for quite a while now, actually," Julie said. "We talk on the phone, and there's even been e-mail since they got a satellite dish. And I think the reason I stayed on in Europe after Dad moved back to the States was to remain somewhat close to her, even though in all the time since she'd left, I'd never been to see her. But it was good to know she was just a few hours away, if something came up, although I admit I put off going to see Ma because it would mean having to see William too.

"Then last April William was injured in a fall, and Ma called me. She sounded so lost and scared I felt like I'd turned into her mother and there was no way I could not help her out since I certainly knew what that felt like, to be left in the lurch by your own mother. The next thing I knew, I was on my way to her. Well, I was on my way after a lot of Byzantine business over the visa and stuff, and believe me, I know what Byzantine is, I worked on the Treasures of the Ottoman traveling exhibit, from the Hagia Sophia. But my boss is a whiz at cutting red tape and arranging transportation—we had this joke going that I was just like the Venus of Cyrene being crated and returned to its rightful owners—and suddenly there I was, and there Ma was, both of us standing in the lobby of this grotty old hospital in Libya." Julie paused and gazed unseeingly at the slow-moving and shady river; she was back in Misratah.

"The first thing that struck me was how well Ma fit in there. She was still wearing Western clothes, but somehow they seemed North African, all these floaty loose layers of cotton. Well, maybe she kind of looked like she was going to yoga class or a poetry reading, I don't know. But there Ma was, talking away a mile a minute in Arabic, telling everyone I was her daughter—that part was obvious—and there we were, walking down this long corridor between the wards where everything looked like a hundred years ago, and it smelled like a hundred years ago, all the smoke and putrefaction, which Ma didn't even seem to notice, not the smells or the weeping and the moaning. I don't think anyone went to that hospital to get better.

"But they had stuck William in a room of his own, which was nice enough and very bright and sunny. Well, of course it would be bright and sunny; it's the flipping Sahara. He had on this very theatrical head bandage, very Marley's ghost and quite grubby. At any rate it didn't look very clean in such severe sunlight, which makes you see everything there just a bit too clearly, in my opinion. Fortunately, William was still unconscious, so all I had to do was just look at him while I had this big inner moral struggle with myself not to wish he was dead, at least not to wish he would die at the same time I was trying to reassure Ma that he was going to be fine. I'm not a complete hypocrite. I was also wondering whether they shouldn't transfer him to a hospital in Rome or maybe even London, but I wasn't sure about his legal status and if he still couldn't go to places where he could be extradited back to the States on all those old espionage charges. And then I couldn't help but reflect how I'd never seen a bigger case of someone having made his bed and having to lie in it, except it's too bad Ma had to join him there. Ma kept insisting all the locals were being perfectly sweet and charming to her, but I wasn't so sure of that, myself. I mean, we were getting some real looks from the locals, that maybe Ma had trained herself not to notice.

"We finally left William when a nurse Ma trusted came on duty, and we drove back to their villa, which sits in a very remote spot among the sand dunes, way out by the sea. I made Ma show me where the accident had happened and explain everything. She said one night, very late, they heard the garage doors banging in a high wind. Their previous servants, who were very nice and reliable, had gone home to Mali to open a restaurant and the new replacement servants from Yemen were being pretty lax about everything, not impeccable like the Malians had been. The new guys persisted in forgetting to latch the doors, especially on very windy nights, no matter how often they'd been told.

"So, William, in a real snit, goes bustling out into the pitch-black night. He had grabbed a torch, but it wasn't working, as it turned out. When he didn't come back, and the garage doors kept banging, Ma went out to find him and she practically fell over him, all sprawled there and bleeding from the head and out like a light. She said he must have stumbled over a big wooden crate of artifacts he'd dug up and was sending to the museum in Tripoli. (He's turned himself into an amateur archaeologist; had you heard about all that? He's such a dope.)

"But when I surveyed the scene of the crime (so to speak), I didn't see how William could have injured himself as badly as he did. I mean, it's nothing but sand there, and from the way Ma described where she found him, he could only have hit his head on the sand when he went down." Julie's own head flopped forward, in partial demonstration of how he must have fallen. She tapped her brow on the spot where William's skull had been broken.

Betsy had been listening to all of this, leaning on an elbow and stroking the moss and thinking that possessing a villa by the sea and having servants sounded rather nice, although of course she could not approve of the circumstances, but still, if one recast the lover and got him back on his feet and if one blurred over the details of the elopement and made sure that no one got hurt as poor Uncle Alden most assuredly had been. She started and asked, "But what are you driving at? Do you mean to say William didn't have an accident?"

"I'm saying William was attacked. I'm saying someone hit him on the head, maybe with one of those stone Roman artifacts he was sending to Tripoli. Oh, and when Ma found the torch later, where William dropped it, it was missing the batteries, which is how she knew he'd been in complete darkness. And they're very careful about keeping a working torch, because their electricity is so spotty, so obviously somebody removed the batteries, probably before William was ever lured outside," Julie said.

"But who do you think would have done something like that?" Betsy asked. She wondered whether Julie wasn't engaging in wishful thinking, inventing dangerous forces whose aim was to do away with William.

"Well, for starters, I'm not too sure about the Yemen guys," Julie said. "They struck me as being very religious and censorious and fanatical. Ma told me not to drink beer in front of them and not to dress immodestly (whatever that was supposed to mean). Or maybe there were some ordinary burglars who had heard there were well-to-do Westerners in the area. Maybe Ma scared them off when she came looking for William. Oh, I don't know; maybe William has been dealing in black market antiquities. I wouldn't put anything past him. Maybe the CIA sent someone out to get him; he's been such a thorn in their sides for years. I'd say there's any number of candidates for the job of coshing William."

"But what about your mother?" Betsy asked. "You told her what you suspect?"

"Yes, of course, or at least I tried," Julie said. "That was when Ma began to insist how sweet and charming everyone was to William and her. But since she's been fooling herself for a long time now, refusing to acknowledge any number of facts, I am not persuaded. At least they're not still living in that remote villa. William recovered consciousness, and they got him so he can toddle around a little and he and Ma have taken a flat in Misratah to be close to the hospital and his physical therapy and other aftercare, such as it is. Personally, I think William isn't going to come out of this entirely unscathed. He has this kind of poststroke affect, in my opinion, but then again, he always walked and talked in a stiff and affected way."

"It sounds awful," Betsy said.

"I'll tell you this; I don't believe for one minute that Ma can be happy, but she just can't figure out a way how to get herself out of there. That's what I think," Julie said. "I think that given half a chance and a good excuse, she'd be out of there in a flash."

LILY HAD COME SUPPLIED WITH string and stakes and a pocket knife so that she could tie up Alden's falling-over phlox, beside the garden path. Tommy wandered over to help and he dug alongside her in the soft dirt, uncovering spring bulbs, which Lily separated and replanted, reaming out Tommy's holes with a stake. She wished she'd brought a trowel, but getting by with a stake seemed easier than asking Alden where he'd last seen his trowel, which was probably in the same place he'd last seen his pruning shears, Lily reckoned, as she paused in her bulb work to untwist a length of deeply rooted volunteer vine from the fence post it had coiled itself around. She rewound the stalk in the opposite direction around the post, for she had read lately that doing so would cause a twining weed to die. She wondered whether this was true. There was so much gardening misinformation on the Internet. Only yesterday she had read that all irises liked lime, which was not entirely true; Japanese iris were an exception to that rule and she mused upon the modern world's many avenues for dispensing flawed information and bad advice. By then she had dealt with the phlox and moved on to stake the peonies that grew in a small plot at the end of Alden's driveway. Well past their prime, they were struggling to hold their ragged heads upright and, more often than not, a stalk released its cup of petals at a single touch from her. Lily was not sure whether she was doing more harm than good, trying to tend to them.

As she knelt there, from time to time she glanced toward Alden. He had been detained at his front gate since the parade's end as he became involved in a series of conversations with one woman after another who, walking past his gate, stopped to say hello to him, and then, prompted by Alden's conventionally polite inquiry, "How are you?" launched into accounts of how very busy they were, how they were run off their feet and always on the go with never a dull moment in their lives because they were so indispensable. They had never felt happier nor more fulfilled, they insisted. These women were all divorcées who at one time or another had harbored hopes about Alden and they did not feel they could now withdraw without making it plain that advances had been made, so they went out of their way (passing by his gate) to let him know what he was missing. All of this meaningfulness flew right over Alden's head, however, and he could only be impressed by how splendid life must be if one was lucky enough to be an unmarried middle-aged woman, resident in a small suburban town.

Lily drove in another stake. She rerouted a length of bindweed around the pillar base of a reflecting ball and leaned back on her heels to see what would happen next. Would the vine uncling; would the leaves turn sallow and drop; would it strangle itself with its own confused convolutions? Her conscience tugged at her as she wondered whether this method brought about a lingering death, and she sawed through the vine's main stalk, just above the roots, with her knife. She glanced up as Harvey scurried past her, on the lam from something; he caught her eye and signed at her to flee as well, but his advice came too late. Babe Palmer was bearing down upon her.

Lily sliced an arm's length of twine from the ball and, unhurriedly, she secured another clump of falling-down peonies, but the ball of twine unreeled away to nothing in her hand when she went for another piece, so Lily had no choice but to rise and see what Babe wanted. Tommy, heretofore her boon companion, took off for the barn as if he too had just remembered he had something urgent to do there, but Penny came over to peck Babe's cheek and declare, "Nice to see you, dear." Babe's late mother had been Penny's cousin, which alone accounted for the kiss.

Babe uncapped a water bottle she carried in a fanny pack and took a long swallow. She had become one of those people who went nowhere without a water bottle, although Lily had heard that 20 percent of all such water bottles actually contained gin. But she recalled that Ginger was her source for this statistic, and as such, Ginger may have based her findings upon an informal sampling among people she knew, so Lily didn't mention anything of this. Thinking of Ginger then, Lily looked across the lawn to her tree-shaded chaise and was relieved to see that Ginger had had the good sense to retreat. The blanket trailed, her book was splayed facedown on the cushion, and her water glass had been knocked over by a hasty elbow, and she was no longer there.

"I take it Alden has a full house," Babe said, indicating the cars parked in the driveway, and particularly letting her gaze fall upon the great hulk of the Winnebago which she regarded as if one of its tires had just run over her foot.

"Almost like old times," Penny agreed happily. "The kids will be staying on; they've all made plans to hang around here for the rest of the summer. We're so pleased for Alden."

This was the information Babe had been angling for. She declared, "Well, if I was Merra Benda, I shouldn't like looking out my dining room window and having a view of nothing but that big awful trailer."

"Oh, but I should think the dining room window is the least looked out window in a house," Lily spoke up. "One uses one's dining room most often at night, if one uses it at all, nowadays."

"If the Winnebago was parked outside Merra's kitchen window, that would be another story," Penny supposed. "I always look out my kitchen window when I'm busy at the sink."

"And then one might very well like to see a bit of extra life going on," Lily said. "While one is peeling carrots."

"Or snipping green beans," Penny supposed.

"May I remind you that we are in the Historic District here, and as such, there are rules about what is and is not permitted to be parked in a driveway," Babe said.

"Well, no, dear, actually not," Penny said. "The Historic District ordinances are very vague and largely unenforceable because everyone is too worried about the resale value of their houses if the new people can't buy them with the idea of putting in swimming pools and adding on new two-thousand-square-foot master bedroom wings. I know. I was on the committee, and I drafted the by-laws. About the only thing you can't get away with in the Historic District is displaying colored lights at Christmas, but it's more of a social pressure not to do that. You'll receive a call of concern from Marilyn Rathbone."

Babe swigged more water and noticed that the Winnebago had grown even larger since its arrival, when she had watched with horror from her folding chair on the library lawn (initially believing the RV contained carnival folk attracted by the parade) as the vehicle lumbered round the green before it heaved itself down Alden's driveway; some cantilevered attachments bulged from either side now, making the thing seem far too comfortable, as if it had loosened its belt.

"Besides," said Penny, who had warmed to the topic, "if I were Merra Benda, I think I'd be gratified to look out my dining room window and see that Brooks and Rollins are visiting. If I were Merra Benda, I'd be conniving ways to have them meet and marry my daughters. I'd send those girls outside to sunbathe, availably, or practice their cheerleading or do Pilates or something."

"The Bendas have granddaughters these days," Lily seemed to recall.

"Same difference," Penny said. "And furthermore, I would even make the argument that some day the Historic District will be putting up signs commemorating Brooks and Rollins. They'll be sticking a plaque on Alden's house."

"Or on the Winnebago," Lily suggested. "They'll park a late-twentieth-century Winnebago in Alden's driveway, open to the interested public, although we won't be here to see that."

"Ah," said Penny. What a shame; she'd have loved to be the tour guide.

"Good. We'll all be long gone," said Babe. At least she would be spared that bitter day when such oddities and horrors would be honored. No doubt even Lily's looming cell tower would be given a plaque. Bristling, Babe went off to have a further word with Alden, deciding to express her feelings about his boys' RV to him. He would not be in possession of Penny's deep and unfair knowledge of Towne ordinances; Penny was such a meddler.

Babe routed Leslie Oates, who had been telling Alden about the genealogical workshop that had been absorbing her of late. She was being enthusiastic about the 1880 census. "Oh, *that,*" said Babe.

Her people were way before 1880; her people were to be found in thumping big vellum-leafed volumes scrawled all over with spider-writing.

Lily and Penny fell into a conversation as to why Marilyn Rathbone should take it upon herself to monitor Christmas decorations, Lily saying she wished someone would make a call of concern to Marilyn about the pair of leopard-skin Capri pants she'd been seen wearing around Towne, and Penny was saying that Marilyn's outfit gave both leopards and Capri a bad name, when Betsy approached them.

"I've completely lost track of Sally, I haven't seen her since . . . I don't know when. I was only down by the river, talking to Julie," Betsy said, her voice rising. "I've been looking for her everywhere," she told them, and in proof of how thoroughly she had been hunting, she held up Sally's forgotten book and Sally's unwanted sweater, which she had ferreted out from beneath the grape arbor and behind the lilacs.

Lily began to form an answer, regretting now that she had not overruled Ginger when she had said not to bother to ask Betsy whether Sally could go off with Cam. Lily prefaced her remarks by saying she was sure Sally was all right.

At that moment, Sally had emerged from the edge of the green and darted across the road. Spying her mother, who was clutching the book and the sweater which Sally recognized as her own, and reckoning they had been found in lieu of herself during the course of a search, Sally dove down and duckwalked along the far side of Alden's wall, followed by Cam who didn't know why they were hiding, or from whom, but she crouched and duckwalked too, like the good soldier she was. They flung themselves through the gate, startling Babe Palmer and spooking Alden as they buffeted the adults' knees like bullets of bundled energy. Alden's automatic assistance, a steadying hand placed on Babe's arm, had been swiftly withdrawn, when Babe yelped as if scalded.

Once within the yard, Sally sprang up and ran at her mother, declaring, "There you are," as if Betsy had been the one who hadn't been where she was supposed to be. The child met Lily's eye with a bland little smile, as if daring her to say anything.

"Wash your hands; Hannah's called everyone for lunch" was all Betsy could think to say. "You too, Cam," she added, for it seemed that Cam was to be included in everything here.

LUNCH WENT ON FOR QUITE A WHILE, spinning out into an ideal sort of meal over which one could linger and nibble at Hannah's savory dishes, or should one overdo it, one could rise from the table and stretch out on a chaise to take a breather before returning to revisit the Cobb salad, having been thinking about the Cobb salad, in the meanwhile. Brooks and Rollins, big fans of Hannah's cooking, asked her if they could buy out her frozen-food company for seven million dollars; their money people had been telling them to diversify. But Hannah said certainly not; she was perfectly happy as she was and she liked to keep busy.

Hannah moved back and forth between the kitchen and the riverbank replenishing empty bowls and introducing new courses; there were nineteen of them gathered at the table and a second table that had been fetched from the house, but she had known enough to provide extra. She was assisted by Petal, who half expected the attractive scene to turn into a photo shoot; she was reminded of a Modality Funds (Life Is Good) print ad in which she had appeared. Petal set down the bowl of minted peas she had fetched from the kitchen in front of Miss Hill (the other old lady was Mrs. Hill, she must remember that).

"Thank you, Blossom," Lily said, which rather hurt Petal's feelings, although as Julie pointed out, at least Lily hadn't called her Bud.

Sally and Cam, who had spoiled their appetites at the Casa di Napoli, sat there itching; Cam constructed a puzzle maze using celery sticks and a pea, and Sally dramatized her discomfort by collapsing her head into her folded arms. Betsy told them they were excused, and they ran off to swing in the hammock.

"We are authorized to go as high as nine point five million dollars," Brooks told Hannah, and Alden asked his son where he had learned to negotiate. Yalta, perhaps? he suggested, which set Harvey off, recalling the events of 1945. He pronounced Stalin "Sta-leen" which Lily thought was affected, and Ginger said she always thought "Sta-leen" sounded like the name of one of the original Mousketeers.

Tarara shuddered at the little girls' shrilled conversation and, turning from the sight of their frantic play, she was affronted by the spectacle of those horrible boys, David, Jason, and Matt, who had bolted down their food and now were huddled round Brooks and Rollins, all of them bent over a laptop computer, their many hands shooting out Shiva-like to depress keyboard points which caused the screen to wink and reresolve upon successive pages of symbols and notations over which they exclaimed and argued. She was being ignored by everyone. Even the ones she didn't want to talk to were talking to someone else, which she particularly resented (that primeval old Lily having quite the conversation with Ginevra about teaching and education), and she endeavored to rise from the table, which was not easily accomplished. She had been wedged into the middle of a backless bench between Julie and Betsy, who, in turn, were bracketed by Alden and Penny, which made five figures fitted onto the plank seat only built for four, but Tarara had been slotted into the center by Penny, who'd been put in charge of telling everyone where to go and who had said Tarara didn't count as an entire person because she was so slender. Straightening her skirt and tossing her hair, Tarara stalked off to find a spot where her cell phone would work.

As soon as she was out of earshot, Julie reached for Tarara's abandoned plate, intending to conduct a forensic analysis of just what such a person actually ate, and Betsy said perhaps they should follow Tarara until she coughed up a pellet like an owl, which they could examine for evidence of, what, breath mints?

"And poppers," suggested Ginger, from the end of the table. She was so happy to have her girls here with her, she felt quite like her old self.

"Let's get you into the hammock," Penny said to Ginger, responding to a nod from Lily, and Hannah signaled to Petal that they could begin clearing the table, but Harvey said he needed Petal's assistance on the croquet project they'd been cooking up between them, so Glover threw a napkin over his arm and offered his services, and Ginevra pitched in; she carried off the fish carcass, which lay sprawled across the platter looking like bears had been at it. Julie and Betsy were also shamed into helping, as Julie put it, since they had failed to be of any use during the preparations. The boys scarcely glanced up from the screen of the laptop although Brooks reached out to snatch a depleted plate of cheese toasts from Betsy's hand, saying it would be a shame to let them go to waste.

PETAL AND HARVEY WHEELED the croquet set from the barn and set up the pitch and began a match, with Harvey remembering the rules as they went along. The little girls, who had been shooed from the hammock, ran over and asked if they could play too. Without waiting for an answer, Sally snatched up the red mallet and ball, and Cam grabbed the blue set. Their favorite colors were not the same, which was fortunate; there was to be no argument over what were, essentially, long-handled hammers and miniature cannon balls. By obliquely observing Harvey's actions, each was able to put on a creditable show of convincing the other that she'd been doing this croquet business all her life, although several times Sally whacked her toes instead of the ball and once Cam shot Harvey's green ball through a hoop, mistaking green for blue, and Harvey said not only did the wicket count in his favor but he won six free turns, while Cam lost her next one and Sally too, because she had failed to prevent Cam's error. Petal, however, received a free pass because she was wearing white, as all proper croqueteers must do. Ginger watched from her hammock, and Lily and Penny sat on the sidelines. Penny had brought her knitting, but Lily was content to be idle, for the moment. Alden picked up the book Julie had given him, and Tommy was asleep beneath the lilacs. He had been generously fed from the table and had no wish to move.

Presently, the Towne Taxi nosed into the driveway. Doris, the holiday driver, tooted the horn, which sounded a rising note of inquiry. The door of the Winnebago exploded open. Tarara emerged and descended the several steps backward, bent and dragging a big, square suitcase, which tipped over the sill and chased her down the stairs.

"Petal? Petal?" she called. "Get your things; we're leaving." Her eyes strayed beyond Petal, for she was sure of her, but she wanted to see how Brooks was taking this. He remained seated at the picnic table holding forth within that cloud of technical boys.

Doris had gotten out of the taxi, a low-slung, big-finned vehicle with writing on the side. She'd been meaning to tell Lily she had all these old Stop and Shop bags set aside for the farm stand which she would drop off next time she drove a fare out that way. It was remarkable how many plastic shopping bags she had accumulated, all stuffed one inside the other like a giant puffball.

"Petal?" Tarara asked again. Petal was just standing there as if planted upon the side lawn. She swayed but she did not move from her spot.

"My dear," Harvey called, swinging his mallet. He had an elegant maneuver in mind, with all the angles worked out. "I shall be forced to invoke the sixty-second rule. If you don't take your shot, you'll forfeit your turn," he warned her.

"Coming," Petal called back to him.

"As if," Tarara said. "As if Brooks is ever going to notice you."

Petal shrugged. As for Brooks—

"Or Rollins. Same difference," Tarara said. "You're wasting your time with him. He won't notice you unless you're a modem. Well, maybe he's a mental dyslexic. Maybe he looks at you and thinks modem instead of model. Ha." She glanced around, seeking someone to appreciate her joke. She was certain had their precious Julie come up with the quip, the family would have rolled about, laughing at her wit.

"Actually," said Petal, drawing herself up to her full height and still standing her ground, "actually, Tarara, you have no idea. Brooks and Rollins are not at all the same person. Brooks may be the genius, but Rollins is the visionary. He sees everything for what it really is and then he thinks about how to make it better."

"Is that the passenger?" Doris asked. Having finished her business with Lily, she jutted a thumb at Tarara. "Is this the luggage?" she asked, nudging the big, square suitcase with a doubtful foot. She had polished her sneakers that morning and she left a white smudge on the side of the bag, like a customs official's mark.

Alden came over to help with the baggage, although Lily thought Brooks and Rollins, one or the other, ought to see off their guest. But then, she did not really understand modern manners, and upon consideration of what she would have identified as the precepts of proper behavior, she decided that this situation was one which would never have arisen in the past, this occasion of such an evidently angry exit from what she could only regard as a rolling harem (for through the Winnebago's door, which had been left swinging open, she viewed an example of what she could only characterize as a piece of very modern art suspended from a wall, which must be an example of what strange things nudes were like these days, particularly where the artist's brush or pallet knife had lingered over the area that Lily chose to think of as the subject's lap).

As Lily worked all of this out, the taxi's trunk lid thumped and its two doors slammed. Doris backed down the driveway, clipping the peony patch and clattering down Lily's stakes as she cut the corner too sharply. Doris had heard the telltale sound of cellophane crinkling in the backseat followed by the slow rip of silver paper and she was preoccupied with fishing the Thank You for Not Smoking sign from the glove compartment, stashed there because the air-conditioning was busted again, and the notice flapped and fluttered in the open window breeze when left hanging on display from the rearview mirror. Doris's mind was divided on whether holiday traffic would be light or heavy and she was glad she had her Yanni tapes with her to make the journey go faster should she not be able to breeze in to Logan, which was where this fare wished to be taken.

Sally and Cam had chased the taxi out to the road waving their mallets and shouting, "Good-bye, Good-bye," to the glamorous lady, and when the vehicle had rounded the green and vanished, they turned their attention to Petal. They didn't wish to lose her too; she was so pretty *and* nice, and they clasped her by either hand to make sure of her and swung all of their arms in a demonstration of joy and satisfaction at the way things had turned out until Rollins came and rescued her from their clutches. He told them he had just spotted a troll, out behind the barn drinking all the milk from the milkweed pods. Sally and Cam didn't really believe him, but they weren't entirely sure he wasn't fibbing, so they took off to see for themselves; that detail about trolls liking milkweed-milk had added a note of plausibility.

Brooks was not unaware of Tarara's departure. Rollins had drawn his attention to the taxi and the luggage and the aggrieved figure who was so obviously lingering in the driveway and he had asked his brother, "Aren't you going to say anything to her?"

"Say anything? To her? Why?" Brooks asked. "What? Huh?"

But afterward Brooks had surrendered the laptop to David May and his friends and taken himself off in the kayak for a moody paddle over dark waters and he indulged in a spell of soul-searching about what was wrong with all of the models and/or actresses of his acquaintance who came on to him so hot and then turned so cold. He wondered whether there wasn't someone out there who could simply be *even* when she was around him, although how he was going to recognize such equanimity he did not know. Perhaps there was a way to plot on a graph a system of factors by which one could predict and identify the desired temperament. He was seeking a nice flat line as far as matters of the heart went, he decided.

"Poor Brooks. He's lost another one," Julie said. She had witnessed the little drama from the window above the kitchen sink as she swished at dirty dishes piled in the soapy water.

"Where do I put these?" asked Becky, who was drying forks with a linty towel and letting them collect upon the countertop.

"Who knows where anything goes in Dad's house," Julie said.

"Over there," said Hannah, indicating a pantry drawer. She was unmolding an ice-cream bombe that had gone rock hard in Alden's frigid freezer compartment, revved up to ten to make all those ice cubes. She set the form in a bain-marie and began to prepare a plate, dusting the rim with grated nutmeg. Alden's kitchen was equipped with a nutmeg grater, but he did not possess a liquid measuring cup.

Glover had set out three bottles of a nice Sauternes. He considered and said, "Uncle Harvey," and returned to the pantry for a fourth bottle. Ginevra carried in a trayful of crystal flutes and set it down upon the island.

"Where did you find those?" Julie asked, rather severely.

"I was doing some snooping in the dining room. I hope it's all right. They looked so gala," Ginevra said. "Are they not correct?" she asked, not that she cared at all about such matters, but she had decided she was going to be very amused by Glover's family; just now she had not thought twice about rummaging through Alden's dining room sideboard with the intention of bringing objects into the daylight in order to let them twinkle and spark for her delectation.

"Oh, yes, of course. I was just surprised. I haven't seen the Orrefors since I don't know when," Julie said. After all the peregrinations and upheavals of the past ten years, she could not remember upon which table, where, and in celebration of what occasion had those goblets last been required. She held a clear, fragile glass up to the light, turning and turning it by the stem to catch the rainbow colors, but all she saw was an empty space defined by a surround of clarity.

"So delicate," said Hannah. "Think of what they've survived. They must have been packed away very well." She turned to Julie. "But that's your area of expertise these days, safeguarding precious and fragile objects while they're in transit, getting them there in one piece and then bringing them back home again safely. What do you think?"

"I think we should break out some champagne, since we've got the fancy glasses," Julie said. "Look in the refrigerator, Glover. What's there?"

"It looks like the better part of a case of Krug," Glover said. "And some string beans I wouldn't answer for."

"A case of Krug?" Betsy asked.

"Yes, Brooks and Rollins sent them out to everyone last winter when their stock split," Julie said. "All of the original investors got a case. It was my idea. I told them to make a nice gesture."

"Your father just stuck all of his bottles in the refrigerator, and they've been there ever since," Hannah said. "Good idea, Julie; these really ought to be drunk up."

THEY REASSEMBLED AROUND the picnic table and watched Hannah flambé a cherry compote, which she dispensed, still smoldering in the ladle, over the unmolded bombe. Sally took one bite of her portion and pushed away her plate without making the anticipated fuss. She had already had dessert at Cam's restaurant. She had spent the last six quarters in her pocket on a slice of red, white, and blue, strawberry and blueberry and frosting cake, which had been delicious, although Cam had raised some sort of funny-language fuss with her mother in regard to the cake, but Sally had been too busy making sure she loaded frosting and a strawberry and a blueberry onto every spoonful she lifted to her lips to follow the particulars of the tiff. Cam had consumed her treat resignedly and when she told Sally not to tell Lily or anyone else about the cake, Sally had said, "Of course not." She had had no intention of doing so for her cake consumption was strictly monitored, and it was nice to get a slice in under the wire.

The Tarara side of the table could relax a bit, with extra leeway for everyone's elbows now that she was gone. Petal, wedged between Brooks and Rollins, who in turn were bracketed by Harvey and Hannah, noticed there was more room across the table, but as she worked it out she understood that wherever she sat, she was going to be the extra person today. At least she was not stuck at the children's annex with the little girls and David May and his friends and, indeed, Rollins had particularly hauled her down onto the bench beside himself and then, when everyone had been served, Miss Hill, making sure of everyone in a general way, observed, "But Petal doesn't have a spoon." Julie jumped up to fetch her one from the kitchen even as Petal insisted she could manage without, although she had no very clear idea how. She would have had to stir lemon into her iced tea with a fork.

When Julie came back, she stood at the end of the table, positioning herself behind Lily and Ginger, holding on to the backs of their chairs and leaning into them as if for support. Lily asked, "Yes, dear?" rather distractedly, for she had never cared to be loomed over, and Ginger said, "What, honey?" and reached up to place her hand on Julie's hand.

"Okay, well, I guess I have an announcement to make," Julie said, almost reluctantly. Faces turned to her, rather concernedly inquiring. As Alden said later, he thought Julie was about to tell them all that she had just seen something nasty in the woodshed.

"What?" Harvey asked. "What?" he complained. He had switched off his hearing aid in an attempt to improve his croquet form; the game had been resumed when Sally and Cam returned from their disappointing troll hunt, and Cam had composed a new poem, *Cro*-quet is *Oh*-kay with *Me*! which, through repetition imposed its cadence upon his stroke to detrimental effect. Now, Penny mimed at him to turn his power pack back on.

"Tell us your news," Ginger prompted Julie. "We love to hear news."

"Certain news," Alden said.

"Yes, we like happy news," Ginger agreed. "In fact, I think we'd all very much appreciate some happy news."

"Okay, well, it's just that I've decided to get married," Julie said.

"What?" asked Alden.

"She's getting married," Harvey spoke to Alden distinctly, the way they all spoke distinctly to him whenever he asked, "What?"

"Yes, thank you. I got that much," Alden said.

Hannah nodded at Glover, and he began to open the champagne, correctly, Hannah noted, not letting loose with flying corks and spewing wine. How calm these people were, punctuating a moment like this with a modulated pop and the hiss of vapor.

"To whom?" Alden asked Julie. "To someone in London?" She had not mentioned anyone in particular, nor could he remember even a general conversation about any recent beaus.

"Yes, it's someone from London," Julie said.

"Why that's not very romantic, with you here and him there," Ginger said. She stroked Julie's arm, as if to warm and comfort the girl.

"Oh," said Petal in a heartfelt manner.

"Well, you know, it can't be helped," Julie said.

"He'd be here if he could," Penny spoke on the young man's behalf. She felt sure of that.

"So, tell us all about him," Betsy said. It occurred to her that she was about to cede her status as the only recent family bride and, as such, she would no longer stand first (or, at any rate, solitarily) in line as the one Lily thought of when she went in for a bout of cleaning out closets and shelves. Not that Betsy was ever greedy or expected anything as her due, but over the years she had become used to receiving, out of the blue, beautifully hemmed drawn-thread bureau scarves wrapped round silver candlesticks or porcelain fruit plates, accompanied by the usual note, *Could these possibly be of any use to you?*

"Is he a nice bloke?" asked Penny, thinking herself clever to have come up with the English word.

"No, I think I'd say he's actually more of a very nice chap," Julie said. "He's called Nicholas Davenant," she added.

"Oh, well done," said Ginger. "I believe I love him already. And what does he do, if he needs to do anything other than to stand around being Nicholas Davenant and British."

"He's a geologist. He looks for oil where, you know, people hope oil will be found," Julie said.

"Why, isn't that useful, in this day and age," marveled Penny. "Oil," she exclaimed. "Oil, Harvey." Harvey nodded, not unimpressed.

"Mom?" David May wanted to drink champagne. He held up a glass.

"No," Hannah said. "Tchah."

"Mummy?" Sally wanted to drink champagne. She held up a mug.

"Certainly not," Betsy said.

"So that's why he's not here, because he has to be in Siberia this summer. Now that it's summer in Siberia, he's just left to join the expedition," Julie said.

"What a pity he can't hunt for oil somewhere more convenient," Penny said.

"Oil is never found anywhere convenient," Harvey said.

"What a pity Nicholas Davenant can't have stopped here en route to Siberia so we could check him out for you," Glover said. "Couldn't he have flown to Siberia via Boston?"

"He went the other way round; it's faster," Julie said.

"Don't they always fly up and over the North Pole to get to Siberia?" Rollins asked.

"I'll hack into NORAD; they'll know how to get to Russia the fastest way," Brooks said. "What a pity he didn't consult us before making his travel plans."

"Oh, stop saying 'What a pity,' all of you," Ginger said. "Now, Julie, I want to see pictures, lots and lots of pictures of your young man."

"At the moment, all my stuff is in Glover's car, behind the Casa di Napoli," Julie said.

"But haven't you even slipped a picture of him into your purse to gaze upon at stolen moments?" Penny wondered. Although she hadn't noticed Julie stealing off anywhere that day—still, she supposed the girl had been kept too busy for any private dreaming and pining.

"No. Should I have one?" Julie asked. "I mean, I already have a pretty clear picture of him in my mind."

"All right, but what about the ring?" asked Ginger. "If your young man is in oil, it ought to be a very good stone."

"I don't have a ring," Julie said. "Not yet," she added as Ginger's massaging hand tightened and slid down her arm to pry back the fingers to verify that none was encircled.

"Is Nicholas Davenant a skinflint, then?" asked Rollins. "What a pity, if . . ."

"The ring is being made. I see so many fine pieces in my work, and there's a particular design being copied by a jeweler," Julie said. "Sixteenth-century Italian, kind of like Cellini, set with rubies."

"Rubies? Oh, well done," said Ginger. "You make me wish I had a ring just like it."

"Of course a girl wants something special," Penny said. She was prepared to take up Julie's cause against anyone who wanted her to settle for an ordinary mounting and stone.

"You can draw me a picture," said Ginger.

Penny rustled about in her handbag and shoved a pencil and a notepad at Julie, which she regarded helplessly.

"How did you meet him?" asked Petal. She always liked to hear how people met; she herself was always meeting people, that part was easy enough, and she supposed what she really wanted to know was how had Julie gotten Nicholas Davenant to linger and talk and allow matters to grow into something more lasting than just a drink before everyone had to race off to keep their next appointment.

"His employer was underwriting a museum show, The Mysteries of the Chukchi—they're a native people of Siberia. I worked on the show, setting it up," Julie said. "The Chukchi weave and carve and make all sorts of things from reindeer," she added, before anyone could ask.

"There's a very strong Siberian theme in all of this, isn't there?" Ginger noted. "I'll have to learn more about that part of the world so I can ask intelligent questions when we all get to meet your Nicholas."

"And when will that be?" asked Betsy. "I hope we'll still be here."

"It will be in September, early. The wedding will be then, just something simple. I've always kind of seen myself being married at Aunt Lily's, in the big field, if that's all right with you, Aunt Lily," Julie said.

"It's perfectly all right with me," said Lily. "Although you may not be aware that the big field has been planted with pumpkins."

"How lovely. Just like Cinderella, just like a fairy tale," said Ginger. "*Magic* pumpkins. I wanted to rent a pumpkin coach for Betsy's wedding, I recall."

"Well, perhaps we can set chairs out between the rows of pumpkins, but I must caution you, they're very large pumpkins," Lily said. "How many guests are you thinking of having?"

"I don't know. I haven't gotten that far. Let's keep it intimate," said Julie.

"Will your mother be attending?" Alden asked, and they all turned to him, those who had been wondering the same thing and those who hadn't thought of Becky at all until that moment.

"Yes. Of course. Ma will have to come," Julie said. "I'm going to insist upon Ma being here. She can't avoid her own daughter's wedding. There's no way she can stay away from that. Is there?"

GINGER TELEPHONED LOUIS AS SHE HAD DONE every night of her visit. The others had gone down to the Towne athletic fields to watch the fireworks. She could hear the first soft reports through her bedroom window, and if she had gotten up and looked out, she could have watched as the highest rockets burst into bloom above the treetops. But as Ginger had explained, declining to join the expedition which had taken off reeking of mosquito spray and lugging lawn chairs, she'd seen enough fireworks in her time.

Louis had spent the holiday alone at his office. He was putting in long hours clearing his desk so he could get away in August and today, without the fax chattering and the phones ringing and his partners bothering him, he'd accomplished a lot. He'd just arrived home, when Ginger called.

"But haven't you eaten?" Ginger asked him.

"I'm thinking about it now," Louis said. The cordless phone was tucked between his chin and shoulder as he studied the contents of the freezer. "What would the green frozen stuff in an unmarked Baggie be, dear?" he asked.

"That's that nice homemade pesto I left for you," Ginger said.

"But there's no spaghetti to put it on. I used the last box and I haven't been food shopping since," Louis said.

"No, there should be some. Try looking in the tall tin on the shelf beneath the island, the tin that says *Cucina, Cucina,* with the embossed purple grapes on the side. There's always spaghetti in that," Ginger said. She heard sounds of rummaging.

"Got it," Louis reported.

"Fill the big pot and boil the water on the right front burner. It's the fastest one."

"I know, you always say that, but . . ."

"That's how they make stoves; it's the most used burner; the others just coast," Ginger insisted.

How clearly she could see her house, which sat long and low upon the prairie, with a winglike lift of roof above the great room. Big, square windows she had never covered with drapes or blinds looked out during the day and gazed within at night. She had liked to say that she had nothing to hide, which was not, of course, true. Nevertheless, she had always been mindful of maintaining appearances, and she had often caught glimpses of herself in the glass doing just that. The main rooms ran one into another, defined by their uses rather than walls; she and Louis had filled in and tiled over an original conversation pit. All of the sofas in her house were beautiful and comfortable and piled with cushions covered in deep colors, and Louis had long been a collector of Sarouk carpets. He was very knowledgeable and kept a stack of books and auction catalogues on a corner of his desk, which Ginger had always made a further virtue of not disturbing when one of her creditable neatening and polishing moods came upon her.

"There's *fleur de sel* in a blue box to the left of the vanilla beans, in the spice rack," she told him.

"Do I like *fleur de sel*?" Louis asked.

"You ought to. It's very nice," Ginger said. "There are those pretty little crystal salt cellars with the little ivory spoons in the left-hand drawer of the sideboard," she added, but Louis confessed, "I'm not being very formal these days," which had given her pause, for in her mind's eye, Louis had been enjoying an elegant bachelor's existence in her absence, lighting tall white tapers and studying his catalogues and listening to the strains of cello music, which could make sorrow and loneliness sound so lovely. Lately, she had ordered the Bach Suites for Unaccompanied Cello, the Casals recording, for Louis; he would know they were from her when they arrived.

"Am I correct in thinking that *fleur de sel* tastes a bit sweet?" Louis asked. He had licked a fingertip and conveyed a few crystals to his tongue.

"Yes," Ginger said. "You've got it."

"How was the parade? Did Sally have fun? Did Alden's brood show up in force?" Louis asked.

"Yes, it was all very nice. The parade was charming. Sally has found a formidable new friend in Cam. Alden's boys are terrific young men, but the really exciting news is that Julie's getting married. I'm just thrilled about it—her young man sounds perfect. Under questioning, she revealed that Nicholas Davenenat plays rugby, reads Thackeray and drives an vintage MG that he restored himself. Oh, romance is in the air. Rollins has a glamour-puss girlfriend but poor Brooks's date got the sulks and flounced off in a snit," Ginger reported. "It was not at all an attractive performance, the way the girl stormed off. If there's one thing I can't admire it's an ungraceful exit. There's really no excuse, and just imagine what everyone will be saying about you, long after you've gone."

THREE *Seeing Round Several Corners*

GLOVER AND GINEVRA WERE SCHEDULED to open the farm stand that morning and they set out early from Ginevra's parents' place in the canoe. They shoved the old aluminum Grumman down an otter slide of embankment and struck off through the cattails. Gaining the current, they floated away from the elder Platt-Willeys' riverside compound, which consisted of an A-frame house, a sweat lodge, an adobe bread oven, a pottery studio, a wind-powered generator, and a guest pod. Each improvement had been set down along the shoreline in the order they had occurred to the Platt-Willeys, who subscribed to the *Utne Reader* and otherwise scouted round the premises of their like-minded friends, from whence grew the almost organic array of low-lying and dun-colored constructions.

Glover and Ginevra paddled through the orchard whose stolen fruits figured in Pratt-Willey cuisine (those dishes called Windfall Profiteroles and Original Sinnamon Cobbler); they glided past the public boat landing where a discarded diaper swirled in an eddy between the pilings of the boat ramp; they skirted the downed tree with its colony of sunning turtles; they skimmed behind the backyards of a subdivision where the chain-link fences ran down to and then continued on into the water, which always made Ginevra wonder aloud what sort of people thought they could fence in a river and Glover always repeated the adage that you can never step into the same river twice, and they would mildly disagree whether Heraclitus or Woody Guthrie had first made that observation.

They found the channel that carried them through a paludal tangle of pickerelweed and bulrushes, where, in the shallowest spots they had to dig their paddles into the muck and propel themselves by force of pushing and shoving. Then, even though they knew it was coming, they were startled when the canoe was seized from their control at the place where the riverbed narrowed and quickened as it flowed through a concrete conduit and they were shot beneath the interstate. The rush of the stream and the rumble of morning commuter traffic roared from all sides, amplified by the vault of the tunnel that closed round them. Glover always thought that this was all he needed to know of what it would be like to go down a drain after the plug was pulled and he always said he would never again wash a live spider down the sink, and Ginevra always rather huffily remarked that he ought never to have done so in the first place.

Seated in the bow, Ginerva kept up the conversation, addressing Glover over her shoulder. She dipped her paddle and swiveled to speak, essaying a single coordinated motion as if she sought to make headway in both endeavors, those of addressing Glover and getting to the farm stand on time. Although at the moment she was asserting that no one was getting anywhere with Julie these days. Several weeks had passed since Julie's announcement, but she was being stubborn about everything that had to do with her upcoming wedding.

"She is refusing to let Betsy throw her a surprise shower," Ginevra said. "Granted, showers are grotesque, but Betsy's trying to act hypernormal about everything this summer, and she believes that's what hypernormal people do; they throw their cousin a surprise bridal shower. She has even bought half a dozen umbrellas at the Ben Franklin which she was going to place upside down on a table and fill with potato chips and bowls of dip. She asked Penny what the form was and apparently that's what Penny said people do." Ginevra gave the river a real push with her paddle.

"How did Julie even know to object, if Betsy was keeping the event a surprise from her?" Glover asked. They should never have given Julie the chance to dig in her heels—they should have just sprung the party on her.

"Julie figured someone would try to plan something and she wrung it out of poor Betsy, who is truly lacking a spine," Ginevra said as she reached and soused her paddle and Glover corrected their course with a tilt of his blade. He didn't understand why food would have to be served in umbrellas; he'd have thought Lily would gladly let Betsy use any bowl or dish she asked for.

"I mean, Julie just isn't acting all that happy and excited," Ginevra said. "I wonder, I only hope, that this Nicholas Davenant is all he's cracked up to be. Aren't you terribly curious about what he looks like? We still don't even know that." She swerved into another stroke, confronting Glover with her question.

"But Julie has pictures," he said. His father had invited him to take a look at Nicholas Davenant's pictures, chucking a portfolio of snaps at him the last time he stopped by the house to pick up a couple of clean shirts and swipe another bottle of Krug. Over the past few weeks Glover had been moving in with Ginevra in easy stages. Initially, he had only gone over there to take a look at the main house's solar panels which were failing to heat the bath water to any temperature past tepidity. Now, matters were quite sufficiently steamy at bath time, as Ginevra said.

"Didn't you notice they were Nicholas Davenant's pictures only in the sense that Nicholas Davenant took all the pictures? And that all of the pictures were of Julie?" Ginevra asked. She had viewed a second set of the photos that was circulating round the farm stand to show to customers who wished to see them, word of the wedding having gotten round somehow.

"You're right. They were just of Julie," Glover allowed. "And of assorted London landmarks," he added. He had been particularly interested in the shot of his sister standing at the future site of the Millennium Wheel. Julie had risen up against the skyline standing on her toes, her arms flung out into a big circle above her head in order to demonstrate how the great Ferris wheel was going to look once it was erected on the spot.

"Except there was that one picture when Nicholas Davenant stuck his thumb over the lens. Julie positively jumped on that thumb, as if it proved something," Ginevra said. "Hey, I wonder whether Brooks and Rollins can invent some kind of technology that can reconstruct an entire human being from just a thumbprint?"

"Well, I think it's touching if Julie was so glad to see his thumb again. And personally, I view Nicholas Davenant as a man of many parts. His thumb's not the half of it, I'm sure," Glover said, and Ginevra flung him a look over her shoulder.

The canoe was passing the high school tennis courts now, where a boy was working on his serve. The steady pock of balls hitting the backboard and the smooth plash of paddles pulsed them onward. They swept below the stone arches of the Bridge Street span. The cemetery rose to their right, parklike and orderly and quiet, and presently they drifted by Alden's house, keeping an eye out to see whether anyone was awake and abroad yet. Empty Glenfiddich bottles and burnt-out tiki-flambeaus littered the crescent sliver of beach below the Winnebago, which had been moved from the driveway and parked broadside with a view of the river. Glover cupped his lips and whooped but he failed to rouse his slugabed brothers.

The river carried them past lawns and gardens and the outflow pipes of sump pumps which intermittently discharged into the water, roiling up clouds of mud. They rounded a bend curtained with willows and continued on, running parallel with the road and a municipal parking lot. They looked up at the rear facade of the old mill building that housed Hannah's premises, prepared to wave at her were she to be seen gazing down upon the river through one of her large upper windows. The current quickened as they approached the dam and spillway, and Glover steered toward a well-trodden place on the embankment. Touching ground, they hopped out and portaged to the other side of Front Street, where they set the canoe down on the pavement in front of Peddocks'. They stopped in there for coffee and corn muffins, sitting at the counter and sharing a left-behind Boston *Herald*. Ginevra remembered she meant to look for bloodroot; Peddocks' featured an aisle of herbal nostrums, but the alphabetized stock jumped from birch cream to blue cohosh, so she enjoyed no luck there.

"What did you want the bloodroot for?" Glover asked when they were back on the water, relaunched below the dam.

"Well, that was just a thought. When my mother called last night, we got to talking, and she thought it might help your aunt Ginger," Ginevra said. "She said our local woods are full of bloodroot, but I'm not knowledgeable enough to gather stuff on my own. I just wanted to read what the package said, if I could find anything at Peddocks'."

"I don't know," Glover said, unhelpfully.

"And I don't know either," Ginevra said. "Mother also mentioned colchicine, which has been proved to naturally inhibit cell division, but it's also very toxic. You can't even get it commercially. Its other name is autumn crocus, but I don't know whether that means you have to wait 'til the fall to get some. Which won't be much help by then, I'm afraid, the way things seem to be heading." She swept her paddle along the gunwale and caught the look on Glover's face. "Mother was just trying to help, in her own way," she explained.

"I know," Glover said. "Please thank her for us." The formality of his tone caused Ginevra to turn away and paddle faster.

They had entered the demesne of an old estate. Ginevra remarked that even the water seemed to be touched with a more silvery glitter here. They floated through a rhododendron forest and entered an Olmsted-inspired expanse of rolling meadow and perfectly sited trees. A mist hovered in a hollow, and several deer materialized from out of the fog to gaze at them. The canoe drifted by stables, a pagoda-like teahouse, a boathouse, and the brick pile of the manor house.

"I think I'd really rather live in that sweet little teahouse than the big house," Ginevra said.

"I wouldn't say no to the mansion," Glover said, and on this particular morning, the realization came to him that he could probably afford to buy this entire property some day or some other country seat just like it, if he decided to go to work for his brothers. He was supposed to be taking this summer to decide what he was going to do next. He had been granted extended leave; he had discussed his options with his CO who had pointed out that the army might be glad to have a close connection to someone so well placed within GLowe Systems and he intimated that Glover's break from the armed forces might not be so complete, if break there was going to be. Glover's brothers had told him they were going to give him China; Glover's colonel had told him they would like someone like Glover to have China. And Ginevra was saying she wanted to live in the Chinese teahouse folly nestled by the river, so perhaps the stars were lining up and trying to tell him something.

The woods pressed closer and darker along this last stretch, where a rare stand of old-growth forest survived. They began to glimpse the road again, or evidence of the road, as cars flashed between the trees; vehicles seemed to be metaphysically speeding through the ancient forest like ghosts from the future. Nearly there, Glover angled his blade, and they skimmed up and onto the shore. They carried the canoe across the road and set it down behind the farm stand, half hidden by crates. Otherwise, Sally and Cam would tease too much to be taken off for a paddle, or they would steal away on their own, crouching out of sight and rocking from side to side to ease the canoe out into the current, although they would have failed to consider that an apparently unmanned craft adrift on the water could excite nearly as much alarm among the grown-ups as one commandeered by small children who had forgotten their life jackets and lost their paddles to the pull of the river. Either way, Glover would have to kick off his mocs and plunge into the water to catch and haul the canoe back to shore, which also would have delighted the little girls, to cause Glover to become soaking wet and perhaps even lose his wallet in the water while rescuing them.

Glover raised and secured the farm stand's shutters, and Ginevra unlocked the cash box. She carried the jelly-jar bouquets, unsold the day before, out to the tap behind the stand and changed their water. Glover filled the ruts in the parking area, shoveling spun-out gravel back onto the bare spots. Mr. DeSouza rode down the driveway in his tractor to drop off the first hot banana peppers of the season; he'd been out in the fields since five a.m. picking a couple of cases, having determined today would be the day they'd be ripe. Lily had left a note in the cash box, telling Glover and Ginevra what to charge for the peppers, per quarter pound. She was asking quite a lot for them because she wanted to make it plain to people that a very little of the very fiery peppers would go a long way. Otherwise, she'd have to worry about everyone burning their tongues, and benumbing their lips, and she already had enough on her mind.

JULIE CARRIED GINGER'S BREAKFAST TRAY up the back stairs. Julie, like Glover, had lately left their father's house and moved in at Lily's, where she was spending most of her time anyway, lending a hand as well as adding to the burdens already on Lily's plate. Lily had been doing her best to work on wedding plans with Julie, but she was finding it difficult to pin the girl down on very much of anything. The first Saturday in September, which was the date Julie had suddenly named for the wedding, would be upon them faster than Julie evidently believed. Earlier in the week, Lily had sat her down at the kitchen table with a checklist and a calendar, but Julie had only wanted to spin the lazy Susan, which was crowded with the household's fads in condiments and seasonings and sweeteners; the spoons in the spoon jar rattled and clinked until Lily told Julie to stop fiddling.

"Who made this strawberry jam? Betsy? Why is it so soupy?" Julie asked, seizing a spoon and scraping it against the side of the jar as she tried to catch an entire berry that still seemed to bear a bit of stem and leaf.

"Betsy added the sugar too soon," Lily said.

"It tastes all right, though," Julie said. She was about to redip her spoon but thought better as Lily gazed at her and then gazed at the spoon.

"Leave that for now," Lily had told her. "What have you decided about the guest list? We *must* send out the invitations and we have to leave time to make hotel reservations for the out-of-town guests. Have you any idea who to count on from away?" She had been about to inquire whether Julie expected many friends from England and to ask, Is Nicholas Davenant's family a large one? By then, Lily hoped she would have worked her nerve up to inquire further, using her most careful and neutral tone of voice, "And what about your mother, Julie?" But Julie had chosen that moment to say she heard Ginger's bell—her ears were keener than Lily's, she claimed—and she had flown up the back stairs, not to return, even though Lily could clearly see Ginger through the kitchen window, seated outside with Sally, the pair of them positioned so the sprinkler would lightly dowse them with its pattering spray on alternate passes as it swayed back and forth over the lawn.

But now, this morning, it seemed Julie was going to have to do something definite about a dress, despite herself, as Lily had said. Penny happened to know *the* place everyone was flocking to at the moment: a chic little shop called Avanda's Off the Avenue. Penny had just been through a big and fashionable wedding with a Nicholls great-granddaughter, and her Nicholls daughter-in-law had been so kind as to go ahead on her own initiative and book a hard-to-get appointment, securing Loretta herself to look after Julie (there being no Avanda at Avanda's, so you had to know it was Loretta you wanted). Julie had been pledged to tell Loretta that Laura Nicholls (now Borodin) particularly said hello and to say that Loretta had been absolutely proved correct about the demi-train.

"Why? Is that some kind of coded message that'll get me access to the secret Vera Wang vault?" Julie had asked.

When she knocked on Ginger's bedroom door and entered with the breakfast tray, Julie knew at once that Ginger would not be able to accompany her today as they had both hoped. Julie set the tray down on the nightstand as Ginger waved it away. She pushed aside a box of tissues and a book and Ginger's summoning silver bell, and she busied herself pulling up the window shades, more disappointed for her aunt's sake than her own. The proposed outing would have been right up Ginger's alley, convening at the appointed hour in the smart little shop to be ushered into a private dressing room where Loretta (herself) would alternately hover and bustle on Julie's behalf as a seamstress stood by wearing a pincushion on her wrist. Ginger would have been able to put to use her knowledge of French seams and pinch pleats. She would have the name of every shade of white fluently on call at the tip of her tongue, starting with alabaster and ending with wishy-washy. Although Lily, who had said she would be available to accompany Julie, if need be, would make a reliable stand-in when it came to determining whether the foliage matched the flower blossom in any floral headdress; no silk godetia leaf attached to a violet's stem would get past Lily, and at the very least, Julie would be able to hold her head up in the fancy chaplet department, as Ginger was saying to Julie now.

"But I still need you to have the last word on any dress," Julie said, sitting on the edge of the bed. "If I come home with something, I want you to honestly say whether or not you like it."

"All right. I'll exercise my veto power," Ginger said.

"Although I'm not so much concerned that I'll choose something perfectly awful so much as I'll overlook something that might be really, really good," Julie said. "Which you would have spotted right away, hanging on its hanger."

"Try on everything," Ginger advised. "You never know," she added as Julie made a face at that prospect.

"I should think bridal shops are used to bridal remorse anyway," Julie said. "I mean, everyone expects me to make all these life and death decisions I'm going to be stuck with forever, and it's not like they even matter, what my china pattern will be, or the thread count on my sheets."

"Well, thread counts are worthy of consideration. They say it's a third of one's life, the time spent in bed," Ginger said. "One way or the other," she added, summoning up a bit of a wink which caused Julie to blink and then blush.

Besides, Ginger had been having a good time, thinking about fine china and remembering just where she had found her own lovely living room lampshades and being definite about the sort of table linens Julie ought to want. Ginger had been considering the question of Julie's kitchen needs and finally made up her mind; Julie must have All-Clad Stainless cookware, Sabatier knives, and a Dualit toaster. Surely, an Englishmen would require toast, and her heart was quite set on getting a Dualit for Julie, although she had yet to home in on the specific model. There was one version that not only toasted bread but also toasted sandwiches; however, Ginger had already settled on a panini maker (a DeLonghi, with an adjustable thermostat), and she'd been further distracted by a Dualit toaster that could accommodate buns, so the entire toaster question was pending. But shopping seemed rather a tame and bloodless sport when conducted (by necessity) online, devoid of face-to-face and gut-level rapturous recognition. It was but a reflection of the real thing.

LILY SEEMED TO THINK SHE NEEDED to hear a weather report before heading out with Julie. (She had been up half the night with Ginger and already knew that she and not Ginger would be going dress shopping with Julie.) She puttered in the kitchen swiping surfaces with a damp sponge as she kept one ear on the radio and one eye on Sally, who was eating cereal. She was eating cereal like Tommy, Sally explained. Her elbows were planted on the table and the heels of her hands were ground into her cheeks as she leaned forward and lowered her face into her deep-sided Lion King bowl. She pursed her lips and breathed in. She and the cereal had been sitting there for a while, and the corn flakes had melted into the milk, making this inhalation method of ingestion possible.

A voice on the radio reported, "In Montana, the jury selection in the trial of the Third Day Brethren will begin with proceedings which are expected to be rancorous."

Sally growled into her cereal bowl, and produced a nice, echoing effect.

"Hush. Listen," Lily said. "They may mention your father on the radio."

"Pah," said Sally. Stupid trial. That stupid trial was everything's fault, why her father wasn't here with them this summer. She studied Lily, who seemed very different this morning. Lily wore a fancy blue dress with shiny buttons and she had on heel shoes. Even her great-aunt's hair had been combed; Sally could trace the tooth marks among the white whorls, set in place by a combination of cold water and Aqua Net.

Lily leaned against the counter, listening to the radio report and touching the sides of the iron, which sat cooling off on the counter beside the radio (the single available electrical outlet drew all appliances to the single spot). Earlier, she had pressed her blue linen dress in an attempt to restore what she recalled had been the crisp and neat qualities that had recommended the garment to her in the first place, for she regarded today's outing as an important one. She had also clasped on her good pearl necklace for this, because Penny had said something about not letting Laura Nicholls Borodin down, not that Penny cared; she was just passing on her Nicholls daughter-in-law's rather uppish remark, for what it was worth.

Lily touched the sides of the iron again, and she judged it could be safely stowed back on its shelf in the broom closet without causing the house to burn down in her absence. She wrapped the cord around the iron's handle; she could not abide dangling cords, which reminded her of mice tails when she came upon them behind a cupboard door.

"Did they say about Daddy?" Sally asked, returning to the matter, her mind having been elsewhere. It was interesting how a radio voice could talk and talk and talk and you would not hear it.

"No, they didn't," Lily said.

"Can I have a cinnamon doughnut?" Sally asked, which seemed the least she was owed for having been deprived of hearing her father's name spoken on the radio as Aunt Lily had practically promised it would be; her hopes had been raised, only to be crushed. Sally whimpered like Tommy, effecting an excellent imitation. Wait until Cam heard—because Cam could do Agnes yowling, *so* realistically that one time Lily thought Agnes had been run over by the tractor and had been very upset.

"*May* I have a cinnamon doughnut," Lily corrected her.

"*May* I have a cinnamon doughnut?" Sally asked promptly, recognizing Lily's schoolteacher voice and knowing, by now, the drill.

"No. Besides you can't," Lily said. "There aren't any."

"What? Why? What?" Sally asked.

Leaving the child to figure that one out, Lily began to rinse dishes in the sink, running them under the faucet and giving them a shake and setting them upside down in the dish drainer. "Are you finished with this?" she asked Sally. She stood behind her, a hand hovering over the Lion King bowl.

"Yes," said Sally. "I mean no."

Too late; the bowl was swept away, and the sponge swiped the tabletop, swerving round Sally's anchoring elbows. She snatched them up as a contaminated spray of dirty sponge water dampened her arms. "Hey," she said. This was not being a very nice morning, in Sally's opinion.

Julie came down the stairs, carrying a tray which she set down upon the counter in front of Lily so Lily could see for herself that Ginger had eaten nothing that morning.

"I hoped she might at least attempt the pear," Lily said. "If not the poached egg."

Sally rose and inserted herself between Lily and Julie, standing on her toes and studying the tray as solemnly as the grown-ups. Wasting food was very bad, and she reached for a slice of toast, only to have her hand slapped away by Julie.

"Hey," Sally said.

"Oh, let her have the toast if she wants," Lily said, but Sally said no, thank you, because Julie had begrudged and Lily condescended, and she'd just been trying to help not to waste Granna's breakfast.

"Aunt Ginger said maybe she'll feel like having the pear later on," Julie said, and she covered the bowl with plastic wrap and opened the refrigerator door. "Gosh, the fridge is so crammed with bits and pieces. What's this?" she asked, withdrawing a saucer containing half a tangerine splayed into fibrous segments.

"A lot of that is Petal's," Lily said. "She has very odd eating habits. I really can't figure her out." She supposed she ought to inquire after the young woman's food preferences and attempt to accommodate them, but everything about Petal's continuing presence in her house puzzled Lily, not the least how she contrived at once to be so inconvenient and yet so helpful. Still, when Petal had come to her as they were packing up the car after the Fourth of July picnic at Alden's and said, "Please, I can't stay in that Winnebago with the guys, Miss Hill," Lily had agreed, "Certainly not," but that was all she had thought she was agreeing to. She had been very much surprised when Petal hefted her suitcase in the trunk and fitted herself into the backseat between Sally and the picnic basket, and she had not bargained on Petal's extended stay in an attic bedroom. Lily had overheard the young woman on her cell phone; they called constantly from New York asking Petal where she was and when she was coming back to work. "I am in the most beautiful place you have ever seen," Petal would tell them. "I am not sure I am ever coming back to work. I am so busy here. They let me weed the lettuce today. Miss Lily has showed me how. They let me help out at the farm stand and I'm going to give Ginger a pedicure this evening. She'll feel so much better with nice cuticles. You know, I really think they all kind of count on me."

"A lot of it looks like it smells funny," Julie was saying, her head stuck inside the refrigerator.

"The pickle and the olive and the grape is mine," Sally spoke up.

"They *are* mine," Lily corrected her. "The pickle and olive and grape *are* mine."

"No, they're mine," Sally insisted. "I saved the pickle and the olive and the grape from supper."

"These cucumber slices are Petal's too," Julie said. "They're the ones she sets over her eyelids to reduce puffiness. She must be saving them, although it's not as if we don't have enough cucumbers around here for her to use fresh ones each time."

"I love Petal," Sally declared. Petal let Sally read aloud to her when she lay on the terrace sightless, with her cucumber eyes. She was patient as Sally stumbled over the hard words in *The Lion, the Witch and the Wardrobe.*

"That's nice," said Julie. "She'll be glad to hear that at least one person in this family loves her. You will give her hope to believe that loving her may be contagious."

"Petal is an angel," Sally said.

"An angel, is she? Why ever do you think so?" Julie said.

"Because you can see on her back where her wings are attached when she is up in heaven," Sally said. "When she was on the lawn in her bathing suit. Cam and I *saw.*"

"Don't be silly," Lily said. She dropped her cell phone into her handbag and checked to see whether she had a clean handkerchief and some cash, just in case. She wished Julie had chosen to wear something nicer than the very short and crumpled sleeveless shift dress of a faded beige linen she had donned for the outing, which raised the question of what similarly draggle-tailed underwear Julie might be wearing. Lily hoped whatever she had on, it would stand up to the scrutiny of the dressing room staff who, no doubt, were used to seeing lacily impeccable lingerie as befits a bride assembling her trousseau.

"Oh, I know exactly what Sally means," Julie said. "Petal's so thin her shoulder blades stick way out and they are sort of winglike. I can see how you'd think they're like vestigial wings."

"She is my angel," Sally said. "Everybody has an angel, and Petal is mine."

"Who told you that everyone has an angel?" Lily asked. "Because that's not quite what we believe, in our church. Angels very seldom appear to anyone at all, and when they do show up, more often than not, it's to inflict some terrible task or trial upon you or, at the very least, to tell you something you really don't want to hear. If I ever saw an angel, I would walk quickly and quietly in the opposite direction and avoid looking it in the eye, and I advise you to do the same."

"No. Everybody has a *nice* angel who *helps* them. It is what I believe," Sally said, simply. "Granna does too—Granna says if I see *her* angel I'm supposed to *grab* it and wrestle it to the ground and hold it down until Granna can get there. Cam says if we each stomp on a wing, we can catch one."

"I thought you were believing in Buddha, these days," Julie said. Lately, Sally had erected a shrine upon her bedroom bureau top. Having modelled a small Buddha from yellow Play-Doh (adding an acorn hat and a scrap-velvet cloak), she set him up in front of a sky-and-sun-and-rainbow backdrop she had painted on a poster board. Offerings had been accumulating in a Lusterware dish: a piece of polished beach glass, an unexploded puffball, and a sheath of sloughed-off snakeskin she had found on the terrace stones one very hot afternoon. She hoped Buddha didn't mind snakes.

"Oh, I believe in angels and Buddha and everything," Sally said. Assorted entities were working hard on her behalf all on the strength of some nice little offerings and a few accompanying words of prayer and petition from her to steer them in the right direction.

"Well, I can't keep up with you," Lily said, and Sally nodded. That was just fine by her if she got to God first, before her great-aunt could interfere.

"What time are we supposed to be at Avanda's?" Julie asked. She'd already been told, but she had a mental block about remembering the precise hour and minute of their appointment.

"Can I come with you? May I come with you? I want to come with you," Sally said. She stationed herself beside Julie with some hope of being generally swept along when the move was made out to the car, and Lily saw now that Sally had been sitting on top of her travel knapsack at breakfast, equipped for an outing. "Please, please, please," Sally said.

"No," said Lily and Julie together.

Sally spun away from Julie and flung herself into a chair, planting her elbows on the table and grinding the heels of her hands into her cheeks. She cast her eyes from beneath heavy brows to see how Julie and Lily were taking this abject posture of hers, but they were just discovering that each assumed the other possessed the MapQuest directions to the place they were going. Lily flurried through a pile of pages snatched from a drawer, as Julie kept saying the place was off some flipping avenue, that's all she knew about it.

"When I buy my wedding dress," Sally announced, "when I go to buy my wedding dress, you two can't come either. Nobody else can come, only Granna. I'll only let Granna be there, when I get married." She saw with satisfaction that she had hit her mark as Aunt Lily and Julie turned away from her, both of them very obviously and most deservedly upset at the thought of that very sad day.

LILY AND JULIE PAUSED AT THE farm stand to drop off Sally, who had been somewhat mollified by being allowed to attach herself to the wedding dress expedition as far as the end of the driveway. Harvey stopped on his return trip from fetching the Samrin kids and the *Wall Street Journal* to discharge Cam. Sally was already at work grading the summer squashes by size even though summer squash was sold by the pound. She didn't like to see the little ones crushed by the big ones. Cam busied herself exchanging the dull cent pieces in the penny saucer for any of the brighter and shinier coins collecting in the till. Mrs. Kariotis, Calliope, the sole customer, lingered to chat with Glover and Ginevra. She and George and the children were flying off to Greece the following week. All that retsina and dancing on the beach, Ginevra supposed, sighing, and then Calliope sighed and said *her* Greek vacation entailed marathon churchgoing and endlessly apologizing to the old folk because her kids were so American, although as far as she could tell, Mike's little cousin Xenophon was equally addicted to his computer games and Twizzlers.

As Calliope selected corn from the bin, Cam kept an eye on her. Calliope examined every ear, holding each one up to the sunlit back window, to what end Cam did not know, but she decided there could be no real harm done. Mrs. Kariotis was just looking. What Cam could not abide were those people who felt they had to open the corn to see what was inside. The sound of ripping and tearing husks occasioned her deepest scowls, although the situation had improved with the recent posting of this sign: "Please do not peel back the Corn. This we look upon with Scorn. If at home you find a Worm, We'll accept its prompt Return—And give you back Double for your Trouble." Cam was convinced she had composed this herself, dictating it one afternoon as Ginevra recorded her words upon a shingle with black felt tip pen. Ginevra herself said that the ideas and the sentiments certainly were all Cam's own though; Ginevra might have just tinkered a bit with the phrasing. Sally was royally miffed that all the glamour of authorship fell to Cam, and she tried to come up with her own cautionary verse but had become blocked in her attempt to rhyme *stupid* and *cucumber,* which she felt ought to work and yet, somehow, could not be made to blossom into poesy. Cam was working on a further piece about the proper handling of tomatoes, getting as far as, If you stick in your thumb / You can't come / Here anymore / Like before / when Lily put her foot down and said there was to be no more hectoring of the customers. One or two little signs were amusing, but beyond that things just looked funny.

Calliope hung around taking up valuable space in front of the counter as she chattered on about her trip to Greece and the several inconvenient international flight connections they must make along the way. Even if there weren't other customers for Mrs. Kariotis to be in the way of, there might be at any moment, and then what? At last, in a spasm of impatience, Cam relieved Calliope of the basket slung over her arm, and she climbed onto the chair and weighed the tomatoes on the hanging scale. She counted the ears of corn, and double-checked the price of red lettuce on the list kept beside the cash box.

The total purchase came to $19.10. Cam wrote the numbers in the ledger and showed them to Calliope, who was still in no particular hurry to pay. She wandered over to collect a pair of summer squash which she had meant to pick up, but she had been put off by Sally's warning hiss; Sally had finished separating the squashes by size, but then she had decided to grade them as well, according to their various shades of yellow.

"These also," Calliope said to Cam, whose face was crossed by a look of disgust. She began to black out the $19.10 she had entered on the ledger page, at the same time kicking the chair back into position beneath the scales so she could clamber up again.

"Just show it as another transaction," Glover said. "There's no need to write it out all over again. Or better yet, just take the squash, Calliope. No further charge," he told Cam, who set her pencil down very patiently and began to bag Calliope's purchases with exaggerated care, placing those controversial squashes on the bottom, tomatoes in between, with a tender lettuce tenderly set on top. The corn was given its own receptacle, individually placed standing up with their blond wisps of corn hair catching the breeze. Sally, who had been offended by the outright giving away of what she had come to think of as her own particular squash, sidled behind the counter to stand supportively at Cam's elbow. Calliope handed them a twenty-dollar bill, which Sally slipped into the envelope where the larger denomination bills were kept separate (as a particular courtesy to any passing sneak thief, Glover said), and Cam counted out ninety cents in the form of two quarters and four dimes, which she reluctantly dropped into Calliope's open palm. So many bright coins seemed like far too much change, even if they added up correctly.

Ginevra decided that Sally and Cam were too full of themselves at the moment to be pleasant to the public, so she told them to go up to the barn and hunt for more shingles. The blueberries would be coming in soon, and they needed to make a sign, she said.

"A rhyme sign?" asked Sally.

"For you. A berry that's blue," Cam recited.

"They make pies like skies," Sally proclaimed.

"We'll see," said Ginevra.

"Mine is best," Cam said.

"Mine is best," Sally said.

"They both need work," Glover said, which united Sally and Cam in a pact against the unkind Glover, and they pelted up the driveway shouting back and forth, trying to come up with a rude rhyme for *him*.

"I only know a nice one," Ginevra assured Glover.

BETSY COLLECTED EVERYONE'S LIBRARY BOOKS, filling her satchel. She scoured Sally's room for *The Golden Book of Crawling Bugs and Flying Insects*, which she at last found fallen down between the headboard and the wall. As Betsy shifted the bed, Sally's copy of *The Lion, the Witch and the Wardrobe* slid out from under the pillow, which explained why her daughter's ear and cheek often looked so red in the morning, from resting all night upon the hard binding. Betsy had also fished out, from the dust behind Sally's dust ruffle, a length of paperclip chain which she dropped into the saucer of offerings at the Buddha's clay feet. She bowed to him with a brief dip of chin to chest just as she had nodded before the altar cross at All Saints' the previous Sunday, when walking up the aisle to take communion.

She picked up Lily's small stack of books left stacked atop the blanket chest in the upper hallway, and she entered Julie's room to fetch *The Shale and Hydrology Handbook: A Survey Course*, which Julie said she was reading for Nicholas Davenant's sake, sitting up in bed every evening, propped against the headboard.

"Why on earth are you bothering with hydrology?" Betsy had asked her. Their bedrooms connected through the new, small bathroom, and the cousins wandered back and forth between their respective chambers, checking to see what the other was up to at the end of the day.

"Don't married people like to talk to each other about their work?

Am I not expected to know all this?" Julie asked. She displayed a *Handbook* page, which bore a bar graph.

"If married people do talk about work, at home, it's more to do with office politics and personalities than any actual work they perform," Betsy said. "Andy will mention some tiff in the faculty dining room."

"Well, that's good to know," Julie said, setting aside her book.

"But what do you and Nicholas talk about?" Betsy asked. She had not, as yet, caught a very distinct idea of him. She could not yet really picture him, she told herself.

"I don't know. Movies. Astronomy. Stuff," Julie said as she slid down beneath her blanket. She clicked off her light with an abrupt reach beneath her lampshade. "Oh my God, I'm sorry," she spoke into the darkness when she heard the retreating Betsy crack her shin against a corner of the desk chair.

"I'm all right," Betsy had assured her, understanding that Julie must have arrived at that exclusive phase of her romance when she had become convinced that no one else could ever begin to understand the smoke and mystery generated by the coming together of herself and Nicholas; Julie wanted only to hug him to herself, whether or not he was actually there for her to embrace; darkness lent itself to dreaming.

Now, continuing her book hunt, Betsy hesitated outside her mother's door. Her hand on the latch, she listened. She pushed the door forward an inch, then a further few inches. "Mummy?" she asked, to no answer, and she advanced into the room. She edged toward the bed. Her mother was breathing; her breast rose and fell beneath light covers. Betsy spied the book she was after on the night table, a seven-day reserve title, stickered to that effect. She lifted the volume and looked for but could find no place marker, although she did not know what she would have done had there been one, sticking up from between chapters; the book was due back that day. She watched Ginger breathe for another moment, holding her own breath as she assured herself that her mother continued to breathe, before she stole away.

Betsy slowed as she drove past the farm stand and called out, "I won't be long," to Glover, who was fitting a case of bright red peppers into the trunk of the car of a runner from Hannah's factory.

The day was such a fine one, everybody who could find any excuse to be was outside. Downtown, the Women's Club was meeting on the lawn of the Congregational Church, and a tai chi class had marched over from their storefront studio to the green, where the students were being put through their paces. Betsy waved to Alden, who was standing at his gate with Tommy, so closely observing the pajamaed combatants as they kicked and lunged that he failed to see her. At the library, Brianna, the high school page, was sitting on the front steps, a book open on her lap; she scrubbed an eraser back and forth across a block of printing penciled into a margin, pausing now and then to blow and brush shreds of rubber from the pages and binding.

"Someone has been revealing the murderers' names in the crime fiction before the end," Brianna said, in explanation of her task. "Like this one, on page seventy-seven, they wrote in who did it, and why they did it. Just when you're far enough into the mystery to be interested in what happened, someone has to go and spoil it. Mrs. Rose says I have to go through every single book on the whodunit shelves."

"Huh," said Betsy. "That's very odd behavior."

"Yes. Mrs. Rose says it's a complete mystery in and of itself why anyone would do such a thing," Brianna agreed. She followed Betsy inside and took her place behind the circulation desk as Betsy unloaded her satchel.

"Was this any good?" Brianna asked of the seven-day reserve novel. "Everyone's reading it this summer," she said, setting the book aside for the next person on the waiting list.

"I don't know. My mother had it," Betsy said.

"I'll have to ask Mrs. Tuckerman, next time she comes in," Brianna said. "Though I haven't seen her in a while, not since last spring. Please tell her I miss her and that I read some Rosamond Lehmann like she told me to. It was *excellent*."

"Yes, I'll tell her," said Betsy, and she headed for the stacks by way of the New Arrivals shelf; not finding anything recent that she wanted to read, she remembered Lily mentioning that Angela Thirkell was very nice, though no one read her very much anymore. Betsy did her best selecting titles for Sally and her mother and herself, and left the library with a satchel full of books.

She ran into a detour on her way home. They were tarring the roads that day, and a man with a rag flag waved her off when she tried to take a right turn onto High Street. She drove on, thinking it was unreasonable to divert and tie up busy midday downtown traffic, and presently she found herself heading out of Towne altogether after she was prevented making the zigzag turn behind the fire station which would have routed her back onto the River Road. She saw the sign to North Andover and recalled a recent talk she'd had with a farm stand customer who said Mossy Stone Farm in North Andover already had their eggplants in, which was not possible, Lily said. Lily said they must have been trucked up from New Jersey, and Betsy took it in mind to do some fieldwork since she was already going in that direction. She would present herself to the Mossy Stone people, incognita, and engage them in a leading conversation. She drove along concocting a likely story about urgently needing fresh eggplants. She supposed she would have to buy something she didn't want, to be truly convincing.

This proposed piece of investigation put her in mind of the library mischief. Surely, it ought to be simple enough to compile the names of those library patrons who had taken out the individual affected titles and determine whose name was common to both lists. Then again, any devotee of the genre (or, conversely, such a dedicated detractor) most likely had received sufficient instruction through their reading on how not to be caught and so would know enough not to forge any incriminating link. Perhaps they slipped the books out of and into the library unchecked, beneath their coats. Or maybe they patronized two libraries, reading at one and misbehaving in the other. But at least they didn't write in the books in ink, Betsy thought. At least they didn't spoil the endings of better books than formulaic thrillers. At least no one had been going through the stacks with their tattletale pencil filling in what was going to happen: Reader, she'll marry him; Madame Bovary swallows poison, Sophie's choice was that she had to decide . . .

A four-way-stop intersection halted her. Betsy glanced in every direction for oncoming traffic and peered further for a landmark of some sort. She had absolutely no idea where she was. Evidently Mossy Stone Farms dwelt among untrodden ways. These local roads had a habit of transmuting from crumble-edged and meandering lanes to strip-malled speedways, buffered in between by residential neighborhoods where the same red Ford Explorer sat in the driveway of the same brick-front Georgian split-level, and she had not been paying enough attention anyway, having lapsed into one of those unaccountable states. Unrecoverable minutes had slipped by with the unintended miles, and she could not have said how she had come to be here, wherever she was. She drove on, searching for anything at all she might recognize, and with a sense of relief, she swerved toward the suddenly appearing marker and arrow pointing toward Route 495. She veered into the loop of the cloverleaf and merged onto the highway in the wake of a big truck. She was pretty sure she could find her way back to Towne from here. She was heading west (Worcester?) but she needed only to reverse direction and travel east again, toward the familiar, having come that way a few weeks earlier when she arrived. But for some reason, she sped past the first exit that presented itself, and then she flew by the next one, by which she could have righted herself, and when she failed to avail herself of a third and a fourth chance to go home, she realized that even if she was no longer lost, she could now be said to have no idea where she was going.

BACK AT ALDEN'S PLACE, Brooks and Rollins were just getting up. They stepped out through the screen door of their Winnebago and carried coffee mugs over to the picnic table, which they had dragged over to sit beside their recently purchased propane gas grill. Alden had been out and about early and he had left a Dunkin' Donuts box on the table, along with that week's edition of the *Towne Crier,* which bore the headline "A Generous Gift Indeed" above the fold.

"Is that us?" Rollins asked as Brooks spread open the paper.

"Well, it's me and somebody. *'Brooks and Roland Lowe have presented the Towne Historical Society with an unprecedentedly generous check for one hundred thousand dollars,'* " Brooks read.

Rollins shook his head and flicked several ants from a jelly stick, reflecting that for a man in his position, his position surely ought to be a better one. Mosquitoes, rife down here by the river, sirened in his ears, and he effectlessly winnowed away at the mist of them swarming round his head.

"Not like that," Harvey told him. Rollins started; he hadn't heard Harvey coming even though they'd been expecting him.

"You let the mosquito begin to bite you and then you hold it there by tensing up your arm muscle and then you stub it out under your thumb," Harvey said.

"The mosquitoes were about to bite my ear," Rollins said. "How do I tense my ear?" he asked.

"Tommy can tense his ears," Brooks said. "Look what he does with his ears when I say his name." Tommy had escorted Harvey down the driveway to the Winnebago and, his duty done, he curled up in the cool, scuffed dirt beneath the picnic table. "Tommy? Tommy?" Brooks called. "See, there goes his ear—the left one!"

"Can't you boys ever make an effort to look presentable?" Harvey asked. He had put on his blue blazer and red tie and a crisp white shirt and sharply creased khakis for this. His loafers gleamed from polish and buffing and seemed misnamed; they ought to have been called strutters. His great-nephews, however, wore swim trunks and T-shirts. *Terry LaBonte 1996 Winston Cup Champion* and *Beastie Boys—Intergalactic*, he read the faded writing on their chests. He had no idea what any of it meant and no wish to find out. "It's only polite to the other party not to come across as a couple of cabana boys," he said.

"Well, you know, we're not going to them. They're the ones coming to us and they'll just have to take us as we are," Brooks said. "Although I protest the characterization of cabana boy. I think that means something different now than in your heyday. The correct and au courant term of disapprobation for us is *slackers*."

"Or *geeks*," Rollins offered. "Which also means something very different now than in your heyday," he told Harvey.

Harvey had unfolded his handkerchief and was whisking off the tabletop, which was covered with a gritty patina of yellow pollen. He lifted up the *Crier* and remarked, "Well, at least you boys made Lily laugh. I don't know when I last heard Lily laugh like that. *'A Generous Gift Indeed,'* indeed." He flourished the newspaper at them. "Kudos," he said. "You skunked that harridan, good and proper."

For Brooks and Rollins had made the donation to the Towne Historical Society in response to Babe Palmer's efforts to evict them and their Winnebago from Alden's driveway. After the parade, she had lost no time undertaking her campaign of banishment, circulating a petition and firing off letters to the zoning board and public works department. (As Alden told Ginger, Babe had become really quite graphic when speculating after waste disposal methods.) She had even approached the police with a noise complaint, for she possessed wonderful ears and she insisted the air of Towne had begun to hum with a *waw-waw*ing emanation she had traced to the Lowe boys' aluminum screen door. She had also fired off a submission to the *Crier*'s guest column ("My Say"), warning that Towne would be taken over with trailer parks; to countenance even a single Winnebago was akin to allowing one mouse into a house, she wrote. Soon, the town would be overrun by a hundred double-wides (or mice), although as Rollins had pointed out, motor homes did not meet and mate and replicate inside dark cupboards and attic insulation. And, he asked, if it's just one mouse on its own, how could it turn itself into another hundred mice—unless it was an agamogenetic mouse, which wasn't likely, as Brooks observed; mice seemed to have mastered sexual reproduction remarkably well, so one should hardly think they'd change their ways.

Brooks and Rollins had, thus far in their short careers, faced down the SEC and stood nose to nose with the Justice Department and gone tooth and nail with the attorneys general of six large northeastern states who had united against them in a class-action suit, so the brothers felt rather Olympian about Mrs. Palmer, whose puny offensive was easy enough to ignore from where they continued to sit—on chaise lounges pulled beneath the shade of their Winnebago's awning, down there by the river, in their father's side yard. Brooks and Rollins were not going anywhere until they were good and ready.

But a recent confrontation between Babe and Brooks at the farm stand had inspired the brothers to settle her hash once and for all. Babe, shopping for shell beans and intent upon rolling every candidate for her stew pot between her fingers to assess the number and the plumpness of the beans huddled inside the pod, had been startled when a tattooed arm darted beneath her nose to snatch a head of curly lettuce. She had exclaimed and stepped back to get a good look at such a rude young person, who proved, not ungratifyingly, to be one of her much-dwelt-upon enemies, whom she had made it her business to study and to know as she drove slowly or bicycled slowly or walked slowly or floated slowly past Alden's house in her rubber dinghy.

Brooks had remained oblivious to the unattractive woman, well advanced into late middle age, who planted herself in his path, and he moved on to select some tomatoes. To get to them he would have to reach over Babe, and he did so, and this demonstration of his high-handedness had so maddened her that she had gone so far as to say something unforgivable about Brooks's mother. ("Babe was bat-mad, she was flaming; she imploded," reported Marilyn Rathbone, who had been there. "Cam saved the day. She told Babe not to use bad language, and she confiscated her basket of shell beans and sent her packing.")

Rollins prised out of Brooks what had happened when Brooks returned from his salad quest in an altered mood. He had flung his purchases into the kitchen sink and hunkered down on the black leather sofa to listen to *The Wall*. (They had invited Petal and the girl from the bank, the good-looking one about whom Brooks was harboring hopes, over for a cookout and Brooks had set out on his errand, whistling "Maybe I'm Amazed.") "What? What happened?" Rollins asked him, and upon being told, Rollins said they must deal with Babe as they had dealt with all those other nuisances: the SEC, the Justice Department, that six-pack of attorneys general. All of them, ultimately, had been paid to go away. Brooks and Rollins had signed the checks, well aware they were being let off cheap and easy relative to the benefits accrued from the original offense, which tended to be such highly original offenses that no one had theretofore thought to forbid them. Indeed, there was legislation pending in Congress, something called the GLoweWorm Statute, which had been misdirected to an agriculture subcommittee and so was not yet in effect.

"I'm not paying for Babe Palmer to go off on a cruise, if that's what you're suggesting," Brooks objected. "Unless we can arrange for some of those Malaysian pirates to swarm on board with daggers between their teeth." He had come up with the more workable idea of thoroughly ingratiating themselves to local authority, as well as conciliating the citizenry, thereby making an end run around Babe and besting her while bettering some civic entity by favoring it with an absurdly large donation. The Towne Historical Society had struck them as worthy and deserving, and Rollins recalled having heard they had a fine collection of arrowheads, which somehow seemed very hometown and admirable.

Their business people had long been telling Brooks and Rollins that they really ought to endow a foundation of some sort, citing any number of excellent financial reasons for doing so. And, they added, had the Lowe Brothers ever considered how much more pleasant it would be to read about themselves in the international business press if they were occasionally identified as "noted philanthropists" rather than "perennial codefendants"? When the air cleared following the precipitating dustup at the farm stand, upon reflection, the brothers had agreed that the experience of giving away so much money had been a positive one (a cabinet had been unlocked at the His. Soc. headquarters, and they'd been allowed to examine those arrowheads, irresistibly tapping the points against the backs of their hands to test how sharp they were, and should anyone ask, they could now say, Not very). As a result, Brooks and Rollins had notified their business people that they would at last consent to meet with the benevolent people. They were ready to go for the good, as Brooks put it.

They had asked Alden to advise them in this endeavor, but Alden had no wish to become a trustee, the proposed position. Reading papers, attending meetings, refusing cocktails at formal gatherings—he'd had a lifetime of that sort of thing, except for the part about refusing cocktails, which was only a recent development and no doubt one which would turn the paper reading and the drawn-out meetings into even more onerous occasions. Besides, there were the demands of his own small firm to consider; he ran interference for select investors in certain central European concerns, an employment designed to keep him not particularly busy while providing suitable cover for turning down other offers, and so he was able to tell his sons he would not be able to devote sufficient time to the responsibilities of overseeing a foundation. "But why don't you ask your great-uncle Harvey?" he had suggested, and when Lily heard that Harvey had, indeed, agreed to take on the job, she had laughed even harder than she would laugh over the headline about the boys' charitable machinations. Had anyone told her that she'd find anything at all to laugh about this summer, she would not have believed them, so in that sense, as well, her young great-nephews were already making the world a better place.

THE TOWNE TAXI PULLED UP BEHIND the Winnebago. Doris heaved her arm onto the sill of the open window to wave Harvey over to tell her what all the fuss was about here this morning. She had had to stand in the shuttle terminal at Logan holding a posterboard sign that read The Merit Group, hoisting the sign toward any deplaning contingent that looked anything like being meritorious, in her opinion, as she waited for her party to arrive, but the hodgepodge of harried travelers that passed in review all fell short when held to that standard. A gray-bearded man in a business suit and a young woman in a business suit slowed as they walked past her and seemed inclined to walk on by, until, her suspicions raised, Doris pounced. "Are you the Merit Group?" she asked.

"Yes?" the young woman answered on a querying note, for she could not imagine who Doris might be.

"You're coming with me," Doris said, stuffing her sign in a trash receptacle and then retrieving it when she remembered she could write on the other side of the posterboard to notify her next airport pickup.

She drove along, wondering whether Merit hadn't something to do with the cigarettes of the same name which her disabled brother-in-law smoked on his fixed income, but she did not sense any wave of invitation emanating from the backseat which would enable her to strike up a conversation and slowly work her way around to asking whether they carried free samples in their briefcases.

Harvey, however, was willing to jaw with Doris, there in Alden's driveway. "The Merit Group? They're some fancy-pants outfit Alden's boys' money people have scared up to help throw the boys' money at so-called worthy causes and the like. I'm here to watch out they don't sign away the store or get themselves mixed up in anything fishy," he explained. The gray-bearded man and the young woman listened to Harvey's account of themselves as they remained in the taxi fumbling at the door handles, which needed to be remotely released by Doris before they would open. This she consented to do after the fare was paid.

Introductions were made, and Harvey, who had known almost everyone in his time, was able to place the graybeard, whose name was Dean Churchard and whose father's cousin George Churchard Harvey had known and known better than Dean himself ever had, evidently, for Dean had never heard the story about George and the artificial eye. The young lady, Cecilia Ruiz, was not related to an Argentinean polo player of Harvey's acquaintance, but he found Cecilia's neat brown pageboy, tucked behind a pale blue Alice band, which matched her pale blue silk blouse, entirely reassuring. His glance dropped to her legs; commendably, she was wearing hose in the heat, he determined, although there he was incorrect. Her skin itself was smooth and brown and as glossy as silk. Brooks and Rollins liked the looks of her too, and they sat down at the picnic table very willingly, taking their places at the rough board bench on either side of Cecilia, who sat up very straight, being mindful not to list into one brother or the other (the tilting angle of the bench lending itself to tilting one way and then correctively leaning the other).

They got down to business. Dean covered the table's gritty boards with several dozen representative brochures, beautifully produced on heavy bond paper, which described and extolled the deeds and aspirations of existing charities and public-spirited institutions. Brooks and Rollins were invited to examine them. The brothers reached and read.

"These're all about *mal*-this and and *dis*-that, and various *-emias* and *-itises,*" Brooks said after a moment or two. "Bummer."

"You've got the diseases," Rollins said. "Here's all the endangered stuff, animals and environments and cultures." He shoveled brochures at his brother, who began to read aloud about the vanishing world of the Bactrian camel, although when the text invited him to try to imagine a world without Bactrian camels, he said he had to admit he had more trouble imagining his world with Bactrian camels in it.

"This one's Eritrean Famine Relief," Harvey said, reaching for a prospectus. His finger traced an embossed crest, and he rustled the sheets of onionskin paper inserted between thick and creamy pages. "Though I'd wager the famished Eritreans would rather have all this onionskin to eat if given their druthers, instead of having such a fancy pamphlet produced about themselves and their troubles," he said. He tore off a corner of onionskin paper and popped it into his mouth where it stuck to his dental work like a shred of communion wafer.

"Yeah, these things aren't our style," Brooks said. "We send out directives against using extraneous packaging material. It's wasteful, not to mention a pain in the ass when you end up with more styrofoam than product, all over your floor."

"Besides, we would rather do good by stealth," Rollins said. "We don't need to advertise how admirable we're being."

"Well, no, we could use some positive press," Brooks said. "IBM's been pretty spooked about dealing with us since that last inquiry by the FCC. I vote we ballyhoo ourselves at least a little bit."

"Have you any idea of the area in which you'd like to make a contribution?" Cecilia asked. She had fired up her laptop, and her hands arched over the keyboard, poised to record any thoughts at all on the subject.

"Brooks and I have been discussing that and we've come up with a list of about fifty possibilities," Rollins said. "It's quite daunting. I mean, if we weren't in a position to do anything useful, we wouldn't have to worry, but since we are, it feels like we'll be failing all the worthy causes we don't choose to do anything about. It feels like we'll be leaving all the other puppies at the pound, even after we've gone home with a really nice dog. You still wonder about the ones you left behind. Especially the ones who aren't particularly cute or outgoing. Because you'd know those were the ones who have good reasons not to trust people, and there you are, proving them right. So it's just very hard to decide."

"Don't go all Hamlet on me, Roland," Brooks said.

"I can take a look at your list," Cecilia offered.

Harvey spoke up. "Before you start, you ought to have some goals in mind, whatever sphere you decide to operate in." He prodded the glossy heap of brochures and continued, "Because it often strikes me that outfits like these here have more incentive to perpetuate a situation instead of fixing it for good. I think they're too mired in the process of thinking up ways to endlessly raise more and more funds. I mean, do you boys sincerely want to cure cancer? Give a lab five years and all the money you've got and let them know you're closing up shop after that, take it or leave it. Don't keep endlessly doling out funds; your true aim ought to be to put your own charity out of business, not to make it a whole way of life with fancy brochures and fancy offices and fancy balls with fancy people milling around congratulating themselves."

"Point taken, in some instances," Dean said. "But then again, there are also eternally recurring wars and always-arising refugee situations and economic inequalities and harsh political realities and endemic dysentery and the like, which will always be with us."

"There's revolution, rule of law, improved infrastructure, literacy, and clean water," Harvey spoke over him, counting off on the fingers of one hand what he'd do about all of that.

"And what about natural disasters?" Dean asked.

"Don't build your vacation condo with a volcano view," Harvey recommended. He leaned forward, like a batter in the box, inviting Dean to toss him another soft one.

"But there are always the human failings that lead to human misery," Dean said, gamely.

"We have prisons for people like that," Harvey said.

They all sat there mulling over Harvey's worldview until Brooks asked, "What was that about sponsoring a revolution somewhere?"

"That's not really an option," Dean said. "There are laws to discourage the undertaking of such activities by private individuals in foreign lands. At any rate, the Merit Group could not represent you in such a venture."

"Too bad," said Brooks. "I mean, that would be something I'd really like to do, you know, go out and liberate some benighted little country and make it good for its people. I'd bring it out of the dark ages and into the twenty-first century. Like, the first thing I'd do would be to make it entirely WiFi ready and abolish all landlines."

Cecilia perked up until she realized he hadn't said land mines. "Why don't you let me take a look at that list of yours?" she asked. "I'm sure there's something there we can all work with."

"WHERE ARE YOU GOING ON THE HONEYMOON?" Loretta asked Julie. "You're going to need a different brassiere." Loretta meant Julie would need a different undergarment to wear beneath the dress she was belling over Julie's head. Loretta had pursued her into the dressing room even as Julie insisted she didn't need help getting into the gown. Lily had made it to the dressing room a few steps behind, less able to run interference these days. She picked up Julie's faded beige shift from the floor, wondering now how Julie had ever managed to cause beige to fade. At least she had worn a slip, if a flimsy and slipping off one she'd borrowed from Betsy. Lily recognized the garment from the clothesline, where it had drooped among Sally's tidy little T-shirts and pajamas and shorts drying in the sun.

"For the record," Julie told Loretta as Loretta fitted her into a gown, "because of my line of work, I'm an experienced mannequin dresser. I am also conversant with farthingales and pantaloons and sixteenth-century Japanese court dress. I know my way around hooks and eyes and underskirts and sashes, so a boned bodice and a tulle train are not a challenge to me," she said. "Nor are they flattering," she allowed as Loretta cinched the last button and spun her toward the mirror.

"Aunt Lily?" Julie stood, her arms held out stiff and away from her body as she inhaled sharply and held her breath, assuming the universally recognized posture for disowning a disliked dress.

"Oh dear," said Lily. "No." She sat down upon a sofa, having decided that this was probably going to take awhile. She gazed round the walls, which were hung with pictures of history's most famous brides, more than a few of whom had gone on to endure infamous marriages, but Lily supposed one was expected to pretend not to know what was to come after the cake was cut and the confetti was flung.

Loretta fluttered tulle and netting over Julie's face as Julie remarked, "Of course, with a mannequin you can just snap off the head, which makes things a lot easier. Don't you wish sometimes you could snap off the brides' heads?" she asked Loretta.

"What does your young man do?" Loretta asked, with more than usual interest in the answer. She had pegged Julie as being not quite her usual sort of client, even though they'd started off on a good foot; this bride had relayed the greetings of that other bride, Laura Nicholls Borodin, and, as Julie was to say later, they had all simpered a bit over Laura and her taste in Malines lace. Loretta's eyes had also gone right to the great-aunt's entirely correct pearl necklace and received that message as well, although the old woman's terrible hands had thrown her. The fingernails had been cut to the quick in an effort to banish the fast-ingrained grime, yet indelible black crescents remained at every fingertip.

"What if he's an *old* man?" Julie asked. "What if my young man is an old man?"

"Is he?" Lily asked. "Are you marrying an older man?" She realized she had failed to ask and Julie had failed to mention Nicholas Davenant's age. Lily had assumed he was suitable, but perhaps there was something Julie had wished not to mention. Really, Julie had not mentioned very much about Nicholas.

"No, I'd say he's fairly young," Julie decided. "Although age is a relative concept, depending on one's own age. I'd say, he's like, about five years older than me? Is that good?"

"An excellent range," said Loretta, who believed the man ought to be older and taller and wealthier than the girl, although you had to be careful who you said that to, and were this not the case, her general remark would then be, What *fun*.

"My niece's fiancé is a geologist for an oil company, who is at present prospecting in Siberia," Lily said. "And he is English," she added, for this rather pleased her. She had always thought well of assorted representative Englishmen: authors, actors, and Parliamentarians, all of whom expressed themselves so beautifully in the mother tongue. Although lately she had become aware of certain loud and loutish Englishmen of the type who, in the past, must have been kept under wraps at home, and it seemed a pity they were being set loose in the world these days to run riot after football matches. Still, she very much doubted Nicholas Davenant would paint himself red and cheer for Manchester United. However, Loretta exclaimed, "He's English!" as if she had been given a gift, and she sent an assistant running off to the stockroom to fetch the *Lady Rowena* model—for all of the dresses were given names at Avanda's Off the Avenue, and, indeed, Julie had just rejected *Juliet*, which Loretta had thought would have been amusing, a Julie wearing the *Juliet*. But as Julie said later, she wouldn't have worn that flipping frock even as a joke, which it would have been.

The assistant returned with a tufted and flounced and panniered creation, which Julie said she would have called Bo Peep while Lily murmured, "Lampshade." Loretta waved that dress away and asked to have *Lily Dale* made available, with a smile for Lily, but Lily dismissed the garment even before the assistant could lift off a protective shroud of muslin.

"What will the groom be wearing?" Loretta asked. "Perhaps that will point us in a direction. Does he have a kilt?"

"God, I should hope not," Julie said. She thought a moment and said, "Picture him in a very nice suit, why don't you."

Loretta thought *Canace* made Julie look like a fairy princess, and Julie asked, "But do I want to look like a fairy princess? Who was Canace, anyway? She sounds all fierce and muddy and Saxon to me."

"Well, how did you imagine yourself, when you imagined your

wedding day?" Loretta asked. She had found there was always some latent image to be coaxed from long-ago rhapsodizing on the subject, and sometimes even a picture to consult, discovered folded in a drawer and colored in crayon with the words misspelled (*mary, huzbint, coopid*). Interestingly, there was seldom a groom figure or, at most, just a sketchy impression of someone in a dark (and very nice) suit wearing a stovepipe hat, the hat often added as a last-minute touch to make the groom stand taller than the bride, Loretta always thought.

"I don't think I did ever dream all that much about getting married. Really, no one's more surprised than me at the recent turn of events. I recall I wanted to run off with one of the New Kids on the Block when I was around fourteen, and marry him without a whole lot of fuss and bother—you know, do something barefoot and spontaneous on a beach in Bali," Julie said. "I was my cousin's bridesmaid once, which was fun. I think it was more fun being the bridesmaid, actually, at *that* wedding."

"How many bridesmaids are you having?" Loretta asked. Avanda's stocked a full line of dresses and gowns for those supporting players.

"None. It'll just be me standing at the altar," Julie said.

"And Nicholas Davenant," Lily reminded her.

Julie turned her attention to a line of dresses, sending one hanger after another spinning along the rack wheeled out from an interior storeroom. She muttered, "No, no, no," as she slid the dresses away with a banishing chop of her hand.

"They are meant to be seen on," Loretta reminded her patiently.

"Oh, but I can see in my mind exactly how things ought to be," Julie said, and she slumped onto the sofa beside Lily. "I really wish there was a mannequin of me to try things on. I'd just send her out to shop in my place. This is so hopeless. Isn't there some closet back at home stuffed full of everyone's old wedding dresses, Aunt Lily? Is Aunt Ginger's dress still there? What did she wear? I'll bet it was something."

"Ginger's dress was ecru charmeuse and it draped like a nightgown," Lily recalled. A very clear image remained in her mind, which she consulted. "There was no veil. She wore flowers in her hair and instead of a bouquet she carried a beribboned staff. I don't know what effect she was going for, although the theory was she meant to mortify

Olive, in which case, she certainly succeeded. Olive was my sister and Ginger's mother," Lily explained to Loretta.

"It all sounds very pagan goddessy," Julie said. "I don't think I could pull off a look like that. I'm not tall enough. Or great enough." She smiled for the first time since entering Avanda's premises.

"I don't even know whatever became of that dress of Ginger's. I shouldn't be surprised if Olive didn't cut it up for polishing rags," Lily recalled. "She was in tears over Ginger's appearance."

"Well, that's something, at least," Julie said. "I was thumbing through a *Brides* magazine, just to pick up a few ideas, and it said that you can know which wedding dress is the perfect one for you if the sight of you in it makes your mother cry. Although that particular yardstick isn't of much use to me, at the moment."

"Olive's tears weren't happy tears, Julie," Lily said.

"Oh, but I should think the tears test still works either way. It all depends upon the mother. It all depends upon the tears," Julie said.

SALLY AND CAM HAD BEEN DIVERTED on their way to the barn by the chance to spy on Mr. DeSouza. They saw him before he saw them and they flattened themselves against the side of his tractor, left idling at the edge of the pumpkin patch, using this opportunity to study him as he paced the field. Mr. DeSouza didn't like kids; this was known, and the fact intrigued them. They had discussed whether Mr. DeSouza was so far gone in his dislike as to glower and grizzle at even the best kid in the world. Were they to locate the best kid in the world and bring the kid to Mr. DeSouza, would Mr. DeSouza tell that kid to keep out of the cornfield and not to use the tomato garden as a shortcut to the herb-drying shed and not ever to touch the milky spore sprayer and mix up the dosage settings? Because Mr. DeSouza never said hello to kids; he would start in right away saying what not to do, whether or not they were about to do it. Had he but known, he put notions in their heads; they would never have thought to fiddle with the milky spore sprayer had Mr. De Souza not told them not to.

"He walks funny," Cam observed.

"I know," Sally said.

As Mr. DeSouza came to the end of one furrow, he turned away from sight of them to proceed down the next row. Cam emerged from behind the tractor and she began to trudge back and forth with locked knees while swinging her arms. She kept her chin stuck to her chest. "He walks like this," she said.

"Like this," said Sally, emerging to stump this way, then that, on stiff legs. She pumped her arms laterally, from the elbows.

They flew behind the tractor when Mr. DeSouza turned again in their direction. They pressed against the thrumming engine, whose insistent ongoingness communicated a single idea to them, and when Mr. DeSouza reversed direction yet again, they scrambled up and onto the tractor seat, or, at any rate, Cam sat in the bucket seat, both hands gripping the unyielding gearshift as she stretched her feet toward the clutch. Sally stood crammed in front of Cam, holding on to the steering wheel as if in command at the helm of a ship, prepared to steer once Cam got them under way.

A shout from the pumpkin field recalled them, and they leaped to the ground and ran for the house. They pelted through the back door and came upon Petal, who was seated at the kitchen table cutting up an apple. Petal sat when she cooked; everyone else stood as they sliced and stirred and assembled dishes. ("*We* hustle round the kitchen, but Petal acts all Zen about it," as Julie had observed. "Don't ask Petal to separate an egg for you," Julie said. "I mean, I think she'll send it out for mediation, first.")

"There you are," Petal greeted the little girls. "I'm making lunch today."

"Where's Mummy?" Sally asked. This was a break from the routine. Betsy always made lunch. She always made sandwiches for everyone. She did so in assembly-line fashion, thumping down bread slices like paving stones and then slathering every other surface with a mortar of filling and mustard. She piled the slices, one atop the other, and sawed through the lofty stack with a serrated knife. To date, the most sandwiches she had cut with this all-inclusive maneuver amounted to ten. Sally and Cam had been urging her to attempt more, an even dozen they suggested, which would probably establish a new world's record for sandwich towers.

"I don't know where your mother is at the moment. Her car is gone," Petal said. "And Miss Lily and Julie are still out dress shopping, so I thought I'd get started on lunch. We're having apple-and-orange-and-pear-and-grape-and-plum salad. And rice cakes. If you want to help, you can cut all the grapes in half. You know where the knives are."

"I am not allowed to use knives," Sally said, but no one was paying attention to her. Cam pulled open the cutlery drawer to fetch two bone-handled steak knives, while Petal just sat there, holding an orange in the palm of her hand, musing over whether the peel would come off easily or, instead, resist her efforts to expose the fruit within.

Sally shrugged, and she and Cam set themselves down across from Petal. Between them was a big yellow bowl that held a layer of browning apple crescents. Petal gave them each a bunch of red grapes. Sally reached for the pair of scissors someone had misplaced in the spoon jar on the lazy Susan and she tried to snip a grape in two, but it only spurted and squashed between her fingers. Sighing, she picked up her knife.

As they worked, Petal told them stories from her modeling career, recounting episodes whose significance mostly flew right over their heads, but they appreciated that they were being let in on something very grown-up and yet also quite distinct from the usual adult experience, and besides, the mention of names like Miu Miu and Badgley Mischka made them squeal and poke each other. *Badgley Mischka.*

"Exactly. Badgley Mischka. Ai-eee!" said Petal. "And the Badgley Mischka dress I wore on that occasion was almost the color of this pear I am now holding. That was their spring collection, which was cast in the colors of nature, which was very good for me, let me tell you, with my complexion. You too, Sally, you could have worn that line. But Cam, I'd rather see you in red or even—I know this is really out there, but I'd like to see you in purple, Cam, with your dark hair and eyes. You'd be stunning."

At noontime, Om and Tru and Thanh trailed into the kitchen. They'd been out picking beans all morning and they flung themselves onto chairs round the table. They seemed surprised not to find a plateful of sandwiches and tall glasses filled with their usual drinks (two Mountain Dews and one Fresca) waiting for them.

"Where's Betsy?" asked Tru. She enjoyed talking to Betsy about California, where she planned to go to college, if she got her way.

"We don't know where Betsy is," Petal said. "And Miss Hill and Julie are out looking for Julie's dress."

"I thought Auntie Ginger was going shopping with Julie," Om said. "Julie's been saying they were going to have a lot of fun."

"No," said Petal. "Ginger couldn't make it."

"Oh," said Om. "That's too bad."

"Is that what we're having for lunch?" asked Thanh, craning to see what Petal was up to as she gave the salad its finishing touch, bestrewing chopped mint all over the contents of the big yellow bowl.

"And rice cakes too," Petal said.

Thanh pushed back his chair and went over to the refrigerator to see what else there might be. He slid open the cold-cuts drawer, and, joining him, Tru rummaged in the bread box. Paper wrappers rustled, and they got down to business at the counter, making the usual sandwiches.

"Well, I still have to make a tray for Ginger," Petal said. "She told me the other day that fruit is really the only thing that appeals to her at the moment. I told her I know; I'm like that a lot too." She retrieved the tray which was kept propped behind the coffee maker and she went about setting a place. Sally slipped her Lion King bowl onto the tray and added an ordinary bowl (Lily's blue Fiestaware) for Cam.

"We will eat with Granna today," Sally said.

Since there was no one to say no to that, Petal decided on her own it would be all right, just this once. She nodded, and Sally and Cam took off up the back stairs headed for Ginger's bedroom so they would be found sitting there, side by side with Ginger, when Petal arrived with their lunch. Then she would have to serve them like a waitress in a restaurant.

Presently, Petal knocked lightly at the bedroom door. She released the legs of the tray and set it down carefully over Ginger's blanket-covered knees, as Sally and Cam, reclining atop the covers and leaning into the cushions they had snatched from the armchair, grabbed for their bowls and spoons.

"What a dainty little birdlike portion you gave me, Petal," Ginger said, looking over what she'd been served. "Thank you. Everyone else tries to stuff me."

Sally and Cam set about plucking the mint from their salads, flicking shreds of green onto the tray. Ginger shook open the napkins Petal had provided and waved them remindingly until the little girls tucked them into the collars of their T-shirts. "What have you two been up to?" she asked. "Tell me all about your busy morning."

"Cam tried to steal Mr. DeSouza's tractor," Sally reported, severely.

"Can you drive, Cam?" Ginger asked. "You're very advanced, if you can do that at your age." Cam, who had started at Sally's treachery, relaxed against Ginger's arm.

"I can sort of drive, Auntie Ginger," she said.

"But I helped. A lot," Sally spoke up, and Ginger told her, "Yes, I guessed as much that you were in on the caper."

"We made the grapes, Auntie Ginger," Cam said, as Ginger lifted her spoon and set it down again.

"Well, I shall have to try one," Ginger said.

"They're in halves," Sally said.

"I shall eat two halves, then," Ginger said, and Sally and Cam watched as she accomplished this.

"Such wonderful grapes," Ginger said, and she closed her eyes as if savoring them.

"We are delicious cooks," Cam said.

The little girls bit into their rice cakes and shared a look of disgust. These things were no more cakes than cardboard was. Petal must have been mistaken about what they were called, they decided, and they chattered back and forth, discussing what the real name must be: rice fakes, rice yucks, rice pukes, until Ginger told them that was enough rice cake talk.

"At least drink all your milk, please," she said, for she could no longer abide the sour grass smell rising from their untouched glasses.

"Aw," said Sally. She had told Petal not to give them milk. She had told Petal they usually had root beer floats at lunchtime, with crumbled Oreos floating in the lather on top.

"Who is the faster milk drinker, Sally or Cam?" Ginger asked, sounding like an announcer at a contest. "Who will be the dairy queen?"

Sally and Cam eyed each other. They always fell for this ploy even though they knew they were being humbugged. But as Ginger seemed to enjoy believing she was tricking them into doing what they didn't want to do, they indulged her, just to be nice. They slid off the bed and carried their milk glasses over to the fireplace, where they stood upon the hearth, which was raised just high enough to suggest a rudimentary stage, sufficient for this performance at least.

"One, two . . ." Ginger's announcer's voice faded.

"Three," Sally and Cam pronounced in her stead, and they tilted their glasses and chugged down milk. Sally had to hold her nose, which placed her at a disadvantage, and Cam finished first, although when she gagged a bit of chalky foam back into her glass, Sally said she was cheating.

"It looked like a tie to me. You're both a couple of champion cowgirls. Now go wash your faces," Ginger said. "And try not to steal any more tractors today," she added.

"What about tomorrow?" Sally asked, to be pert.

"Let's just get through the rest of today," Ginger said. She pushed effectlessly at the tray. "And send your mother up to me, please."

"Mummy isn't home."

"Not here? But where is she?"

"*I* don't know," Sally said.

BETSY WAS ON THE TURNPIKE NOW. If Route 495 was determined to hold her in its grip, she had hoped to stop and to speak to the toll booth operator who oversaw the entrance ramp to the pike. She had hoped to confide in someone, *I am completely turned around and I very much need to go the other way.* She had hoped to be allowed to make the necessary U-turn against the oncoming toll plaza traffic, which would be briefly halted by a helpful hand raised to assist the lone young woman with the out-of-state license plates who freely admitted, I am such an idiot, as the toll taker, becoming a bit fed up, beckoned to her, Go on then.

But a toll slip had been automatically dispensed to her from an unmanned station. The lowered bar, which she had regarded as a protective, restraining arm, lifted itself as she drew the ticket (which reminded her of a stuck-out tongue) from its slot. The horn of the vehicle behind her had blurted as she hesitated and so she could only drive on as if pushed and pulled along by all the other fleeing cars which sought to stream past one another, again and again. Overtaken, Betsy felt compelled to overtake whoever had hurtled past her; she jousted with a white van for miles and miles. The landscape blurred at the edges of her vision, which had narrowed to a keen awareness of the pavement whose pocked and pale gray surface would turn suddenly slick atop fresh black-top repairs, and even though she did not reel into a skid, she feared she might.

But I am always going too fast, Betsy thought. I was too fast to grow up and I was too fast to get married and I was too fast to have Sally— and all the while, she had had no clue what any of that was leading to either. Oh, but she knew where this summer was headed, and these summer days were flying away from her most rapidly of all. She could not face the rest of the summer. She could not turn around to face what she knew was coming.

She became aware of a plaintive note sounding below the drum of traffic and engine roar and rushing wind. It was her own voice; she had begun to utter, over and over, a refrain of wordless syllables. She recognized then that she was repeating the same sequence of sighs and whimpers that escaped from Sally at the child's worst moments. "Uh huh huh huh," Betsy was raggedly breathing, as Sally would raggedly breathe. She was blinking back tears, as Sally would blink back tears. Provoked, or bored or inconvenienced by some passionate refusal or insistent stand on Sally's part, Betsy had often enough mocked her daughter. "Oh, boo hoo hoo," Betsy had drily cried, not convinced of Sally's griefs and only sure of her excessive display. But I shan't do that again, Betsy thought. I shan't do that if I ever see Sally again. If I ever see Sally again, I shall never be impatient with her, she pledged.

She wondered whether she was about to follow after her aunt, after Becky, who had also driven off one day and never come back. What harsh desert will receive me? Betsy wondered. How will Sally and Andy fare without me? she asked herself. Andy would remarry; most likely he would turn to the colleague who so often figured as his ally and supporter when he spoke of university politics at home. He would fall into her arms as readily as he had fallen in with her ideas to reform the graduate school honors thesis requirements. As for Sally, Sally seemed set already (bright, pretty, well tended; her first six years had been golden), and if an early loss, or early losses, tempered a certain certainty the child possessed by nature, the world would be too dangerous a place for her to venture into, in the years to come, without a strong measure of doubt and an abiding memory of pain to accompany those further steps. Perhaps there's a case to be made, Betsy thought, that her Aunt Becky's defection had shaken the boys and Julie out of their prior complacency. Her cousins had been awful kids, and yet they somehow had turned out very well, which no one had foreseen. They were all so successful, and decent too, and their mother had left them early. Was that what it took to make someone finally grow up? Was that final sacrifice required of all mothers? Betsy wondered. Must they all go away and leave their families to learn how to fend for themselves?

She again spied the white van, which she thought she had shaken. It sought to steal past her in the right-hand lane. She accelerated instantly; every instinct she possessed was setting her off on another fruitless chase. She leaned into her pursuit and fumbled blindly in her satchel, feeling for the roll of Life Savers she knew was in there, somewhere among the library books and the other clutter. She was hungry. What time was it? She glanced at the dashboard clock, which the glare of the sun rendered unreadable. Her cell phone rang then. She felt the resonance tremble against her fumbling hand before she heard the chiming and she seized the phone at once and held it to her ear asking, "Yes?"

It was Andy. There had been another ruckus at the courthouse and another delay in the trial. "The Third Day Brethren are revolting," he said, and Betsy almost smiled at his usual joke.

"So, I'm just standing by, gazing up at the mountains, which look particularly clear and close today, and deciding whether to have lunch at the Mexican place or the Mexican place," Andy's voice said.

"I'd try the Mexican place," Betsy said, because that was what she always said.

"So, what's going on where you are?" Andy asked. When she did not answer, he asked, "Are you busy at the farm stand? Have I interrupted you with a customer?"

"No," said Betsy. "No." She knew she could not begin to explain to him what was occurring and where she was, wherever she was.

"I hope you're wearing a hat, if you're out in the fields," Andy said. "The DA had a Band-Aid on his nose today. It was a skin cancer."

"Oh dear," said Betsy. "I hope he'll be all right." She watched the white van disappear up ahead around a bend and she let it go.

"He'll be fine," Andy assured her. "And he's bought himself a natty new Stetson to keep the sun off his face from now on."

"I'm wearing a hat too," Betsy said. "I'm out in the highbush blueberries. They're only just getting ready to pick, so you have to hunt a bit. A lot of them are still quite green."

"Are you going to make a pie?" Andy asked, just as Betsy thought to say, "I'm going to make a pie."

"How's your mother doing?" Andy asked.

"Oh, she's having a very good day. She's out on the terrace. I can't quite see what she's up to, but she has some project that's absorbing her," Betsy said.

"Good. Good for Ginger," Andy said. "And Sally?" he asked. "What's Miss Sally up to?"

"Sally? She's right there on the swing. The guys put up a rope swing for her, from a branch of the really big maple, the one on the lawn. Now what? She's hopped off. Oh, she's gone and fetched Mummy. She wants Mummy to push her. I should tell her not to bother Mummy when she's busy, but Sally can't hear me from here. And I guess Mummy doesn't mind; she's going over to the swing," Betsy reported. "But now she's not pushing Sally high enough."

"No one can ever push Sally high enough," said Andy. "According to Sally."

"Ah, there she goes. Mummy just gave her quite the shove. Sally almost shot off the seat," Betsy said.

"But she'll have had the ropes wound twice around her wrists so she could hang on. I taught her that," Andy said.

"Yes, that must be what kept her on," Betsy agreed.

"Well, I won't keep you from your pie-making activities," Andy said. "I'm at the restaurant now anyway."

"The Mexican one or the Mexican one?" asked Betsy.

"Yes," said Andy. "That's the one."

"Okay, and I've got to get going too," Betsy said. She had just spotted a sign that read Next Exit in 5 Miles and resolved to take it so she would not have lied to Andy. She was going to hurry home and make everything she had just told him become true.

AS THEY DROVE AWAY FROM AVANDA'S, Julia abused each dress she had tried on, embellishing her previous criticisms of their excesses in the frills and frippery department and happily ripping them to even smaller shreds. She had tried to spare Loretta's feelings during the appointment and held back on delivering her best remarks, she said. Lily had laughed at some of her comments (she could not help herself) and despite the nonsuccess of their outing, she and Julie were not having a bad time. In that spirit, Lily had drawn another deep breath and broached another difficult topic that she knew she had to raise and that had been nagging at her conscience for some time. Lily felt obliged to mention to Julie that she was in possession of her mother's jewelry; everything Alden had ever given to Becky had been hurtfully returned—or honorably relinquished, depending upon one's point of view. It had all had been packed into two shoe boxes and mailed from Prague (the city from which Becky had vanished) for Lily to take possession of and keep safe until some future time when Alden's children would have need of rings and things.

Lily had only briefly looked at the contents, checking on the top layer of several layers of Tiffany and Shreve, Crump and Lowe boxes in order to know just what she had received. She had then resecured the paper wrappings of the two packages (in no mood to steam off the pretty Czechoslovakian stamps for her album) and conveyed them to the attic where she buried them in an ancient barrel of sand, an old fire fighting precaution that was once as commonly found in people's houses as cannister-style fire extinguishers are today. She was quite sure no thief would think to look there, nor anyone else she had realized, and so she had made a note of what she had done, scribbled on the last page of her will should anything happen to her before she had a chance to tell the interested parties what she'd done with the jewels (aside from Alden, but he could not be relied upon to remember things like that).

Lily eased into the subject. "You'll need to wear something old and something new," she reminded Julie. "And borrowed and blue."

Julie had snorted a bit at the traditional formula, nevertheless, she agreed that she would have to come up with suitable items to wear. Her shoes would be new, she supposed, and as for blue—something would turn up, she supposed. Betsy wore a lot of blue, and she had some very nice scarves.

"Your mother owned such lovely aquamarines," Lily mentioned.

Julie slumped down in the front seat (she was Lily's passenger, although she had offered to drive since she needed practice handling a car on the wrong side of the road). She stared at the road ahead.

"I have them at the house. I know your mother would like you to have them. She always wore such lovely things. Why don't you just look at them?" Lily suggested.

But Julie had flung a hand over her eyes as if the very idea of seeing her mother's lost brooches and bracelets was too blinding and she spoke forcefully, "No."

So Lily let the matter drop. She turned on the radio to listen for a weather report as she wondered whether she would have better luck interesting the boys in the contents of the buried boxes. There was a particular engagement ring, up there in the attic, that had passed from hand to hand within the family and which their mother had quite properly handed back. It would look well on Ginevra's finger, and it would be entirely suitable for Petal, Lily decided, and consulting her own feelings about the eventual disposition of the heirloom ring, she realized that she would be very happy to hand it over to either one or the other of the two young women.

THEY RAN INTO THE CORNFIELD, ducking in and out between the bristling stalks, which rose up taller than people and clenched the earth with wiry roots that held onto the hard ground like the talons of birds. As Cam and Sally rushed past, the stalks swayed and rattled and struck at them with projections that were scissor-sticky and glue-sticky, all at once—repelling them as if following Mr. DeSouza's orders to keep kids out of the cornfield, the little girls half believed. They ran on, dead set for the far reach of the last row, where they broke free of the almost unbearable press of sharp and dusty verdure. They ran on through a fringe of tough and entangling weeds and pitched themselves onto a stone wall. Without losing momentum, they scrambled up and over the stones, which felt hot and cool and rough and smooth and solid and unsteady all at once beneath their scrambling hands and knees.

For seconds then, they were confounded; they were now in the woods, which were thick and dark and impenetrable here except at a single point where a child-wide path of their own stamp began and to which they were always mysteriously blind, at first, and were only permitted to behold after their eyes adjusted to the permanent twilight that had settled beneath the trees.

"Here," said Cam and she vanished, a wag of fir bough indicating which way she had gone to Sally, who called, "Wait, wait, wait," as she followed. They ran faster; the ground lay so porous and buoyant underfoot that their feet sprang up with extra liftoff, making them run so fast their legs could not keep up. Waving their arms as if to catch themselves, they were drawn forward and deeper into the woods, racing on and on through a miniature forest within the forest of feathery and immaculate ferns, past the stinky swamp and on beyond the raccoon's hollow stump until the broad trunk of a giant hemlock reared up and stopped them. "Oof," they said, colliding with the hemlock, although Cam had pulled herself up short and only pretended she had crashed into the broad trunk, while Sally ran on full tilt into the tree. They dropped onto a spreading apron of moss, a lush expanse of the smooth, cool, velvet kind. Cam rubbed her hand back and forth across its softness to pick up the green earth scent as Sally laid her flushed cheek against its surface to absorb some of its coolness. Cam plucked a sprig of Solomon's seal and tucked it behind her ear.

"I am stunning," she said.

"You are stunning," Sally agreed.

They picked themselves up and trudged on. The path rose and led them out of the darkest part of the woods into a less densely canopied and brighter section. The trail turned rockier too, with tumbled boulders evident among the trees. One in particular, bigger than all the others, crouched there like Aslan; they could make out his massive and leonine head, and then the formation tapered down to lithe, tensed haunches. (Although one day, when they accompanied Alden and Tommy on one of their walks through Lily's woods, Alden had said everyone had always called that rock The Sphinx, but neither Cam nor Sally could even begin to say that word, each having lately lost a loose front tooth while sharing a box of saltwater taffy at Harvey and Penny's house.)

Now, Sally and Cam picked up the thread of an ongoing argument.

They were both having a *The Lion, the Witch and the Wardrobe* summer, vying in their love for the book, and there was a critical point upon which they very much differed concerning the fate of Aslan and whether, after he was killed and torn to pieces by the bad queen's minions, he subsequently came back *as* himself or if it was another lion *like* himself who showed up to finish the fight.

"But even if he was another lion *like* Aslan, he was still just like Aslan, so he wasn't really just another Aslan; he *was* Aslan," Sally said.

"No, he wasn't. You don't understand," Cam said.

"Yes, he was. You don't understand," Sally said.

"If I killed this ant," Cam said, stooping and swiping up a specimen who conveniently came to hand, sitting fat and shiny atop a rotting log, "if I killed this ant and pulled him all to pieces and gave the pieces to you, you couldn't make him an ant again. You'd just go get another ant and try to tell me it was the same ant as before, but I wouldn't believe you. That's what you'd do and that's what I'd *know.*" She knelt and let the frantic ant scuttle across her fingers and disappear into the underbrush.

"Well, anyway," Sally said after she watched all of this ant business from a fastidious remove, "Aslan is always alive the next time you read the book again, so doesn't that make him the same Aslan, over and over again, even if the other Aslan was at the end of the book, if that really was another Aslan, isn't he, um, the same Aslan at the beginning?"

"Huh?" asked Cam. "You are crazy. What does Auntie Lily say when she reads that part to you about Aslan? Did you ask *her*?"

"She says it's all just a made-up story," Sally said.

"What does Julie say?" Cam asked. She had figured out, lately, that Julie now stood as second-in-command around here.

"*She* says she'll stop reading to me if I don't stop asking stupid questions," Sally said.

"See. Julie says your question is stupid," said Cam.

"No. Julie is stupid," Sally suggested.

"But what does Auntie Ginger say?" Cam asked.

"Oh, Granna agrees with me," Sally said, which Cam didn't quite think was true, and she believed Ginger would agree with her, instead, should Cam ever have the opportunity to explain the opposing point of view regarding Aslan.

They soldiered on, letting a gap grow between them as each resented the other's presence; Cam, half running, led the way as Sally lagged behind. Cam was energized by disagreement, whereas dissension gave Sally the sulks.

She caught up with Cam, who was pacing at the edge of the High Field. "Look," Cam breathed and she held out her arms as if to embrace what she saw; the Queen Anne's lace had blossomed into a froth of fancywork unfurled across the meadow.

"Can we walk on it?" Sally asked.

"If we're careful," Cam said, and she advanced a few respectful steps.

"No. Walk like this," Sally said as she glided forward at a bridal pace. She cupped her hands in front of herself, holding an imaginary bouquet (for she would no more have picked a flower here than she would have torn apart a veil). She and Cam had been practicing being bridesmaids in an attempt to convince Julie to let them join the wedding party. They were going to prove to her they could do everything beautifully.

"Oh, Cam," Sally remembered, "last night I told Julie that Nicholas Davenant called when she wasn't there and I answered the phone, and he told me that you and I were *supposed* to be the flower girls and Julie had to obey what he said or else he would divorce her."

"What did Julie say?" Cam wanted to know. She would not have thought Sally had the guts to lie to Julie.

"*She* said she knew for a *fact* I never talked to Nicholas Davenant and that I was a flipping brat and now we'll be lucky if she lets the both of us sit at the back of the wedding with duck tape over our mouths," Sally said. "*If* we even get to go to any wedding at *all,* Julie said." Sally wasn't sure why she was confessing all of this to Cam, except that it was a very powerful story.

"Why blame me too? I didn't make anything up about Nicholas Davenant," Cam said. That didn't seem fair but, then again, perhaps it was; Sally had lied on her behalf as well.

They had come to a buttressing leg of the cell tower. They flung their heads back to gaze up into the intricate superstructure, shading their eyes from the dazzle of sunlight that sparked off shining steel beams and crosspieces. Cam said, as she always said when she and Sally stood here, "I watched the men build it. We all came up and watched. The men had a crane and a helicopter and everything."

"So?" Sally said, as she always said. Just as so many interesting events seemed to have occurred before she'd even been born, so many other interesting things had happened at Aunt Lily's before she'd ever gotten there. Someday, she'd like to arrive some place first and get to be the one to tell everybody else how much good stuff they had missed.

They picked up the service road, a dirt track bulldozed through the woods to allow GlobaLink's maintenance truck access to the tower. They were heading downhill now; the road was very steep in places but followed the most direct route, and before long they emerged onto the River Road, well out of sight of the farm stand, as they'd intended, and very near to the old railroad bridge that had been their destination all along.

Looking left and right to make sure they were unseen, they darted across the road and batted their way through the underbrush to get to the section of riverbank that curved just above the bridge. They peeled off their sneakers and waded into the water, proceeding up to their ankles and then to their knees. Cam gave a hop and dove in, headfirst, while Sally sat down suddenly, the water rising up to her neck, and they swam in their fashions (Cam's tidy crawl, Sally's churning butterfly) out into the current. They allowed the flow to carry them to the pilings of the bridge, which they caught and hung on to as the river tried to sweep them away. Their legs were snatched up and they floated as if they were flying in the air instead of the water, the river gliding over their shoulders and along their backs like an endless Superman's cape that streamed for miles and miles until the ocean.

Sally did not particularly care to swim in her clothes; she possessed a lovely Little Mermaid bathing suit, but Cam, more used to makeshift expedients than she, didn't seem to mind. Besides, should Auntie Lily, or anyone, come along and catch them, they could say they had fallen into the river—or Cam planned to say Sally had fallen in and she was rescuing her. Sally said she would prefer they say she was rescuing a drowning Cam, but Cam reminded her that no one would ever believe that version of events.

They were splashing and shouting so hard (having revived the Aslan argument, Sally pointing out that even though she and Cam possessed different copies of the book, the same Aslan still showed up in both volumes) that they failed to hear the approaching kayaker's soft plash and skim across the water. "Little girls," the lady called to them. "Little girls," she said, pulling up against a pillar of the bridge and turning her craft sideways to hover there, "you aren't swimming here all alone, are you?"

Sally floated out of sight behind a screen of debris caught among the pilings, but Cam bobbed nose to nose with the boat's prow, caught. She thought quickly; everyone always knew who she was, whether or not she knew them (she was very famous here in Towne for being that little Cambodian girl), and she didn't doubt inquiries could be, and would be, made. This lady had the aura of an interferer; Cam saw she had been scooping up discarded beer cans and bottles as she paddled along, collecting them in a plastic bag balanced on her bow.

"My big brother is here," Cam said. "But he had to go into the woods to pee." She was treading water, and energized by her inspired fabrication, she shot upward like a leaping fish.

"Oh," said the kayaker. She really didn't care to hear about that sort of thing. "Well," she advised, drifting off, "go sit on the bank until he returns. He shouldn't have left you alone and unattended in the river."

"He was in a big hurry," Cam began to explain. "He really had to go. He had diarrhea too."

"Out of the water," the lady ordered, and she kept watch over her shoulder, prepared to wheel her kayak around and reinvolve herself in other people's business, and so Cam retreated to the riverbank, where she sat shivering, her wet clothes clinging to her skin so much more clammily than a wet bathing suit. Sally floated from the hiding place and climbed onto the embankment. "You are awful," she told Cam. To say what she'd said about Thanh.

"Let's go," said Cam. They had to dry themselves off before anyone else saw them and asked more questions. They retraced their steps, walking up the service road and across the High Field and back into the woods, where they veered from the regular path and made their way to a rocky outcrop they knew of where the sun would bake their clothes stiff and superdry. Here, they flung themselves down flat, arms and legs outstretched.

"We are just like Petal," Sally said. Petal offered herself to the sun at every free moment, composed and inert upon a towel spread out on the lawn, listening to Sarah McLachlan CDs with a bottle of Evian water close at hand. "La la la la la," Sally sang until Cam picked up the imaginary radio and threw it over the edge of the outcropping.

"La la la la la . . . ai-eee," Sally sang and then shrieked, and they kept this up for quite a while, Cam throwing fifteen more imaginary radios from the cliff before Sally finally shut up. Then they bickered some more about Aslan, Cam making the point about the time that Tommy came over and they helped themselves to a skein of yellow yarn from Lily's knitting bag so they could wrap a mane of yellow yarn round and round Tommy's head, did Sally really think Tommy was Aslan or didn't she understand that it was all just pretend?

GINGER HAD BEEN KNOWN IN THE PAST to express a desire to spend an entire day in bed. To avoid some uncongenial obligation, she would announce that she must regretfully retire, for she feared she was coming down with something (like terminal boredom, she would be thinking). And sometimes she had longed to stay in bed all day for the sake of love, and almost as compelling, there had been all those occasions she had not wanted to get up because she wished to be left in peace to read some really good book, to remain lying propped on pillows and tucked beneath a blanket in a posture of complete receptivity and ease, consuming chapter after chapter as the rest of the world got on perfectly well without her. At present, she was wondering where her current book was; she thought she had left it on her night table, but someone must have moved it to set down a tray. (Overloaded trays were always upsetting her arrangements around here.) At any rate, she felt like reading now. Often she revived a bit later in the afternoon. She perked up for the cocktail hour, she would say. Old habits died hard, she would remark.

She sat up and slid her legs over the edge of the bed and stood up. She allowed herself a moment not to be dizzy and then she began her prowl around her room, searching the bureau top and dressing table and the mantel. She felt behind the chair cushions thinking that Lily may have sat there reading beside her last night while she slept.

She heard voices on the terrace below her window and she looked out and down upon Om and Tru and Thanh, who were seated at the old wrought iron table filling glassine envelopes with dried herbs. Lily had a new little sideline going this summer. She supplied a few fine food shops in the area with only the freshest of dried herbs. When Lily had first showed Ginger the proposed design of the labels, which told only the name of the herb and where it had come from written in plain black print on a plain white background just like the labels on generic-brand tin cans, Ginger had told Lily they could do better than that. She had recently arrived in Towne and just being there had raised her out of a previous low state. Ginger possessed no little talent for sketching, and Lily had produced pastel pencils and good paper, and, to enable Ginger to draw from life, she bought bunches of basil and sage and tarragon and dill and mint and thyme at Stop and Shop (for this was in the spring and her own crop had only just been sown). Now each label bore a botanically correct and really quite exquisite rendering of a single leaf or frond, and old-fashioned script-writing promised the customers, Herbs, Picked in their Prime, Dried by Nature and Hand Packaged with Care. Lily hadn't let Ginger get carried away with saying Hand Packaged with Love, but she had permitted her to bestow the appellation The Farm Stand Herbary, even though that seemed pretentious—herbary. Then again, one could charge more for herbs from a herbary, particularly if one pronounced the *h*'s when on the telephone with the store owners. Ginger had thought of starting a Web site, offering herbal recipes and bits of herbal lore *(It is said that dill will increase a mother's milk)*, but by then, she was running out of steam. The initial benefit she had sought and believed she had found under Lily's wing had not lasted out the spring.

Ginger leaned on the sill and watched from her window as Om tilted measured scoops of dried basil into the bags and Thanh crimped the tops and sealed them shut with a device that melded the edges together with heat and Tru pasted on the labels, making sure each went on centered and straight. Petal came into view bearing a list and a carton; she was packing up a stock order for the My Life, My Joy, My Food Shop, over in Wenham.

"They want twenty-five units each of whatever's available," Petal said.

"Hi," Ginger called down to them.

"Auntie Ginger?" Tru asked. "What is it? Do you need help?" She jumped to her feet. A sheath of labels flurried from her lap.

Ginger motioned reassuringly, her hand performing a leveling glide. *(Sit down. Calm down.)* She had become used to being met with alarm, although she would never have guessed that being ill so often obliged one to make other people feel better.

"I'm fine, dear," she said. "I'm just looking for a book I lost and it occurred to me that Betsy might have it somewhere. So, now I need to find Betsy. Do you know where she is?" The faces turned up to regard her. Viewed through the mesh of the window screen, Ginger had the look of an old photograph.

"No," said Petal. "She's still not back yet from wherever she went."

"Not back yet?" Ginger asked. "I wonder where she could be."

"Here she comes now," Om reported. Betsy's station wagon was racing up the driveway. She parked on the edge of the lawn and jumped out and made for the group on the terrace, for Petal had called her over.

"Yes, Petal?" Betsy asked. She shifted her heavy satchel from one hand to the other, impatient to get to the kitchen to begin baking a pie.

"Your mother," Petal said, gesturing upward.

"What?" Betsy asked. "What's happened?" The satchel fell from her hand and onto her foot, but she didn't seem to feel it.

"Up here," Ginger called. "I'm fine, dear. I was just looking for my book. It was on my night table. Have you seen it?"

"Oh, but I returned that book to the library. It was due today. It was just a one-week, on-reserve checkout. I told you when I got it for you," Betsy said. She stepped back for a less foreshortened look at her mother. "You were asleep this morning when I took it, but I checked for a place marker, so I figured you were through with it."

"I stopped reading on page two twenty-seven, which I knew I'd remember, since it's your father's birth date. Two twenty-seven," Ginger said. "Because I lost the scrap of paper I was using for a bookmark." It had been borne away, stuck to the bottom of a tray.

"I'm so sorry, Mummy. Maybe the library will let you have it back again for another day or two? Will that be long enough for you to finish it?" Betsy asked. "I think the library's open for another half hour." She picked up her satchel and rattled through the contents for her just-deposited car keys. "I don't think it's too much to ask for a little more time for you to finish—"

"Please don't bother," Ginger said. "Truly don't."

"But don't you want to know how the book ends?" Betsy asked.

"That happened to me once, Auntie Ginger," Thanh spoke up. "My mother sent a book I was reading to the cousins in Cambodia who want to learn English, and I never found out whether the Antareans destroyed the Earth and became the rulers of the universe, or if the proton bomb the earthlings were rushing to build was able to wipe out the invasion fleet."

"Well, of course the proton bomb worked," Om said. "Because *you* were reading the book—on the Earth."

"The story was set in the future," Thanh said. "So none of it had happened yet, so you can't be sure."

"I'm sure Auntie Ginger's book was a much more worthwhile and interesting one concerning something far less predictable than Earth versus the Aliens," Tru said. "Because the Aliens never win. The Earth, and by the Earth I mean we, the United States of America, always find a way to overcome the Aliens."

"I read this book once," Petal said, and everyone turned to her inquiringly and turned away again when she failed to elaborate further.

"What was your book about, Auntie Ginger?" Tru asked, after a moment. The heads all peered up at her window.

"Oh, it was an atmospheric tale about a woman who has to decide whether to marry a very eligible suitor or to follow through on her life-long dream to become a missionary in Africa," Ginger said.

"Can't she do both?" Om asked. "Can't the suitor go with her to Africa?"

"No, he won't go. He's an embittered financier who lives and breathes the acrid air of the boardroom. He can't be transplanted," Ginger said.

"He doesn't sound very nice," Petal said. She was filling the carton with herb packets but kept losing count and she had to start over, twice.

"Oh, but Victoria (she's the heroine) makes him be a much finer person when she's around him, so that's part of her dilemma," Ginger said. "She fears for his very soul, should she abandon him to his baser instincts."

"So then she has to decide between saving one soul or a thousand souls," Om said.

"Very nicely put," Ginger said.

"Actually, I've seen that book. Everybody's reading it at the beach this summer, and I read what they say about it on the back cover," Om confessed.

"Well, I can see why so many people like it," Ginger said. "Victoria is very religious, of course, but then again, she also really tears up the sheets with that financier of hers. And even when she's in her Jesus mode, she comes across very church militant. I mean she swears like a sailor and believes women should be priests, and there's this whole naughty choirboy subplot. It's very prurient and uplifting, all at once, you know, simply brimming with good parts, in every sense."

"But don't you want to know what Victoria decides to do?" Betsy asked. "What if I run out and buy you your own copy? The Book Stop will still be open downtown."

"No, please don't. Either she'll marry the fellow, or she'll go to Africa, and I rather like having the opportunity now to decide for myself. I don't know why these authors get to call all the shots. I suspect a lot of them just flip a coin," Ginger said. "Though I understand they get paid more for churning out a tragedy than a comedy, so naturally they cheerfully doom everybody."

"So, which should it be, Auntie Ginger, one soul saved or a thousand?" Tru asked.

"Well, on the one hand, I'd say she should go for the single soul, in that the financier really seems to be her soul mate, and as such, love trumps all. Besides, I don't know, the prospect of saving a thousand souls makes it all seem like just so much mass production (Mass production, hah!), and as such, it feels inherently soulless, to me. But, on the other hand, renouncing a great love for a higher calling, that's always a crowd pleaser, and maybe in the last paragraph, Victoria can be met at the airport in Mbandaka by some dishy maverick priest. Well, there's the sequel for you. They'll be tearing up the cassocks in that one," Ginger said.

"You can read that next book, the sequel, when it comes out," Petal said. She regarded Om, mystified. Om had just kicked the back of her chair.

"Where's Sally?" Betsy thought to ask then. "And Cam?"

"Here they come now," Om said. The little girls were running toward the group on the terrace, relieved that Cam had not missed her ride home. They knew they were late; the red light on top of the cell tower had switched itself on, timed to blink warningly in the winter darkness but discernible in the late summer daylight if one binoculared one's hands over one's eyes. They had run all the way from the rocks, through the woods and across the cornfield and over the lawn.

No one thought to ask them where they had been, since they'd returned safely from whatever they'd gotten up to. Betsy reached for Sally, who swerved away, but Betsy caught her. "You're so damp," Betsy said. "You've been playing too hard on such a hot day, poor baby." She stroked Sally's hair, gently undoing the tangles.

Sally and Cam shared an amazed glance, and Cam wiped her brow. "Phew," she said, as if she too was very hot, although she was really signifying her relief to Sally. It was as if they had a secret language.

"Phew," Sally echoed her.

"Come up and see me," Ginger called to the little girls from her window. "I still feel like reading something, so bring me one of your books. And I don't need three guesses which one it will be."

"Okay," Cam answered for them both. Here was her chance; she was quite certain Auntie Ginger did not really agree with Sally about the true nature of the restored Aslan, and even if she did lean in Sally's direction, Cam was pretty sure she would be open to persuasion.

BETSY STOOD BEFORE THE KITCHEN SINK running a sponge over stainless steel surfaces and suppressing the froth of iridescent bubbles that tended to erupt from the drain of the just-emptied sink. Supper had been very late, and dessert, the pie Betsy had been able to bake only after she had run outside to pick a Revereware bowlful of blueberries (for that was what Lily's handwritten recipe called for, *Mound the middle-sized Revereware bowl with berries*) had only just been pulled from the oven and was going to be too hot to eat until breakfast, although Sally found it hard to believe they'd let her have pie for breakfast. She was sure her mother would sleep on the promise and wake up with the cold word *cereal* on her lips. She eyed the pie sitting on the counter atop a cooling rack, some tin foil stuck underneath to catch the drips, for the pie oozed blue, and she sighed.

"Buck up, little one," Julie told her.

Julie sat at the table with Sally, helping her to order a sprawl of playing cards into suits. Sally had been discovered using the cards, which had pretty paisley backs, as coverlets for a dormitory of paper doll beds, the cards and the beds and the paper dolls themselves all existing on a correspondingly flat plane, and this alternate use for the playing cards had quite naturally suggested itself. Lily was sure Sally had managed to misplace at least a part of the deck, although Sally had argued back passionately that she had not. She had shouted and stamped her feet, and Sally's punishment for that (rather than for the misuse of a deck of cards) was to remain at the kitchen table until she had verified every suit was complete. Julie ought not to have been assisting her, but Betsy could only think that too much fuss was being made over those particular playing cards, which were so old and individually bent and broken that one could survey an opponent's paisley-sided hand and recognize much of what they held there. She and her mother had passed several recent evenings playing a notably transparent form of gin rummy, further aided by Betsy's knowledge of her mother's fondness for face cards and the aces, while Ginger bore in mind Betsy's attachment to even-numbered runs of twos and fours and sixes and eights. Tomorrow, Betsy resolved, she would drive down to the Ben Franklin and buy a new pack of playing cards (and then come right back home) so that there would be a bit more mystery and fewer foregone conclusions.

"Ladies," Rollins's voice addressed them. No one jumped, for they had heard him coming; he'd blundered into a stack of tomato cages piled in the back hall. "Care to join us? We're heading off to the Dock. Brooks and Glover and Ginevra are waiting in the car."

Betsy said she was expecting a call from Andy later, and Julie said she was going to spend a quiet evening reading, Lily having lent her a copy of *The Small House at Allington*, and besides, she didn't like cold beer.

"You can order a beer and let it just sit there getting all warm and furry and English," Rollins suggested.

"Not at the Dock, a beer won't just sit there," Julie said. "From everything I've heard, the Dock is a real dive."

"I want to go," Sally said. "Can I? I mean, may I? Please?" she added.

"No, you may not, and furthermore, you cannot. You are an underage child," Rollins said. "Brooks and I will be arrested for leading you astray, and think of the headlines, just as Brooks and I are getting our acts together. 'Noted Philanthropists Implicated in Child Alcohol Scandal,' " he quoted.

"Aw, flip," Sally said, and Betsy shook her head to remind the child what she had been told about saying words like *flip* even though Julie said it all the time.

"Hey, how did it go with the charity people today?" Julie asked, although she had already heard Harvey's version, and having heard Harvey's version, she wanted to know what had really happened. Harvey had hunted Lily and Julie down in the yellow-bean patch, where they had gone out picking after they returned from the dress-buying expedition, which had been a complete failure, so it was nice to do something simple and straightforward like fill a colander full of beans for supper. Harvey had stood over them, occasionally throwing some bean he liked the looks of into the colander, as he recounted what the Merit Group had said and what the boys had said and what he had said, giving himself all the good lines and the benefit of his long wisdom culled from real-world experience.

"We decided we're going to start a foundation that funds underfunded foundations which we think are doing good work," Rollins said. "Like, we'll be helpful to the people who are being helpful to whales or helpful to the illiterate."

"You can help illiterate whales," Julie and Betsy suggested, at the same time.

"Yes, well," Rollins said. "But I think we're mostly going to be of assistance in sudden emergencies like floods and fires and famines, or even when there's just someone in the paper who's had a personal disaster and you think what they really need now is enough money to rebuild their house after the tornado hit, or go back to school to learn computers now that they've lost the use of their limbs. We're going to call it the Flash Fund."

"I like that. Truly I do, Rollins," Betsy said. She wondered whether Becky knew what decent human beings her sons had become, and she asked herself whether it would be all right to send Becky a letter. She would tell her about the boys, and perhaps she would express how very much she hoped her aunt could attend Julie's wedding, which was, perhaps, none of her business, but Betsy felt she understood Julie's feelings on the subject better than anyone else and could convey them to her aunt. And she thought she would include a photo of Sally and a newspaper clipping about Andy and his work on the trial, and she had no idea how much, if anything, Becky knew of Ginger's condition, but she thought Becky ought to know how things stood there. She did not think that matters between the sisters-in-law should end in such silence as had fallen.

"I think you should call it the Kitten Up a Tree Fund," Julie said.

"Or maybe The Baby Down the Well Fund," Betsy said.

"Mummy, you are awful," Sally said. She was hunting unmethodically among the heap of playing cards for the six of clovers. Julie flipped the missing card to her from across the table.

"Yeah, well, Brooks wanted to call it the No Balls Fund, since we're not going to get all bogged down in fancy parties with socialites and such, but that got shot down fast," Rollins said.

Petal had been watching from her attic window, keeping a careful eye on what she could view of the driveway as she leaned on the sill and at the same time applied makeup by the waning natural light. She held a square of mirror in one hand, which was awkward, but she made do. She had thought a great deal about her hair and at last decided to wear it down and hot-combed smooth and flat (simple could be as much work as complicated). Now she was descending the back stairs. They all turned to the careful clump of her high heels, which reminded Julie of the metered pace of the peg leg of a pantomime Long John Silver but she held off saying so. Petal appeared; she wore a short silver skirt and silver sandals and a cropped and off-the-shoulder T-shirt with the word *ChaCha* picked out in rhinestones across the front. Sally had never seen anything so wonderful and she had to stand up to take a better look.

Petal expressed her surprise at finding Rollins in the kitchen. "Rollins, what are you doing here?" she asked. "Is there any more coffee?"

She had equipped herself with a coffee mug and claimed to be in search of a refill before settling down for the night with a good book. She held out, in proof, the volume she had just plucked from the upper landing bookshelves on her way down, *The Consolation of Philosophy,* which no one was buying, Petal dipping into Boethius, but Julie gave her credit for making a good effort. Props were a nice touch; they gave one something to do with one's hands while spinning a line of guff.

"But I thought we had a date," Rollins said.

"Well, you didn't actually say," Petal said.

"Do I have to say?" Rollins asked.

"Yes, you do, you dope," Julie answered for Petal, who looked nervous when Julie called Rollins a dope on her behalf.

"Well, he did sort of tell me maybe he'd be seeing me," Petal said.

"What, like sometimes you're invisible and sometimes you're not?" Julie asked. "*Maybe* he'll be seeing you?" She smacked her brother with a rolled-up newspaper.

Petal would have said that it was more like a sensation that she had moved from darkness into the light whenever Rollins was around but she understood one didn't talk about personal feelings around here. In that instance, one would suddenly become inaudible.

"Have fun," Julie called after them as they departed. She made it sound like a command.

"I have finished my punishment," Sally announced. "And *all* of the cards are there."

"Good, now go kiss Granna goodnight," Betsy said. "But gently, please, remember."

"Of course," Sally said, sliding from her chair.

"My brother is socially inept," Julie said. "I don't know what Petal sees in him, but obviously she sees something."

"What about Nicholas?" Betsy asked. "Is he very thoughtful and considerate? That's how *I* see *him*. Julie, if it were up to me, I'd conjure up the nicest guy in the world for you to marry."

"Yes, well, thank you. I hope I have accomplished that for myself," Julie said. She had picked up the restored deck and was shuffling the cards, expertly letting them flurry into realignment, smartly tapping the pack and cascading it again. Betsy decided her cousin must have played a lot of poker, or something, over there in England.

THE DOCK WAS AN AFTER-HOURS CLUB located two towns away in an old factory complex where shoes had once been manufactured. Any car entering or exiting the parking lot rumbled and rocked over an abandoned railroad spur where a final freight car was outlasting the elements and the work of vandals and the arson fires and the leafless poplar tree that had grown up through its bed and now seemed to be dying there. The building was windowless and asphalt shingled. Up on the flat roof sat a searchlight whose many beams swept the night sky with lacing and unlacing ribbons of light.

The club was entered through what had been the loading dock. A raw wooden staircase rose shoulder high to the lips of a steel platform. Several smokers were lingering there in the open air, not that smoking wasn't permitted within the Dock's premises, but, as Ginevra observed, smokers had been turned into feral creatures lately; even when they were allowed inside, they preferred lurking in doorways and alleys.

"You singing tonight?" one of the smokers asked Ginevra. She had been performing at the Dock off and on this summer, backed by a local band called The Remedy.

"No. Only once a week. The management's too cheap for more," Ginevra said.

They entered the premises and walked the length of the crowded bar, where they noticed the Marry-Me-Nomar girl sitting by herself and watching an away game on a silenced TV. She was listening to the radio play-by-play through a headset clamped over her veil, which made the material splay up and out, creating an even more off-putting cordon of bouffant netting. The stools on either side of her remained empty and a remembered tag of poetry came to Ginevra: . . . *how everything turns away / Quite leisurely from the disaster.* She thought she might write a song using that line as the chorus.

They crossed the dance floor, stepping around the clenched couples who swayed and shuffled to the strains of that summer's incessantly popular anthem. Ginevra was recognized and she acknowledged nods and greetings with nods and greetings of her own. However, Petal caused the greater stir; heads spun to take her in, and Ginevra felt the attention shift from herself like the sudden cessation of a sweet-smelling breeze.

They found a table, and the brothers tilted back in their chairs passing around the beer menu. Softly, Petal sang along with the song that was playing, "I kno-ho dat my hut weeeel go ahn."

"You know who makes surprisingly good beer?" Brooks asked.

"The Turks do," he answered himself, when no one took him up on his question.

"Nee-ah. Fah. Wheer-evra yew rrrrr," Petal sang, her voice swelling and her hand gesturing near and then flaring out, farther away. "Dere is sohm luv dat weel nut go a-waaay."

The brothers decided to sample a beer listed as a product of a local microbrewery, Tad's Really Quite Terrific Ale, and if it was any good, Brooks said maybe Tad would be really terrific and let them buy his company in order to diversify their holdings. The ale proved to have shreds of wheat and flecks of orange peel suspended in the suds, which they all decided they rather liked; it seemed nutritious. Patti, the waitress who usually just plunked and departed, lingered to pour their orders into glasses, for she was aware of whom she had at her station. The two guys who were squinting at the menu and scratching their heads were Ginevra's fella's brothers, the ones who had invented QPyramid and were millionaires, or possibly billionaires—the Dock staff had gathered by the salad station to debate this point—but either way, Patti expected to earn a far better tip from this table than her other ones. The landscaping crew sweating over their nachos, the auto body shop guys getting grease on her apron when they grabbed for her attention, the mall clerks celebrating a twenty-first birthday with a Sara Lee cake (they had asked for a knife and nine plates and forks) would have to hold their horses. She would get to them when she got to them.

"My parents tried making mead once. It had bits of bees floating all through it," Ginevra recalled. "Then they got ahold of a lot of plums and tried their luck with slivovitz."

"Which, if you can't pronounce it, you've had too much," Brooks said.

"No, if you can't pronounce it, you haven't had enough," Rollins said.

"I want to make a toast," Glover said, holding up his glass. "To the Flash Fund. Nice work, guys. Well done. I mean it."

Brooks and Rollins shrugged, and Brooks said, "We'd better drink to the success of the VeeCube so we can pay for it all. Uncle Harvey's officially on the lookout for worthy causes and dire emergencies. He's licking his chops over hurricane season. He's hoping all of Miami will be blown away, though I am not clear whether he'll release funds to help them build a new one."

"But you'll have another triumph. You have those select boy geniuses you hired to test the VeeCube for you, David May and his pals Jason and Matt," Ginevra said. "I saw Hannah at the farm stand, and she was saying David hasn't budged from the living room sofa all summer. He just plays games and schedules teleconferences with your designers and engineers in California so he can tell them all how lame they are and generally read them the riot act and tell them what to do. Apparently they hang on his every word."

"I know," Brooks said. "David's a tough customer. He got Sally and Cam to play Horror Hunt one day, just to prove it's so stupid that even six-year-old girls could reach level three without even trying, which they promptly did."

"Well, I'm not sure whether that wasn't a case of their both trying extra hard to dazzle David May and not so much a reflection of the game itself," Ginevra said. "I think they both L-I-K-E him."

"I hadn't heard about any of that," Rollins said. "But here's an idea. Maybe we should reconfigure Horror Hunt. You know, make the graphics go all pink and unicorn-y and call it My Little Monster."

"I always suspected this was how corporate America functioned," Ginevra said. "I mean, I've always said I believed the universal remote could only have been thought up late one night in a bar."

"Anyway, I'll make a toast now," Rollins said. "To Petal and her ChaCha shirt, which I cannot take my eyes off of."

Petal, who was used to being gazed at, received this tribute graciously, and because everyone had turned to her (Brooks openly admiring, Glover giving her one of his calm and reassuring smiles, and Ginevra looking amused, but then Ginevra always seemed to regard her with amusement), she raised her glass. She too had thought of something to drink to—and usually the best she could come up with was "To You" or "To Us," so, really, she almost felt like making a toast to her own excellent toast. She drew a breath and declared, "I want to say, 'Here's to Julie finding her wedding gown.' "

"Oh? Julie got a dress today? Really? Did she really?" Ginevra asked. "Well, well, well. I wish I'd known that. I'd have run into the house to see for myself just what she's come up with."

"No, no. She didn't come home with anything. I guess I should have said, 'Here's to hoping Julie will find a wedding gown, next time,' " Petal said. She held up her glass again, less exultingly.

"No luck, huh?" asked Rollins. "But our sister has never been easy to please, so it's fortunate that everything I've heard about Nicholas Davenant makes him sound like quite the paragon. Explorer. Scientist. Julie told me the other day, he has an especially soft spot for cats—that was to rebuke me for giving Agnes the gentlest shove away after she bit my hand."

"Almost too good to be true," Brooks agreed. "Which he'd have to be, to get past Julie—and not to mention us."

"Miss Lily said Julie tried on twenty gowns and nitpicked at every one of them," Petal reported. "Miss Lily came home very discouraged. She said she just can't figure out what's going on in Julie's head at the moment. She's just not acting like a normal bride-to-be."

The brothers shrugged. Their sister had always been a rather prickly girl.

"Now me? Can I make a toast?" asked Ginevra. She lifted her glass and swept it toward the bar and the Marry-Me-Nomar girl, who still sat there intent upon the televised ballgame. "Okay. Here's to *all* the imaginary boyfriends," she declared, and she sat back, regarding the brothers and Petal with a look of challenge.

"What's that supposed to mean?" asked Rollins. "I'm real enough." He offered Petal his arm. "Pinch me," he said.

Petal refused to do so. Instead, she stroked his cheek; he had as good as declared in front of everyone that he was somebody's boyfriend and that could only mean he must be hers.

"Oh, come on. We're all thinking the same thing," Ginevra said. "Aren't we?"

"Are we? Enlighten us," Glover said. "Please."

Ginevra propped her elbows on the table and leaned forward, taking them all into her confidence. "Are you telling me that you're all perfectly convinced that there really is a Nicholas Davenant?" she asked. "For goodness' sake, just listen to how we always refer to him by both of his names. Nicholas Davenant. Like Oliver Twist. Like Ethan Frome. Like he's a fictional character. You guys must have sensed there's something fishy going on, even if you don't know you know."

"But Julie's going to marry him," Petal insisted. "Honestly guys, don't listen to Ginevra. She's just being . . ." The word she wanted was provocative, but she didn't think of it until later that evening. However, Glover and Brooks and Rollins had fallen silent and thoughtful.

"One might make something of there being no pictures of him, at all," Glover allowed, after a moment.

"Nicholas Davenant is the only one who knows how to use their new camera," Petal said. "I asked Julie about that. And don't forget; there was the picture of Nicholas Daven—of Nicholas's thumb."

"Did she carry on about that thumb with everyone?" Rollins asked. "Like we're supposed to be able to reconstruct the entire Nicholas Davenant from that one little part the way paleontologists project how dinosaurs looked on the strength of a fossilized tooth."

"And there's no engagement ring," Ginevra reminded them.

"They're having one made. Modeled on something Julie saw in one of her museum exhibits," Petal said. "Why would she bother to make up all of that? I mean, wouldn't she have just shown up with a big fake diamond otherwise?"

"Oh no, she'd never get a big fake diamond past Aunt Ginger," Brooks said.

"Then how is she going to get a fake boyfriend past her?" Petal asked.

"Ginger's a bit off her game this summer," Ginevra said. "Oh, or maybe she's particularly receptive to otherworldly presences at the moment. I don't know."

"The no-ring thing is plausible," Glover said. "If circumstantial. You can find reasonable explanations. But something has seemed a bit odd, about a lot of it," he admitted.

"But this is absurd. We know for a fact Nicholas Davenant exists," Brooks said. "Or a Nicholas Davenant, at any rate, who seems to possess the correct professional affiliations and is the presumably appropriate age. Rollins and I Googled him first thing."

"Because you were suspicious, " Ginevra said.

"No, we pretty much Google everybody. Not that there was very much information on him, but enough," Brooks said.

"Enough for someone clever to have fleshed out," Ginevra said. "Maybe Julie just got there before you in order to find him and present him as a likely candidate."

"But Julie's been reading all those big books about Siberia and shale and the history of Standard Oil so she can talk to him intelligently about his work," Petal said. "Why would she do that if she didn't have to?"

"So she can talk to us convincingly about his supposed work?" Glover suggested.

"Sending him to Siberia was an inspired move," Rollins said.

"I think it was a bit obvious. He had to go either there or to Antarctica," Brooks said. "There are very few ends of the earth left where you can keep someone virtually incommunicado for months at a time."

"No, Antarctica wouldn't work. Nicholas Davenant would still be locked in there by the long southern winter. Julie couldn't plausibly get him out in time for a fake September wedding," Glover said. He'd been an Antarctica buff since high school and knew how hard it had been to extract Admiral Byrd from a perilous situation on the ice shelf.

"She could have stuck him in prison until she needed him," Brooks suggested.

"Please. Our sister has her standards in imaginary beaus," Rollins said.

"Well, maybe he's a brave and courageous freedom fighter who ran afoul of the powers that be," Brooks said. "If he's a political prisoner, that'd be cool. That'd be acceptable."

"All right, but excuse me," Petal said. "What would Julie be doing all this for? She doesn't need the attention. You people all look up to her. You all defer to her in everything. I've noticed that. She told you to come here this summer; you came. She tells you to stay here; you stay."

The brothers shrugged, and Brooks nodded at Patti, who had been hovering in the vicinity semaphoring with her tray her willingness to bring them another round.

"You know perfectly well what Julie is up to," Ginevra said. "Maybe she's sick of having to act like your mother. Maybe she's trying to lure Becky back home. Oh, don't look at me like that for speaking her name. Who is she, Lord Voldemort?" She was impatient with them all, they were like a classroom full of students who repelled knowledge like waxed jackets repelled rain.

"I have wondered whether Julie doesn't know something she's not telling us about Ma," Glover said. "Ever since she went to see Ma last spring, I've wondered just what happened out there, but Julie hasn't been very forthcoming. She just told me a lot of tourist stuff about all the camels and some Roman ruins she took an excursion to one day when Ma was having her hair done and William was having therapy."

"Oh, this has everything to do with Ma," Rollins said. "Anything that isn't right—it all goes back to Ma. So here's an idea. Maybe now Julie has arranged everything. Maybe she's collected us and brought us here and set us up like one of her museum exhibits. We'll all be standing around at her so-called wedding, all cleaned up and in our good suits (didn't you get her memo about buying a good suit?). She'll have us arranged like figures in one of her reconstructed museum tableaus, and suddenly Ma will walk in and it will be perfect. It'll be like we were waiting for the final exhibit to arrive, like Ma was a precious Vermeer held up at customs. And then maybe Julie thinks Dad and Ma will suddenly decide to get married again, out there in the magic pumpkin field. She's probably arranged for a pumpkin to turn into a horse-drawn carriage. I wouldn't put it past her."

"Ma's married to William now. Julie knows that," Brooks said.

"But does that count? Do we even recognize stuff that happens in Libya?" Rollins asked.

"What, do you think Ma could just click her heels three times and say, 'I divorceth thee, William'?" Brooks asked. "Was it a Muslim wedding? I don't think I ever heard whether or not it was."

"I'm not saying Julie has thought through this part of the plan very well," Rollins said. "She is not that sort of thinker. Many's the time I have come across her painted into a corner, figuratively speaking, you know, like the trip to Colorado when she hauled herself up that big cliff and threw all the ropes and stuff down for Uncle Hap to come follow her."

"Right, and that piton chunked him in his arm," Glover recalled. "Which is when we radioed for a helicopter to come to generally sort matters out, stranded sisterwise, injured unclewise. And long-suffering Ma-wise."

"Well, I'll believe in Nicholas Davenant before I believe in Ma and Dad getting back together again," Brooks said.

"But can't somebody just ask Julie what's going on?" Petal asked. "Although one way or the other I think they're just going to make her very, very angry, whoever asks her about this. I'm certainly not going to. I'm certainly not going to tell her how you've been talking like this behind her back."

"Nobody is going to tell her anything. Nobody is going to ask her anything. Who's to say we'll get a straight answer? I mean, if she knows we're suspicious, she's just as likely to tell us any real Nicholas Davenant is a fake, as much as she'd insist a fake Nicholas Davenant is real. I vote we don't say anything to Julie. I say we just let her proceed with whatever it is she may or may not be intending," Glover said. "Most of all, I say we ought to trust her. Whatever's going on, let's count on Julie to do—what? What is she doing?" He was not sure how to characterize what Julie may or may not have been attempting to accomplish.

"The wrong thing for the right reason?" suggested Ginevra.

"Yes, that rather sounds like our sister," said Rollins.

FOUR *Passing Through Doors*

" 'THE SUN MAY COME OUT BY NIGHTFALL? The sun may come out by nightfall'?" Harvey asked. "What kind of ragtime is that weather fella talking?" Harvey wanted to know. He scowled at the kitchen radio, a blandly gray little cube that also brewed coffee and would detect carbon monoxide should there ever be any of the stuff wafting about the house silently and scentlessly trying to kill him. An alarm would go off to rouse him and Penny from any too deep sleep they may have fallen into.

"The weather fella means he hopes it will stop raining, later in the day, toward evening," Penny said reasonably, and Harvey turned to gloom at her. He gave her no credit for actually understanding the weather fellow and his ragtime.

"Perhaps we will get to see the stars tonight," Penny said. "And, if you think about it, many of those stars may very well serve as suns to other beings, out there in the galaxy." She cast an inspired eye in the general direction of the universe, but Harvey felt it was too early in the morning for Penny to start being marvelous. There was only one sun that mattered, and he wished she would allow him to grizzle at the radio if he wanted to, for the rain had been falling for the better part of a week and such a long string of dreary, wet days was enough to get anyone down and it was particularly discouraging for those who lived in a glass house as he and Penny did. Even if the mind knew better, the body shivered and bent a bit at the sight of the endlessly rivering and blurring and polishing and spattering of rain upon all of one's windows and walls and skylights.

"Lily says much more of this wet weather will mean the end of the shell beans. They're turning rusty on the vines," Penny said.

"Rusty?" challenged Harvey.

"I am just repeating what Lily said."

"She must have said *musty.*"

"Perhaps," Penny allowed, even though the word Lily had used was *rusty,* and Penny had known what she meant.

"Or most likely, she said *muddy,* which you misheard for *musty,*" Harvey said. "Which you then misremembered as *rusty.*" He liked to get to the bottom of things and was satisfied he had done so, in this case. He was incorrect but he'd been rather clever, so Penny gave him a pass.

They were seated side by side at their breakfast bar, as yet unbreakfasted. Harvey fiddled with the sugar bowl, and Penny turned her plate upside down and studied the mark on the bottom; they might have been stuck at the counter of a luncheonette after the waitress had wandered off with their order, muttering something they hadn't quite caught but which had evidently been important.

The weatherman quit his yammering, and a spot ran on the radio, an advertisement for an online home mortgage company that touted the ability of customers to access the status of their mortgage applications twenty-four hours a day. Harvey observed that any person who was wide awake at two o'clock in the morning and seeking information on an impending loan was asking to borrow too much money, and he rejected Penny's suggestion that a person could find himself joyfully awake at two a.m., too excited to sleep and too busy mentally arranging where the furniture would go in his dream house. Didn't people have jobs? Harvey wanted to know. Didn't people have to get up in the morning? If they didn't have to get up in the morning to go to work, how could they afford to buy a house? No wonder their consciences woke them up at two a.m. Harvey was satisfied he'd won his argument, too, and he signaled his success by tracing an exclamation mark in the sugar he had spilled on the breakfast bar.

"Oh good, here she is," Penny said, who had been keeping an eye out.

Sally had appeared at the edge of the woods, revolving a pink umbrella over her head, which made it seem a more actively effective rain deterrent, in her opinon. She crossed the terrace and pulled apart the sliding doors and entered the kitchen backward, relinquishing her umbrella only at the last minute, allowing it to be snatched from her hands by a slight wind which escorted it across the terrace bricks and secured it beneath the legs of a garden bench. Sally had learned lately there was nothing unluckier than to carry an opened umbrella into a house. Cam's sister Om's friend's cousin had known a boy who had carried an open umbrella into his house and he had *died*. She and Cam had run this information by Julie, the only available adult they could find at the time, and she had said yes, she'd also heard that about opening umbrellas inside a house from a friend's cousin's sister. One could not be too careful when such authority spoke.

Offered to Penny, then, was the knapsack on Sally's back, which could not be shrugged off without courting disaster. There were eggs inside the backpack.

"Six!" said Penny, extracting half a carton. She broke two eggs into the bowl of pancake batter which, earlier, she had not been able to finish mixing without eggs. A quick call down to the big house and an inquiry as to the egg situation there had caused Sally to be sent up through the woods with fresh provisions. Everyone (Granpa, Julie, even Aunt Lily) had asked her where her red cape and basket were, but Sally had already found her umbrella and hitched the pack over her shoulders, although she supposed she could fetch a basket from the farm stand but she didn't have a very firm line on where she could get her hands on a red cape.

She had thought about wolves as she tramped up the path to the Ridge House while being slapped by soaking branches which hung low and heavy all along the way, but she was not worried. Wolves abounded in Siberia, where Nicholas Davenant was spending his summer. (Also abounding in the region were reindeer and sable and the nerpa—an encyclopedia had been consulted first thing the morning after the fireworks so everyone would be able to speak intelligently about Russia's easternmost region—or at least ask sensible questions.) And since all the wolves lived over there in Siberia, they could not live here because no one could be in two places at once, which Sally knew for a fact because that's what her father kept telling her over the telephone when she complained that she missed him so much and wanted to know why he could not be here, with her.

Harvey boosted Sally up onto the counter stool beside his own perch. Of course she would be staying for pancakes. She curled her hand around the glass of milk Penny set down in front of her and she wobbled her head as she took a little sip. Whenever she sat at Uncle Harvey and Aunt Penny's kitchen bar, she liked to pretend she was a intoxicated person ensconced in a real bar.

"Oh, I am so drunk," she said.

"You're starting early," Harvey told her.

"How is your grandfather settling in?" Penny asked. Louis had arrived in Towne a week ago. Everyone had been saying he brought the rain with him, which was not accurate; the clouds had already been assembled in place to greet him upon his arrival. Only Doris, who'd met him at the airport, had gotten it right. "Oh, Mr. Tuckerman, I truly believe someone up there *knows* what you're going through," she said referencing the gloomy skies, and then she had hugged him, right there in the taxi rank, as Louis hoped that everyone in Towne would not feel the need to wrap their giant arms around him. He knew Doris meant well, but such a demonstration helped her a great deal more than it helped him.

"All Granna and Granpa want to do is just sit there and hold hands," Sally reported, severely. Tru Samrin had lately taught her how to play cat's cradle, and her grandparents only occasionally consented to let her practice on them and were not very patient when she forgot, as she usually did, just how the yarn was supposed to go and so had to run and fetch the diagram Tru had drawn as her co-player sat there, entangled.

Penny bustled around her nice modern kitchen, which had been ergonomically designed for old people. She and Harvey had surpassed themselves, anticipating every likely infirmity, which was why they had two ovens, one installed low in the event they ended up in wheelchairs, and one set high, should torticollis rob them of their ability to stoop, although as Penny admitted, at the moment, neither height was just right since she and Harvey remained quite fit and there was nothing very special about their needs, at least not yet.

Now, Penny stood at the griddle, which was fuming smoke at her as she held her spatula aloft and wavering. She was picturing Ginger and Louis just sitting there in Lily's little parlor, holding hands like a courting couple, and she had to be recalled to her task.

"Aunt Penny," Sally said. "You are burning."

"How about if I sprinkle chocolate chips on your pancakes?" Penny asked to cheer herself up in a roundabout way (the child needed a treat).

"Sure," said Sally.

They had to remain very quiet as they ate. Harvey needed to listen to the news, which the little gray radio was about to report at the top of the hour. Harvey was monitoring disasters, great and small, local and national and international, on behalf of the Flash Fund, although nothing very terrible had happened since the boys launched their foundation. Harvey supposed that was just as well. The stationery he had ordered had not yet come back from the printer's and he was still negotiating for local office space, and then the authorities had suddenly swanned in and involved themselves, snowing him with forms and fill-outs, all of which he shoved into envelopes and sent on to that Merit Group gang from New York, written over with his red-scrawled queries and instructions which were as confidently illegible as the signature of a monarch; but let them divine his wishes, Harvey said. Besides, Brooks and Rollins were away at present, and Glover too, all of them having flown to California for a few days. Glover had lately made up his mind to transfer to the reserves and go to work with his brothers, and although the deal had been done, his brothers meant to cinch the matter by impressing him with a tour of their corporate headquarters. Perhaps they planned to dangle the Calder mobile in front of him, as Alden had remarked to Ginevra after they saw the boys off to the airport. (Doris was keeping busy that summer ferrying the family back and forth from Logan.)

"Oh, Jesus, the guys own a Calder?" asked Ginevra, and she had wondered whether she wasn't in over her head, running around with such people.

Sally slipped down from the counter stool. The pancakes had not been a notable success, the sweetness of the maple syrup embittering the chocolate, and she had gouged out the chips and dropped them into her glass of milk, meaning for them to melt there, only they hadn't done so. They had subsided to the bottom and lurked like pebbles, which had been off-putting because pebbles had no business sitting at the bottom of a glass of milk.

"Wash your hands, please," Penny said as Sally made for the wall of kitchen windows onto which she planned to breathe a white fog field where she could draw flowers and write a message with her fingertip (Sally Was Here). She veered toward the bathroom, a visit to which was one of the high points of any call upon the Ridge House. Uncle Harvey and Aunt Penny's bathroom was wonderful.

"And don't touch anything until you're clean," Penny said. There was not enough Windex in the world to keep her windows bright and shining, she was fond of saying, and she said so now.

Sally held her arms up over her head so she would not accidentally leave sticky prints on a lamp or a table or a chair as she ran across the living room and skidded around a corner and hied into the bedroom, where there was a very big bed that reminded her of a trampoline and which she always had to pause to admire before she ducked into the bathroom.

The bathroom did not have a door as such. You walked one way through an opening and keeping a shoulder tight against a cool, glass block wall, you curved round the other way and popped out by the shower stall. This was called a snail door because snails used a similar arrangement when exiting and entering their shells; not that Aunt Penny and Uncle Harvey were snail people, but Aunt Penny said she and Harvey appreciated not having to fiddle with door handles in the middle of the night when they had to get up.

Sally stood on tiptoes at the sink and nudged on the hot faucet with her wrist and as hot water flowed, she turned a cake of soap over and over in her hands which were so dirty the soap itself had become grubby, and she had had to wash the soap as well. She rinsed everything beneath a lovely warm spray of water (for the rain had drummed down so cold upon her umbrella she had nearly forgotten how nice warm water could feel against her skin). She filled her palms and emptied them one into another like the cascading bowls of the fountain in the park back at home in California, for which she was particularly pining at the moment (home, that park, her dollhouse aquarium). Brooks and Rollins and Glover had refused to let her accompany them on their California trip, even though she had boasted to Cam that she was going along too. Sally had laid it on a bit thick, insisting what a fine time she and her big, grown-up cousins were going to have, and she'd been avoiding Cam for the past two days, neglecting her work at the farm stand and even being obliged to disappear beneath the dining room table, at one point, when she had heard Cam's voice coming from the kitchen asking Aunt Lily whether lunch was ready, and if so, what were they having?

GINEVRA'S MOTHER HAD CALLED HOME the other evening to say that she had promised to provide a thousand origami white doves for a

Pax and Lux Festival in British Columbia, and they needed to be delivered by the end of the week. Mrs. Platt-Willey had been sitting on a mesa meditating upon a Southwestern sunset when she remembered that she had made the commitment some months earlier. She had seen a dove, she said, and had known at once that it had been sent to remind her of something.

"Pax and Lux mailed me a box full of paper and folding instructions, which I carefully set aside. They are definitely somewhere in the house," she recalled.

"That dove didn't mention where?" Ginevra asked. Her parents' residence was formidably cluttered. Such self-sufficiency as they had striven to achieve required a great deal of apparatus and arrangements; one could never just push a button. One turned a crank or lit a fire or primed a pump or trimmed a wick or sloshed a bucket. Ginevra had pointed out to her parents that they themselves were no more than cogs in a machine, as enslaved by their emancipation from the national grid as those people in the subdivisions who were subject to their dishwashers and automatic garage door openers. Her parents decided they had done wrong by letting their daughter receive a public school education, but that was an old regret and one past remedying. Ginevra had pleaded to be sent to the Meadowbrook Elementary School; she had longed to ride in the big yellow bus that stopped for other children at the end of the road. She had yearned, as well, to have hot dogs and macaroni and cheese and green Jell-O for lunch.

After her mother rang off, Ginevra had wondered whether white doves were native to Arizona, and she decided that the one her mother had seen must have escaped from a magic act performing at some nearby Indian-owned casino, in which case, perhaps her mother would be moved to insist that the manifestation truly had been something of a mystical nature. She hoped her mother wouldn't spot a runaway white rabbit on the lam from a magician's hat and take off across the desert in pursuit of it.

Subsequently, Ginevra had run into Petal at Peddocks', where Petal was picking up the August fashion magazines. Petal appeared in several print ads inside the slim summer issues and she always liked to see whether she was more prominently featured on the page than the tube of lip gloss or the bottle of vodka being touted. Ginevra was buying a bottle of Advil, the homespun remedy she had come across in her mother's pharmacopeia cabinet having failed to relieve her rather stiff headache—maybe the label on the vial of betony had been wrong, in which case, Ginevra hoped it had not been some sort of purgative or sleeping potion or hallucinogen she'd ingested in error.

She was also trying to find one of those rubber sheaths that slipped over the index fingertip to facilitate work with slippery paper. Mr. Peddock, appealed to, knew what she meant—they were those things that bookkeepers used to wear when leafing through ledgers—but he did not carry them. He would have told her to try Towne Stationers, who may or may not have had a box of them in the storeroom, but they'd gone out of business shortly after the new Staples opened over in Danvers and he couldn't speak for what Staples might or might not stock.

"What do you need that finger thing for?" Petal asked, after Mr. Peddock went off, shaking his head. She and Ginevra had fallen into a conversation about the guys, comparing their news from California and figuring out whose news was fresher. (Ginevra had known that Brooks and Rollins were taking Glover to see a house out there that they thought he maybe ought to buy, and Petal had been able to report that Glover had returned from the expedition saying he was looking for someplace larger and with a more cook-friendly kitchen.) Since Petal had nothing else to do and because Ginevra seemed overwhelmed, she had offered her assistance with the origami project, and Ginevra could not think of any reason not to thank her and say yes. She supposed one might even say she and Petal were friends by now. She had no idea when that could have happened, although it may have had something to do with the intelligence Petal had just imparted in regard to Glover's requirements in a residence; Ginevra knew for a fact he did not cook, whereas he was perfectly well aware that she loved to bake, and furthermore, when he said he wanted a larger house, just how large would larger be, although that was an unanswerable question unless one knew the dimensions of the passed-on dwelling. The place might have been a hobbit hole; then again, would Brooks and Rollins steer their elder brother to a hobbit hole? Ginevra thought not since the point of the California visit was to wow him and she was inclined to believe that the brothers had collectively turned their noses up at four or five thousand square feet of living space.

Now, this rainy morning Ginevra and Petal had gotten down to business at Ginevra's parents' house, seated at the great-room table with a pile of flimsy paper squares scattered in front of them. Ginevra read the directions aloud, "Fold corner A to corner C, adjust the paper a quarter turn and repeat." She peered at the diagram supplied by Pax and Lux. "Is that very clear to you?" she asked.

"Repeat what?" Petal wondered. "Do I fold old corner A to old corner C, or does turning the paper give me a new corner A and a new corner C? Because I've already mentally labeled the unturned-to corners as B and D. Oh, plus I forgot; I mentioned to Miss Lily how you were looking for something so your finger wouldn't slip, and she gave me her old leather quilting thimble to give to you. She's not sure it will be any help, though, but she doesn't want it back. She says she's never going to be quilting again. She was never that keen on quilting anyway, she told me, so don't worry about her giving it up."

Ginevra slipped the thimble onto her index finger and although it didn't do much for her one way or the other in regard to her present task, she kept it on because she found she was unaccountably pleased that something of Lily's fit on her hand so well.

After spoiling a dozen or so sheets of paper between them, they got the hang of what they were doing, and the shapes they folded even achieved flight when lofted up into the rafters (the Platt-Willeys' A-frame was a log house and rustic). Ginevra wasn't sure what the Pax and Lux Festival people in British Columbia were actually going to do with the doves once they received them, but Petal didn't feel this was a bad way to spend a rainy day, engaged in mindless but pleasant work with an opportunity to chat more freely than had lately been the case at Miss Hill's house, where they were all glued to the television set hoping to catch a glimpse of Betsy's husband on The Justice Channel. Well, Petal could understand that. Her folks had been the same when she had a Pantene commercial running a couple of years ago; they'd sat through the entire Tony Awards program for her sake, waiting for her ad's premiere airing, and they weren't at all Tony people, although her father had had to admit that Bebe Neuwirth certainly was a talented girl.

Hunkering down for a good, long session—she was brewing a pot of coffee using the complicated method by which coffee was made in her parents' house and she had some shortbread baking in the wood-fired oven—Ginevra asked whether there had been any new developments on the wedding front. The subject intrigued her for so many reasons, on so many levels, some so deep down she had not yet sufficiently plumbed them.

"Miss Lily told Julie that she absolutely had to write up whatever she wants put in the newspaper for the engagement announcement. Miss Lily thinks last-minute notices look, you know, too last minute, and people get the wrong idea," Petal said. "If you know what she means. I mean, I knew what she meant, and Julie knew what she meant and she got sort of insulted, and Miss Lily said, well, it wasn't her wrong idea, but it was the Babe Palmers of the world who would get the wrong idea and why give her anything to get excited over?"

"It's very sweet of Lily to worry about appearances, in this day and age. My cousin and his wife waited to get married until their youngest son was old enough to be able to have a good time at the reception," Ginevra said. "But I wonder whether it's a crime, or at least some sort of offense, to submit a fake wedding notice, if that's what's holding Julie back."

"I'm sure that wouldn't be illegal. It would just really be sad," Petal said.

"Well, I wonder what all Julie's problem is, that she just can't give Lily something for the paper, fact *or* fiction," Ginevra mused. She tossed another origami shape onto the table to join the several dozen they had fashioned so far.

"Wouldn't something like these doves look nice at Julie's wedding? Like if we put them in all the trees? I think you could stick them onto individual leaves, with straight pins. Don't you think that'd look nice?" Petal asked. Well, she thought doves in trees would look nice even if Ginevra couldn't quite see it, although whether she was unable to picture Julie's wedding at all or was just incapable of envisioning that specific element, Petal didn't know.

"I've been keeping an eye on the clock," Ginevra said. "It takes me ninety seconds to fold a single dove, and you can do one in seventy-five seconds. Just how long is this going to take us?"

"Don't look at me. We'll have to ask Cam to do the math," Petal said. "In the meantime, I suggest we'd just better sit here until we get the job done." Ginevra agreed that was the wisest course.

NOT MANY PEOPLE WERE OUT AND ABOUT on such a stormy day. The weather was such that, even when you got where you were going, you thought twice about stepping out of the car, and the few cars that drove by the farm stand kept on driving. Raindrops dented the surface of the swollen river like hammer taps on tin. Cam said she wondered whether all the poor fish were getting wet, and Julie knew what she meant.

Some crops liked rain, and some did not. Eggplants rose in a pyramid display, beautifully shiny and black, but the raspberries had furred over with mold overnight, and Julie had thrown them all away. The Sorry All Out sign was propped in the empty space on the shelf.

Wrapped in a cardigan Lily had left behind the day before, Julie inventoried the items in the Hannah's freezer and filled out an order slip, blowing on her icy fingertips as she counted boxes and made check marks on her list. Cam set about straightening a tangle of donated plastic grocery bags, separating the Stop and Shop ones from the ones from Shaw's and from the Market Basket. She bundled the maverick bags (Osco, Blockbuster, Staples) and set them aside for emergency use only, she said.

"Thank you, Cam," Julie said after she had been bidden to admire her arrangements. "I'm not sure what else there is for you to do. There's not enough happening here to keep us both busy."

However, Cam had thought to supply herself with a tennis ball, which she produced from a back pocket, and she played a game of seven-up, bouncing the ball off an interior wall onto the hard-pack dirt floor, bouncing it again and again and again, dogged in her ambition to perform all of the prescribed seven-up maneuvers in a single, flawless sequence. One time, she got as far as six-up before she had to start all over again from one-up just because she had clapped her hands once and spun around twice before she caught the ball instead of clapping her hands twice and twirling round for a single spin.

When Mr. DeSouza stopped by with a few more bushels of corn in the back of his truck—there was a glut of corn at the moment, for it had to be picked—Julie, who could no longer abide all the thumping and clapping, asked him to drive Cam back up to the house.

"Auntie Lily will find something for you to do," she told Cam.

Cam pulled Julie's head down so she could whisper in her ear. "Mr. DeSouza doesn't like kids," she reminded Julie.

"Well," Julie could not disagree. "But it's an emergency?" she hazarded, and Cam accepted that. Off she went in the truck, where Mr. DeSouza made her sit in the front seat because there was only a front seat in Mr. DeSouza's truck. Cam worried so much about being crushed by a deploying air bag that she failed to annoy Mr. DeSouza in any of her usual ways, neither staring at him nor nervously giggling over nothing, and he only had to tell her once not to rebound her tennis ball off the dashboard.

Left on her own, Julie sat behind the counter. She pushed the jam jar bouquets out of the way; a bunch of Eden roses picked several days earlier trembled on their stems and fell apart with a flight of petals that adhered to the damp wood of the counter. They looked very bridal strewn there, Julie determined, as she set out her laptop and snapped the case open. Perhaps rose petals would put her in the mood for the task before her. She was under orders to attend to any number of deferred and neglected wedding details and decisions; Lily had embarked on rather a crusade to get things done. She had, on her own volition, paid a visit to the rector of All Saints', the Reverend Penworthy, and secured his services for the first Saturday in September. She had also committed Julie to a series of counseling sessions, marriage being a sacrament which the Episcopal church still seemed to take seriously. At present, Lily was concerned about making hotel reservations for the out-of-town guests, which, of course, was her way of nosing out information about Becky's plans without having to come right out and ask Julie about her mother. Lily was treading lightly there, but she did so like someone who had removed her shoes and yet was still betrayed by the creak of old floorboards.

Julie opened a file and retrieved the page on which she had started to draft an engagement notice the night before. She had only written, *Alden Lowe of Towne, Mass. announces . . .* and then she had not known what she was supposed to say about her mother. She had given up and gone to bed to read a very interesting book by two English lady academics who were convinced they had encountered Marie Antoinette while on a visit to Versailles in 1901. Julie wasn't sure just what had happened to the women; she accepted the ladies' versions when they told of their experience, yet she found herself nodding at the naysayers' footnotes, which proposed a very different explanation for the events the women described. Oh, but people were so willing to believe what they wanted to, she was well aware.

Having resolved to get it over with, Julie swiftly typed, *Alden Lowe of Towne, Mass. and Rebecca Baskett of Misratah, Libya, announce . . .* No, that would not do, linking her parents like that. They had not acted in concert over anything for years. She moved the cursor and inserted a comma. *Alden Lowe of Towne, Mass., and Rebecca Baskett of Misratah, Libya, announce . . .* but she saw at once that a mere comma could not begin to acknowledge the gulf that existed between her parents. Furthermore, neither parent was actually announcing anything. That burden had fallen upon her shoulders, along with everything else, and she decided to take a different tack. She tapped out, *Julie Lowe is to be married . . .*

And then, there was the matter of her own name. She was, in fact, also a Rebecca, or Becky, or Little Becky really, but she'd always hated being Little Becky and she had taken to calling herself Julie and refused to answer to anything else for the past nine years. Nevertheless, the change had never been made official, and when she signed stuff (contracts and leases and the like), she remained Rebecca.

She typed this: *"Julie" Lowe . . .* which struck her as looking slightly shady.

She typed this: *Julie (Rebecca) Lowe . . .* and she decided she liked that version, with the Rebecca side of herself acknowledged, but sitting on the page looking contained and incidental.

She continued to type: *Julie (Rebecca) Lowe, who is the daughter of Alden Lowe of Towne, Mass., as well as Rebecca Baskett of Misratah, Libya, is to be married to . . .*

Yes, she thought, that would do. The phrasing was awkward, perhaps, but then the entire situation was messy. That "as well as" referenced all sorts of imperfectly repressed wellings-up, in her opinion, and let the readers of the Social Notes page in the *Crier* stumble and wonder over her announcement.

She went on: *. . . is to be married to Nicholas Davenant, son of Mr. and Mrs. . . .*

Her fingers stalled again on the keyboard. She had no first name for

Mr. Davenant. How was she supposed to know? Was it reasonable to expect young people in love to sit down and compare their family trees?

"HOW DO YOU THINK THE TRIAL IS GOING?" Lily asked Louis. Lily, Louis, Ginger, and Betsy were in the little parlor watching The Justice Channel's coverage of the case against the Third Day Brethren. Sally came and went; her fascination with seeing her father on television had waned, for Andy was only fleetingly on view when the camera happened to take in a wide shot of the defense table. He never got to stand up and talk, and the people who did speak never said anything interesting. Their long and complicated words glanced off her ears even when she really tried to hear them, and Louis said he hoped for Andy's sake that the defense had seated a jury full of Sallys, who would sit there yawning and fiddling and irresistibly following the flight of any bumblebee trapped behind a courthouse window.

"I still don't know who I'm rooting for," Ginger said. "Because I'm very certain that peculiar man stole all that gold, but since Andy's on his team, so to speak, am I very wrong to hope the accused gets away with it?"

"Andy's real role will come into play after there's been a conviction. He'll try to have the sentence mitigated by placing the crime within the larger context of the Brethren's belief system," Betsy said. She sat on the hassock beside Ginger, who lay upon the sofa, propped on pillows and covered with a light blanket. Betsy picked up the cup of broth Ginger had set down upon the hassock and forgotten about. She offered the cup to her mother, who shook her head.

"Here, Sally," Betsy said. "Granna doesn't want any more of this now. Take it to the kitchen and cover it with plastic and put it in the refrigerator, please."

Sally rose from the floor in front of the TV where she had just flopped herself down, positioned to reach up to touch the screen with a fingertip wherever her father's image appeared. She accepted the cup, aware that she was continuing her morning's work of being helpful and good. Just lately, she and Lily had had a long talk in the herb garden about what an important contribution Sally was making to the household, which Lily hoped Sally knew was very much appreciated even if sometimes the grown-ups forgot to thank her. But then again, the satisfaction of knowing oneself to be behaving well should be reward enough, Lily had gone on to explain, and Sally had told her about a certain sensation of lightness and happiness located just behind her rib cage which she associated with the knowledge that she had just done something good. Yes, Lily agreed, that was probably an example of what she was talking about, that rather glowing feeling Sally had just described.

Buoyed along by the very idea of herself, Sally skipped across the center hall. The broth swirled in the cup and a spurt of soup erupted from the depths of the eddy and splashed over her hand, which she licked clean as she walked on more circumspectly.

In the kitchen, she busied herself tearing plastic from the roller and taking too much but, entrusted to safeguard her grandmother's half-consumed snack, she wished to do the job thoroughly. She wrapped the see-through plastic round and round until the cup beneath could no longer be seen.

"What are you doing here?" Cam asked her. She had been standing just inside the back door, dripping in her yellow slicker and watching Sally for the past few minutes, mulling over this development. "You're not in California," she accused her.

"Yes, I am," Sally said.

"No, you're not," said Cam.

"I mean, I just got back," Sally said.

Cam slid out of her slicker and rendered her opinion of Sally's alleged adventures with the motion of a single shrug. She did not necessarily not believe Sally, but she refused to be interested one way or another. She hung her slicker from the low hook, which she considered to be her own. In order to do this, she had transferred Sally's slicker to a different peg.

They mooched around the kitchen for a while. They fooled with the egg timer, playing a game they had invented which mandated the completion of a task before the timer, set at sixty seconds, pinged. *Quick*, exchange the contents of the apron drawer with the contents of the dish towel drawer. *Quick*, eat ten Saltines and then whistle. *Quick*, put Agnes's Meow Mix box upside down on the cupboard shelf and slide your fingers underneath to open the top flaps so all the food would fall out when the next person reached for it. After that, they ran out of good ideas, and the balance of the day stretched before them needing to be filled with incidents and amusements.

"Auntie Lily says rainy days are made for reading," Cam recalled.

"Aunt Lily says rainy afternoons are made for reading. This is a rainy morning," Sally said.

ALDEN DROPPED BY WITH A QUESTION for Lily concerning the status of the wedding plans, about which he remained largely in the dark. Nevertheless, he wanted to give her some money, for he felt all of this ought to be costing him something. Tommy, who accompanied him, had bolted from his side and tracked down the group in the little parlor, and a chorus of greetings (Louis in particular was taken with what a good dog Tommy was) told Alden where everyone was. He stepped out of his wet moccasins; he'd been standing just inside the front door, adhering to a square of old carpet and waiting to see whether he could conduct his business from there, having inquired, "Lily?" rather cautiously, not wanting to disturb Ginger were she resting. Evidently she was not; he could hear her voice extravagantly praising Tommy, telling him how very, very handsome he was.

Lily, looking weary, was reclining in the Barcalounger. Ginger was stretched out on the sofa underneath a blanket, and Louis sat at the end with her feet propped on his knees. Tommy pressed against the sofa cushions longing to hop up there and wedge himself between those two warm people, but Betsy, now seated on the floor below her mother, held him by the collar as he continued to strain and yearn toward Ginger. They were all far more interested in what was occurring on the television screen than in finding out what Alden wanted. He was only briefly acknowledged; indeed, Ginger waved him out of her line of sight, and fearing that some fresh disaster must have just occurred somewhere in the world to so transfix them, Alden asked, "What has happened?" He dropped onto the desk chair and hitched it toward the TV prepared to be shown the worst.

"Supporters of the defendant are shouting scripture and throwing dirt on their heads," Louis told him. "A brief recess has been called, and the demonstrators are about to be escorted from the courtroom."

"Ah. That," said Alden. He'd not forgotten about Andy's trial but he'd not been following it since the boys had taken off for California. They had very much enjoyed the proceedings, which they'd been watching on the flat screen TV they suspended from the side of the Winnebago. They had lounged on chaises lined up beneath an awning and played a game which required them to swallow a slug of tequila every time someone asked, "May I approach the bench?"

"So then we have to approach the bar, Dad," as Brooks had explained.

"But really, Betsy," Ginger was saying, "when you talk to Andy tonight, remember to tell him that it can't be a very good idea for the followers of someone who stands accused of digging a tunnel to rob a bank vault to be seen in possession of so much dirt to throw on their heads. It's entirely too suggestive."

"That's exactly what I was thinking. I'm sure the jury can't help but wonder where they got all the dirt," Betsy said. She held up a glass of water inquiringly, and Ginger took a sip through the straw. Tommy watched, his tail thumping.

Alden had brought his check ledger with him, which he now spread open across the desktop. "Lily," he said. "What have you spent so far on Julie's wedding? Tell me what I owe you." He uncapped his fountain pen.

"You don't owe me anything," Lily said.

"No, I insist," Alden said.

"But no one's spent anything," Lily said. "Julie still hasn't found a dress she likes. And she says she's going to pick flowers from the gardens for her bouquet. She seems to assume that Ginevra will provide the music, though I'm not sure she's informed Ginevra of that. She says everyone takes so many photos and movies these days that she doesn't need a professional photographer. Hannah has volunteered to cater as her gift to Julie, but Julie won't commit to a menu. She keeps saying every dish Hannah proposes sounds just fine to her, which of course leaves Hannah nowhere." That Lily could so fluently reel off the status of the arrangements betrayed how they occupied her mind; she'd never known such a casual bride as her grand-niece.

"Well, I'm glad she's not fussing you," Alden said, and Lily didn't attempt to explain to him that fusses went with the territory, whereas Julie was displaying what she regarded as an eerie calm, while Lily herself was growing increasingly leery that all of this was going to come off in any coherent way. She could only imagine Julie sending out for Chinese food on the big day, after she got a head count of those who had stuck around following the ceremony to which, presumably, they had been summoned by a last-minute e-mail message.

"Suppose I leave you a pile of blank checks," Alden said. "I'll sign a bunch and leave them here under the blotter."

"As you wish," Lily said. She motioned to Betsy; Ginger's blanket had slipped to the floor, and Tommy was treading it into a bed for himself.

Above all, Alden had intended to ask Lily whether there had been any word from Becky in regard to her plans. Had he gotten Lily alone, had she answered his call from the front door and come to speak to him as he stood in his wet mocs, adhering to the carpet square, he would have mentioned Becky after he'd concluded the other matter about money, presenting the query as a mere afterthought that had struck him on his way out. "Oh, by the way," he would have prefaced his question and he'd have gone off into the rain with his answer, whatever the answer was to be. Even to be told that the matter remained unresolved would have been sufficient. The day's great achievement, in his view, would have been to have asked at all.

JULIE RECKONED SHE HAD MADE enough progress on her announcement to be able to report somewhat truthfully to Lily that she had only to add a few finishing touches to the text. She wished Lily wouldn't work herself up into a tizzy in regard to these small details. She had always credited her aunt with possessing an infallible sense of what really mattered, and upon reflection (the lulling thrum of rain upon the farm stand roof encouraged meditation), Julie supposed that all this agitation about dresses and flowers and alerting the media stood to express another anxiety entirely, and one which Julie shared to such a degree that nothing needed to be said on the subject.

Then again, there was that one thing to be brooded over. A record of correspondence about the wedding between Julie and her mother had accumulated over the past weeks, which Julie now summoned with the press of a key; a scroll of messages and replies resolved across the screen of her laptop. Julie was reminded of the court case playing itself out upon the little parlor TV of which she had caught snatches. Her mother could not answer a simple question with a simple yes or no. One had to study the transcript to determine just what had been confessed and what had been denied, and so it was in a prosecutorial mood that Julie reviewed the record:

Dear Ma, I am writing to you with exciting news. I am going to be married. The wedding is going to take place at the end of the summer. Aunt Lily says of course I can use the field and she has already been rifling the china cupboard, looking for bud vases and punch cups and this really awful bride and groom cake topper—the groom's face is all disintegrating and indistinct. I think someone shoe-polished in his hair at some point. I don't know whose it was—yours, everybody's? Well, it's seen a lot of action, tfs.

Oh, I should tell you about the guy. It was all rather sudden, deciding to get married, just before I took off for the States. Total whirlwind. Hard to believe, actually, but still— His name is Nicholas Davenant and he is a geologist at present prospecting for new sources of oil in Siberia (watch out, Libya!). It is very hard to describe him. I'd reference my "feeble pen" and its inadequacies, were I using a pen—but I believe he is everything you would hope him to be for me. Well, I don't know who'll be more surprised at the end of the summer when all of this comes to the boil. Everyone's going to be here, Glover, Brooks, Rollins. Everyone. Betsy and her family too. (Oh, I'll tell you all about her little girl at another time—I can't say she's all that pretty, which was a surprise when you consider Betsy and Aunt Ginger.)

Anyway, the wedding will be on Sept. 4, so I am giving you ample time to make all your arrangements for getting here in time. You may notice how calmly and confidently I am assuming you will be present. I refuse to countenance difficulties—they are all in your mind—you can choose whether or not to entertain them. Of course you'll find a way to come. You have to be here.

Dear Julie, What extraordinary news. I am of course so very happy and I long to meet the young man who has won your heart. Please give me more details, however awkwardly expressed. I myself just went a bit B. Cartland, with that "won your heart" remark. "And of His sign that He creates for you mates out of yourselves, so that you may find tranquility in them, and He has planted love and kindness in your hearts." There, perhaps the Prophet Muhammed can better express what I feel.

My dear, I have begun to actively look into the possibility of being there with you. As you are aware, such an undertaking is very involved, and all of one's ducks must be in a row. The appropriate agencies have been consulted, and we must hope for the best. In the meantime, I long to hear of all of your plans. Make me feel as if I am there. I want to know everything.

You did not ask how William is but you must remain aware that many things depend upon his condition and the course of his recovery which at present is going slowly . . .

. . . How is William? Of course I hope and pray he is improving every day.

Initial inquiries raise definite red flag about the certainty of my being allowed back into Libya.

I'll have Uncle Harvey ask his congressman pal to lean on somebody . . .

I am very much afraid American congressmen hold no sway here.

I am sure they will let you back into their country. Really, that's just an excuse. If you are worried about seeing everyone, please don't worry. A lot of time has passed. . . .

I would stare down bears for your sake; that is not the problem.

There is no need to bring bears into this if you think everyone's claws will be out and there will be roaring. I mean, Dad will be just fine. He practically has a girlfriend these days. Remember Hannah?

Yes, Hannah, what a lovely person she was. But are you really sure about Nicholas? You still haven't told me much about him. Your reticence on the subject has me concerned. No one knows better than I the consequences of making a mistake in the matter of marriage. Please tell me more about him.

What do you want to know about him? Fire away.

Where did he attend university? What interests do you have in common? Do you agree upon politics, for example?

Oxford. We are interested in each other. Yes; we both like Tony Blair and, oh yeah, moonlit walks along the beach. But please do not change the subject. Have you booked your flight?

Tripoli is sitting on the necessary paperwork. But please do not change the subject. I am very fond of Tony Blair myself, but one cannot base an entire marriage upon—

Julie welcomed the interruption when a car pulled up to the farm stand. Mr. Penworthy, the rector of All Saints', emerged from his VW. Hatless, he was one of those individuals who seemed to think one could run between the raindrops if enough evasive maneuvers were made. He professed pleasure at finding Julie, for he had driven out this way specifically to see her and to pick up some lettuce while he was at it.

"These'll do," Julie said, dropping two green heads into a plastic bag, feeling free to adjudge the requirements (Boston and curly) of the Penworthy household. She had already crammed in the three requisite premarriage counseling sessions Lily's interference had let her in for, dropping by the rectory on successive nights, an intensification of the usual schedule, which had forged a bond of sorts. "Here's Julie," Timothy Penworthy had called into his father's study when Julie appeared at the door on the third evening, and he had lingered then to ask her about the VeeCube and her brothers and whether it was really true they were paying David May and Jason Schmitt and Matthew Cavalieri to play video games all summer to test them for GLowe Systems. David and Jason and Matt had been going all over Towne bragging they were working for Brooks and Rollins, but no one believed them.

"Well, it's true," Julie said. "They're drawing paychecks and having teleconferences with the Vee team and they want to drop out of junior high school and move to Montecito, but none of their parents will allow it."

Seated in the rectory parlor, Julie had clutched a *Christian Marriage* pamphlet and gazed at the drawing of the happy young couple that must have been gracing the front cover for the past decades, the two of them spending a quiet evening at home, conferring over which LP to place upon the hi-fi turntable. Mr. Penworthy's eye had caught Julie's, and he saw they were thinking the same thing. "Those old-style LPs remind me of the giant currency they have on Yap Island," Julie said. "I always used to worry my parents would move us there and I'd have to trundle my allowance around in a wheelbarrow." Then again, Mr. Penworthy allowed, perhaps their thoughts were not running along parallel lines.

Julie seemed forlorn in a way he could not specify, but there were several good reasons, that summer, for her to be dispirited, which had nothing to do with the subject under discussion. However, when he asked her whether she had any particular questions, she had answered, "No, no, Mr. Penworthy, not about this," and his answering query, "Anything else?" had (rather stubbornly) been taken for an offer of more iced coffee, his wife having left a pitcher on the coffee table, along with a plate of fig squares she had baked.

Julie had done her best to speak for her absent intended, but the rector wondered just how meaningfully the young couple had discussed their future together. Julie's representations on her betrothed's behalf needed fleshing out before Mr. Penworthy could be entirely satisfied he had done his duty by the pair, and at the conclusion of the final session, he had asked Julie how he might best get in touch with Nicholas to continue the conversation. Julie explained that the oil prospecting expedition had recently moved to an even more remote encampment, which was incommunicado from the rest of the world but for a helicopter that came and went dropping off supplies and mail according to no fixed schedule. Mr. Penworthy had said in that case he would "set a paper" for Nicholas, and so he had done, inviting the groom to concur with or to refute or merely to demonstrate an understanding of a selection of essays and statements and verses, scriptural or otherwise, which spoke of wedlock and companionship and love. He had thoughtfully included a blue book and a No. 2 pencil—he had gathered that the groom was a studious type, Julie having attributed to him an active "life of the mind," as she put it—and he felt the young man could settle down and apply himself better amidst all of the distractions of the vast Siberian wilderness, were he to find himself in possession of the usual test-taking tools. However, there could be no wrong answers on this particular examination, although the possibility existed for the submission of some troubling ones.

Mr. Penworthy stood before the farm stand counter and shook himself off. Then he showed Julie a large manila envelope stoutly taped along every seam and he asked for Nicholas's address at that remote Siberian encampment. The rector's next stop today was going to be the post office.

"Oh gosh," Julie said. "It's such a complicated address, all consonants and diacritical marks. You know how when you can't even pronounce something, it's impossible to keep it in your head—but I've got everything written down up at the house. Leave the envelope with me, and I'll see to it." Mr. Penworthy contained his disappointment, for he'd been looking forward to causing a stir at the post office, showing up with a parcel destined for such a remote corner of the world. Nevertheless, he could not send Julie running up to the house for her address book. She had the farm stand to mind and, besides, she'd been leaning over her laptop when he arrived, obviously deep in thought. He'd leave her to her musings. He gathered up his bag of lettuces.

"I've advised Nicholas that he can drop his responses off at the rectory when he arrives in Towne at the end of the summer. I look forward to meeting him," he said.

"Okay, so you're not looking for a reply in the meanwhile?" Julie asked, just to make sure.

"No, no, you needn't chivvy your young man along on my account," Mr. Penworthy said. As he took his leave, he noticed how distinguished the bank of eggplants looked; their purple-black hue was decidedly ecclesiastical, the color to which a bishop's robes faded as both the man and the cloth grew ancient together. He would have bought one, not to consume, but just to keep on his desk as an object of contemplation, had Julie not already forgotten all about him and returned to her study of her laptop screen.

You did not ask how William is. He continues to suffer from the aftermath of his terrible accident.

. . . So Ma. Tell me. How is Wm. doing? Has the feeling returned to his feet?

ANDY APPEARED BRIEFLY ON CAMERA, massaging shuttered eyes with his thumb and index finger. The defendant was just settling himself into the witness box, and Andy could not bring himself to watch.

"Darling Andy, he told the defense team not to put the accused on the stand under any circumstances," Betsy said, and Ginger patted her shoulder.

Nevertheless, Ginger always found trials in which the villain did not take the stand in their own defense to be unsatisfying, all chorus and no star turn; one wanted one's money back. That last time she and Louis had indulged in a New York theater week, she'd felt very let down by one notable no-show even as her heart had gone out to the understudy, who must have heard the grumble of disappointment that had greeted the announcement of his last-minute assumption of the role. Although upon reflection she had posited that a person in the arts had to possess the hide of an elephant and the ego of a peacock and would relish any opportunity to shine, however come by, and perhaps even go so far as to hope for an illness or an accident or a death in the family of the leading actor to occur at some time during the course of the run, and even if Ginger could not definitely impute an active desire on the part of the stand-in for something unfortunate to happen in the life of the greater name, she had supposed the understudy's heart had leapt rather than fallen upon being informed of the event. All in all, Ginger had not responded simply to the absence of the starry personage she had hoped to see; still, she was inclined to believe that her mind would not have wandered so widely along those other lines during the performance were the featured, listed player shining forth up there on the stage.

Lily signaled to Betsy; Ginger had slipped down among her pillows, and Betsy restacked and plumped them. Tommy tried to leap onto the sofa and rearrange himself among the cushions, offering his own back as something for Ginger to lean upon, but Louis caught him by the collar and scrubbed him under the chin, which induced a sort of ecstasy in the dog, who strained against Louis's knee seeking more of the same attention.

Alden observed that the fellow who had just entered the witness box looked like an awful ruffian, and he said he failed to see how anyone could follow him anywhere, let alone to an armed compound in backwoods Montana. Betsy said that as Andy had explained it to her, criminals were often very charismatic people; they felt that they were above and beyond the laws which keep the rest of us in check, and these inflated self-estimations were picked up on by others, who took these charming individuals at their own value. Alden said he'd never thought of it that way but it made sense, and he grew thoughtful.

"Well, psychopaths give charming people such a bad name," Ginger complained.

The front doorbell jangled and Betsy went to admit the visiting nurse, who was dropping by every day now. Betsy led Norma back to the little parlor, where Norma watched the trial for a few interested minutes, hoping to catch a glimpse of Andy; catching a glimpse of Andy seemed to have become part of the program here, and she kindly attended to the TV even as she noted Ginger's color and posture and assessed her level of engagement with all that was going on around her. Then Andy appeared on camera for the better part of ten seconds as he clicked open his briefcase and extracted a document which he shot down the table to the lead attorney, who had momentarily lost his train of thought as he interrogated his own witness. The defendant had departed from the script when fashioning a reply. Norma said Andy was wearing a particularly nice tie that day which, if Lily's TV color was properly adjusted, looked to be blue.

"Now, if I may just steal my patient for a minute," she added and she got Ginger to her feet and led her across the hall to the big parlor. Tommy crept onto the vacated end of the sofa, where he would keep Ginger's space warm, everyone said, and his tail began to thump when he understood he was not going to be shooed from his spot.

When the prosecuting attorney asked permission to approach the bench, Alden thought of his boys and their drinking game and he decided he half felt like having a drink himself. Lily sighed as deeply as Alden, although for a different reason; she had wanted rain, but not an entire week of foul weather. Julie had put Sally and Cam up to doing a little rain dance one afternoon, after Lily had remarked how worrisomely dry the summer had been up until that point. Julie stuck grackles' feathers in the little girls' hair and marked their cheeks and foreheads with bars of red lipstick and showed them how to prance round in a circle while bowing and leaping and saying, "Woo, woo, woo." Lily supposed she ought not to have laughed at Julie's ceremony; perhaps her niece had known what she was doing. She may have come across some ancient parchment in one of those museums of hers and learned some ancient mystery.

"What now?" Louis asked as the judge beckoned the opposing counsel to come join in the discussion, and he and Lily and Betsy and

Alden speculated uninformedly, basing their conjectures upon the body language of the conferees (prosecutorial and defensive postures in evidence) until both teams of lawyers were rounded up and ushered into the judge's chambers, and The Justice Channel ran a backlog of commercial messages, most of which touted prescription medicines to alleviate any number of only hinted-at conditions. As Lily remarked, one should be grateful not to have been told outright what the diseases were, the intimations being dire enough.

Betsy thought that Norma and her mother were taking longer than usual that day to conduct their business and, concerned, she excused herself and knocked on the double doors of the big parlor, which had been imperfectly pulled shut so that, through a gap, she could view the patient and nurse, who were at present looking at family pictures, a number of which stood upon a velvet cloth–draped table, mounted within frames in sore need of dusting. Ginger blew upon surfaces, raising little clouds as she picked up one or another likeness, and, prompted by Norma's questions, she explained who had been whom and remembered this or that about them, offering recollections of a mild and minor nature, so different from the usual tales of past battles and strange behaviors she had formerly relished in the retelling. Ginger and Norma were discussing old Grandmother Hill, Ginger holding her picture up to what light that was available beyond the rain-streaked window in an attempt to determine the era of the wallpaper in the background, which would give her a clue to the identity of the squalling infant being balanced on that unaccommodating lap. Ginger had previously insisted to Betsy that the baby had been herself and that Grandmother Hill surely must have just dropped her (Look, is that a bruise on my head, or a shadow?) or left a diaper safety pin unclasped and sticking into her side, which proved that from the beginning there had only been ill will and loathing there.

"My grandmother always smelled of violets," Ginger was telling Norma, which was news to Betsy. "And she was very fond of peppermints. Anything peppermint appealed to her."

"She looks so sweet and old-fashioned," Norma murmured, and Ginger made a little sound of agreement. Since when had her mother started to like all these dead people, Betsy wondered, and though she had not always bought the former characterization of her great-grandmother, she wasn't convinced by this rosy new version either, but when she pushed through the door and began to object, "Mummy, I thought you despised her," Norma, used to moments like these, cut Betsy's objection off by asking Ginger, "*Who* is this handsome man?"

"Wasn't he attractive? That's Great-Uncle Howard," Ginger said, and she picked up that photograph huffing at the dust on the frame and holding him toward what light there was, for a closer look.

SALLY AND CAM MOVED QUIETLY through the front hall, shushing and pushing each other as they passed the door of the little parlor undetected; everyone was turned toward the television set. But adults had a way of becoming arbitrarily demanding, and neither Sally nor Cam had any wish to be caught empty-handed, so to speak, and then stand accused of having nothing better to do than to interrupt the grown-ups' important attendance on the trial. Inconvenient children would be sent to the barn where they could stay out of trouble culling the rusty string beans from the good string beans. (For Lily had been going on about those beans to everyone; she would just be looking for an excuse to trap a couple of unwilling workers in her snare.)

They grabbed the newel post and swung themselves onto the stairway, which they climbed with elaborate demonstrations of just how quiet they could be. Sally crouched and crept; Cam sat down on the bottom step and, remaining sedent, hitched herself up and up from tread to tread. At the top, they startled Agnes, who was coiled in sleep on the lid of the blanket chest; she jumped up and stalked off to a less discoverable resting place beneath Lily's bed.

"I think it is awful how Agnes sticks her nose under her tail when she sleeps," Sally said.

"I know," said Cam.

They made their way to Sally's bedroom, which Sally had turned into her own little lair over the past weeks. She'd been collecting rocks and feathers, which she arranged on the windowsill, the rocks anchoring the feathers by their shafts. One fine day, she and Julie (just them) had taken a trip to the Plimouth Plantation, and Julie had bought her the Tabletop Nine Pins game that they sold in the gift shop there; it was either that or a Pilgrim Girl bonnet, and now the nine pins were always set up in anticipation of a game. Sally had been drawing a lot of pictures, having come to believe that she could draw exceptionally well (local landscapes were a specialty); the best ones were masking-taped to her walls, and since Sally looked upon all of her work as her best, the walls were covered. Her dolls had been sitting slumped and largely ignored on their shelf. Sometimes she felt sorry for them and allowed one or another to accompany her down to the farm stand or into the woods, where Tianna the Tooth Fairy got herself lost. Lily said she must have met up with some of her own kind and gone off to live with them, and Sally had decided to accept that explanation; otherwise the loss threatened to be a very sad one. She wished Tianna hadn't been wearing her crown, though, when she went away. Her Twist 'n Turn Barbie doll would have been next in line to be promoted to princess, were the tiara still available.

Cam gave a nod to the bureau-top shrine, acknowledging Sally's yellow Play-Doh Buddha, and she stood by respectfully as Sally, who was denied candles and matches, flicked on a pencil-thin flashlight. She had fashioned a flame of red tissue paper wrapped around the bulb end but she had yet to come up with a way to create smoke without fire. She wagged her fingers in the air and said, "Woo-oo," which was the best she could do to effect the mystic connection between earth and sky sans smoke.

"There," she said, and she shot a sharp look at Cam, who sometimes tried to conduct business of her own here at Sally's altar; if there was something Cam wanted, she could ask her own guy back at the Casa di Napoli.

They flung themselves upon the bed, which skidded and thumped against the wall. Cam slipped Sally's copy of *The Lion, the Witch and the Wardrobe* from beneath the pillow. A braided bookmark dangled from the spine; beads, worked into the plait, clicked.

"We cannot read in the morning," Sally reminded her.

"I don't want to read it. I have read it over and over," Cam said. "Now I think I would rather *be* the lion, but not the witch and the wardrobe, and I'd like to be Peter and Susan and Lucy, but not Edward," she declared.

"What? How?" asked Sally. She was shoving the leg of her Strawberry Shortcake pajamas back under the pillow, disowning them, for they were childish.

"Julie says that what a wardrobe is in England is a closet in America," Cam said. "She told me."

Sally understood at once what Cam was driving at, and they raced each other to Sally's closet. Cam got there first and wrenched open the door, which allowed Sally to slither through ahead of her. They trampled the shoes on the floor, which leaped up and kicked back at them, and they batted through a tangle of shirts and skirts and dresses. The closet was a small one, and wedge shaped, and they crammed themselves into an interior corner, their shoulders pushing and pushing, their cheeks crushed against cool, chalky plaster.

"Not this one," Sally spoke through the side of her mouth.

"Auntie Lily's room," Cam declared, as if that should have been obvious to them in the first place.

They sprinted down the hallway and tore into Lily's closet, flurrying her pressed and serried garments, causing the hangers to squeal along the rod with the sound of something happening. The little girls slammed themselves, with every expectation, against solid wall. Sally, who had decided on her own that the preferred method called for diving headfirst into Narnia, fell back and buried her stinging face in the soft plush and powder scent of Lily's bathrobe, which hung from a hook. She arranged the sleeves around her neck like a stole and adjusted the mirror-backed door so she could see how nice she looked. Cam stepped into Lily's sheared sheepskin slippers (a gift from Ginger) and joined Sally at the mirror to admire herself. If worse came to worst, they could devote the rest of the day to playing dress-up, and thinking along those lines (of high heels and white gloves and hats with brims and ribbons), Cam recalled, "In the book in the closet they had fur coats."

"Which turned into fur trees in the woods in Narnia," Sally remembered. Whenever Lily read the story aloud to her, she looked up and smiled and made of point of saying again, "fur trees," inviting Sally to imagine what those would be like. Sally considered a moment, and then she said, "But I know where all the fur coats are kept."

Heretofore, Cam had resented Sally's full-time residence in Lily's house, and Sally had lorded her advantage. (She knew where the Oreos were hidden in an upper kitchen cabinet, and she would retrieve them only when Cam had covered her eyes.) Now, however, Cam was glad that certain solitary prowls had taken place and borne this fruit, as Sally, being a bit officious with her shushes (for who was there to hear them?) led her up the attic stairs. At the top, they barged through the plank door and into a corridor which was crowded with more doors and the shrouded shapes of unrelated objects stacked in transfiguring arrangements: a sofa table, a hassock, and a music stand draped with a sheet made a camel; a cheval mirror propped in an armchair and flung over with a blanket looked like someone sitting there being sad. The drenched daylight spilling through smeared and distant windows was dim and only aided these visions.

Sally studied the doors and selected one. They entered a room tucked beneath the eaves where the roof came down low and almost met the floor, a dimension instantly attractive to small children; two hands shot up and irresistibly tagged the ceiling. They looked about the room to fix its elements in their minds so they would know they had come back to the right place upon their eventual return. A camp bed without a mattress, a marble-topped table that tilted, a treadle-foot sewing machine, and a bamboo bookcase with shelves too narrow to hold books any way but sideways—these signposts were made sure of and remembered. The closet, to which they then turned, was fronted by another plank door secured with a wrought iron latch which would not budge until Cam struck it a glancing blow with a flatiron that suddenly came to hand.

The fur coats were suspended along a rod, just as Sally said, svelte pelts and scruffy ones, crinose and shaved, with long cuffed sleeves and shawl collars and lovely frog fasteners. The coats were lined with satin, or satin tatters and shreds, and several silk scarves, worn the last time, dangled from pockets and collars and sleeves, pretty once and pretty even now.

Cam caught the waistband of Sally's shorts with a restraining finger, believing they should both pause and think for a moment. She pointed out that the book said it would be winter when they got where they were going and she thought they each ought to select one of the coats to wear. At the very least, they should leave a note where someone would find it, atop Lily's pillow or on the kitchen table secured beneath a jar of honey, she suggested.

"But in the book they were only gone a minute," Sally said. "There won't be any time for them to miss us."

"But in the book they were gone for years where they were," Cam said.

"Julie said Narnia years are our minutes; I asked her why Susan and Lucy and Peter didn't grow old," Sally said, and she hitched herself free of Cam's hold and plunged in among the coats.

"Wait up," Cam cried as she followed. "Can't you?"

The closet proved to be a deep one. The assembled coats pitched and grabbed at them with their empty arms to keep them from going forward, but the little girls fought on with fervor and battled their way beyond only to smack into a second barrier, which at first seemed solid against their pressing and pushing but then suddenly proved to be not so impenetrable after all. Surfaces turned soft and the wall began to sway, and when shoved and rammed at further, this obstacle melted and parted to allow them to slither through a slot so narrow that a breath could neither be drawn nor expelled, which somehow only seemed the correct phenomenon to be occurring as one passed from this world to the other, to cease to be (for a bit) in the interim. But no sooner had they emerged, restored to respiration and reaching for each other so that neither would be first into Narnia (or perhaps each wished to make sure she would not be entering Narnia alone), yet another impediment reared before them and this was one that would not yield to the force of their shoulders and pounding of their fists at any point, high or low, along its length.

"Was this part in the book?" Cam asked, which set them off arguing whose fault it was that they had forgotten to bring the book with them to consult along the way. Cam pointed out that since the missing volume in question belonged to Sally, it had been up to her to remember, which made unanswerable sense to Sally, who, in lieu of framing a rebuttal, reeled away and flung herself at the obstructing surface one final time (after which she intended to fall down and cry with frustration). However, as her head banged against the wall, her cheek struck the projecting lever of a latch, and the glancing impact released a door which creaked ajar on stiff hinges.

"Wait," advised Cam, and she and Sally peered out into a small and shadowy room that contained a desk missing its drawers and a table lamp without a shade and a pillar of brick chimney. Rain drummed on the roof, and water seeped through the roof in the vicinity of the chimney; tea-colored drops trembled, clutching the ceiling as if too frightened to fall so far to the floor.

"Flip," muttered Sally as Cam, who was taking a few seconds longer to realize where they were, inquired, "Mr. Tumnus?" with her faintest voice, not wishing to be answered but knowing that she had to ask, like questioning Who's there? when it was late at night and she heard something crash downstairs in the empty restaurant.

Nevertheless, Sally and Cam turned to each other, prepared to be convinced that something had almost happened to them just now. They did not believe that any kids had come closer than they had to reaching Narnia, at least not since the book.

"Maybe next time Petal can go with us," Cam said. With the experience safely behind her, she was willing to try again; only she thought next time they each ought to wear a fur coat and pack a picnic lunch and persuade an amenable adult to join the expedition.

"Or David May can come instead of Petal," Sally suggested.

"Yes, because he is a boy," Cam agreed. "That would probably be better."

They then conducted a postmission review, inspecting the opposite side of the closet they had just passed through. The soft-sided and yielding interior wall proved to consist of two garment bags, tightly crammed together, and Sally got busy tugging at a long balky zipper as Cam knelt and held the bottom of the bag taut to keep the teeth from entangling with the facing as Sally worked the zipper all the way down.

They delved and probed among an assortment of itchy wool jackets and itchy wool trousers and itchy wool skirts, dragging them from their hangers and tossing them onto the floor after they held the clothes up to their shoulders or waists, although upon inspection some of the buttons proved to be very nice little knots of leather or discs of shiny brass embossed with crests and crowns, and one of the jackets held a note in its pocket which read *3 o'clock, Friday.* Sally and Cam wondered whether they should tell somebody about this, but who to tell and how to explain the circumstances of the note's discovery was too complicated to work out, and besides, Sally had come upon a highly interesting dress jammed into the back of the bag. She slapped Cam away from the emerging prize, a longer-and-longer-growing dress of white and shimmering fabric trimmed with lace and beading and a satin ribbon sash.

Cam tried to tell Sally that this wonderful white dress must belong to the White Witch, but Sally had instantly forgotten all that Narnia business. Obviously, this was a wedding dress, and she was aware that over the past weeks a great deal of discussion had been devoted to the subject of wedding dresses and whether Julie would ever make up her mind over which one to buy, and if not, she would have to be married in her underwear, as Ginger predicted. Sally had been horrified on Julie's behalf at that prospect. Obviously, this was the dress, the very dress that had been missing all summer and that nobody else had been able to find except for her and which must immediately be presented to Julie.

AS GINEVRA FLEXED HER FINGERS before she began to fold and crease yet another dove shape, she decided she and Petal were like the cigarette-factory girls in *Carmen*, their repetitive work of manipulating scraps of white paper made more interesting by a flow of gossip about boyfriends. However, she did not mention this thought, which had visited her in one of those illuminative moments when art can be applied to a real-life situation, for she knew she would become mired down in an explanation about gypsies and toreadors and old Seville, and she did not wish to distract Petal from the subject under discussion at present. Petal was allowing herself to be drawn out further on the subject of Glover's requirements in a yet-to-be-purchased house, which so evidently had not been met by the dwelling viewed in California the previous afternoon. Ginevra had asked whether anything had been said about the number of sinks in the master bathroom, and, getting back to the kitchen, had anything been said about a preference for an electric oven for baking with a gas-fired cooktop for sautéing? And had Glover expressed strong feelings (as relayed by Rollins during the course of what must have been a very long phone call) over the matter of local recreational opportunities? Must there be a canoeable river, a walkable woods, a vibrant musical scene nearby? I really don't know, Petal kept repeating.

"Did he say anything about wanting to have some sort of folly on the grounds, you know, like a gazebo or a grotto or a teahouse, or anything?" Ginevra wondered.

"Well, he prefers a detached garage," Petal said. She remembered Rollins saying that.

"Oh, so do I," Ginevra said. "For how many cars, do you know?"

"Four," Petal said, just because she was tired of saying she didn't know.

"Four?" Ginevra asked, and she worked out just which four vehicles those might be: Glover's sports car, a sport-utility vehicle, a man-of-the-people pickup truck, and what else? He would probably need a big black Mercedes for formal occasions.

"The next time Glover calls, you can ask him everything you want to know," Petal suggested, in the event that Ginevra had not figured that out for herself. She tossed a completed dove onto the heap accumulating on the tabletop; the force of its landing flurried several other doves, which skidded and fell to the floor.

"What about if we scattered doves in front of Julie, when she walks down the aisle?" Petal said, for she remained convinced there had to be some way to make use of origami doves at the wedding.

"I don't think so," Ginevra said. "I can just picture her storming through them and kicking them aside and holding everything up while she fetches a broom."

Petal wished Ginevra hadn't summoned up that image of such a wrathful Julie lashing out at whatever stood in her way. "I have been so worried about what to get her for a gift," she confessed. "Julie hasn't registered anywhere, and I know I'll choose the wrong thing and I so want to get her what she likes. I'd feel bad if she felt she had to force herself to be nice about something she hated."

"But she keeps saying she doesn't want any presents and I'm inclined to believe her," Ginevra said. "Because I really think she knows she's going to have to give them all back, when Nicholas Davenant doesn't show up."

"Oh, how you go on about that," Petal said. Her concentration faltered and she misfolded a slip of paper, mistakenly producing a stealth-wing bomber plane (she thought).

"Or maybe she doesn't want presents because she can buy anything she wants, all on her own," Ginevra said. "I mean, you do appreciate that she's as well off as the rest of them. Brooks and Rollins signed over the patent to her for this invention of theirs—I don't know what it's called, but every time anyone anywhere in the world uses an ATM machine, Julie makes a thousandth of a cent or something like that.

Which starts to add up, when you factor in the population of Earth all lining up in front of ATM machines."

"Oh, isn't that nice. Rollins never told me," Petal said. "He's so modest about his accomplishments."

"Well, Glover told me in strictest confidence, which is how I'm telling you now," Ginevra said. She tapped her lip with her thimbled finger.

"I wonder whether Nicholas Davenant knows," Petal said. "I'll bet he doesn't. I'll bet he loves her for herself, which must mean he really, really loves her since she's not the easiest person to get close to. You have to make an effort with Julie, you really do. So imagine how surprised he'll be and imagine how happy Julie will be, since she knows she can be sure of him. It's like when in *A Little Princess* Sara Crewe finds out she's really not poor and everything is happy again. Or it's like in that episode of *Crown Point*—have you ever watched it? No? Well, Samantha's sweet but plain cousin comes for a visit, and Justin really, really falls for her, even though she's not his usual type. And then it turns out she's an heiress; only then she dies. Oh, but first he marries her, except I don't think people would still watch *Crown Point* if Justin was permanently married, so you could see it coming, that the cousin was going to have to die. She had this real bad cough, and the music was sad when they were on the beach, on their really sad honeymoon. I mean you could just tell it wasn't going to be good."

"Yes, this is all like something from a made-up story," Ginevra said. "Which is exactly what I've been saying all along."

GINGER AND BETSY RETURNED TO the little parlor in time to witness the return of the defense and prosecution teams to their respective tables and to hear the judge severely pronounce that the proceedings had just ended in a mistrial; convincing evidence of an attempt to suborn a juror had been brought to his attention. Andy could be viewed snapping his briefcase shut and standing up and shaking hands with assorted court personnel and heading for the door in the midst of a scene of general agitation and confusion; he was a tall man, and one could follow the top of his head as he made his way outside. He seemed to be the only sensible person in the courtroom, the only one who accepted that the trial was over.

"How disappointing," said Lily. "I was quite curious to see how this was all going to turn out, and now what? Will they have to retry that unpleasant man all over again, from the very beginning? Won't that be an advantage to the defense, to know what the evidence and the strategy against them is to be?"

"Who knows?" said Louis. "They may not even bother to do anything. Or they may accept a plea bargain, if one is offered. Or the state may come up with some additional charges and try him on those, if they're determined to get him on something."

"Call Andy," Ginger told Betsy, indicating the little parlor telephone. "Find out what's going on."

"This means he can come join us now. That's all I want, more than anything," Betsy said as she picked up the phone and punched in the numbers. "Although who knows what this will mean for Andy's book contract. It's mostly all written, but he just needs the last chapter, which was going to be an analysis of the verdict, one way or the other. Oh well, he'll think of something, I'm sure."

The television screen was now showing the front of the courthouse, where supporters of the defendant were gathering. Andy had just emerged; he stood beside a pillar, patting his several pockets and withdrawing his cell phone. He smilingly answered, *Betsy;* they could all read his lips, for they had had a pretty good idea of what he was going to say.

Ginger waved at him, and she said to Betsy, "Tell Andy I just waved at him."

"He says he saw you," Betsy reported, and he waved back from the courthouse steps.

Alden was making sure of the checks he had tucked beneath the blotter; sometimes one stuck to the back of another, especially in such damp weather, but he saw he had signed them all. Still, he lingered. Tommy had to take his leave of everyone, wandering from Louis to Lily to Betsy to Ginger, offering his head for a final caress. From Ginger he also received a kiss on the top of his nose just between the eyes, which Lily hoped was not unwise, but then she decided it was more important at the moment for Ginger to cherish a pet than to worry about any opportunistic germs and infections she might pick up. Then,

Alden lingered a while longer to give Lily a chance to rise and see him to the front door, where he would have a final opportunity to put the deferred question to her, asking (pausing and turning and addressing her as if in afterthought, he would strike just the right note of casual interest) whether or not Becky had been heard from and if so, what had she said, and if she had said anything, did Lily think they could count on what had been said based upon a close examination of whatever may have been communicated? But The Justice Channel anchor was reporting the details of the jury-tampering charge and explaining its implications and, listening to this, Lily failed to notice that Alden wished to have a word with her, or if she was aware of his hovering shadow, she chose not to involve herself with any more of his concerns at the present moment.

CAM HAD TAKEN A SECOND LOOK inside the garment bag, hoping that something else remained in there, long hidden away and only awaiting detection by her; she was not about to cede to Sally all the glory of discovery. Burrowing deeper, clattering past the emptied hangers and flurrying aside a clutch of frayed, flannel bathrobes (too shabby to wear but too well worn to discard), she came upon a suspended drawstring bag, plumped full with something. The bag swayed at her touch, swinging one way and rebounding the other to collide weightlessly into Cam, who, braced to be clobbered, decided it was very odd for such an overstuffed sack to be so airy. She reached up and scrabbled at the drawstring knot, which relented enough to allow her to insert a finger through the top, and a crook of that finger snagged enough of an end of a fabric, which she carefully conveyed up and up, caught upon her fingertip, and snaked out through the narrow opening. When enough had been tugged free and began to uncoil itself and then to froth from the bag as Cam pulled and pulled with increasing enthusiasm for her task, the stuff billowed into a length of white lace veil. Sally had to concede that Cam's veil was almost as good a find as her dress but Cam contended her discovery was better. She undertook to demonstrate how lofty all that lace was by flinging it up into the air by the armful and transforming the little attic room into a diaphanously cloudlike tent; Sally could not begin to do that with the dress.

They made their way down the stairs, bundling and conveying all that finery with as much commotion as if they had corralled fair-weather clouds up there in the attic and were wrestling them back to earth. They flowed into Julie's bedroom, where they arrayed the dress upon the bed, nipping in the waist and belling the skirt. The veil was fixed to a bedpost and fluffed to cascade over the dress. They stepped back and assessed this presentation, exchanging nearly satisfied glances, and Sally ran off and returned with her Anne Shirley doll, whom she stuffed down inside the neckline of the dress with only the head poking out, for she and Cam had already established the very interesting fact that Julie and Anne of Green Gables must be twins, for their red hair and freckled faces were so alike and both their sets of eyes had a way of rolling up toward the tops of their skulls when Anne was dropped on the floor or when Julie was pushed too far.

"Wait until Julie sees," Cam said, which made them realize they could not bear to wait for Julie to turn up on her own. That wouldn't happen for hours, not until she wandered upstairs to wash her hands before supper and the matter pressed too urgently to languish until suppertime.

"How will we get her back up to the house?" Sally wondered. "It has to be a surprise," she added. "We can't spoil the surprise by telling her why."

"Let's call Julie at the farm stand and tell her there is an emergency in her bedroom," Cam said, which struck them both as a brilliant idea.

They surged into Lily's room and picked up the receiver of the bedside telephone and dialed Julie's cell, whereupon Julie kept them on the line, at first scolding them for bothering her at work and then by attempting to guess the nature of the emergency that required her attention.

"Is there a fire? You nitwits, if there's a fire, get out of the house at once, and I'll call the fire department," Julie said.

"It isn't a fire," Sally said.

"Is it another bat? If there's a bat flying around my room, just open the window screen and shut the door and leave the poor thing alone. There's no harm in a bat," Julie said.

"It's not that either," Sally said, and she grimaced at Cam; there had been a thrilling incident involving the appearance of a bat swooping all around Petal's attic bedroom in the middle of the night, and Sally was not impressed by Julie's present insouciance on the matter. Julie had shrieked as loudly as everybody else, except for Aunt Lily, who had been the only calm one; she had placed a handkerchief on top of her head and bravely entered Petal's room to wrench open the window screen.

"Well, if you and Cam have been fooling around with my stuff and spilled my bottle of Ombre Rose, I am going to have to murder you. How many times have I told you not to steal my perfume? Haven't you figured it out that I can smell you two coming from a mile away whenever you get into my cosmetics?" Julie asked. "And do you really think I don't notice your crimson lips?"

"No, that's not what's happened either," Sally said, and she resisted reminding Julie that she and Cam had meant for everyone to admire their lipstick.

"Then what have you spilled all over my library books?" Julie wanted to know. "Ink? Paint? Root beer? Glue? What?"

Sally held her hand over the receiver and told Cam, "Now she thinks we spilled again on her library books."

"Tell her yes, that's it," Cam advised. She was becoming tired of this, since she wasn't the one who was getting to talk to Julie and listen to her being so mad and so funny about stuff.

"Yes, that's what we did," Sally told Julie. "Nail polish. Like the last time." She held the receiver away from her ear as Julie's voice, amplified and angry, soared at her. She dropped the receiver onto the cradle then and told Cam, "Julie's on her way."

JULIE HUNG HER DRIPPING RAIN SLICKER on a hook in the back hall. She stepped out of her moccasins and tilted them over the set tub, draining off a trickle of cordovan-colored water before slipping them back on. She had left Tru and Om in charge of the farm stand, having called up to the barn where they were packaging herbs to ask if they'd spell her for a while.

Lily was in the kitchen warming soup for Ginger and assembling tomato sandwiches for everyone else; she had forgotten who had said they wanted mayonnaise and who had said they did not, so she was making half with and half without. The kettle shrilled and Julie poured the boiling water into the big pot, because hot tea was what this day called for, Lily said. Julie inquired after the events of the trial and expressed surprise at what had happened; how swiftly the proceedings had unraveled and all come to nothing. And Andy had let Betsy know he would be arriving by the end of the week; so the house is filling up, Lily said, which observation may or may not have been intended to nudge Julie into letting her know who else she could expect to appear on her doorstep later that summer for the wedding. For Lily had placed a possibly meaningful emphasis upon the words *filling up*, which on another afternoon Julie might have seized upon, although most likely not to any useful end; Lily held no high hopes for any response other than a flare of temper or an exasperated sigh. Still, she could not not try to find out, and the nature of the sigh or the timbre of the temper might be analyzed for some hint of which way events were tending. However, Julie's thoughts lay elsewhere at the moment.

"Do you know what those horrible children have done now?" she complained to Lily.

Sally and Cam had been watching for Julie. They had knelt at Lily's front-facing bedroom window muttering, "Come on, Julie, come on, come on," until they spotted her trudging up the driveway; she was swinging her arms and stamping her feet and her head was bent low in a ferocious posture, which was all to the good, for the madder Julie was now, the gladder she was going to be afterward. The little girls had followed her progress across the lawn. They raced from upper window to upper window, making sure of her as she stalked around the side of the house, keeping track of her whereabouts until she passed from view below the porch roof, but they heard the back screen door creak open and slap shut. Then they crouched at the top of the back stairs and listened to Julie clump into the kitchen and denounce them to Lily, who said that if the little girls were plaguing Julie too much she would send them out to the barn to dehisce a bushel of shell beans for Penny, who had come down with her annual canning bug. Penny had wiped out Peddocks' supply of jar bands and lids and she was steaming up all the windows of that glass house of hers with every pot she possessed, and several others that she had borrowed from Lily, bubbling away atop all of her stove burners.

The tennis ball, which had been stuffed into Cam's shorts pocket all the while, erupted from its confinement as Cam lay down flat, her ear to the floor all the better to hear Sally and herself being discussed in no uncertain terms. Cam snatched, but the ball rolled out of reach and began to bounce down the steps with a painfully slow and obvious series of thumps. Julie, waiting at the bottom, caught the ball on its final hop and recognized it from its earlier appearance at the farm stand. She headed up the stairs.

A minute later, Sally galloped down to the kitchen, calling, "Aunt Lily, Aunt Lily. Julie needs you at once."

Betsy, who had come to tell Lily that she had persuaded her mother to eat a buttered Pilot cracker with her soup (Betsy having played the Andy card, reminding her mother that she wanted to be feeling well enough when he got here to be able to quiz him thoroughly about all the behind-the-scenes courtroom drama that the camera failed to capture), took over the luncheon preparations. Lily removed her apron and tied the sash around Betsy's waist. Sally danced about the kitchen as if she believed her own agitation could make everyone else hurry and Betsy was to observe later that Sally had demonstrated just what the expression "being beside oneself" meant.

Sally darted up the stairs ahead of Lily and raced halfway down to meet and to pull at her slowpoke great-aunt before flying up again.

"They're in Julie's room," she told Lily and she fell into step behind Lily, making shooing motions with her hands.

Julie stood before her long mirror wearing the veil and holding the dress up against herself, securing it by the shoulders like a paper doll's costume. She was eyeing her image critically, but more with a sense of hope than discouragement; thus far she had spotted nothing wrong as she reviewed some mental checklist of all the things she didn't like and didn't want in a wedding gown.

"Oh, Aunt Lily," Julie said. "Look at what Sally and Cam came across, fooling around up in the attic. I'm really inclined to think it's quite nice. Do you think it will fit me? I think I'll try it on except it's all hooks and eyes down the back. I'll need some help doing it up."

"I'm not sure about this," Lily said. "Is it even clean? It smells musty, and is that a bit of rust on the skirt?" Her thumb rubbed a spot which proved to be a shadow cast by a fold of the cloth.

"I should at least try it on," Julie said. "Go away, Sally and Cam, just while I'm changing." They stood on either side of her, mirroring her own expectant posture as all three gazed down upon Julie's reflection.

"We will close our eyes," Sally said.

"We'll close our eyes and turn our backs," Cam said. This was the formula for providing privacy in her own crowded home.

"And we'll cover our ears," Sally promised as well, for if the dress did not please her, if it did not fit, Julie might very well say something they ought not to hear.

"No, be nice and go away for a minute, and if I like the dress, I'll do something nice for you," Julie said. Lily clucked her tongue; she did not believe in bribing children to behave, however Julie was inclined to be more realistic about the efficacy and necessity of negotiation to facilitate the smooth conduct of most human exchanges.

"Will you take us to see *Muppets from Space*? Tonight?" Sally asked, and Cam held her breath. Every grown-up of their acquaintance had refused to sit through the *Muppets* with them. Julie herself had told them no three times, and the last time they had asked she had said she would feed them to the tigers if she heard anything more about it, which had raised the question just where Julie was going to get tigers to feed them to; nevertheless, they had not entirely not believed her threat.

"Yes. All right. If that's what you want to see," Julie said now. "Damn it." She scowled, but the scowl was softened by the sight of herself. She adjusted the held-up dress; she belled the skirt with nudges of her knee and noticed how pretty the sleeves were as they emptily, lacily fluttered.

"Off with you," Lily said, and she shut the door behind the little girls, who huddled just outside, their ears pressed to the jamb and their eyes screwed shut with the effort of listening, but they could overhear nothing aside from the creak of floorboards as Julie and Lily stepped back and forth. Sally jabbed Cam, and they crept into Betsy's room and passed through to the connecting bathroom to kneel at a different door, though with no better result, and so they turned to inventing their own new hair care product at the sink, pouring drops and drips of all the existing shampoos and conditioners into an empty aspirin bottle they retrieved from the wastebasket. On another day, they planned to wash Agnes's tail.

Lily lifted the veil from Julie's head. "You had this on backward," she said, lifting it off.

"Well, Cam stood on the chair and just sort of flung it up and heaved it over me like she was netting a giant tuna," Julie said. She placed the dress upon the bed and turned it inside out to investigate the seams in a knowledgeable way. She gave a little grunt of approval. "But whose dress could this have been?" she wondered. "Not my grandmother's because I've seen pictures of her wedding, and she looked like the cake. Not Aunt Ginger's, because this isn't like a piece of lingerie like you told me about. I know it can't be Ma's, because I threw her dress out when I helped Dad unpack the boxes after he moved into his new house. I sent all of Ma's stuff to Goodwill." She glanced at Lily, wondering if Lily would consider it to have been wrong on her part not to have hung on to her mother's wardrobe. But nothing had been folded properly or sent to the cleaners before being stuffed into cartons, and moths had gotten to a lot of things, so Becky would not have been happy, anyway, to be reunited with her wardrobe. Julie had only been able to salvage some pewter buttons from a boiled wool jacket and a rather battered Burberry, which she had kept for her own use.

However Lily only said, "It's a mistake to keep things." She deflated the veil with kneading and folding motions and set it upon the bureau top where the buoyant material began to rise and puff again as soon as her back was turned.

"I know Uncle Harvey has been married four times," Julie said. She was still puzzling. "I mean, not to say that this was his dress, but one of the brides'? I'm going to say this garment was made sometime in the forties. I can tell from the way it's sewn because, don't forget, I worked on the Duchess and Dior exhibit. Who in the family was the right age, fifty or sixty years ago, Aunt Lily, for getting married in a dress like this? But look, it must never have been worn. The basting stitches are still there. That's peculiar." Julie leaned over to bite and release a thread, which she pulled free and wound around her thumb after judging the strand too long to drop to the floor. "So, I guess I should really be asking, who in the family was the right age *not* to have been married fifty or sixty years ago?"

Lily, who had not betrayed her shock of recognition and subsequent perturbation over the surfacing of this particular gown, now allowed herself to display a measure of exasperation with Julie's ongoing mystification. Julie was turning the neckline inside out, hunting for a name tag or a laundry mark, and Lily laid her hand upon her niece's hand to indicate there was no further need to wonder. She patted Julie's arm in a resigned and forgiving manner, which caused Julie to blame herself at once, for having been obtuse.

"Oh gosh, Aunt Lily, forgive me. I didn't realize. What happened? What happened to you? Did the guy die? Did the guy die in World War Two?" she asked. She put this question rather eagerly, for she believed a fiancé killed in battle to be, all in all, a moving sacrifice and historically interesting tragedy.

"No, he just changed his mind, even if it was rather late in the day for that," Lily said.

"What? Why? How horrible. What a horrible person, to do that to you," Julie said.

"Well, he was very nice, really. Quite intelligent and serious," Lily recalled.

"Okay, I suppose he must have been worthy enough, for you to have liked him," Julie allowed. "But still."

"He changed his mind after his previous fiancée changed her mind about not marrying him after the man she had dropped him for refused to come up to scratch. That man was interested in someone else. It was quite a convoluted situation and no one seemed to have been very sure of themselves at the time," Lily explained. "At any rate, the first fiancée wrote to our mutual fiancé, as I suppose he was, and she said she was sorry and she wanted him back and he told me he was sorry because he wanted her back as well. The other fiancée even came here to the house so she could sit in the big parlor letting me see how sorry she was and so I could feel sorry for her for having put her in the position of having to be so upset about upsetting me, especially at what was supposed to be the happiest time of her life which it wouldn't be of course, unless I was prepared to be forgiving. By that point I was sitting back and observing everything as if it was happening to somebody else, so I was very aware of everyone's roles and how we were all supposed to play them," Lily said.

"Yes, I know how that feels," Julie said. "I think it's a survival mechanism that lets you see everything that's going on with hyperclarity even as your emotions are disengaged, so to speak."

"Yes," Lily agreed. "Well, let's see how this looks on you. Let's see if it will even fit." She lifted the dress from the bed, and Julie stepped out of her T-shirt and shorts. She seemed to be wearing another T-shirt and pair of shorts underneath those, which Lily didn't even bother to stop and think was odd as she lowered the skirt over Julie's head, which emerged from the sweetheart neckline after a moment of tugging and adjusting; the T-shirt sleeves, bunched, were rolled up into the shoulder seam. Then Julie held her breath, and Lily worked at securing the hooks and eyes; somehow, she had misaligned them, but her error was not very apparent; they were just going for the general effect at this first fitting.

"But I can't possibly wear your dress," Julie said. She plucked at the skirt and gazed into the mirror. "You don't want to resurrect all those old memories," she asked Lily. "Do you?"

"I doubt anyone will even remember. Although at the time I thought I'd never live it down, but now even I can't recall every twist and turn of what went on," Lily said. "I do recall my former fiancé was very petty about the ring though, which technically I didn't have to return since I was the injured party, although I chose to do so. It was your grandmother who tried to convince me to sell it so we could both go to Bermuda on the proceeds. I should have listened to her; that would have given the story a better ending, at least when I retold the tale. 'Then Olive and I set sail for the tropics,' I could have said. But it has just occurred to me, at this very minute, I am sure the other fiancée badgered him about the ring. He wouldn't have been so adamant, I am sure. I was so apologetic because I'd already misplaced the ring box since I had pledged never to remove the ring from my finger, which was much the usual vow. Although I later came to think that such a big stone would have gotten in the way, particularly in the garden. I'd always have felt obliged to be careful." Perhaps if she had married she would have been forced to go in for carefree shrubs and low-maintenance perennials and small container plantings. She would have become someone to whom she rather condescended, in her unspoken thoughts, when invited to admire a landscape that contained a pot of petunias and some juniper bushes and a flock of pachysandra, just that and nothing more.

Julie turned and craned her neck to see how she looked from behind. The dress fell in such a long, graceful line she hardly recognized herself, not that she spent a lot of time thinking about how she looked when leaving a room—she had problems enough organizing the effect she made when entering one. "Maybe I could just say this dress is vintage, should anyone ask," she said.

"Wear the dress," Lily said. "I should have showed it to you earlier but I think I had some idea that it would be an ill-fated and unlucky and unhappy choice. That's why I never mentioned it when you asked."

"Oh well, at least I'll have a good excuse; if my guy doesn't come up to scratch, we can blame the dress," Julie said, but Lily told her she mustn't say such things, even in jest. Julie's reply, if she made a reply, was muffled by the fall of the veil, which she had slung back on atop her head, once again getting it backward; it was as if the flipping thing insisted upon being worn the wrong way round.

AS GINEVRA SLOWED TO MAKE THE TURN up the driveway, she and Petal glanced toward the farm stand, which was shuttered against the weather. The overhanging trees, bowing and blackening beneath the rain, grazed the roof shingles, and the bright blue tarp that covered a mound of unsorted squash was dripping down all its sides with an affluence of streaks and streams. Penny's seated figure was visible through the door, bent over a piece of knitting which so occupied her that she didn't look up to see who had turned up the driveway as they drove past.

"She heard about a Rumanian orphanage that needs sweaters," Petal said. "She's been teaching me how to do ribbing, and next she's going to show me how to set a sleeve, which I think will be pretty hard, but it doesn't seem right to send little kids just a sweater vest. Vests are for old people. I don't even think Gaultier could carry off a vest. Well, maybe if he did one in shredded and cropped leather with rivets, and while I wouldn't recommend fringe, as such, I'd suggest maybe he could do some thin lashes of leather braiding swinging off the yoke. I mean, I could possibly see a vest like that, although it still wouldn't be suitable for a child."

Ginevra said she understood that adopting Rumanian orphans was actually rather in vogue at the moment, so it only seemed appropriate that someone like Petal was going to help dress them, and Petal observed that, indeed, she was spending an unexpectedly busy and eventful summer here, what with just now folding all those origami doves to secure world peace as well as knitting for the underprivileged children of the world (funny how many opportunities she was getting this summer to make the world a better place). Not to mention she had her work at the farm stand providing people with fresh and healthy fruits and vegetables; everyone asked her what *she* ate and she was always happy to chatter on about diets. Besides that, she had been trying to be of help to Miss Lily up at the house with her various guests and responsibilities, as all the while poor Miss Lily was also endeavoring to plan a big wedding. Whether the wedding was to prove to be imaginary or not (Petal held up a hand to prevent Ginevra from saying anything more on that subject), Petal had still been set to work searching the china cupboard and other cabinets to accumulate the two dozen scattered bud vases which were going to sit upon all the tabletops, filled with baby's breath and Bow Bells roses. These vases, when rooted out from their corners, all had to be washed and more often than not they contained the distinct and dried remains of a spider or fly, and sometimes both. Petal reckoned the spider must have caught the fly in its web; otherwise the fly could have just flown out of the vase as easily as he'd flown in, although in the case of the spider, she wondered whether it couldn't or wouldn't leave. Perhaps it had become too fat and complacent to clamber up and out from its retreat, gorged on all those flies. She could not decide whether it would be quite terrible to live out one's days in a bud vase, or merely cosy.

At any rate, Rollins had led her to believe Towne would provide a more spalike retreat for someone seeking a bit of a break after a spell of hard work, Petal said, although she did not now seek to blame him for her very different experience of the place. Ginevra could not think of a way to ask Petal what could possibly be onerous about being required to stand around in beautiful clothes all day as everyone exclaimed how beautiful she was, without betraying that she believed the answer to the question could only be, *Not much*. In a case like Petal's, Ginevra would have said that lounging about and sitting still on a spa vacation while having her nails buffed and her skin exfoliated would have seemed like more of the same and perhaps turned into a more tiresome exercise than a relaxing one, so she had nothing to complain about, not that Petal had been complaining. Actually, Petal had been sort of marveling at how rewarding her summer holiday was turning out to be.

Ginevra parked in front of the barn, and she and Petal ran for the back door, sharing the cover of a single umbrella between them, neither proceeding very gracefully as they pulled apart and then collided, each dashing one way and another in the effort to bypass puddles and to avoid treading upon the slugs that were oozily abroad and ambling along the stone walk (for they loved this weather, Petal said, and Ginevra, who didn't step on slugs because of the sickening way their sac of insides popped out beneath the pressure of her foot, supposed that Petal was sparing the creatures because she imagined they were out and about visiting their cousins and picnicking with friends, but she couldn't think of a way to ask Petal this without sounding satirical, which she didn't mean to be).

Sally and Cam were seated at the kitchen table, busy with a project. They reached into a basket piled high with mushrooms and toadstools, selecting among the beige and black and red and spotted specimens. The various mushrooms had smooth or ruffled edges, and some were as small as thumbnails while a few had sprouted to the size of saucers although most were of a size somewhere in between. The little girls worked at the stems, tugging and twisting them off with practiced moves, and then they inspected the underside of each cap detecting, or failing to detect, some characteristic display which either recommended the mushroom to them or disqualified it for their purposes. Sally tossed a rejected top back into the basket, and Cam had to remind her to throw it into a plastic basin set out for that purpose and into which they also tossed the discarded stems.

Sally sighed and drew a sheet of black construction paper to the edge of the table, settling it just below the tip of her nose. She peered at the paper nearsightedly, not that her eyes weren't perfectly fine, but what she was working on was so exacting that she was not convinced that her usual powers of sight were sufficient and she emulated the squints and furrowed brows of her elder relatives, who often found that their bifocal, and sometimes trifocal, eyeglass lenses failed to afford a true view, at any interval, of a line of newsprint or a bird in a tree. Cam aligned a sheet of black construction paper in front of herself as well, but she gazed upon its surface more calmly and with the air of someone entertaining an inner vision.

"Where is everybody?" Ginevra asked them. She had a peremptory manner with children, which Cam and Sally accepted. Ginevra would never have come here just to see them.

"Auntie Lily has gone to bed with an ache, so we are being very quiet," Cam said.

"And we are being very quiet for Granna too," Sally said. "She has gone to bed with an ache."

They turned their faces toward Ginevra and Petal so the young women could see just how good they were being at the moment. To have an audience at such a time was quite gratifying, and each vied to be more quiet than the other; Cam picked up and put down a pair of scissors without making a sound, and Sally scowled at the refrigerator, which had suddenly whirred on to manufacture ice. She pantomimed in its direction, *Shhhhh*.

"What's that you're doing?" Petal asked. She too was whispering and she unsnapped her jacket buttons with a conscious effort not to let them click too loudly.

"Oh, I know, I used to do this too," Ginevra said. "They're making mushroom art. You arrange mushrooms and toadstools on top of a piece of black paper, which you stick away in a dark cupboard to sit undisturbed for a few days, and the spores drop onto the paper and leave pretty patterns. Well, you can have your pick of mushrooms at the moment. They're springing up everywhere, all over the lawns and in the woods and even up under the eaves of the farm stand, I noticed the other day."

"But is it at all safe to pick mushrooms and toadstools?" Petal asked. "Aren't they poisonous?"

Ginevra leaned over the basket and considered the assortment. "I guess some of them could be," she said. "Don't put your fingers in your mouths," she told Sally and Cam. "And if either of you starts to understand what the refrigerator is saying, go find an adult. Just be sure to remember to wash your hands thoroughly when you're finished," she added.

"When we are finished, Julie is taking us to see *Muppets from Space*," Sally told her.

"Tonight?" Ginevra asked. She and Petal shared a look of dismay. "But we need Julie to go somewhere and do something with us tonight."

"Well, she can't," Sally said. She was very sure about that.

"Julie has promised us," Cam said. She picked up a mushroom cap with two hands and held it above her sheet of paper as she meditated upon the proper placement. She allowed the mushroom cap to drift a bit one way and then the other above the page in search of the spot where it wished to settle, as if this were a collaborative effort.

"Where is your mother then?" Ginevra asked Sally.

"What?" Sally had to recall herself from her contemplation of Cam's work method; the first mushroom to go down was obviously the most important one, and depending upon Cam's decision, Sally was either going to copy or to better her design. "Oh, Mummy is in Julie's room; they're all talking about Julie's dress," she said. "Julie's wedding dress," she clarified. "It is beautiful."

"Beautiful," echoed Cam, and on that note, she plunked down her mushroom. Sally craned for a look at what she'd done, but Cam curled a barrier arm around her paper.

"Julie has found a dress? She's found a dress at last?" Petal asked. She turned to Ginevra with an air of triumph; surely, one would not go so far as to commit oneself to a beautiful dress if one had no intention of wearing it. Petal could not begin to imagine anyone doing that.

"So, Julie's got a dress," Ginevra observed. "Well, well."

"What does that mean?" Petal challenged her.

"I'm not sure," Ginevra said. "But I'm starting to wonder whether she suspects that we suspect what she's up to, and she's trying to make us blink first." She went off to see for herself just what Julie had come up with. Petal lingered for a moment, regarding the basket of mushrooms and the basin of mushroom parts and the busy little hands, snatching and manipulating the mushrooms, and she thought of issuing another warning about the possibly poisonous nature of their work materials to the little girls; however, she concluded that repeated cautions only made the forbidden seem irresistible. She wondered why that was so and she supposed that something first had to be attractive in order to be dangerous, for why else would one so willingly be drawn too close to the edge of a cliff or the scorch of a fire or the banes of the earth if, at first, one had not felt their fascination?

BETSY AND JULIE WERE TO BE FOUND in the upper hallway. Julie stood upon the lid of the blanket chest attired in what could only be a wedding gown as Betsy knelt below her, pinning up the skirt with a show of finicky folding and evident second thoughts about the evenness of her emerging line; the tilt of the lid of the blanket chest was making things difficult. Ginevra told Julie she looked just like the *Winged Victory of Samothrace,* which was not to say that Julie was winged and armless and lacking a head, but coming upon a pale and commanding female figure balanced upon a pedestal at the top of a stairway just sort of reminded her of being at the Louvre. At any rate, the figure of Julie seemed impressive and immense as well, at least in that sense of making it impossible to notice anything else in the vicinity, Ginevra said.

"Uh huh," said Betsy, who held pins in her mouth. She was not much good at sewing, she had informed Julie, but Julie was of the opinion that anyone could fix a hem, and besides, there was no one else available and the act of self-hemming was an impossibility unless the dress was to be very short and one's arms were very long.

"What shoes are you going to wear?" Petal asked. "If you don't mind my saying, it's the usual thing to have on the shoes you're going to wear, when a gown is being fitted."

"Oh, flip, I don't know," Julie said. "What about heels about yea high?" She raised herself and swayed on the balls of her feet.

"Those'll be two-and-a-half-inch pumps," Petal informed Betsy, as if that was going to be of any help. "Are you sure you want two-and-a-half-inch heels, Julie? That's kind of extreme if the wedding's outside and you'll be dancing on the lawn, afterwards."

"Well, it's a gorgeous dress," Ginevra had to admit. "Wherever did you find it?"

"It's vintage," Betsy said, talking around the pins in her mouth. Julie had told her the full story of its origin because of course Betsy had to be clued in, and Ginger already knew something of what had happened (she had been alive at the time but not anywhere near old enough to be involved) but she had learned a few new details from Julie's account. No one ever spoke of the incident, Ginger said, but the end of the stick she had gotten was that Lily had called the whole thing off because the young man had worn Bermuda shorts to Evening Prayer at All Saints', although she'd always figured that aspect of the tale was apocryphal. Now she understood how Bermuda had factored into some overheard conversation, half caught and scarcely remembered. She thought it was a pity Lily and her mother had not installed themselves in the Princess Hotel for a week on the proceeds of the sale of the ring; Lily would have loved the birding and botanizing, and Olive could have stocked up on English china and Scottish cashmere. The lesson in all of this is to have your fun when you get the chance, Ginger advised Betsy and Julie, and although she did not feel sorry for herself when she said this, Betsy and Julie had both received her words with a measure of sadness and seriousness, which weighed upon them until they became distracted by the insight that the sculpted form of the redeemed dress gave them into Lily's former figure. She must have been something, as Julie said. She plucked at seams which stretched at certain points and sagged at others, this occurring rather in reverse to the places one would wish a garment to pull tight or hang loose upon oneself.

"Well, I've really come to ask a big favor," Ginevra began to say. She recalled that she had come here on business.

"It's more of a fun favor," Petal said.

"Is that Ginevra I hear? Is that Petal?" Ginger called from her bedroom. Louis, exiting with a tray of untouched toast and tea, told them all to go in and keep her company; she was feeling a bit brighter.

Julie hitched her skirt and hopped from the top of the blanket chest as Betsy kept a fold of fabric pinched between her fingers, not wishing to lose her place on the hem; they moved to Ginger's room, where Julie climbed onto an ottoman and Betsy resumed pinning where she had left off. Ginger patted the bed on either side of herself, bidding Ginevra and Petal to sit with her. Petal, by now accustomed to the air of the sickroom, alit gently on the bed, but Ginevra, who had only encountered Ginger when she was up and about, hesitated. She affected an interest in the view from the front window, which was limited by the trees, for Ginevra would have guessed that the top of the Unitarian steeple could be viewed from this vantage.

"Only in winter when the leaves are gone," Ginger said when Ginevra mentioned this.

Then Ginevra consulted her watch. The business that had brought her here pressed, and she remembered her errand. "It's like this," she explained. "I received a call from Terry, down at the Dock, not an hour ago. He claims he told me that tonight was going to be Motown Night, which he never did; he's such a pothead, but that's neither here nor there. I'm going to be Diana Ross and what I need is some Supremes to back me up in a big hurry."

"And you thought of us?" Julie asked, unconvinced.

"I understand you're busy tonight," Ginevra told her, and Julie shrugged; a deal was a deal.

"Then how about it, Betsy?" Ginevra appealed to her. "I'm desperate."

"Well, since you asked so nicely," Betsy said, a bit put out that she was Ginevra's second choice. "Yes, I suppose so."

"I'm going to be there too," Petal said. "I have the perfect outfit upstairs, and we'll find one for you too," she promised Betsy. She had been thinking all summer that she'd like to see Betsy dressed in something other than a denim skirt and an untucked cotton blouse. "And your hair . . ." Petal said, thinking hard about putting a beehive on Betsy, but she was also tempted to go with a flip.

"Damn, it's starting to sound like fun," Julie said. "Now I'm really going to have to hate *Muppets from Space,* I mean, even more than I was already planning to hate it."

"Okay, so I thought I'd sing 'My World Is Empty Without You,' 'You Keep Me Hangin' On,' and 'Love Child.' I think there's a kind of narrative logic to that set," Ginevra said. "Here, I went online and printed out a bunch of lyrics as soon as Terry called." She pulled sheets of paper from her satchel purse and distributed them all around; she had made extra.

"But what a sad song 'Love Child' is," Julie said, reading down the lyric. "It's not the love child's fault it's a love child, but look how the poor love child says right here about how she's been scorned by society and always feels second best. That's just sad. Oh, I know. I know how we can fix it, so I can come too. What if we dress up Sally and Cam in tatters and rags and let them come along to represent the poor love children? They'd like that even better than a Muppet movie."

"No," said Betsy because she could picture all too well what enthusiastically obliging urchins Sally and Cam would make. No one would ever hear the end of it.

"But are you going to have enough Supremes?" Julie persisted. "Because I'm pretty sure there were three of them."

"There were, but not at the same time. Florence Ballard exited with hard feelings, though I forget what the whole story was. And then I'm afraid things ended badly for her," Ginger recalled. "Mary Wilson was the other original member, and she was joined by Cindy Birdsong. I always liked that name, Birdsong, which I don't believe she made up, even though it sounds made up."

"Oh, I want to be Cindy Birdsong. Can I?" asked Petal, and Betsy looked as if she would have liked to put dibs on her too, except she had all those pins bristling between her lips. She sputtered them into her palm and held them like a cache of tiny fish bones encountered in an inexpertly filleted shad.

"Though I scarcely carry a tune," Petal confessed, as she surveyed her lyrics sheet, running a finger below all the lines of lyrics labeled *Chorus*, of which there seemed to be worrisomely many.

"That's all right; almost anyone can sing adequately. I can teach you a few techniques, and besides, *you* can get away with just standing there looking beautiful," Ginevra said. Ginger winked at Betsy; they were very fond of Ginevra but they felt she made an interesting study of someone who had been raised in an atmosphere where frankness and openness were valued to the exclusion, perhaps, of sensitivity and reserve in certain areas of discourse. Then again, no doubt Ginevra would know exactly what to do and say when meeting the Dalai Lama or, say, a person who lived in a tree.

"You girls stay right here with me and practice," Ginger said. "I'm an excellent audience. And come over where I can reach you, Julie, and I'll unhook your dress." Julie obliged, sitting on the edge of Ginger's bed. She shivered; her aunt's fingertips felt very cold as they touched the back of her neck.

Ginevra placed Petal and Betsy on the fireplace hearth and she ordered them to stand up straight; Betsy always stooped and Petal tended to sway, she said, criticisms which stemmed from a prior assessment of their usual postures and here now was her chance to remedy their deficiencies. Then she poked them in their midriffs to make them understand just where their diaphragms were located which was where, Ginevra claimed, one sang from. Betsy complained that if she could only appreciate the fact of possessing a diaphragm when the diaphragm had been made sore, she would rather not know anything about it. Petal seemed to admire Betsy for speaking up but she did not go quite so far as to agree with her assertion; Petal had never been very much of a student and she had never liked to draw attention to herself lest she be called upon to recite.

Ginevra produced a pitch pipe from her satchel and huffed on the opening, summoning a note which Betsy and Petal replicated to the best of their abilities before they broke into song at a nod from Ginevra, who listened with narrowed eyes, tapping the pitch pipe against her upper lip so she could whistle them to a stop at any moment. Betsy and Petal thought they must not have done too badly when Ginevra didn't cut them off; however, Ginevra had only let them go on so she could know the worst. She told Betsy she had problems with her diphthongic vowels; the long *i* sound in "Love Child" must be put over has *ah-ee*. As for Petal, Ginevra accused her of committing a *coup de glotte,* and Petal said she wasn't doing anything on purpose and please not to poke her hard in the *glotte,* wherever that was located on her body.

"Just get us through the evening without disgracing ourselves," Betsy told Ginevra.

"Of course," Ginger spoke up, "my favorite part of any Diana Ross and the Supremes song came when they had to express some thought or idea that was so serious and so important, they had to cease singing and begin to speak the lyric. That's how they used to perform the line, 'Scorned by society,' for example. You should say it like this, '*Scorned* by . . .' with deep stress on the *scorned*. And then give *society* all four of its syllables with equal emphasis. *So-ci-e-ty*. And there's a longish pause after you say " '*Scorned* by.' "

" '*Scorned* by,' " Betsy and Petal said, " 'so-ci-e-ty.' "

"Yes, that's very good, but try speaking '*Scorned*' with more scorn," Ginger advised.

" '*Scorned* by,' " Betsy and Petal spoke, scowling, " 'so-ci-uh-teee.' "

"That's even better. I mean, just remember, you are black and illegitimate and you live in the blighted inner city and here you are vowing not to repeat your own mother's mistakes by refusing to follow the road she took as you attempt to fend off the amorous advances of your own young man," Ginger said. "Even though the road your mother took led her to having *you,* so I suppose the subtext of the song is really about the wish for self-annihilation and how the singer will not allow herself to yield to love, because she fears that love will lead to life. Oh, one can hardly bear it, how wrong a child can get things sometimes and how much of the burden of what happened in the past before they were even born they take upon themselves. One simply cannot bear it, how wrong a child can be, sometimes." She fumbled at the last of the hooks and eyes on Julie's dress and she gently pushed her away. "There," she said. "Go now and try to wiggle out of this."

Ginger settled back among her pillows and indicated her willingness to listen to the evolving performance. She shut her eyes, the better to hear, and when Betsy and Petal and Ginevra, believing she had drifted away from them, tried to steal quietly off, she told them to keep singing. "You still need a lot of practice," she told them, although she added that she had every confidence they would be just fine in the end.

THE PLAN (OR A REFINEMENT OF THE ORIGINAL PLAN) was to have supper at the Casa di Napoli when they dropped Cam off at home after the early movie. Om, waitressing that evening, steered Julie and the little girls into a booth in the back as Sally and Cam gushed into both her ears telling her what a wonderful movie she had missed. Om was among the many whom they had failed to convince to accompany them to the Cineplex, prior to Julie's capitulation.

"I'm sorry I missed it," Om said, deciding to be nice since she was off the hook and there was no point in revisiting an expired argument.

"Then you can take us next time," Sally said. Having enjoyed *Muppets from Space* once only left her eager to enjoy it again, especially since she now knew how much she was going to like it.

The theater had been empty when they arrived, and it remained empty, which was rather thrilling; Sally and Cam were able to pretend that the entire auditorium belonged to them: the soaring ceiling, the soft-tiled walls, the two hundred seats with adjustable backs and armrests and recessed cup holders, the sloping center aisle, carpeted in a pattern of blue and gold, down which they irresistibly ran toward the big white screen, which possessed all the untapped powers of blankness. This could be their house; they could live here all the time, sitting in every seat and eating Raisinets for breakfast and watching movies every minute of the day.

"Uh huh," said Julie, half listening to the little girls' amazing plans. "Oh flip, I'm not going to sit in the flipping front row. I don't even know why they have to put front rows in movie theaters." She plunked down in a seat directly behind Sally and Cam and settled back to read her book, *The Small House at Allington,* by the directed beam of a clip-on book light. She thumped a toe against the back of their seats whenever incidents of silliness penetrated her consciousness, but Sally and Cam felt tremendously grown up, having been left almost on their own at the Cineplex, and they had comported themselves with what they believed to be dignity, picking Junior Mints from the big box Julie had shoved at them, with their pinkies raised and their mouths pursed to take dainty bits. They refrained from talking during the movie except when comment was absolutely necessary. There were times when wit would not be denied.

Now, in the booth at the back of the Casa di Napoli, Julie slid onto the bench beside Sally, who had wanted to sprawl over her own side of the table without having to share with anyone, and she slithered underneath and surfaced next to Cam to ensure that Cam would not get her own side either. Sally had not bothered to ask Julie to move and sit beside Cam, knowing the suggestion would only try Julie's patience, which she had specifically ordered Sally and Cam not to do prior to starting out on this expedition, and at this midpoint of their evening, Julie had gone so far as to remark that Sally and Cam had almost behaved like humans.

"We are humans," Sally informed Cam, who failed to be impressed. Cam reached for a menu even though she could recite, word perfectly, every item listed under Appetizers and Pizzas and Pasta Specialties and Beverages and How About Dessert?

Om approached them, a pencil poised above her notepad, and Sally spoke up. "Pizza, french fries, orangeade, and a Coke," she said.

She and Cam glanced over at Julie to see whether she would allow this, but Julie only asked Om if she could have the Greek salad without olives but not to worry if there were already olives; she would eat around them. Cam didn't bother to place an order because members of the Samrin family were automatically served whatever dish wasn't selling well at the moment; from time to time Mr. Samrin cracked open a cookbook and deviated from the set course. But Julie told Om they wanted a sixteen-inch pizza and when their order arrived she divvied it up between the two children, so nobody had to eat Mr. Samrin's codfish cakes, although Julie stabbed a bite of one with her fork and said they were pretty good. Besides, Om brought extra french fries.

After the dinner rush (when Julie found herself nodding at and acknowledging half the customers she served at the farm stand, which made her wonder what they were doing with all the produce she sold them because as far as she could tell, most of Towne was dining or ordering out that night; then again, it wasn't up to her to ask everyone why they weren't eating their vegetables), Mrs. Samrin emerged from behind the cash register and came over to say hello. She sat down with a hot and smokily aromatic cup of tea; the cup possessed no handle, and Mrs. Samrin half raised and half bowed to it in order to sip. Julie told her what a doll Cam had been all evening, as Sally, not singled out for a compliment, kicked Cam underneath the table. Mrs. Samrin signaled to Om to fetch an apple pie from the case and enough plates and forks for everyone and she let the little girls tell her all about the movie. She asked sensible questions, which showed she was listening, although as Julie pointed out, sensibleness didn't really enter into a discussion of a Muppets movie.

Presently, Sally and Cam fished in their pockets and discovered that between them they had enough quarters to feed into the Casa di Napoli's jukebox. They excused themselves, and it didn't take an argument for them to agree to punch the button for "Livin' La Vida Loca," to which they danced a slippery dance across the floor, slick from all the walked-in rain.

"How is your Aunt Ginger?" Mrs. Samrin asked Julie. "I have not seen her lately. She used to come in last spring every morning for her beignet and coffee but not now. We sat and had some good talks. She is a very interesting person, and an interested one as well. So many experiences. The children tell me your uncle has arrived at last. That must please her very much, to have him there. I know how much she missed him and all of you. She was very much looking forward to having all of you come to be with her, she told me. She was so happy, knowing that you were all on your way."

Julie burst into tears then, unable to hold back a harsh and sudden onslaught of weeping. Her face betrayed that she was horrified at herself and she turned toward the back wall and mopped at her eyes with napkins pulled from the dispenser. When she could speak, she apologized. "I don't know what came over me," she said and she set about shredding the tear-dampened napkins into confettilike particles, an occupation which seemed to require her full attention.

Mrs. Samrin signaled to Om to bring a second cup of tea. She wished she had more to offer Julie, although Mrs. Samrin supposed that her own life story and her presence here on this rainy evening in this brightly lighted place could serve as proof to Julie that there was always cause for hope. She smiled encouragingly at Julie who sipped at the tea, which was somewhat bitter and which she did not very much care for, at least at first. "I am sorry," Mrs. Samrin said. "I had wondered, but I did not fully know what the situation is."

Sympathetic words caused Julie to well up again but she snuffled aggressively, drawing up her top lip and furrowing her forehead, which gave her an expression so suddenly fierce no one would doubt that she could be very brave when she had to be.

"Look at those two," Mrs. Samrin said, understanding that the matter was closed. Sally and Cam were showing off on the dance floor, for all they were worth; they were cadging songs from the other customers, who, drawn by the hand to the jukebox and shown which button to push, were surrendering the quarters they had received in change.

"Those two," Julie agreed. They were so funny and so annoying.

For they really couldn't let Sally and Cam harass people in that way, and Mrs. Samrin called, "*Cam,*" and Julie crooked a finger at Sally, who had spun to see what Cam was in trouble for, what they both were in trouble for, evidently. They hopped over to the table (this method of locomotion was a hilarious carryover from something seen in the movie), and Sally climbed onto the bench seat beside Julie and knelt there so she could study Julie, who obviously had been crying; her brown eyes, washed a deeper brown, swam beneath reddened lids, and her spiky, dark lashes held little droplets on their sharp ends, and there were salty streaks where tears had run down her cheeks, and her nose breathed stuffily, and the tip of her nose was mantled as bright a red as her eyelids, and her voice, when she spoke to tell Sally to quit staring, had that muffled head cold sound about it, nasal and dampened. Sally was prepared to begin quite the conversation about Julie's troubles, for she had seldom seen an adult weep and never had one sitting beside her so available for study. Sad grown-ups retreated to their bedrooms and remained there very quietly, in her experience.

"I bit into a hot pepper," Julie told Sally. Sally knew all about hot peppers having found out the hard way down at the farm stand that even though they came in such pretty shapes and nice colors, peppers did not taste like candy; they scorched like dragons. You would have to drink the *river* to make your mouth stop exploding, should you ever eat one.

"Oh," Sally said. "That was stupid."

BACK AT HOME, GINGER AND LOUIS's bedroom door was shut, and Lily's as well, and their lights were off (because in Lily's house doors fit imperfectly within their frames, and one could tell if a lamp was burning). They would all have to wait until morning to hear about the movie. Nor had Betsy and Petal returned from their outing at the Dock, so it fell to Julie to put Sally to bed, a process much imbued with ritual. Sally needed a glass of water from the kitchen faucet to rinse out toothpaste and she had to locate and kiss Agnes and then she raised an impromptu fuss about not liking any of her pajamas, which continued until Julie gave her an old Union Jack T-shirt to wear as a nightgown. After that, Sally retired to her bed willingly enough, since the prospect of sleeping in a flag dress seemed quite glamorous. Julie stood by the bed and covered her with a blanket, lofting it and letting it drop over Sally several times as Sally's legs scissored to kick away the descending blanket before Julie became bored by this. A population of stuffed animals displaced by the initial hoist of the blanket lay scattered where they fell across the floor, and Sally insisted that they all be restored to the bed.

"No story tonight, it's very late," Julie told Sally, stooping and flinging plush creatures at her.

"Is this the latest I've ever stayed up?" Sally asked.

"I don't know your entire history, so I'm not in a position to say," Julie said. "My familiarity with you is just recent, if intense."

"Is this the latest you've ever stayed up?" Sally asked.

"I have been known to stay awake the whole night through," Julie said.

"Really?" Sally asked. She sat bolt upright, and Julie plumped her back against her pillow and tucked the blanket more firmly in place around her.

"Tell me about how you stayed awake the whole night through,"

Sally said and she squirmed free of the too-tight bedding and rolled onto an elbow, receptive to being told a tale after all. She had had every confidence she would get to hear a story, one way or the other. She pushed a Care Bear out of the way to make room for Julie to sit.

"Oh, I've done it my fair share of times. On train rides and plane rides," Julie said. "I get around, you know."

"On train rides and plane rides," Sally repeated dreamily.

"And I've pulled more than a few all-nighters before exams, after the coffee and the panic kicked in," Julie recalled. "I remember the first time I ever stayed up all night was to read *The Diary of Anne Frank* secretly by flashlight so my parents wouldn't stop me. I was so into it and I had to know what happened, although I think I must have been the only person on earth who read that book without already knowing what happened to her in the end. Then I was so shocked that I couldn't fall asleep, even when I wanted to. Okay, and then there was this time I stood in line for thirty-six hours to buy tickets for a U2 concert and yes, I admit it, another time I stood in line overnight to get Spice Girl tickets, but we'll keep that little episode secret, just between us, all right? I lost a bet, so matters were beyond my control. I mean, you have to honor a bet; otherwise the entire system of pub culture and office pools would collapse, utterly."

"Honor a bet," Sally repeated, as she drifted off. Presently she emitted a bleatlike snore. How she would hate to be told she snored, Julie thought, but the night contained many perils and revelations. She regarded the child, wondering whether she would ever want a child of her own, although she had yet to lose any night's sleep over that question. Perhaps the time would come.

"Because it happens to everyone," Julie said, speaking softly and to herself, for she had to finish the story. "Everyone experiences what is known as a 'real dark night of the soul.' That's when you lie awake listening to a clock tick or the rain fall or to somebody breathing next to you, and you can't stop thinking of every mess you've ever made and every awful thing that's ever happened to you as if they're happening to you all over again. It's like your entire record is right there before you, written in black ink on the black night, but you can still read every word and you just have to stick it out until morning and daylight make your mind go blank again."

She rolled Sally's head from the flattened end of her pillow, resettling her upon the stuffed part. The child sighed and sank down deeper into her dreams, whatever they might be. The REM-induced flutter of her eyelids quickened, which was how Julie knew that Sally was off and running after rabbits, or if not rabbits, then she was hot on the trail of something else.

BETSY AND PETAL RETURNED LATE, thoroughly pleased with themselves and the evening they had had. They came upon Julie in the big parlor, where she lay stretched out on the camelback sofa, with the yo-yo afghan draped over her length and a sherry glass of Lily's Manzanilla (poured from Lily's very cloudy dining room sideboard decanter) and her book (only a few pages of the Trollope to go now) propped upon, respectively, her breastbone and her stomach. Julie stared at her cousin, who was wearing Petal's short silver skirt and silver sandals and her cropped and off-the-shoulder ChaCha T-shirt. Petal wore a near-matching outfit, except her skirt, sandals, and T-shirt were gold in color, and the words on the T-shirt read *GotCha,* and Julie wondered how Ginevra had been outfitted. She guessed there must be a platinum version of the ensemble and no doubt the sequins spelled out *WotCha* or some such.

"Did anyone take a picture of you, looking like that?" Julie asked.

"Yes, Mummy insisted before we left. She got out her fancy new camera and made everybody strike poses for her, together and individually," Betsy said.

She and Petal plopped themselves down in facing chairs and proceeded to tell Julie all about their evening. A Smokey Robinson impersonator had been on the bill as well and, his usual Miracles having let him down, he had enlisted Betsy and Petal and Ginevra, too, to fill in as his backup singers on very short notice.

"But I think we pulled it off," Betsy said. "Smokey, aka Calvin, gave us sharp jackets and Ray-Bans to wear."

"Yes, that'd work," Julie said. "I'm sure you passed for elegant black men."

"I just sang whatever Ginevra sang, a half a beat behind," Petal said. "Only she kept thinking she was hearing feedback and she kept inching over to give the speaker a kick. Well, the chorus to 'You Really Got a Hold on Me' was easy enough to remember, since it's just singing,

'You've really got a hold on me' over and over while you snap your fingers, except I seem to have this complete inability to snap my fingers. Watch," she said, as she bounced her thumb off her two forefingers, which only evoked the sound of silk softly brushing on silk. "What am I doing wrong?" she asked.

"Nothing. I think it must just be you," Julie said.

"I have to say, though, I preferred being a Supreme," Petal said. "I really think we captured more of their sensibility."

"That's what Andy thought too. He said we really pulled off being Supremes," Betsy said.

"Andy?" Julie asked. "How does Andy figure in all of this? He's still in Montana, isn't he?"

"He listened over my cell phone. He was so sorry he was going to miss my maiden performance as a pop star, and then I realized he didn't really have to. The Marry-Me-Nomar girl was there tonight and it turned out she is actually a very nice person. She obliged by holding my phone up to the stage," Betsy said.

"So now you've gone and gotten mixed up with the Marry-Me-Nomar girl?" Julie asked. "I knew I shouldn't have let you two go off on your own."

"Her name is Tina. We ought to call her by her proper name," Betsy said. "Petal and Ginevra and I had a very fascinating talk with Tina between our sets."

"I really think Nomar would adore her, if he gave her half a chance," Petal said.

"Oh, but she doesn't want to marry him at all. It's just a sort of project," Betsy said. "She's really a theater major at Northwestern but she had to take this past year off to make money for tuition, and she got so crazy-bored working as the Houghton-Hortons' au pair she decided to do the Marry-Me-Nomar thing as a piece of performance art. I think she confided in us because she looks upon us as her fellow artists." Betsy paused to look pleased. "Anyway, at the very least she says she's going to get a good audition monologue out of everything that's been happening to her, you know, about how she's been treated by people and what she's learned about being a celebrity in America, not the least of which is how easy it is to become a celebrity in America."

"Well, I must say, that's a useful gambit she came up with. You can do something completely idiotic and make a total fool of yourself and then claim you were just being a performance artist all along, and everyone says bravo," Julie said.

"Tina's really a Cubs fan," Petal said. "Red Sox fans drive her batty. She thinks being a Red Sox fan is like being in a weird cult."

"Anyway we ended up sort of inviting Tina to your wedding, Julie. I hope you don't mind," Betsy said. "I thought Mummy would get such a kick out of her."

"And besides, Ginevra thinks Tina may be just flaky enough to appeal to Brooks and vice versa," Petal said.

"No, no, I don't care who comes to the wedding," Julie said. "The more the merrier, just as long as she doesn't rag on Brooks. Tell her she can't go making performance art out of my brother. Then again, I suppose if Brooks wanted to, he could turn her into a hologram or something, so maybe it would be a fair enough fight."

"And Tina mustn't show up at the wedding wearing the same thing Julie's wearing," Betsy said. "We have to remind ourselves to tell her to leave the veil at home. We can't have Julie's wedding turning into a complete farce."

"God no, we can't have that," Julie said, and she drained her sherry glass. Her arm swung over the side of the sofa and she hauled the decanter out from underneath the skirting. "Anyone else?" she offered, before tilting a thin stream of any remaining liquid into her glass.

Petal found herself wondering whether Betsy knew what Julie was really up to in regard to the wedding, if indeed Julie was up to anything. Had Julie confided in her cousin? Why had Betsy spoken of the possibility of farce at Julie's wedding? Was she simply referring to what appeared to be this family's evident propensity for subverting any serious occasion, or was some more specific commotion planned for the day? Possibilities swarmed, but Petal was unable to suppress a yawn. The day could not contain another incident or surprise, although she had to say she had not been surprised that Betsy turned out to look so nice when someone just took the trouble to dress her properly and add a little color to her face.

"Well, I'm off to bed," she announced, yet she sat there, too content to move.

"I'm too wired to sleep," Betsy said. "I don't know when I've had so much fun, standing up there in front of everybody and going, 'wo-wo-wo,' and 'oh my-oh my-oh my' while everybody just kept applauding us. No, all in all, it was a very good day, an excellent day. That absurd trial finally ended, or at least they put a stop to it, and Andy will be getting away as soon as he can and he should be here by the end of the week. And then we discovered that Tina isn't really pathetic, so we don't have to feel sorry for her anymore, and on top of that, Julie found a beautiful dress, and even Sally got to see her silly movie without my having to sit through it too."

Julie dragged her sherry glass to her lips and muttered that some people were flipping Pollyannas, which Betsy didn't catch, for she had sprung up, declaring, *"Sally."* She had to run up to Sally's room right that very minute. She would stir the sleeping child awake so she could behold her mother, kneeling beside her bed all silvery and smiling and aflush with success. Sally would never believe it otherwise, and she might not even believe it anyway, in the years to come should anyone ever mention and remember how her mother had been so shining and so happy and so young that one last time, on that one late August night.

FIVE *Tell Me*

OVER THE PAST FEW WEEKS, LOUIS AND ANDY HAD ESTABLISHED a morning routine. They each rose early. Andy would be roused by a concentus of birdsong that swelled around a single treble note sounding from somewhere high up in a tree. He slid out of bed, mindful to let Betsy sleep on; she remained deaf to the racketing birds but was attuned to Andy's restlessness, and she looked so untroubled as she slept, her cheek cradled by a relaxed hand that consciousness would clench to take on the demands of the day. Louis, who dozed shallowly and alertly, had been watching for the dawn. Then it seemed safe to leave Ginger's side for a while. Were she to awaken without him, she would know, without being bewildered, where it was that she found herself as familiar forms emerged from the darkness, dim and gray at first (in the gloom and without her glasses, a lineup of pill vials resembled the towers and turrets of a toy fortress), but presently color and clarity would return in full to the pictures hanging on the wall and the roses leaning over their vase and all of the paraphernalia of illness that cluttered the desktop.

Nothing was ready to receive them in the sleeping house. The percolator had been programmed to begin brewing at half past six, and the newspaper still lay at the bottom of the driveway, where it had been tossed from the truck, so it only made sense for Louis and Andy to walk down to the road to collect the *Globe* and then to draw out their walk to fill in the half hour or so until the coffee would be ready to pour. Besides, the air was fresh at that early hour, and one morning they had spied a fox trotting across the lawn, his shock of tail waving and his tidy feet almost dancing along, and Louis and Andy subsequently kept an eye out for him because that first encounter had been so unexpected and so interesting. The fox hadn't minded them nor they him; they were all just figures occupying the same landscape at the same moment in time and no one meant harm to anyone.

They headed down to the end of the driveway where Louis would bend to pick up the paper and shake out the pebbles that had lodged between its pages during its landing skid across the gravel. He would read the lead story down to the fold and go no further no matter how compelling or urgent the news was on any given morning: *The president threatened to . . . The top rate on capital gains will drop from . . . Tragedy was averted when . . .* Louis balanced the paper on the crown of the mailbox so he would not forget to retrieve it on their way back. They passed the shuttered farm stand, always remarking on what an unanticipated success Lily had made of the venture, and they followed the river and the River Road as far as the railway bridge. There they slipped between the cement-block barriers and stood upon the open framework of trestle and track, where, transfixed by the flow and stir of the current, they gazed down at the water, which endlessly split apart at the pilings and then seamlessly repaired itself as it glided on its way.

Each would rather have been alone. Andy would have walked faster and further on his own, and Louis would have preferred not to have to talk; nevertheless, Andy adjusted his pace, and Louis would offer remarks of an inconsequential nature, generally pointing out things that Andy had already noticed for himself. A bedspring discarded in the woods, any particularly large tree branch that had fallen overnight, the flattened volute of a run-over snake were all perhaps given more than their due in passing, although one had to wonder about the snake and whether he had seen or heard or felt the car bearing down upon him. Andy seemed to think the snake would certainly have been aware that something big and calamitous was coming its way and would have attempted to avoid it, however uselessly—it would have gone out on a note of panic and flight—but Louis believed the course of events must have been so swift and overwhelming that the snake would have had no sense at all of what hit it; one instant it had been slithering across the smooth, warm pavement and the next instant, nothing.

THE PREVIOUS DAY, LILY HAD STOPPED by Alden's place on her way back from the ribbon store (weddings seemed to call for the purchase of many ribbons of various lengths and widths and materials with which to link and cinch and embellish the components of the ceremony and its surrounding hoopla—they were going to create an allée of ribbon-tethered helium-filled balloons, for example, which would direct guests from a parking area on the lower lawn up toward the house, lest anyone be inclined to wander off in the wrong direction and become lost in the woods). She had left behind a note weighted down by a rock on the picnic table for Brooks and Rollins to discover after a knock on the Winnebago door and a stroll down to the river, and a peep inside the barn, had failed to find them. She wanted them to come by her house at ten o'clock the following morning. She did not, on the note, tell them what it was she needed them for because she could only scrounge, from her purse, the back of the ribbon-store sales slip to write upon, briefly, and at any rate, her intentions were too involved and complicated and not entirely worked out enough in her own mind to describe.

But by the following morning when Brooks and Rollins showed up, Lily had all of her plans in place. She greeted them with the sort of smile which often accompanies a request for the undertaking of an uncongenial task (really more of a tightening of lips over teeth than any smile, paired with a corresponding sharpening of the nose) and she had even called them her "dear boys" because they were so punctual; just as the clock in the big parlor was striking the notes of the hour she had glanced out the window and there they were on the doorstep, reporting for duty.

"Where's Petal?" Rollins asked, but Lily wasn't going to let him change the subject.

"She is busy," Lily told him, and then she led them out to the pumpkin field, where, this year, she had planted the variety Giant Moon, which had flourished, the vines sprawling and the fruit rounding and mounding into great globes which were no longer green but had not yet become orange. At present, they were tinged with what could only be viewed as a rather funny flesh color.

"This is where Julie wants to have the ceremony," Lily said.

"Here?" asked Brooks. The spot did not look promising.

"Why?" asked Rollins. He'd been thinking that the terrace would be a nice place to hold a small wedding, although he wasn't necessarily thinking of his sister's arrangements.

"She says she has her heart set on this very field," Lily said. "She is being intractable on the subject, so you must find some way to set up the seating and make it all workable. We shall have a practice run today and decide where the aisle and the altar are going to be."

She conducted them to the barn where the fifty wooden folding chairs she had borrowed from All Saints' parish hall were being stored for the moment, although she had no idea whether fifty chairs would be enough. Because Julie had been so slow in sending out the formal invitations and since news of the impending wedding had somehow gotten round regardless, any number of people had been unofficially asked. Down at the farm stand, interested friends (and mere acquaintances who were perhaps swept up in the excitement) would inquire just when the wedding was going to be so they could save the date, and when they learned that the date was to be so soon upon them and they hadn't yet received their invitation, there would be an uncomfortable pause before a verbal invitation was issued by Lily or Betsy or Julie herself, all of whom were now a bit hazy on the names and the head count of those appended to the list, and, indeed, there was confusion over whether an individual had been sincerely asked or instead was expected to understand that they had been the recipient of an air kiss-off (as Ginger put it, although she had to explain to Lily the etymology of her newly coined phrase).

Lily told Brooks and Rollins that the fifty wooden folding chairs from All Saints' could be supplemented by the kitchen chairs and the dining room chairs and the hall chairs and the deacon's bench and perhaps even those two tabourets from the big parlor, if the ground wasn't too damp (for they were very old and rather precious). She said they would have to agree upon a discreet signal should there be a need for additional seating, and she demonstrated the American Sign Language gesture for *chair,* which neither Brooks nor Rollins quite caught but they reckoned should Lily catch their eyes and waggle her fingers at them above the heads of the other guests, she could only mean that one thing.

"I shall leave you to it," Lily said and she went off to brainstorm with Mr. DeSouza up in the potato patch; that year's yield of Bliss Triumph potatoes was so far proving to be a bit of a disappointment and she had some ideas of how they might fare better next year with Quaggy Joes.

Rollins and Brooks put their backs to their work, at first unaccountably touched that their great-aunt was relying upon them in this matter. They noted that neither Glover nor Andy had been recruited and confided in and made privy to the secret high sign (which, upon reflection, Brooks could *almost* replicate), but soon enough they concluded that Glover and Andy must have had the good sense to weasel out of the job. For the fifty chairs were to be carried the not inconsiderable distance from the barn to the edge of the field, and this journey could only be accomplished by taking a roundabout route which the lay of the land relative to the location of the barn door made half again as long as it had to be; a small pond, the walled herb garden, and an unexplained (but to be avoided) miasma of voracious gnats intervened. The temptation was to carry four chairs at once, two tucked beneath either arm; the chairs' weight allowed for this but not their loose and clattery construction. Grasped, the chairs contrived to free themselves, lashing out with a leg or an arm or seizing up and pinching fingers or any exploitable lappet of flesh between their slats.

Julie, who was lounging on a chaise pulled to a shady corner of the terrace (for the day was melting into a sizzler), paid her brothers scant attention, only sometimes lifting her eyes from the pages of her book to mark their progress. That she failed to encourage them as they trudged back and forth grappling with chair after chair puzzled Brooks and Rollins, who were, after all, doing this for her benefit, but her attitude caused them to redouble their efforts to please her because, as Rollins pointed out, they were the products of a broken home and as such had turned into the self-appointed fixers of the world (and thinking along those lines, he observed that this time it could be said Julie had gotten first dibs on being the fixee). As well, they were paying Julie the compliment of believing for the moment (or, at any rate, acting as if they believed) that an actual wedding was going to take place here in five days' time, although they could not point out this particular courtesy out to their sister, who reclined among cushions steadily reading *The Eustace Diamonds,* for Lily had set her off on a Trollope kick.

After all of the chairs had been conveyed to the edge of the field, Brooks and Rollins did their very best to arrange them in six rows of eight with a central aisle; however, the obvious impediments of so many giant pumpkins—which could be shifted but only as far as their tethering vines would allow—coupled with the unsuitability of the terrain underlying the foliage, which was a maze of trenches and hummocks, made the formation of straight lines and orderly spacing an impossibility. Brooks wondered whether some kind of a raised plank walkway could be constructed in lieu of any sort of discernible aisle, but Rollins advised him to take a moment to think of how that would look—a bride walking the plank. Lily, who had been monitoring their progress from a remote spot, now appeared at the edge of the field with Julie in tow so that Julie could see for herself that the pumpkin patch was not going to be a suitable site for a wedding ceremony. Brooks and Rollins understood then that this had been the point of the exercise all along, as Lily explained to Julie just how none of this was going to be possible.

"It will look as if your guests have all dragged and skidded their chairs around to position themselves farther away from people they don't like—like a bunch of kindergartners. And everyone's shoes and stockings will be ruined," she said. "The ladies' heels will sink down into the earth, and and they will all twist their ankles."

"Well, maybe Brooks and Rollins just ought to try harder," Julie began to say. She waved an airy hand as if the solution was so obvious she needn't bother to go into details.

"No, we'll be in the kitchen getting something cold to drink," Rollins said.

"We're parched," said Brooks.

"Don't drink all my diet Moxie," Julie warned them, and Rollins told her a less necessary sentence had never been spoken.

Then, sighing because she had to do everything herself, Julie entered the pumpkin patch to demonstrate how easily it could be walked through, but her legs were tugged at and entangled by the vines. She paused (pretending that she had meant to pause) and pointed to various pumpkins and suggested they could serve as small tables; the guests could set their cocktail glasses down upon the pumpkin tops during the service.

"People don't drink cocktails during the service," Lily said.

"Well, they'll be able to, at my wedding." Julie said.

"No, dear," said Lily. "I'm telling you, you're not going to be married in the pumpkin patch. I'm very sorry, but that's not going to happen."

Julie looked almost amused and then her face darkened. "Oh, all right, do whatever you like," she said. "It doesn't matter anyway. I don't even care anymore about any of it," she declared and she stalked off, headed back to the terrace. By the time she had resettled herself in the chaise, she was very much regretting that she had snapped at Lily, of all people. However, she knew she would be forgiven. Julie knew Lily knew she felt far worse about the outburst than Lily and she waited for her aunt to seek her out to let her know she ought not to brood. But when this did not happen, Julie began to resent Lily all over again for this failure to relieve her of her bad conscience. She snapped open her book and read; her lips moved as she continued to mutter random, resentful thoughts.

For her part, Lily had every intention of holding the girl to her word now that she had forced Julie's hand and at last been given the carte blanche she required to get things done. Thus far, every decision referred to Julie had only been deferred or, if decided at all, had been decided incorrectly. When Julie had bestirred herself to propose a hymn to be sung during the service, she had come up with *Now from the altar of my heart, Let incense flames arise / Assist me, Lord, to offer up / Mine evening sacrifice.* Even Ginger had agreed with Lily, the choice was not entirely appropriate although Ginger had pointed out they should only be grateful that Julie didn't want everyone to sing *See, the Conqueror mounts in triumph.* Lily had mentally penciled in *O perfect Love, all human thought transcending*; it went without saying that this was the safest choice, to sing of transcendence.

She had further need of Brooks and Rollins; those chairs had to be transferred from the pumpkin field to the upper lawn, and she went to fetch the boys from the house. They viewed her without enthusiasm as they sat at the kitchen table, slumped over glasses of cold water. They'd been discussing where their great-aunt's vitality had come from and they determined it was because she had perfected the art of delegating. They were thinking of inviting her to spend a month or two at GLowe Systems headquarters knocking heads (as Brooks said), although Rollins cautioned she might set her sights upon them and try to whip them into shape while she was at it.

"Julie has agreed. We'll be setting the chairs out on the lawn," Lily told them. "After you boys mow it for me," she added.

"That blows another theory," Brooks said to Rollins. They had also been speculating why Julie was so set upon having everyone assemble in the field, and they had decided that she wanted the guests to become tripped up and tangled among the vines and be unable to give chase when she announced that the wedding was off (and, in fact, had never been on). Julie would have a head start as she made her getaway—especially if she could dash down the plank though that bright idea lay more or less dead in the water. Brooks and Rollins knew there would have had to be a plank to make the pumpkin field a viable site.

"But I don't know," Rollins told Brooks. "I still kind of picture Julie sticking around for Hannah's cake, no matter what happens."

"What's that?" asked Lily. She had decided the least she could do was to make tomato sandwiches for her two helpers and she was sawing through the recent loaf Petal had baked in the adobe oven over at Ginevra's parents' place. Lily flicked off some bits of straw and ash and she gouged out a pebble baked into the crust. She dropped the pebble into the dirt of the windowsill pot in which Sally was hoping—and was being encouraged to hope—to sprout the pit of an especially delicious peach she had eaten.

"Nothing," Rollins said. His attention strayed to the refrigerator door, where a newspaper column was secured by a magnet. The engagement notice had finally run at long last in the past week's edition of the *Towne Crier.*

Further intelligence had been prised from this fresh material. Nicholas Davenant's parents lived in Cheltenham and his father's name was Stephen. An advanced search and mere minutes at the PC confirmed that a Stephen Davenant did live in Cheltenham and, furthermore, he may or may not have been the Stephen Davenant who had written a letter to the *Times* (of London) to impart the information that the first breeding of the Atlantic puffin occurred at four years of age and that a *single* egg was produced. From this, Brooks and Rollins had surmised that someone had gotten part, or perhaps all, of this puffin poop wrong elsewhere in the *Times*'s pages and they agreed that were this candidate for Pops Davenant-hood to show up for the wedding, after all, he would most certainly fit in with his in-laws.

"Although we must bone up on puffins. As a courtesy," Brooks had said. "Plus we still have all that Siberia material to work into our conversations with Nicholas Davenant."

But the brothers had a further question. "Aunt Lily," Rollins asked, "why is the photograph in the engagement notice of just Julie by herself? All the other announcements in the paper showed the girl and the guy together. I mean, I know Nicholas Davenant is in Siberia and all, but he could have sent us a picture and we would have Photoshopped it with the picture of Julie. We could have shown the two of them together. We could have posed them underneath Dad's grape arbor or standing by the farm stand. We could have put them in front of the Taj Mahal, if it comes to that."

"Or flying over the Taj Mahal in a chariot pulled by swans," Brooks said.

"It's a very modern practice to include the young man," Lily said, "although it doesn't seem right to me. I think the picture should just be of the young lady. It's really her moment, and besides, I don't think it's very manly to sit there trying to look like you're in raptures, as the girls do. Though most of the young men strike me as being rather sullen and uncomfortable."

"You discussed all of this with Julie?" Rollins asked.

"Oh yes. She particularly doesn't like the typical arrangement which seems to be popular, where the young man stands behind the young woman with his arm slung around her throat. She thinks it looks odd and artificial and agressive," Lily said.

"Like he's demonstrating a wrestling hold," Rollins agreed.

"So Julie and Nick were just being tasteful by not having a picture of him, too?" Brooks asked. "You'd go so far as to say that Julie and Nick are a traditional young couple, would you, Aunt Lily?"

"Are we calling him Nick now?" Rollins wondered.

Lily set a plate down in front of him. "What an interesting sandwich," he said. A large opening created by an air bubble in the top slice of bread let him see through to the tomato filling. He thought, on the whole, this was a very good thing, for it saved him the effort of prying up a corner in order to ascertain what was inside. And condiments could be added directly through the hole, he noted, reaching for the salt shaker.

"It was Petal who baked that bread," Lily told him, meaning to disown the stuff (she hoped she had removed all the pebbles, and she watched her nephews chew, hoping neither would break a tooth), but Rollins thought she was just being honorable and giving credit where credit was due for a really excellent loaf.

BUT WHAT OF BECKY? LILY AND GINGER AND BETSY had discussed that subject earlier in the morning when Betsy brought Ginger her breakfast tray. Lily had joined them, carrying up a small dish of jam scooped from the jar Penny had just sent down to the house via Harvey with the message that Ginger would be certain to find it irresistible. "This is damson plum jam from a fancy shop in Newburyport," Lily explained, where Penny had tried to buy some sort of pale and bridal candied violets to add to the Jordan almonds and pastel meltaway mints in the netted and beribboned favor parcels she was assembling for the wedding guests. Penny had been directed to the shop in Newburyport from a shop in Ipswich, being sent on quite the wild goose chase in the midst of a whole lot of late summer beach and tourist traffic, and she had had to settle for buying white chocolate nonpareils in place of the candied violets, which she hoped no one would mind. Since no one had asked her to do any of this, no one felt they were in a position to have an opinion about the makeup of the guest favors, although privately, among themselves, they regretted that Penny had not been able to follow through on her original candied violets scheme and they wished she had not mentioned them at all, unless she had been entirely confident of their procurement.

"Although you have to be very careful that no pesticides have been used on edible flowers," Lily said. She placed the saucer of jam on Ginger's tray, and Betsy spooned some onto a corner of an English muffin, which she offered to Ginger, who shook her head.

Lily did not like to see Ginger doused in shadows and she pulled up the window shade too vigorously and thus too high. Ginger winced and held her hand over her eyes. Betsy sat on the edge of the bed and peeled an orange, absentmindedly eating a segment before offering one to her mother, who took it and held it up to a sun-bright window, which exposed the umbrae of several seeds whose presence caused her to lose interest in the orange, because of the anticipated effort and bother of eating around the seeds.

"You see a lot of nasturtiums in salads on the West Coast," Betsy remarked.

"Too pretty to eat," Ginger said setting down the piece of orange, and she seemed satisfied to have come up with an excuse to leave things on her plate. Another orange segment was inspected. This one was encased in the most delicately scrolling membrane and she set it down.

Lily remained by the window, gazing out. The sight of so much clear and infinite blue sky made her remember, "Nicholas is flying in tonight."

"Yes," said Ginger, "and I am on tenterhooks over meeting him. Do you think he'll like us? I hope he likes us."

"What about Nicholas worrying whether we like him?" Betsy asked.

"But we already do. We love him; he sounds too wonderful," Ginger said. "Julie says he is entirely kind to young children and animals."

"She volunteered that information?" asked Betsy. "I mean, I can't ever get much out of her."

"No, or not exactly, she didn't tell me. I was drawing her out and I asked her, what about Nicholas's attitude toward little ones and pets," Ginger recalled. "I was attempting to divine whether they plan to have children of their own some day, but she gets a bit skittish when any serious subject comes up, so I framed the question as a general query about dumb and defenseless creatures, so to speak (Julie and I were both making a fuss over Agnes at the time). It was my hope that the conversation would lead to some sort of revelation."

"And did it?" asked Lily. She wasn't sure which she would find more concerning, a childless Julie or a Julie briskly and brusquely overseeing a brood of (she pictured them now) scrappy, spikey-haired boys who would always be in need of a bath or in want of a warmer jacket. Perhaps Nicholas would be the more nurturing parent, but Lily couldn't quite see how that would work out if he had to spend half his time in Siberia and such places.

"Julie said Nicholas once had a dog named James," Ginger said.

"Just like in *The Railway Children*, their dog was called James," Betsy said. "He looks like a dalmatian in the illustrations—Sally used to make me read that book to her all the time before her current C. S. Lewis fixation began."

"Apparently, James the Dog Davenant was also a dalmatian," Ginger said.

"Huh," said Betsy. "Well, people often name their pets after characters in books." She remembered that Agnes had been called after a Brontë heroine; she was pretty sure it had been the idea at the time.

"One way or another we shall all satisfy our curiosity about Nicholas tonight," Lily observed, and she had a feeling everything would go well on that front. But another, less congenial meeting loomed. "I'm just not at all sure what will happen when Becky arrives, if indeed she is even going to come," Lily confided. "We continue not to know whether she'll be here, because Julie still hasn't said. The last time I dared to inquire she just looked miserable and wouldn't, or couldn't, say. I don't want to badger her; besides, I'm not the right person for her to confide in over the matter. She knows I've taken sides (how could I not?), and I cannot discuss Becky in the proper spirit. I really don't want her here, for our sakes, but still, Becky *must* come, for Julie's."

"Still, I have to suppose that Julie's gotten used to not having Aunt Becky around. Perhaps she won't mind as much as you think, if she doesn't show up, after all," Betsy said.

"But special occasions can have a way of resuscitating old feelings," Ginger said. "You can feel like you've lost someone all over again in a whole new way no matter how long they've been gone from the scene."

"Longer can even be worse," Lily said, "when you realize how much time has passed without someone being there and you look back over how much they've missed out on and then you suddenly see that you've even allowed yourself to forget about them sometimes."

"And then it's like a cloud has passed over the sun," Ginger said.

"Well," said Betsy. She didn't like the sound of any of that and she wished her great-aunt and her mother would not go on so about absent presences or whatever it was they were driving at. "Your tea is getting cold," she reminded Ginger.

"It was too hot," Ginger complained; she'd taken a single sip earlier.

"So perhaps now it will be just right," Lily suggested and she and Betsy watched as Ginger lifted the cup and drank a bit and sputtered. Their eyes followed the cup as Ginger set it back down upon the saucer. "What?" Ginger asked. "What's going on?" Why were Betsy and Lily hovering by her bedside this morning and acting in cahoots, trying to get her to drink her tea?

"It's just that Mrs. Samrin gave me some tea for you to try," Lily confessed. “She dropped by the farm stand yesterday with a little box. She was quite shy; she says it’s a sort of a traditional Cambodian folk remedy, not that the Samrins were ever so-called folks when they were back in Cambodia, mind you. She told me she and Mr. Samrin met when they were both students at the Sorbonne, which I never knew. However, she said she personally witnessed some inexplicable results from traditional remedies during the days of Pol Pot, when life was so bad, and she learned a few things. Well, she had to, didn’t she, and I must say, they all managed to survive somehow. Just don’t mention any of this to the older girls. Mrs. Samrin says they’re very embarrassed when she brings up anything from the past, although whether that’s a cultural indisposition or a more general teenage angst, she isn’t sure.”

“I thought something smelled funny,” Ginger said. She sniffed the cup and pulled the same face Sally made when told she must try to like Grape-Nuts pudding.

“I think the tea smells like flowers,” Betsy said. “Try a little more.”

Ginger took another sip and washed the decoction over her tongue before she swallowed with an idea that to do so would give the remedy every chance. She drained the cup, and they all waited for something to happen.

“There are leaves left in the bottom of the cup. Perhaps we’re supposed to read them for further instructions,” Ginger said. She peered. “I’m detecting a very Rorschachy-looking crab.”

“Really, Mummy,” Betsy said. “I believe one’s attitude is almost as important as the elixir, with remedies like this.” She confiscated the cup before her mother could see anything else in its depths.

“You’ve turned into such a Californian,” Ginger complained.

“Mrs. Samrin left the entire box, you’re supposed to keep drinking it,” said Betsy. “The effect must be a cumulative one.”

Ginger crooked a finger and snagged a shimmering little gobbet of jam off the English muffin top, which she sampled, as Betsy and Lily exchanged rather pleased looks.

“But what have we decided to do about the Becky question?” Lily asked. That matter pressed above all others.

“I think you should talk to Julie,” Betsy told Ginger. “You and she get along so well these days.” Indeed, she had noticed, not without a pang, what friends her cousin and her mother had become. Ginger seemed to love everything about Julie: her fascinating museum work, her London life, her bright red hair, and Nicholas Davenant, of course, although he almost sounded too good to be true, in Betsy's opinion.

"Oh no, I just let Julie come to me with her concerns if she's so inclined," Ginger said, "and she hasn't confided in me over this one. No doubt she's being delicate and doesn't want to put me in an uncomfortable position because she knows how savage I can be on Alden's behalf." She leaned back among her pillows and shut her eyes as if the very thought of how fierce she was prepared to be for her brother's sake had worn her out.

"Maybe we can put Petal up to asking," Betsy said. "We can make her in charge of accommodations for the out-of-town guests and we can very casually remind her to ask Julie whether Aunt Becky needs a reservation at the Academy B&B."

"No, Betsy. That wouldn't be at all nice. We can't take advantage of Petal's eagerness to please us," Lily said. "Any more than we already have," she added.

"Whatever happens, whatever Aunt Becky may or may not have done, I'm going to feel terrible for Julie, and for Aunt Becky too, if she can't be here for the wedding," Betsy said.

"Then that's why you're the correct person to speak to Julie about this," Ginger spoke up. "You're the only one who can console her or be sincerely glad for her, whichever way it turns out to be."

"Yes," Lily said. "I really think this is a job for you alone, Betsy. You're the one who has to come through for the rest of us now."

BUT BETSY PUT OFF SPEAKING TO HER COUSIN. She needed to run a few errands first and she was obliged to have Sally and Cam in tow, which would make everything she had to do take twice as long, since no one else had time for the little girls that morning. Lily's morning plans did not include child minding, and Penny couldn't keep them with her up at the Ridge House because she was polishing the floors. She had hired a machine from the Home Depot and read the directions on the back of a bottle of liquid wax twice over and sent Harvey down, out of her way, to help out at the farm stand, which was why Glover and Ginevra weren't able to keep an eye on the children: they were monitoring Harvey's activities; he just made up prices for things and got into arguments over the correct length of time to boil corn, insisting upon twenty seconds and no longer. Sometimes he refused to sell a dozen ears to someone who was so unwise as to disagree.

And Betsy was mindful that Andy was holed up in the little parlor waiting for a teleconference to begin; new charges were going to be filed against the Third Day Brethren, something having to do with Internet credit card fraud. He had invited Louis to listen in, guessing that his father-in-law would enjoy musing over the list of offenses. Nor could Petal be distracted from her alteration work on Julie's dress. She was taking in the bust and letting out the waist, which, as Julie said, was rather demoralizing, being shaped like a Pez dispenser, although Petal seemed to think that Issey Miyake would just adore her figure. Julie, pleading exhaustion, was sitting out the final week of wedding preparations and was in no mood to be saddled with Sally and Cam at the moment. Besides, Lily had warned Betsy that the state of Julie's disposition was about to take a turn for the worse, pending the showdown in the pumpkin patch.

Sally and Cam were delighted to be told they were going downtown and they piled into the car more than willingly. Betsy parked in the lot tucked behind Hannah's building, where the production line was turning out desserts that morning. An exhaust of caramelized sugar and chocolate was blowing through the ventilation fan, and upon their release from the backseat of the car, Sally and Cam darted to stand beneath the vent. They made a show of deeply breathing in and in and in, and Sally clamped her arms and legs tight and closed her eyes; she was a piece of candy being covered in chocolate, she said.

"So am I," said Cam, offering up her face to be drenched.

Betsy hooked a finger under the collar of each girl's shirt and propelled them around the corner and in through the door of the Ben Franklin store. They dawdled for a moment by a new display of back-to-school supplies, Sally putting first dibs on a Sabrina the Witch loose-leaf notebook, which Cam didn't care about anyway, having zeroed in on a Kermit the Frog three-ring binder. They tore off to visit the goldfish offered for sale in the square aquarium located at the very back of the store. When they tapped upon the glass sides of the tank, a spew of bubbles erupted from a small interior pipe. The coil of bubbles, which they summoned again and again, tickled the fish, who shimmered and looped-the-loop sliding on their stomachs along a crest of silvery effervescence.

Betsy went in search of a sticky-backed felt pad for her mother to attach to the vamp of a newly purchased shoe which she planned to wear to the wedding. When Ginger had practiced walking in her shiny pair of sling-back pumps (for the heels were very, very high and she wanted to make sure she could manage to move in them), the right shoe rubbed at just the wrong spot across her instep, where the skin was stretched too thin above a trident of visible bones. Betsy could not quite picture the item that Ginger required, but Ginger insisted that such a thing existed and would either be found in the notions department or in the Dr. Scholl's display kiosk perhaps. She had warned Betsy not to let anyone try to sell her bunion pads because they would not do the trick.

When neither of her mother's suggested sites panned out, Betsy dedicated herself to a review of every corner of the store. She wandered up one aisle, past the cleaning and polishing supplies, and she wandered down another, past the buckets of silk flowers and baskets of wax fruits. She paused at a pile of brightly colored nylon headscarf squares of the sort that wearers triangled and knotted beneath their chins. A mirror suspended above the counter invited her to see how she looked in a yellow daisy-printed kerchief which had caught her eye as something suitable for Lily, or maybe even for herself. Perhaps the silvered old mirror just knew some flattering angle and was used to casting back a pleasing image to any would-be customer, but Betsy thought she didn't look half bad in the scarf. She experimented; there was a way of crossing the untied ends of the kerchief beneath the chin and knotting them behind the head, catching and securing the flyaway vee of fabric, for a more sophisticated look, which was enhanced when she slipped on a pair of large, dark-lensed sunglasses plucked from an adjacent revolving rack. Betsy turned her head and propped her chin upon an elevated shoulder, aiming an affronted glare at an imaginary paparazzo.

Sally and Cam, who had had enough of the fish (there was a sameness to goldfish antics; it was all back and forth with them), bustled past Betsy on their way to another department of interest in the Ben Franklin store. They froze and spun around, openmouthed. They had not recognized her until the usualness of her denim skirt registered with them, a lapsed second later. Cam didn't care that Mrs. Happening had assumed a disguise, but Sally's lower lip trembled, and her backward glance, as Cam pulled her away, was forlorn and blameful at once.

As she slipped off the sunglasses and unknotted the scarf, Betsy decided to buy them for herself and, returning to the object of her original errand, presently discovered the item Ginger required. They were called Comfi-Feet and were displayed on a shelf between the ladies' stockings and the tube socks, in the hosiery section. She spotted some cute white nylon socks with a double row of lace on the cuffs, but they didn't come in Sally's size; they were intended for much smaller feet, a realization that brought her up short.

The little girls rushed back to Betsy's side then, desperate for her to buy them each a Lil' Sir Lancelot ensemble, which was comprised of a molded plastic sword and shield and helmet. The pieces were affixed to a stiff cardboard backing which was imprinted with a picture of a dreamy castle and a moony maiden and a lingering knight balanced on a horse and equipped with finer versions of the sword and shield and helmet that Sally and Cam coveted.

"I don't know," Betsy said. She prodded a sword blade, which had been fashioned from a blunt and hollow length of flimsy plastic, and she decided the sword itself would receive the worst of it when put to use smiting any enemy whose head or arm or leg would surely prove to be the harder surface.

"But what do you want this for?" she asked.

Cam was about to blurt something, but Sally cut her off. "It's educational," she claimed.

"Is it? How? Educational in what way?" Betsy asked.

"About the olden days?" Cam suggested, taking note of the dreamy castle's unmodern moat and spire-topped towers.

"Do your parents let you play with weapons?" Betsy asked her.

"*All* the time," Cam promised.

"Are you sure?" Betsy asked. She rather thought Buddhists were particularly nonviolent people and she didn't want the Samrins to regard her as a bad influence.

"*All* the time," Sally echoed Cam.

"Well, you must give me your word you won't pretend that Agnes and Tommy are lions and bears and attack them. Or that Mr. DeSouza is an Efreet or an Orkney or a Woose," Betsy said. She hoped she had named all the eligible members of the monster rabble who had murdered Aslan.

The little girls swore they would not go after Agnes or Tommy or Mr. DeSouza, agreeing so willingly and with such evident relief that Betsy understood she had not yet guessed what mischief they were plotting. "You can't play swords and helmets at Julie's wedding either," she said. "Just imagine what Julie would have to say if you did anything unkind to Nicholas."

"Julie would say, 'You flipping kids, I'll kill you,' " Sally said. Her hands clutched and wrung an invisible neck, for she believed Julie would most likely wish to strangle her and Cam.

" 'I'll flipping kill you, you flipping kids,' " Cam added, snarling as she knew Julie would snarl.

Leaning against Betsy's legs and pushing her forward, they herded her to the cash register, where Betsy reached into her satchel and withdrew a small square of plastic from her wallet that she presented to the clerk, who, in turn, shoved a slip of paper and a pen across the counter. Sally reached for the pen because she was showing off and wanted Cam to think she always got to sign for the money, but Betsy knocked her hand away.

Then Betsy marched the little girls back to the car and piled them into the backseat, where they sat, very satisfied, each hugging a big billowy bag containing her Lil' Sir Lancelot kit, which they were forbidden to open until they got home. The least rustle or tear of plastic earned them a stern look delivered via the rearview mirror, where Betsy's right eye floated, all seeing and formidable. As well, Betsy took it upon herself to criticize their behavior in the store, where they had recklessly raced up and down all the aisles. They would have to perform better at the library, their next destination on that morning's round of errands.

On notice, Sally and Cam took off across the library lobby like race walkers, mindful to keep the sole of one sneaker or the other in contact with the floor at all times so that, technically, they could not be accused of running. (They had, one exasperated day, taxed Lily to give them an exact definition of just what did and what did not constitute running.) They veered toward the spiraling staircase which rose to a gallery that encircled the space beneath the library dome, and Betsy stopped at the circulation desk, where she pulled book after book from her satchel: her own, Ginger's, Sally's, Lily's, and Petal's recent reading.

"I need to renew this copy of *Sugar Busters!* for Petal," Betsy told Brianna, who was on duty at the desk. Brianna swiped her scanner over the line of bar code affixed to the spine and then she settled down on an elbow to read the copy on the flap.

"Maybe I should try this diet, Mrs. Happening," she said.

Betsy pulled a list from her skirt pocket and drifted over to the Fiction/New Arrivals shelf. Ginger always consulted the Sunday papers' reviews and jotted down titles, although lately she had informed Betsy she could no longer read anything written in the present tense; to do so now left her breathless because she never knew where to pause to take a mental breath as the action rolled on and on. Betsy opened a new novel at random and read, *I go to his room and I find him there waiting, he takes me in his arms and I say, No, stop, and he says, Yes, start, which makes me laugh, so I say All right, but only if you promise and he promises me before I say what it is he must promise me, because he says he promises me everything and anything.* Betsy saw what her mother meant and she stuck the book back on the shelf. Lily had also made some specific requests. She was rereading Jean Plaidy in chronological order and she only needed to read *Gay Lord Robert* and then she'd be done with the Tudors, so if Betsy happened to spot *The Captive Queen of Scots,* she was to grab that as well, since Lily was keen to revisit the Stuarts.

Betsy headed for the stacks. She wasn't looking for anything for herself because she and Andy and Sally would start their long drive home, cross country, the first thing the following Monday morning, once the dust of the wedding had settled. Between now and then, she would have little time to read, being occupied with the wedding and its attendant fuss, not to mention continuing with the subtle execution of a campaign she had undertaken to persuade her mother to come to stay with them in California for as long as she wanted. That was the careful phrase Betsy used; for as long as she wished to remain with them in Santa Barbara, they would be very happy to have her. She had already looked into the arrangements that could be made to fly a very ill person cross country.

Up in the gallery, Sally and Cam admired the gold-leaf star shapes arranged in the configurations of constellations spread across the cobalt blue field of the arching dome. They were on their way to a screened alcove in the gallery's darkest reaches, where an artifact of mid-nineteenth century taxidermy, which no one had had the heart to throw away (nor quite the stomach to have to gaze upon every day), lingered on inside a glass display case. A finely crafted coach was being drawn by a brace of high-stepping squirrels who galloped along, forever frozen in fleet, tail-flourishing attitudes. A liveried chipmunk commanded the coach, grasping silver ribbon reins in one exquisite little paw as he held on to his stovepipe hat with the other. A family of mice, finely dressed in gowns and capes and suits and bonnets fashioned from scraps of silk and lace, rode inside on tufted seats—although the youngest mouse child rather perilously hung out an open window; he seemed to want to have a word with the chipmunk. Sally and Cam had never seen anything more wonderful. They always tapped upon the glass because they were not quite certain that one day the darling creatures wouldn't reawaken and take off on their interrupted journey, breaking through one of the glass walls with a shower of sparkles and glitter and go flying off round and round the gallery. Cam was convinced the mice family was going to their grandmother's house, but Sally was pretty sure they were headed to church, and with their noses pressed against the glass, the girls argued their cases for these views, until Cam noticed, as she never had before, a small placard half tipped over in the soap-shavings snow of the foreground which read, in faded writing, *Off to the Races.* This effectively proved Sally wrong but discredited Cam's own theory as well, so Cam pronounced herself suddenly bored with stuffed squirrels before Sally could spot the sign for herself. Cam decided she would prefer that they both not win the argument than both be proved the losers; she would have answered back that a loss shared is not a loss halved; rather, it was a loss magnified, should any adult get ahold of her and try to tell her otherwise. Sally only minded that Cam had thought to be bored because a certain superiority was implicitly expressed by tiring of an activity first, which mimicked, perhaps, a more general sense that in life one was always outgrowing something, and, indeed, both she and Cam were committed to looking over their shoulders to make sure how fast the other one was gaining on her.

"Come on then," Sally said.

Low bookcases filled with retired encyclopedias and foreign dictionaries and bound volumes of a hundred years' worth of annual *Towne Reports* ran around the outer wall. The inner ring of the gallery was fronted by a low balustrade supported by urn-shaped posts, and here Sally and Cam elected to sit, their feet swinging in the open air as each straddled a post and gazed out above the railing. They overlooked a grid of bookshelves whose never-dusted tops were littered with flung or fallen objects; mittens and pens and twists of paper and broken-backed books created a world of long-forgotten things, the contemplation of which made them thoughtful.

Today they had discovered, left behind on the gallery's study table, a square block pad of notepaper and several pencil stubs used for noting call letters and reference titles. They had appropriated this material; the pencil stubs were particularly attractive, for the little girls loved anything pared down to size. They tore off sheets of paper and crumpled them into balls, which they tossed onto the tops of the bookshelves to take their places among the other lost objects. This was harder than it looked. More often than not, even if a paper ball was properly aimed and landed satisfactorily, it would bounce along and jounce off onto the floor, and presently this pastime threatened to became not very interesting. Sally had an idea then. She picked up a stub of pencil and scrawled something upon a piece of paper which she showed to Cam. Sally had written *BOM*. She crumpled the paper into another ball and pitched it over the balustrade. They followed its descent; it wedged itself between a couple of books on the Returns cart.

"Pow," Sally said.

"Ka-pow," Cam said. They had to whisper about explosions because they were at the library.

They tore off multiple sheets and inscribed and dispatched multiple bombs, strafing the tops of the shelves and landing missiles in the big wastepaper basket behind the checkout desk, and they hit all the Reading Is Fundamental posters stuck to the walls, which, according to Cam, had to be struck in specific order going from left to right around the perimeter of the lower gallery, and if you missed one you had to start all over again, beginning with Mr. Rogers and ending with Mrs. President Clinton. Sally sighed and settled down to work.

Below them, in the General Fiction section, Betsy carried a small cache of Jean Plaidys tucked under her arm. The stacks, ungenerously spaced and not very well lit, were the last place anyone should wish to run into Babe Palmer, as Betsy now did, coming suddenly upon the older woman as they simultaneously turned down the opposing ends of Row Br-Coz. There wasn't sufficient room to sidle past each other in such tight quarters, at least not in Betsy's opinion, for although she and Babe were not at all big people, Betsy had no wish to be familiarly breathed upon by Babe nor to brush up against her breasts or bottom (whichever aspect was presented), so Betsy reversed direction. This about-face meant they were now going in the same direction, and Babe fell into step just behind Betsy, forgetting for the moment her wish to lay her hands upon something to read by Maria Corelli, an authoress of whom she approved when Miss Corelli wasn't trying to be too artistic. Babe bore down upon Betsy, who had quickened her pace and was heading for the brighter lights and wider spaces of the lobby where she could be less easily cornered, as Babe questioned her (questioned the back of her head, the pale loose swirl of bun caught up in a silvered clasp) about the particulars of Julie's wedding, which Betsy had no intention of divulging, for she almost believed that Babe would take any nugget of information given to her and spin mischief from it; she would blight the flowers, embitter the wine, and break the strings on the violins like an evil fairy godmother, if given half a chance. "And what about Becky; will she be there?" Babe asked, which was particularly galling to Betsy, who wanted to know why she had become everybody's go-to expert on that subject.

Cam nudged Sally as Betsy and Babe came into view and halted hard by the glowing copy machine, directly below their swinging feet. Cam snatched up a piece of paper, scrawled across it with her pencil, and creased it into a ball, which she aimed with dead-on accuracy to land on top of Babe's head, where it stuck in the middle of the whorled and messy parting of the waves.

For several wonderful seconds, Babe failed to react. Intent upon quizzing Betsy, she reached up slowly and prodded the wad of paper for an additional second or two before snatching it from her hair. Whether or not a normal person would have thought to unfold and investigate further such a randomly fallen object is an open question, but Babe did so. Cam, in her eagerness to land a BOM on Mrs. Palmer, had neglected to close the top of the *O* so that the message read, to Babe's eye, *BUM.* She breathed in sharply and held the revealed text between extended fingers like the nasty thing that it was as she glanced around in every direction save that of above. Sally and Cam, who had swiftly retracted their legs, crouched and peered down from behind the cover of a more substantial baluster (every tenth baluster of the gallery balustrade was a thicker, bracing one). They thrilled for a moment over their lucky escape from Mrs. Palmer, who would have been sure to come stumping up the spiraling staircase to stage a confrontation had she spotted them. That Mrs. Palmer had no idea at all of their involvement emboldened them to scurry back down to the lobby so that they might parade themselves in front of their unenlightened victim, which would be, they agreed, a great deal of fun.

By then, Betsy had changed tactics. In response to a rather sneering inquiry about Nicholas Davenant, she now found herself relaying an excess of information of a nature intended to annoy Babe, telling her that, in fact, Nicholas owned the oil company whose business had taken him to Russia and for good measure she let it drop that he was the nephew of an earl. She was quite sure Babe and Nicholas would never meet, so there seemed to be no harm in making up stuff about him, and even should there be some day of reckoning, should Babe ever encounter Nicholas on the sidewalk of High Street and put further stiff questions to him, Betsy herself would be long gone and far away from the scene, and besides, Babe would be blamed for getting the wrong end of the stick rather than Betsy for applying, as she was at present, the needle.

Sally and Cam materialized, bubbling over with some happy secret. They stood in front of Betsy, loosely leaning into her in such a manner as to make her feel aproned by the little girls. They stared, and persisted in staring, at Babe, with wide grins stretched across their faces. All of this attention began to unnerve Babe; she knew perfectly well she was nothing much to look at and certainly no one in whom to take such evident delight (she was no Penny Hill, who could always be counted upon to have sweets and trinkets in her handbag). She lingered over dark thoughts of Penny (the way she wore all those T-shirts with uplifting messages scrawled across her drooping bosom); however, she was unable to sustain this rather comforting buttress of the considered failings of others. For she was being irresistibly revisited by the second of her first impressions, which had struck her upon becoming an object of such fascination to Sally and Cam, and she could not successfully suppress what was for her a revelation: the fact that there was no good reason for anyone ever to be happy to see her. Her feelings had been hurt, very thoroughly and very complicatedly. She felt as if all the wind had been knocked out of her, and she could not summon sufficient breath to remind the little girls it was very rude to stare. She took her leave abruptly, and Betsy squeezed Sally's and Cam's shoulders in gratitude for running off Babe. However they had accomplished that feat, she wasn't going to ask questions.

She checked out her books. They left the library and piled into the car. They were going to drive just halfway around the green and pull into Alden's driveway, which Betsy said was a terribly lazy thing to do, and they were not going to tell anyone they hadn't walked across the Common from the library. Sally and Cam, who had sat in the backseat displaying just how lazy they were being (Cam faked slumber and a snore; Sally sprawled like an understuffed rag doll), leaped from the car when they got there, calling for Tommy. They ran off in search of him as Betsy unloaded the trunk.

There had been considerable discussion over who was going to get to keep Nicholas Davenant for the few days prior to the wedding. He could not stay at Lily's, where there was no room for him unless he was put in with Julie, which possibility no one was about to suggest to Lily. Penny had offered to let him camp out on a sofa up at the Ridge House, although the Ridge House had been specifically designed and built to discourage guests; there was just one of everything for the two of them, as Harvey pointed out, and he did not know what the English fella would use for a towel rack. Brooks and Rollins offered the Winnebago; the pool table would do (had done) as a bed in a pinch, and they said they would make sure that Nicholas enjoyed a very jolly final few days of bachelorhood. Glover and Ginevra put in a bid as well.

There was the guest pod attached to the main dwelling at Ginevra's parents' place which would be quite comfortable, providing Nicholas wasn't unusually tall. "How tall is he anyway?" they had asked Julie, who said she only knew the figure in centimeters. Sometimes she pulled rank because she had been living abroad for ten years.

But obviously Alden's house had been the only choice or, at any rate, would have to be made to do, and Betsy's final errand that morning was to deliver supplemental items to upgrade Alden's guest-room amenities, such as they were. Glover and Brooks and Rollins had lately been showing up around town attired in Izod tennis shirts and madras shorts, Alden having off-loaded the overflow contents of the guest-room bureau upon them in order to make the drawers available for Nicholas and his unpacking. Lily gave Alden full marks for thoughtfulness, and she was also pleased with her great-nephews' improved appearance. Today, employing Betsy as her factotum, she was sending over lavender-scented bedsheets, an electric fan, a reading lamp, and several extension cords to link the fan and the reading lamp to the guestroom's sole electrical outlet. She also wanted to be sure that Nicholas had his own working flashlight, which she had told Betsy to leave standing conspicuously upright on his bedside table, for Lily remained haunted by the dark-and-stormy-night-plunge-down-the-stairs-and-fall-through-the-trapdoor-and-drown-in-the-well scenario, which she had envisioned so clearly the very first time she entered Alden's house.

Sally and Cam had chased Tommy beneath the Winnebago where he had retreated once he caught wind of them. He could not be enticed out from his hiding place, and so it only made sense to enter the Winnebago in order to stamp upon the floor just above where he lurked in an attempt to drive him out from under.

"Helloo?" the little girls had called first, through the screen door, receiving no answer, which suited them. They hopped onto the glass-topped table and jumped off with all their might several times, running to the window in between to check whether Tommy had emerged under this assault. Then they gave up trying and settled back on the black leather sofas to fool around with the prototype VeeCube Brooks and Rollins had lately installed.

Upstairs in the guest room, as Betsy remade Nicholas's bed (Alden having used two top sheets and mismatched pillow slips), she hoped Nicholas would not awaken in the dark and sit up too quickly, for he would crack his head upon the lowest part of the sloping ceiling and show up at the wedding with a big bruise on his forehead. She swept a litter of dead hornet husks from the windowsill, lifting the screen and brushing out the husks as she looked about for living hornets; most likely there was a nest beneath the eaves and she wondered whether Alden ought not to spray lest Nicholas be stung repeatedly and show up at the wedding with red and swollen features.

She noticed, however, that Alden had taken a stab at brightening the room. He had covered the bureau top with pictures of Julie taken at all ages and stages of her life. Displayed was her dental history (crooked teeth, braces on, braces off) and her hair color and haircut histories and her various past fads for horses and the ballet and only wearing black, even in the summer, even on Christmas Day. Chronicled was her evolution from cute to awkward to Julie, and if Nicholas did not fall in love with her all over again, and fall in love deeper and harder, Betsy thought as she picked up and put down photos, he could not be made of flesh and blood.

"Anything else?" Alden asked, after the lamp and fan were plugged in and turned on and off, just to make sure of them. The flashlight batteries were fresh as well, Lily having seen to that.

"I suppose Nicholas has been living rough all summer in a yurt or whatever," Betsy said, thinking out loud as she surveyed the room, which Alden accepted as an endorsement. What Betsy meant was, This beats a yurt, so that was all right.

Betsy tracked the little girls down in the Winnebago. She didn't care that they had finally figured out how to activate the VeeCube and were about to figure out how to access the initial portal—she had no idea what that meant and she didn't care. She bundled them out the door and shooed them into the car.

"Wait," Sally cried.

"What now?" Betsy asked, braking.

"Where are my library books?" Sally asked. She had been rummaging through the satchel and only finding grown-up things to read. "I wanted to read *No, David!* again."

Cam giggled. David.

"There won't be time for you to read and return books to the library. We're going home right after the wedding," Betsy said.

"Home?" Sally asked.

"Home," Betsy said. "You and Daddy and I are driving home, first thing Monday morning."

"What?" Sally asked.

"You knew that," Betsy said.

"No, I didn't. Can Cam come too and live with us?" Sally asked.

"Certainly not. Her family would miss her and she'd miss them. They'd all be so sad," Betsy said. Cam shot a blameful look at Sally, for wanting to make everyone unhappy.

"I didn't say good-bye to the goldfish," Sally complained. "I didn't say good-bye to the squirrel."

"What squirrel is that?" Betsy asked. She had never been a child in Towne, so she didn't know about *Off to the Races.*

"I didn't say good-bye to Library Brianna. I didn't say good-bye to Mr. Peddock," Sally said. "I didn't say good-bye to . . ."

"Mrs. Palmer," Cam suggested.

"Mrs. Bomb-Head," Sally said, and they shook with laughter.

"Now you're just being silly," Betsy said. "And you have almost a week to see everybody one last time. We'll make a list, and Daddy and I will drive you around to say good-bye."

"Not good-bye to Granna?" Sally wailed then, and Cam smiled. So, she would have Auntie Ginger all to herself once again.

"I don't know; we'll have to see about that," Betsy said.

Upon their return to the house, Sally and Cam flew from the car hugging their sword sets. They jettisoned the big plastic bags, which lifted and lofted across the newly mown lawn until chased down by Brooks and Rollins, who resented this intrusion upon their neatly arranged folding chairs (six rows of eight chairs, with a center aisle). They were working on the board-and-sawhorse altar, steadying the structure with wooden shims and rocks, but no one would see all of that beneath the white damask tablecloth that would ultimately be draped over their rough construction. Betsy collected her book satchel and Ben Franklin purchases and the several empty pie plates Alden was returning—whenever Lily baked, she remembered him.

Betsy followed the shrilling of Sally's and Cam's voices around the corner of the house and onto the terrace, where they had discovered

Julie, who sat in her chaise, reading. She was sipping Evian water from a liter bottle through a bobbing and flexible straw. The little girls had just asked Julie the questions which, suddenly and brilliantly, had occurred to them to ask her, of all people.

"Which way is England, from Aunt Lily's house?" they needed to know, because they had finally figured out that the reason they had almost, but not quite, found Narnia that day in the rainy attic closet was that the closet in the book was located in England, whereas they were starting out from an American closet and had obviously taken a wrong turn. When they made their next attempt on Saturday (dressed in their wedding finery so they would look very nice when they got there and armed like knights with their swords and shields and helmets and accompanied by David May, whom they planned to convince to come with them or maybe they'd have to trick him or kidnap him or something), they would know which direction to take to get to Narnia from Lily's house.

"Which way is the UK?" Julie mused. "I guess it's east and sort of north of here, which is, which is, which way is that?" She made some mental calculations involving the locations of Rte. 95 and the Atlantic Ocean relative to her present situation. "Thataway," she declared, pointing in the general direction of the cell tower.

"Thanks," shouted Sally and Cam, and they took off, skidding through the French doors, which they left swinging open behind them.

Betsy lowered herself and her bundles onto the end of Julie's chair. Julie's knees made room in a welcoming way and she set down her book, the place marked with a length of thread she had been worrying from the hem of her shorts as she read.

Betsy showed her the scarf and sunglasses she had bought, putting them on to model them. "What do you think? Cute, or what?" she asked.

"On a foggy down-and-out waterfront with 'Gymnopédie No. 1' playing on a café jukebox after an abortion, they'd do," Julie said.

"Oh dear," sighed Betsy, stuffing the items back inside the bag. She didn't think she had quite deserved that comment.

Julie became interested in submerging her drinking straw deep down in the water bottle, but it kept surfacing whenever she removed her restraining fingertip.

"Nicholas's room is all ready for him," Betsy reported. "Well, he won't be spending much time there," she added, not very encouragingly. "And then it's off to your secret honeymoon destination," she concluded more brightly.

Julie had been claiming it was bad luck to divulge one's honeymoon plans, which was not a superstition anyone had ever heard before, but Julie claimed it was a personal superstition, which she believed she was allowed. She had even asked Andy whether there wasn't some sort of anthropological clearinghouse where one could register a new practice or belief so every time a bride refused to say whether she was going to Paris or Cancún, she, Julie, would earn a nickel.

"Let's just make it through the ceremony first," Betsy advised. She lounged as best she could on the end of the chaise, and the friendly knees ceded more space. Betsy felt as if she had not sat down all summer long, which was not entirely true, but she had seldom sat down without a chore or a purpose in view, and she had a purpose in view now, which was one she had been pushing farther and farther off, but she had been unable to lose sight of it.

"Okay, I have to ask you something. I've been deputized to talk to you," she began. Julie's knees tensed, but Betsy pressed on. "It's about your mother. We really have to know, one way or another. Will she be coming, or won't she?"

"No," Julie said, and she took a long pull on the straw as if to dilute the bitter taste of her answer. She worked at the fallen hem of her shorts, fraying the fabric further.

"Oh Julie, I'm so sorry," Betsy said. "Oh, I wish it were otherwise."

"It's for the best, really," Julie said. "I mean, I don't know what I was thinking trying to get her to come. Can't you picture how terribly, terribly polite everyone would have had to be? I mean, steam would have been coming out of everyone's ears, and we'd have had to call a crane in to unlock everyone's jaws just so they could make small talk."

"I'm not so sure it would be like that. After all this time? Hasn't everyone moved on?" Betsy asked. "I've been thinking that perhaps the worst thing of all might be for Aunt Becky to come back home and see how well you're all getting on without her."

"That wasn't Ma's reason for staying away. I think she was prepared to brazen out seeing everyone again, for my sake, and she really, seriously looked into how she could manage to get here but in the end she couldn't get reassurances from the flipping Libyans that they'd let her back into the country once she left. Oh, I don't know. Maybe she was just stringing me along about all that. Or stringing herself along, more like it," Julie said. "She finally told me a few days ago. She rang me up the other night and said how awful she felt about it." Julie pulled a face which presumably expressed just how bitter she perceived Becky's remorse to be.

"How's William been doing with all of this going on?" Betsy thought to ask.

"Apparently he's still quite woozy, wobbly, whatever. I really think he's emerged from his accident, or whatever it was, kind of brain damaged," Julie said. "God, it's such a shame he just can't die."

"You mustn't talk like that," Betsy said. To do so seemed to her to be unlucky. One ought not to invite the death of anyone, no matter whom. Once summoned, death could very well decide to stick around and take on a life of its own, or, rather, a death. "That's a terrible thing to say," Betsy told her cousin.

"Well," Julie grumbled a bit. She plunged her straw deeper down into the water bottle and snapped her finger away. The straw shot up and over the rim, and she gave a satisfied grunt. Evidently she'd been trying to make this happen all along.

"Maybe there's another way," Betsy said. "I mean, if you can talk to Aunt Becky on the phone, and all."

"Any time I want to, really," Julie said. She squirmed and produced her cell phone from a pocket. "Ma sounded quite wistful; I'll grant you that."

Betsy considered for a moment and then she spoke. "Well, then I don't know why Brooks and Rollins can't hook up some sort of live video link directly from the wedding to Libya. She has a computer? Yes? Maybe she can watch the whole ceremony while it's happening. I'll hold the camera. We don't even have to say what we're doing, so no one will get all in a twist over it. Everyone will just think I'm one of those people who can only experience reality after the fact when watching it on film. What do you say? I'm sure it's possible."

She could not tell whether Julie liked the idea. Julie was squinting into the sun (a cloud had just shifted) and she was more methodically pulling threads from the hem of her shorts, which she really needed to throw away; they were worn and stained and ragged in a way peculiar to the demands of farm work.

"What if I run the possibility past Brooks and Rollins?" Betsy asked. "They might need a few days to sort it all out, technically, you know, figuring out how to bounce the signal off the cell tower to some satellite somewhere."

Julie did not come right out and say no to that, which Betsy took as a positive sign, although she knew her cousin was just as likely to insist she had never said yes either, once the arrangements were in place. But that would not leave her optionless at the last minute, should she undergo a sudden change of heart. Betsy took her leave to go check on her mother and to report the results of her conversation with Julie to Lily and to find out from Andy what new trouble the Third Day Brethren found themselves in. She was not unsatisfied. If her scheme to include Becky in the wedding came off, she would feel that at last she had earned the right to sit at the grown-ups' table here at Aunt Lily's.

EARLY IN THE AFTERNOON, HARVEY RETURNED TO the Ridge House. To keep out any interlopers while she was waxing the floors, Penny had locked all the doors, which otherwise were never locked because neither of them fussed with carrying keys, and Harvey's immediate assumption was that the unyielding back door must be broken. Then he was briefly afraid that Penny was trapped inside the house, sprawled out helpless and confused on one of her excessively overpolished floors, for she had taken several minutes to respond to his shouts and pounding while she was making up her mind whether the floors were all right for him to walk on. They were all right for her, but she was a different, daintier case, sliding around in clean white socks, like a dancer on ice.

Harvey was in a lather to change his clothes from chinos and a checked shirt suitable for serving at the farm stand into chinos and a different checked shirt and a nice navy blue summer-weight wool blazer suitable for conducting business down at the Flash Fund offices, which had been opened the previous week. He had rented space on the floor above Peddocks' premises, an ideal location just a hoot or a stomp away from the cappuccino machine and the fresh doughnuts under a dome on the lunch counter, and there was usually someone available, a high school kid or a software company CEO buying a bag of pretzels or paying for gas whom he could commandeer to help him when the fax machine jammed. Penny had promised to stop by one day a week after her Bikram yoga class to deal with any correspondence that had accumulated until Harvey got around to hiring a part-time assistant. Word that he was on the lookout for someone had not yet circulated around Towne, and Penny felt that the position would be ideal for a former daughter-in-law. Everyone seemed to have one or two of those somewhere in the background.

However, the office furniture and machines were in place now, and a dozen of the world's newspapers had been subscribed to and were showing up stuffed into the PO box, newly acquired for that purpose. The stationery had arrived in a big box, trundled up the stairs on a dolly. The writing paper bore the Flash Fund's logo, a stylized flame, which Lily had pointed out was very similar to the Camp Fire Girls' insignia. She said she wished someone had consulted her prior to placing the order at the printer, although Brooks and Rollins didn't seem too worried that the entities would be mixed up as both they and the Camp Fire Girls went about their business.

Harvey had worked himself into his present lather because the Flash Fund was about to make its inaugural contribution in the form of a very large check to be sent to the Red Crescent on behalf of the victims of the earthquake that had struck Turkey two weeks ago to the day. Bingo, Harvey had said when he caught the first disaster footage on the television screen playing soundlessly behind the cash register of the Casa di Napoli as he was picking up a pizza on Penny's Towne Planning Board evening (when he became a bachelor and had to forage for sustenance). He had stopped and watched images of those particularly discouraging ruins of the homes of people who didn't have very much to lose in the first place. The survivors were sitting on rubble or picking through the debris as, all the while, one of those very clear and very blue skies which so often dawn the day after a calamity arched overhead.

Poor buggers, Harvey had said, and he'd been working ever since to position funds and to follow protocols. A congressman pal of his had been running interference in Washington and the go-ahead call had just come through on his cell phone when he was down at the farm stand telling a very interested lady about the special way he liked to prepare parsnips. He wasn't sure the very interested lady had quite believed him when he told her he had to run down to his office to disburse a very large charitable contribution but no matter. He had to cut the check and catch the next-day delivery collection at the post office. The sooner those hard-luck Turks got their money, the better, Harvey told Penny, when at last she unlocked the door and let him come inside, after he'd removed his shoes, which he'd planned to do anyway, since he was going to change into different trousers. She said if he'd give her a minute to unplug the floor polisher she'd go downtown with him to make sure that he included enough zeroes when he filled in the amount on the check face. Nor did she want Harvey to include too many. Those nice boys of Alden's had told him he could spend five million dollars, no more, no less.

EVERYBODY WAS AT THE BEACH that late-summer afternoon, Sally and Cam assured Andy when they arrived there. Their experienced eyes took in the scene. The lifeguard was sitting on her low web-and-tubing chair, slumped and looking like she was asleep behind her dark glasses, but she'd be on her feet and shouting, fast enough, when any kid was dunked or pulled under by another kid. A grid of floating plastic lines defined the spaces for separate activities and abilities. The under-fives were having their swimming lessons on the far side of the boathouse, splashing behind kickboards. The teenagers were being exclusive out on the raft. A cluster of Sally's and Cam's contemporaries were playing a game in the shallows that involved a beach ball and popsicle sticks, and Sally and Cam ran off to join in, shedding their backpacks and T-shirts and flip-flops on the fly. Andy followed them across the sand, retrieving their effects. He saw that his daughter and her friend were among the bossiest children in the mix. The beach ball and popsicle stick game, rather listlessly played before their participation, turned energetic as they swarmed into the midst of the action. They splashed at their opponents, which was, evidently, not a permitted strategy; nevertheless the other children began to splash back and soon the drenched and writhing figures resembled a Bernini fountain, Andy thought. The lifeguard stood and yelled, "Knock it off, Advanced Beginners." But perhaps she was not an art lover.

Andy remembered that Betsy had read him the riot act about being sure to spray Sally, and Cam too, with sunblock, so he called to them. He was surprised when they didn't ignore him, for someone had just cornered a frog sheltering in an area of encroaching spatterdock and Sally and Cam were instantly engaged by the frog hunt. But Andy was in favor with the little girls at the moment. Accompanying fathers were a relative rarity on weekday afternoons at the Towne Pond and the glow of having just lately been on TV had not entirely faded from him, Sally and Cam felt, so they came pelting over and presented their arms and legs and backs and shoulders and faces willingly enough as Andy pumped on a protective coating. They even withheld their usual protests that the substance stung and burned and smelled because they were being so agreeable. Besides, Sally was still smarting from the last time she had shrieked and carried on a bit too much when Betsy accidentally spritzed sunscreen into her eye. Betsy had asked her if she'd rather have skin cancer someday, and when Sally said yes, Betsy had hauled her home from the beach and put her to work scrubbing carrots in the barn.

"I'll be sitting right here," Andy told Sally and Cam. He pointed to a picnic table set beneath a grove of pines. He had brought his laptop and he hoped to get some work done. He would have to hit the ground running once he got back to Santa Barbara, where the academic year was about to begin. Indeed, it was going to start without him since he would be missing the first week of classes, but that could not be helped with all that needed to be seen to here, and his university was being compassionate, under the circumstances.

"Andy?" A voice recalled him and he glanced up at the woman who had addressed him.

"Calliope?" he asked. He wasn't quite certain, for she looked younger and sleeker and more assured than the Calliope of old.

"I thought that was you," Calliope said, settling herself and her bundles (everything crammed into straw baskets) beside him on the bench. "But it's been ten years since you lived here and came to the restaurant.

You were my favorite customer because you were so patient, listening to my very bad English. Remember? Well, of course you remember," she said.

"Betsy's caught me up on you and George. She said you've been away visiting family in Greece," Andy said.

"We just got home yesterday, and wouldn't you know, the kids begged to go swimming," Calliope said. They could not wait to wash away some sort of old world crust they must have believed they had taken on during their time in Neapolis.

"Which ones are yours?" Andy asked, and Calliope indicated a pair of dark bobbing heads, Mike and Lindy, afloat between the intermediate swimmers' lines.

"Don't tell me they prefer this piss-colored pond to the wine dark sea," Andy said.

"Oh, but they do," Calliope said. She waved at the stock-still figure of Cam, who had been staring, trying to make out who was talking to Mr. Happening. Cam notified Sally, *Mrs. Kariotis,* and they performed for her, standing on their hands in the water, which was an unsatisfactory method of performance since, when immersed, they could not see how Calliope was taking them.

"How is Miss Hill?" Calliope asked, and Andy recognized the line her thoughts had followed. She was thinking Lily must have had a lively summer with Sally and Cam underfoot. He was able to report that Lily was still carrying on, as strong as ever. She had spoken the other day of growing Christmas trees in the field beyond the barn. "You're branching out?" Andy had asked her, which, it turned out, was the same joke Alden had come up with and so Lily had not expanded very much on the subject.

"And Ginger?" Calliope asked. "She is better after a spell of sunshine and good food and good care?" Again, Andy followed the way her thoughts were going. She had assumed that time spent in Lily's company, in Lily's care, in Lily's realm, could only be beneficial. Lily, with her cat up there in the woods on her hilltop tending to her gardens and living in that house which seemed to expand to accommodate everyone who showed up on her doorstep requiring rest or shelter—anyone might come to believe that all the elements were there to effect some charm, once again.

But Andy only shook his head, his expression telling Calliope enough, and her smile faded—for she had been smiling at the idea of Ginger restored to her usual form.

"Although Lily told me the other day that no one expected my mother-in-law to see out the summer," Andy said. "So who can say what will happen, and when? The theory is that there's been so much going on this summer that it's all just too fascinating and she can't bear to miss anything."

He watched, taken aback, as Calliope fumbled at the collar of her blouse. For a brief, intrigued moment he thought she was about to tear at and rend her garments in a traditional display of grief. But she was just trying to unlatch the stubborn clasp of a necklace. At the release of the fastening, she snatched the chain and its pendent object, reaching down into her cleavage. Then she held out her hand to Andy, showing him an Eastern Orthodox cross with its three horizontal bars. Andy knew they all meant something, although he couldn't just now remember what.

"The Patriarch blessed this," Calliope said. "I want Ginger to have it."

"Oh, no," Andy objected. The relic was too valuable in the weight of its gold and its evident antiquity, and no doubt Calliope attached even greater worth of a different nature to her talisman, which Andy understood, even if he did not assign such significance to iconographic objects that had been submitted to the fleeting touch and mumbled prayers of some divine. (Andy taught a seminar on Magic and Religion, which was open to students who had passed Magic and Science I.)

"Please," said Calliope. "For Ginger," she reminded him. The decision to refuse the gift was not his to make.

"Of course," Andy said, and she lowered the cross and the chain into his open palm. He wished he had a handkerchief to wrap them in; direct contact with his pocket contents seemed disrespectful, the cross rattling round with his car keys and loose change. He hesitated, then clasped the chain around his own neck. "For safekeeping," he explained as he let the crucifix drop down his shirtfront. Whatever the Patriarch would make of Ginger and however Ginger might feel about the Patriarch, Andy understood that the rood had been made sacred by the act of Calliope's sacrifice and, as a cultural anthropologist, he suspected he had just witnessed and, indeed, participated in a very authentic moment. He made a few notes on his laptop after Calliope left him to round up Mike and Lindy who were due at a Little League game and gymnastics practice; she had to drop them off at opposite ends of Towne at the same appointed hour, but she'd grown skilled at being in two places at once.

LATE IN THE AFTERNOON THE FARM STAND WAS BUSY. Cars filled the wedge of parking lot and spilled out along the road. Glover and Ginevra were still minding the store, and Ginevra was also trying to work on lesson plans using the hull of the overturned canoe, out behind the farm stand, as a work space. School started for her the following week. The breeze off the river lifted and rustled the pages of her open ring binder as if hurrying her along, although she knew well enough that the summer was almost over. She set a securing rock upon her open notebook page and, rising from the lawn chair in which she had been sitting sideways to the canoe (there was not room for her legs because of the gunwale), she went to help Glover sell off the bounty of the harvest which was being sent down from the barn and the fields, thick and fast. Mr. DeSouza and his crew were bringing in the red potatoes that day, and Om and Tru were up in the barn removing the dirt from their skins with soft brushes so that the redness of the red potatoes would be featured.

"That always happens," Ginevra said as someone selected an onion from a pyramid of onions and sent the rest spilling off the shelving and across the dirt hard pack of the floor. She and Glover and several of the customers, regulars here, chased and gathered them up. A bruised onion seeped its juice onto her fingers and she plucked a bunch of parsley from a basket to scrub away the smell.

"We're almost out of shopping bags," Ginevra said as she stuffed a cantaloupe and two turban squashes into a single plastic sack. "Careful," she warned the customer, who seized the parcel by its flimsy handles. They broke, sagging and snapping, but the customer understood she would not receive another bag.

Glover listened to a complaint about a beet which sounded more like a problem with an ill-cooked beet than an ill-grown one and he said so, not as a criticism but in an effort to get to the truth of the matter, but it was impossible; the evidence had been eaten, though not enjoyed, and the customer left in a huff, which was neither here nor there. Lily did not encourage manifestations of what she referred to as "personality" (as opposed to "character," which nice people possessed, Ginevra supposed), and there had been a considerable weeding out of undesirables over the past few months so that now almost everyone who came by to shop figured as a friend of the farm stand or at least had made the cut. In the wake of the beet incident, everyone present clustered around Glover to describe the many excellent beets they had purchased and prepared that summer, the best way being to roast and slice and toss them with with fresh corn and crumbled chèvre and a drizzle of vinaigrette, which was Hannah's method as relayed by Ginevra. Further discussion followed on the unrivaled excellence of overripe tomatoes, just picked and warm from the sun, which could be bitten into like an apple after taking a lick of salt sprinkled on the back of one's hand. There was no other way to eat a tomato.

"But have you noticed the chill in the air at night now?" someone asked.

"The leaves on our swamp maples are just starting to turn," someone else mentioned.

"I am leaving for the West Coast right after my sister's wedding," Glover was explaining. "I'm not sure how Lily will run the place in the fall. The Samrin kids will all be back in school. Perhaps she'll operate on the honor system and let everyone help themselves." There was general speculation then on just how honest the general public would be, although everyone agreed that nowadays you could just assume security cameras were trained on you almost everywhere you went, not that anyone intended to do anything devious; but say you were in the home remedies aisle at Peddocks' looking for cold medicine and digging into a pocket for a tissue at the same time (natural enough if one suffered from a cold). You felt you had to pantomime that you weren't stealing anything, because there was even a camera at Peddocks', installed when the ATM machine went in.

Upon their return from the beach, Andy stopped at the end of the driveway to let Cam hop out of the car as she requested. She and Sally had been spatting in the backseat. Sally was about to get started on making a hooked pot holder, her just-thought-of wedding present for Julie and Nicholas Davenant, and she wanted Cam to fix the fabric loops onto the metal teeth of the loom frame, which was the hard part of the process. Cam had long since completed her own gift for the bride and groom, a pair of spool-crochet bookmarks individualized with sewn-on beads, and she was not about to be dragooned into doing Sally's last-minute work for which Sally would take all the credit; Cam was as certain of that as she was that the sun would rise in the morning. Besides which, Cam had not yet checked in on the farm stand that day, and no one else could be trusted to see to certain details. She steeled herself against the shambles she would find there, for she knew Mr. Harvey had been allowed to assist earlier in the morning and he always interfered with the setting on the scale, recalibrating the dial hand back to the point which he perceived to be zero, but it only looked that way to him because he stood in the wrong place as he nudged the needle, a mistake Cam could never make him understand no matter how hard she explained.

She entered the farm stand, and on the strength of her sighs, Cam dispersed the cluster of customers who were uselessly chattering and not shopping. She saw at once that the onion pyramid had been seriously degraded, and no one had changed the water of the jam jar bouquets of asters and zinnias nor that of the big and radiant dahlias standing upright in individual Sprite bottles; their water was cloudy and the submerged leaves, viewed in magnification, were becoming black and slimy. She watched with extreme disapproval as Ginevra weighed out and returned Mrs. Snowdon's yellow peppers to her, sans a bag, along with a frozen Hannah's entrée. Mrs. Snowdon balanced the peppers on top of her Spinach Lasagna, unsuccessfully. A pepper tumbled to the floor, which Glover snatched up and exchanged for a "clean" pepper and he lobbed the fallen pepper through the back window for the skunks to eat.

Cam slipped behind the counter and dragged out the box in which she had stashed away a hundred accumulated odd-lot shopping bags for such an emergency. She flourished a handful at Ginevra, blamefully; she had *told* Ginevra about the bag storage system, she said. The child's snippiness toppled Ginevra all the way over into the blue mood she had been fending off all day, although her depression was really about Glover, of course, and how soon he would be in California and she would be back in Worcester, back at school and back in her apartment, with nothing very definite decided about the future.

"I'll leave you in charge," Ginevra said to Cam, and she returned to the overturned canoe and her interrupted lesson plans.

Taking Ginevra at her word that she was now in charge, Cam pulled a chair into the correct position beneath the hanging scales. She climbed onto the seat and aligned her eyes with the dial, ignoring the way the surrounding scene swarmed and swayed at the margins of her vision, refusing to be distracted by all of that. She was exasperated, yet gratified, to find that the setting of the scale had been tampered with. She had caught Harvey at his usual tricks, and the weighed orders were coming up short by one-quarter of a pound so that every four purchases of tomatoes lost the farm stand an entire pound's worth of tomatoes, which came to three entire dollars lost and not earned. Cam did the sums in her head. She had long wished Lily would invest in a digital scale so that the farm stand measurements would enjoy accuracy down to the nearest fraction of a gram (at the restaurant they weighed out the pizza dough and the cheese and the sausages on a digital scale because at the Casa di Napoli they practiced quality control), but Lily said she did not care for the metric system.

"Why is Auntie Lily mad at the metric system?" Cam now asked Glover.

"I don't know; perhaps the metric system is afraid of commitment and responds to every serious inquiry about the future with some off-putting joke that it can't seem to stop itself from making, no matter how hard it tries to" Glover said, which made no sense at all, although Ginevra, listening through the back window, exclaimed, "Ha."

Cam turned her back on him and picked up a magic marker and a shingle with which to make a new sign that read Apples; they were going to have apples in by the end of the week. She wasted the first shingle she wrote upon, running out of room before she got to the *s*, and she slid the spoiled shingle out of sight beneath a pile of discarded cabbage leaves. Glover leaned his elbows on the windowsill and had a conversation with Ginevra about what to do with a large order packed for Hannah's production line; two stacked crates of lemon thyme, exuding a sharp citrus scent, awaited collection by a runner from the factory. Glover had understood that Hannah needed the thyme ASAP and he wondered whether there had been some mix-up about the pickup. Ginevra kept saying unhelpfully that she knew nothing about it because no one ever told her anything.

Cam worked on a poem about apples, feeling there was a lot to be said about them and she knew she could make something of her topic. She came up with Take a bite of our apples, please / We grow them ourselves, from Trees. She recited this verse to Lily when Lily drove down in the golf cart towing a load of red potatoes for which there was no room on any of the farm stand's shelves; the trailer was to be backed up right next to the door and left there. Cam ran to and fro avoiding the fishtailing trailer and shouting the lines at Lily, who, when she came to a stop, seemed to think the poem was a very good effort and she said they would post it above the new apple bin Mr. DeSouza was going to build. Cam got down to business with the magic marker and another cedar shingle. Ginevra, appealed to through the back window, helped her to spell *ourselves,* which they agreed was a fourth-grade vocabulary word and so there was no disgrace in being uncertain about the second *e.*

After a while, Alden dropped by on his way up to the house to find Julie so he could report to her that his Nicholas Davenant arrangements were complete. He had just purchased loose tea and a strainer, Weetabix, Lyle's Golden Syrup, Yardley soap, and a hot water bottle covered with tartan flannel at the Britannia Mart's going-out-of-business sale, over on Main Street. They were going to shut down for good that very day, at sunset, and then Angus and Ewan would be retiring to Ibiza (so there went Alden's Thursday morning golf threesome).

"Julie's not there," Lily said. "You've missed her. She and Petal are at the hairdresser." She studied her nephew. She had called him as soon as Betsy informed her that Becky was definitely not coming to the wedding. He had thanked her and been disinclined to say anything more.

"Oh. Good," said Alden now. "Excellent." He had been wondering whether Julie oughtn't to do something different with her hair.

"Yes," Lily agreed. Julie had finally consented to have her hair restored to a sensible color. Petal, whose opinion had been sought, had recommended a shade called Honey-Honey and she had given Julie a long swatch (charmed from Stacey at Hair Today) to carry around and become accustomed to in various light and shadow conditions, holding it up to the side of her face, fluffed over her cheek. "Petal said they were going to be awhile. There's rather a lot that needs to be undone before they can even begin the main process," Lily explained. "Excuse me." Her cell phone was ringing. (She was going to have to remember to recharge the thing that evening; the little power ticks were fading away.)

Alden watched, not unamused by Lily's ease as she flipped her phone open and attached it to her ear. She was the rare person who did not raise her voice when on a cell, although Alden wasn't sure whether this indicated Lily's confidence in the technology's excellence or reflected the fact that Lily never raised her voice under any circumstances. But whatever the murmured conversation was about, Alden saw that he was going to be involved. Lily crooked her index finger, bidding him to stay put; she had need of him.

"That was Hannah," Lily said at the conclusion of the call. "Someone forgot to collect her special order, and she really has to have it. Will you be so good, Alden, as to make the delivery?"

Glover, directed by a further crook of Lily's finger, lugged out the crates of lemon thyme and stowed them in the trunk of his father's car between the golf clubs and the spare tire, and as Alden was about to drive off, Lily thrust a bunch of dahlias at him through the passenger-side window, their dripping stems wrapped in a newspaper cone.

"Also for Hannah?" Alden asked, startled, and Lily, who had meant for them to brighten Nicholas Davenant's room (Betsy having told her that the chamber still needed "something"), agreed, "Yes, they're for Hannah." She hoped Alden would not too scrupulously credit herself as being behind the offering of flowers. Hannah would be disappointed to learn they had not come from Alden, Lily felt, even though, in a roundabout way, perhaps they had. Then again, one would not be doing Hannah any favor to encourage her to think that Alden was capable of coming up with flowers entirely on his own. Then again (again), were Alden prepared to be a bit sly about their provenance, Hannah might have reason to hope. Most certainly, Hannah would be most interested to hear that Becky was not going to attend the wedding after all and on the pretext of alerting Hannah that Alden was on his way so she could keep an eye out for him (as if he might become lost between here and there, all on a late-summer afternoon),

Lily flipped open her phone and tapped in Hannah's number. She delivered her update on the lemon-thyme's whereabouts, and then she said, "Oh, by the way . . ."

As she rang off, Lily reflected that she had not done that very gracefully. She feared she had only flustered Hannah, who had said "Oh" and "Well," when told about Becky, giving no elucidating emphasis to either word, and Lily wished she had not interfered. Ginger would have been the proper person to relay such information about Becky, coming round to the subject by way of some elegant conversational construction of linked and linking observations which would build to the natural mention of news of a sensitive nature. One could be told something startling (or stirring or disturbing) by Ginger and only later appreciate the convoluted yet revelatory import of her art. Lily supposed now that she had never given Ginger enough credit (or even any credit at all) for being so good at what she had always been so evidently good at—at being exactly who she was, Lily understood, an accomplishment which was, at once, both great and fragile. Lily shooed Cam out from behind the counter. She felt the need to sit down for a while.

The van from Senior Village had just turned into the parking lot. Cam stepped forward to receive the group; these people always needed assistance. They asked her which eggplant was better or which carrot, presenting the choices held in either hand as Cam selected one and confiscated the other. As the ambulatory seniors exited the van, Glover stood by to clasp elbows, reaching out discreetly in the case of the men, while the women relished his courtesy and made a fuss of being made a fuss over. The driver activated the hydraulic lift and lowered the wheelchairs. Rosalie Chubb, who had lately acquired a new electric-powered model took off, inexpertly steering into the side of Marilyn Rathbone's Subaru wagon, but Marilyn was intent upon rooting around in the deep freeze for a third and fourth individual-serving-size portion of Chicken Kiev and cursing her luck; she was having a small dinner party and intended to pass off the entrée as her own. Rosalie chugged away, casting a not-to-tell glare at Anna Webster, who was still wheelchair bound. Her ankle hadn't healed properly, and as a consequence of remaining stuck at Rosalie's level, she often found herself at the receiving end of scowls and mutters. Anna had embarked upon a reciprocal campaign of relaying smiles and encouraging nods to Rosalie, but pleasantries seemed to be less potent than malice, she decided, although why this should be so, she could not say. She did not want to believe that evil was a stronger force than good but maybe that really was the way of the world.

Anna's sister-in-law, visiting from South Carolina, had descended from the van beside her on the powered platform, their combined weights causing the mechanism to whirr and burn hot. Ruth stood behind Anna, clutching the handles of her chair. "Forward," said Anna softly. "More to the left," she advised. Ruth wore blackout glasses over gauze bandage pads. She had recently undergone eye surgery to correct a double-vision problem, and she and Anna were recuperating together, their daughters having decided on behalf of their mothers that this was a good idea, although they had not really thought through just what would happen when Anna dropped her front door key in the gutter and Ruth had to set about retrieving it.

"Go a bit to the right, dear," Anna said. "Oh, never mind, here's Glover," she said as he took over, pushing and bumping the wheels of the chair over the threshold of the farm stand. He placed Ruth's hand on his forearm to guide her steps alongside himself and Anna.

Cam, who had just put an end to Marilyn Rathbone's depredations among the freezer contents (apprised of the situation, Cam wrenched free a family-size Pork Chops Zingara which, paired with a mixed green salad, would be perfectly adequate for any dinner party of Mrs. Rathbone's, in her opinion), advanced to set a shopping basket in Anna's lap. She gazed at Ruth, free to stare because the blind lady couldn't know that she and her complexly drooping chins were being closely studied. Cam was thinking how the folds of skin ought to be pinched into neat pleats to be made to look nicer and she touched her own throat but her flesh was pulled too taut above the windpipe to fiddle with.

"Do don't let me be in the way. Ah'll sit aback of the fray and visit with this little person here," Ruth said. She reached out and claimed Cam, cuffing her on the head and letting her hand drop onto Cam's shoulder. Cam gasped and jumped free.

"Ah could hear you breathing there," Ruth explained.

"Yes, Cam," Lily said. "Why don't you look after . . ."

"Mrs. Malcolm," Anna supplied the name, which was her own maiden name. Ruth had married Anna's brother and kept him down there in Charleston, all those years.

"Of course," Lily said. "Chat with Mrs. Malcolm here at the counter, Cam."

Cam was jealous of the space behind the counter, but she consented to let this Mrs. Malcolm be seated on a stool, off to one side. Doing her best to be entertaining, she read aloud her new poem about apples, which Mrs. Malcolm said was a piece of very fine writing, although she pronounced *fine* in a funny way, which Cam had to listen to again, repeating the remark inside her head and filtering out Mrs. Malcolm's peculiar accent before she understood her.

"Thank you," Cam said, and then she became busy. Mr. MacNally wanted to buy half a cauliflower, and she told him he could if he found someone willing to take the other half. After he wandered off, Rosalie Chubb rolled over and tossed an ear of corn at Cam.

"Look at that," Rosalie commanded, and she indicated a larval worm bored into the cob. The creature flexed when she poked it with a fingertip, and Cam was prepared to believe that Mrs. Chubb had worked it out beforehand with the worm to perform this most unnecessary demonstration.

"You're supposed to just throw away the bad ear and tell us about it, Mrs. Chubb. You don't have to show us," Cam said. "We believe people here."

"You have to give me back double for my trouble," Rosalie reminded her. "That's the rule."

"I know. It's my rule," Cam reminded Rosalie, and she recorded the transaction on the debit side of the ledger page, which she never liked to have to do and which Lily said wasn't necessary, but Sally couldn't figure out at all how to write down about the money, so the exercise possessed the added value of putting Cam one up on Sally. Cam was keeping a running tally on that score as well.

Lily returned, carrying Anna's shopping basket. "Weigh this all up, please," she told Cam, and she turned to ask Ruth, who was just sitting there, neglected, the conventional question, "Are you enjoying your stay here?" even as she was quite certain that Ruth must be having a rather thin time. If one could not see the sights, did travel offer anything except a strange bed and uncertainty (if not anxiety) over where the teapot and the aspirin and everything else were kept? Or maybe, Lily thought, seeing family was a different matter which required a different set of senses and she wasn't sure that actual blindness might not, in fact, be an asset since there was so much one chose to overlook where one's family was concerned.

"And Ah've noticed there's such a nice breeze in the evenings around here," Ruth was saying. "Anna and Ah make sure to catch that lovely breeze every evening." Between them, she and Anna would make their way down the elevator and through the double doors out to the Senior Village terrace, where they walked and wheeled over the unevenly set slate surface to the far corner upwind of the lingering smokers. There, they waited for the breeze to arrive, tarrying on the terrace as if in expectation of a favored but unreliable visitor, like some Southern sort of beautiful young man, Anna privately thought, and she blamed her sister-in-law for introducing the idea of him on those evenings when he could not be bothered to bestir himself and failed to materialize.

"A nice breeze," repeated Lily, distractedly. "Cam, where do we keep the string?" She had noticed that the geraniums in the planters out front were flopping and flailing about and needed to be staked and tied.

"Here is the string, Auntie Lily," Cam said. "And here are the scissors." She had anticipated Lily's next question as she delved into the very useful drawer that slid out from beneath the counter. Had Lily also required a ruler or a red crayon or a magnifying glass or a foil-wrapped stick of gum (the extended drawer was redolent of Juicy Fruit), Cam could have provided any of those, although Lily wouldn't want the gum. She often said that the only difference between a young lady chewing gum and a cow chewing its cud was that the cow had a thoughtful expression on its face.

"And Mrs. Webster has to pay twelve dollars and three cents, but I'll take the three cents from the penny saucer," Cam said, so Mrs. Webster wouldn't have to fumble in her change purse with her bent fingers. Mrs. Webster said she couldn't straighten out her fingers except sometimes first thing in the morning if she was lucky.

"Cam," Glover called from over by the freezer. He had the top open and was prodding the contents. "I think someone's knocked out the plug again. Will you check behind the post?"

"Okay," Cam said. She ducked down to the floor, and there was a scrambling sound as she followed the snaking cord, one among a network of cords converging upon the outlet panel.

Ruth had been taking in all of this activity with interest and approval, drawn into this little slice of life. She already felt that she half knew these people; Anna had sketched them for her. Actually, Anna had rather thoroughly filled Ruth in on how Lily had so surprisingly made a success of her farm stand business just as her contemporaries were cutting back and slowing down, although it was so sad about her niece, who was said to be in a very bad way, going just as her own mother had, thirty years earlier, and they still couldn't do very much for some women. But a wedding was in the works, so that was happier news, and one could not forget about those rich-as-Croesus boys, whom you'd never guess to look at them were such captains of industry, not that Ruth could look at them in her present situation, but Anna had supplied a description of Alden's younger sons and she had, while she was about it, also discussed poor Alden's recent history and the running away of that confounding wife of his, of whom everyone had been so fond. No one quite understood what had happened there, but one could never know what really went on between two people which, of course, was not a reassuring thought.

"Auntie Lily," Cam reported from the outlet panel. "I can see shiny wires."

"Bare wires, do you mean?" asked Lily. "Remind me to call the electrician tomorrow."

"Yup," said Cam. She retreated carefully from her wedged-in spot behind the post, and stood, slapping her hands free of dust against the sides of her shorts.

"That's a real fine little Yankee girl you're raising up. She's so practical and so helpful and so good," Ruth remarked to Lily. She had hesitated a bit before speaking up because where she came from Yankee was not a term of approbation, but up here everything seemed proudly to call itself Yankee-this and Yankee-that (like Yankee Dog Grooming, Ruth had had to smile at that one). "I mean, she's doing you folks proud," she said, just to make herself clear.

"Well, actually," Lily began to explain, for poor sightless Ruth had obviously gotten the wrong end of the stick about Cam. "Well, actually," Lily said again, and then she looked down. Cam stood by her elbow, sidling in close and peering up at Lily with her little praised face. "Well, actually," Lily said, "I don't know how we'd get through the day without Cam."

ALDEN CARRIED THE CRATES, stacked and awobble with the bouquet balanced on top, onto the floor of Hannah's commercial kitchen. A woman approached to relieve him of one crate, and he followed her bearing the other to the side of a stainless-steel-encased dehydrating unit. She hauled open a hatch and began to flurry sprays of lemon thyme onto tiered mesh trays.

Alden left her to it, but she called him back. He'd forgotten the flowers. "Unless they're for me," she said, but Alden would not be drawn into a bantering session.

Another dozen or so women clad in bright cotton coveralls and skull caps were clearing up at the end of their shift, scouring stainless steel surfaces and restoring pots and other implements to cupboards and recesses. Didi Wells, who came round to clean Alden's house every other week, emerged from the walk-in freezer where she had been loading the day's output of Hannah's—In A Hurry? Sweet Things onto pallets.

"Oh hi, Alden," she said. "I'll be seeing you Saturday."

Alden was uncertain whether Didi meant she was coming to housekeep (he lost track of her schedule) or had Julie invited her to the wedding? Perhaps Didi planned to be present as part of the catering staff Hannah was going to supply. Delicious things would be whisked among the guests on silver trays, he recalled her having told him, and then they were all going to be expected to sit down to eat even more delicious things.

"Excellent," Alden told Didi, in any event.

"You'll find Hannah in the test kitchen," Didi directed him. She'd noticed the ruffled edges of the flower heads poking from the top of the newspaper cone he was holding upside down and absentmindedly slapping against his leg, and she wanted him to get them to Hannah before he entirely shredded her nice bouquet.

Alden knew the layout of the premises well enough. Hannah had sought his advice over the past few years when making capital expenditures. Initially he had protested he was not the best person to give her advice; the relatively small scale of Hannah's operation would not be able to withstand the level of risks and liabilities he was used to imposing upon more substantial entities, losses leading to gains, ultimately, but certain intervening lean times had to be survivable along the way. Hannah said she understood; to convert a recipe for eighty into a recipe for eight required more complicated calculations than simply dividing every quantity by ten, but that was where art entered into the equation. Once Hannah revealed to him that she relied upon the machinations of art to arrive at business decisions, whether effected by her own hands or by his, he knew he could not refuse her his help. Besides, this was all occurring at the same time Lily was recovering from hip replacement surgery and Hannah was being a brick. She'd become Lily's one woman Meals on Wheels purveyor, and Lily said she was content just to lie there on the hospital bed temporarily installed in the little parlor wondering what dish Hannah would tempt her with next. In that context, perhaps a scheme to appeal to Alden could be said to have been something that Lily and Hannah had cooked up between themselves. At any rate, Alden had not done badly by Hannah; her production level grew and her physical plant expanded into an efficiently and optimally used and attractive space featuring exposed and old bricks and beams. Alden had been heard to say that Hannah's—In A Hurry? had evolved into quite the sleek and elegant little corporation.

Lily's just phoned-in revelation that Becky would not be attending the wedding after all had thrown Hannah, although not in any way Lily might have anticipated. Hannah had, in fact, been rooting all along for the return of Becky to Towne, for she was convinced that the living and breathing woman could not begin to fill the void in Alden's existence which she was credited with having left behind her. Surely, Hannah believed, Alden clung to a much-inflated appreciation of Becky's prior virtues even as he struggled to come to grips with the enormity of her subsequent sins. Hannah had so very much looked forward to the reappearance of Becky that she had formed a definite picture of what she must now be like. She would be older, of course, and marked by her experiences. (That Becky was going to seed in the sand had been Lily's assessment.) And whatever would Becky wear? Hannah had wondered, and she saw someone oddly attired in the best the bazaar could offer, arriving at the wedding via Towne Taxi, which final leg of a long journey would bestow a final measure of frazzle upon the traveler, who would be viewed at last by all as a diminished beauty and a punctured monster whose presence after such a long and great absence would finally allow room for someone else to come into Alden's life.

In the test kitchen, Hannah adjusted the flame beneath a copper sauce pan and she made an entry on the notebook page left open on an unfired burner of the stove. Hannah was experimenting; she wanted to include a fish course in a newly established institutional line of frozen entrées and she had yet to find a variety that could stand up to poaching, steaming, or sautéing (she had tried them all) and then subsequently endure freezing, thawing, and reheating without losing texture and flavor. At the moment, she was testing yet another species of fish and concocting a light sauce of butter and lovage and something else. A table was littered with bunches of herbs and jars of capers and pignoli and the like, all candidates to be that something else whisked into the saucepan.

When Alden wandered into her kitchen, Hannah was chopping porcini mushrooms and half humming and half singing the few words she knew of the song that was currently stuck in her head, "Dust in the Wind"; the production line had been listening to a *Seventies Solid Gold* CD compilation all afternoon. Hannah was well occupied and she had recovered from her disappointment over Lily's news. The only person who truly mattered in any of this was Julie, and Hannah thought she understood now the reason behind Julie's strange reluctance to settle upon wedding details. Julie must have known all along that the day was not going to be perfect no matter how much effort went into matching the rosettes on her shoes with the roses in her hair, and Hannah wished that she had not been so impatient when Julie had been difficult about the cake. The samples Hannah had cut into and bid her to taste must have all tasted like cotton in her mouth, poor child.

"Thank Lily for me, for the flowers," she told Alden briskly before a formal presentation could be made. "Stick them in the sink, will you, and run a little water for them to sit in until I can find a vase."

Alden did as he was told, although he felt a bit miffed when Hannah had automatically failed to assume the flowers came from him. He had left them in the passenger seat and had had to go back for them, lugging those crates of herbs one way and then the other. An effort had been made by him on the flowers' behalf.

He released the stems from their newspaper wrappings, and the individual blossoms sprawled and scattered. Alden wondered whether he ought not to have left them confined and contained. Besides, he didn't know where to throw the crumpled and soggy newspaper. Hannah recycled religiously, and there was a protocol to follow; plastic, tin, metal, and the burnables all had their own receptacles, but Alden wasn't sure whether wet paper counted as a burnable. Plus, newspapers had their own bin at the dump, but it was not necessarily the correct place for used and *wet* newspapers. His general uncertainty communicated itself to Hannah, who had just realized she remained in the grip of a renouncing mood; she had spent the past weeks primed to "have it out" with Becky, in one way or another. She wondered whether she ought not to wash her hands of Alden entirely, if only he hadn't cluttered up the sink with dahlias, cutting her off from the soap dispenser.

The sauce Hannah had going on the stove smelled particularly wonderful. Alden came over to see just what the shining copper pot held. He peered through haze; the surface of the sauce gathered itself, surged, and then subsided. It was working itself up to the boil, if Hannah would let it. She set down her knife and reached around Alden—he was standing in her way—to reduce the flame.

Alden lingered. He noticed a large fish sitting upon a marble slab. The creature was bewhiskered and in general looked deep-sea and zoological, but Alden had confidence that Hannah knew just what to make of it.

"That's a monkfish," Hannah said as he approached it.

"Oh. Yes," Alden said. He knew about monkfish, although he didn't know that he'd ever seen one whole.

The sauce had reached some critical point, and Hannah snatched the pot from the heat. She clapped a sauté pan down onto the fire and splashed in oil. When a sizzling sound informed her, she lowered a portion of fish into the oil, and Alden saw that the monkfish's tail had been lopped off. (Alden had been regarding the fellow, eye to eye.)

"Well, then," Hannah said. "Thanks for dropping off the thyme." She'd been remembering back to what had brought Alden here as she wondered what was now keeping him. Had some other arrangements been made that she'd forgotten?

But Alden was disinclined to leave. He asked, inconsequentially, how the new ten-gallon mixers were working out, although he was already aware they were working out just fine, and Hannah did not feel like having yet another conversation with him about appliances.

She prodded the sautéing fish with her thumb and then fetched a plate from the cupboard. "You can tell me what you think of this recipe," she told Alden. She gave the fish another prod, as she half hummed and half sang, "All we are is dust in the wind."

"Almost there," she interrupted herself, to tell him.

"It will be delicious," Alden assured her, and Hannah supposed she should be gratified that he always professed such confidence in her abilities as a chef, but sometimes she wished he would first take a bite.

JULIE HAD TAKEN OFF FOR THE AIRPORT ALONE, refusing the offers of all those who had volunteered to accompany her. She had turned her father down rather gently and she had brusquely told her brothers, No way. She was to meet a ten p.m. flight, which seemed an odd hour for an international arrival (from London, where Nicholas was said to be reporting his findings to his company as well as picking up a decent suit of clothes). Julie said he had gotten a good deal from some kind of meandering charter airline. He would save $150 and get to spend some time in Iceland.

"Either she really is going to meet Nicholas Davenant, in which case she understandably doesn't need all of us horning in on their beautiful reunion," Brooks said. "Or else she's not going to the airport at all. She'll hang out in a diner for a few hours, thinking up another story to tell us."

"Maybe she's headed back to the airport to catch a flight to London and she'll just go home and pretend none of this ever happened," Rollins said.

"Are you two still going on about that?" Petal asked.

"I hope Julie's not intending to do a flit. I lent her my car. She'll have the keys and the garage stub with her, not that I'll even know where she parked," Glover said.

"Maybe she'll just keep on driving through the night all the way to Florida with the top down," Ginevra said.

"Don't you encourage them," Petal told Ginevra.

They had gathered in Lily's big parlor. The French doors were open on to the terrace to admit what breeze there was, and the moths were wafting in to thud and scramble against the lampshades, but the alternative to not having moths was not to have air, so they put up with them. They had settled down for a long wait. Rollins remembered Lily's house was well-stocked with board games, and he had found the Monopoly set. He was organizing the money, and Petal was separating the houses from the hotels from the game pieces. Whoever had last played the game had made a mess of things. She picked up the board, searching underneath for the players' pieces, most of which were missing. There were only the top hat and the flatiron.

"We'll have to improvise," Rollins said, and between them, he and Petal came up with a peppermint from the covered dish on the mantel shelf and a paper clip and a lithium battery scrounged from Brooks's pockets.

"Julie did say she was stopping here, first, at Lily's before dropping Nicholas off at Dad's?" Glover asked.

"Yes. You told me she said so," Brooks said. "Didn't you?"

"I thought you told me," Glover said.

Petal could only find one die and she was pretty sure you needed two for Monopoly. She hadn't played in a while. The directions were printed on the underside of the game box cover, but someone had written all over them, some long-ago child misbehaving with a black crayon: A-L-D-E-N; Petal made out the name in a sprawl of letters.

"Just one dice?" asked Rollins. "We'll roll it twice."

"Maybe we should go up and say hello to Aunt Ginger while we're here," Glover said.

"Will she still be awake?" Brooks asked. The mantel clock had just chimed ten round, golden tones, and as the last note faded, Petal and Ginevra said as one, "I love that clock."

"She's staying up especially tonight," Petal said.

"So Julie must have told Aunt Ginger she and Nicholas were dropping by the house," Brooks said.

"No, I think Ginger said Miss Lily told her," Petal recalled. "Although what Miss Lily said to me earlier was that it would be nice if Julie stopped by on the way back from the airport."

"Get Julie on her cell and tell her Ginger's sitting up waiting for her to come," Ginevra said to Glover.

"Good idea," Glover said. He snapped open his phone and wandered out onto the terrace to place the call. Returning, he reported, "I could only get her voice mail."

Petal had finished organizing all the property cards and she fanned them out in a wheel, compatible with the distribution of colors around the board, an arrangement which impressed Rollins with its neatness and utility.

"Okay, let's play," he said.

"What? Do we have to play?"

"Do we have to sit on the floor to play?"

"Yes. Yes."

"I'll be the battery."

"There's only one die? Well, what if we throw the one die once and double whatever it says. That would be less bother than throwing it twice."

"No, because in two-dice Monopoly if you roll doubles you get another turn and I like getting extra turns."

"Well, if you roll one six, then a second six, isn't that doubles?"

"I suppose so, but I like the click of dice."

"We'll provide sound effects."

"Oh, all right. Who goes first?"

"Me."

"Me."

"You have to roll for it."

They applied themselves to the game until Tommy came nosing into the big parlor. He snuffled at the board, sending the tokens skidding, and he stepped all over the bank, which did not matter; the bills were already so creased and bent they would not stack crisply; instead they sat atop one another like layers of a mille-feuille.

"Dad must be here," Glover remarked.

"Maybe Julie told Dad to meet her here," Brooks said.

"Was I on Indiana or Illinois Avenue?" asked Ginevra.

Rollins rolled a four and then he determined he had rolled a five after he retrieved the die which had spurted beneath the skirt of the picture frame table. Petal counted under her breath as he danced the top hat onto Park Place.

"Ah," she sighed. She had been hoping and hoping to land there with her paper clip. "Well, aren't you going to buy it?" she asked, feeling as let down as if she had been bettered in some real real estate deal.

"Purchase Park Place? Never, my dear," Rollins said. "Can I tell her?" he asked his brothers, who considered his request and nodded their permission.

"Tell me what?" asked Petal. She braced herself. She hoped she wasn't going to hear anything unpleasant about Park Place, not to mention Boardwalk.

"We have an old family secret for winning at Monopoly," Rollins said. "Mark this well; we only ever buy slum properties and railroads. That's the only way you can make money when somebody lands on you; that's all the rent and penalties anyone can ever afford to pay out, without throwing in the towel."

"Which is why I don't ever like to play with you guys," Brooks said. "Nobody in this family can play Monopoly with each other, and now you've gone and spilled the beans to Petal, not to mention Ginevra."

Petal was thinking. "But we can fix up the slums, right?" she asked. "We put in nice houses and nice hotels?"

"Sure. And plant a few trees," Glover suggested. "We can line Baltic Avenue with teeny little bonsai trees."

"And we can establish Enterprise Zones," Rollins said. He pictured tiny factories turning out tiny components.

"How about improving the schools, while you're at it?" Ginevra asked.

"Well, okay," Petal said. "I guess that's all right then, so long as you make everything as nice as Park Place."

"Who has the die?" Brooks asked. "Whose turn is it now? Has anyone even been paying attention to who goes next?"

They had to hunt for the die, which presently turned up; Glover had been sitting on it.

"COME BE BY ME," GINGER SAID, and Louis stretched out beside her on the bed atop the coverlet. He folded a pillow between the back of his head and the headboard. Ginger's hand moved out from beneath the blankets and sought his hand. Two armchairs had been carried into the bedroom, and Lily sat in one, Penny the other. They were knitting away at a pair of newly begun projects which did not yet depend from their plying needles in any recognizable form, but Lily's was going to be blue and Penny's persimmon. Betsy was propped on the windowsill reading a humorous piece in the *Smithsonian Magazine* about the sorts of silly things people collected, which Ginger had been passing around (as if the Smithsonian was in any position to tease anyone else about their acquisitiveness, she said). Andy remained within earshot in the upper hall where he was planing the threshold of the linen cupboard, which caught at the bottom of the door in damp weather. Lily, who could not remember this not happening, was thinking it would be quite an advantage to enjoy easier access to the towels on rainy days.

"Has she settled down?" Betsy asked her father. Sally had wanted Louis to read to her that evening from *The Cryin', the Itch and the Snoredrobe,* as Betsy had taken to referring to that summer's sacred text. She wanted to smack stupid little Edmund every time he threw his lot in with the White Witch and her minions.

"Yes. Yes," Louis said. Sally behaved herself when in his custody. Tonight her teeth had been thoroughly brushed; Ginger had been kissed with minty tenderness; Agnes, encountered by the blanket chest, emerged from that meeting unprovoked. If Sally had not said her prayers, as such, she had placed a double-fused green bean, before her bureau-top shrine and bowed to her clay and acorn-hatted Buddha above a tangle of fingers, vigorously petitioning him. Louis had tried to find out what was so important to her. Was the benefit within a grandfather's ability to bestow? Sally had considered telling him. Louis had known he was being estimated and he had known, as well, that she had concluded his powers would fall short and he would not be able to grant what she wanted, which must have been something beyond a doll or a bicycle or anything else she could have circled in a catalogue.

"Julie's hair looked very pretty when she came home from the salon," Ginger said. "But I thought her previous fire-engine red color suited her too."

"Nicholas must not have minded it," Penny remarked, "although he may have been attracted to her despite her spiky red hair."

"He saw through to her inner worth and beauty," Ginger supposed. She began to cough as she spoke that last word. Lily set aside her knitting and went over to hold a glass of water to her lips, administering sips.

"Oh, I am so excited about meeting Nicholas, I can hardly stand it," Penny stated. Harvey, however, had rebelled when she asked him to come with her down to Lily's to wait for Julie's young man to arrive. Harvey had groused that the fella had been keeping them waiting all summer and he was prepared to keep on waiting until tomorrow to see what he looked like, or the day after tomorrow, for that matter. The bloom was off, Harvey said.

Betsy set down the *Smithsonian* and told Ginger, "Very funny, Mummy." Ginger returned her smile and closed her eyes then. She had been watching Betsy, gauging her reactions as she read the article. She had hoped Betsy would take its lightly made point about the way people persisted in holding on to things better let go of.

Betsy remained at the window. Light spilled through the open French doors onto the terrace below, and she heard voices, if not words, coming from the big parlor. So, the others were down there, also waiting. Every exterior light had been switched on in a welcoming way, along the paths and at every door. She would be able to spot any car first, as it climbed up the driveway, its headlights flashing between the trees. A car was approaching at that moment, but it was too soon for Julie and Nicholas to have returned from the airport. That will be Uncle Alden, Betsy guessed, and presently she heard her uncle in the upstairs hallway asking Andy what he was working on (Andy had taken the door off the hinge and was standing in a little heap of wood shavings). They conferred; Alden said he had a better planer back at his house that Andy could use, but Andy thanked him and said he was getting on well enough with the means at his disposal.

Alden wandered into the bedroom and he sat down on the dressing table bench, his back turned to the mirror. He had nodded to everyone but not spoken, like someone entering church after the service had started. Tommy found them all, after a while. He hopped onto the end of the bed and curled up at Ginger's and Louis's feet. "Bad boy," said Penny and she shooed at him with her dangling piece of persimmon knitting, but Ginger said to let Tommy stay where he was; he'd keep her toes nice and warm.

"Petal has completed the alterations on Julie's dress," Lily told Alden. "Would you like to see how it turned out?"

"Well, I sure would," Penny answered for him. "After all the trouble that dress put us through before Julie finally found it," she complained, in a mild way.

Lily jammed her yarn and needles into their basket and she crossed the hall to Julie's room, where the dress ought to have been found hanging from the front of the armoire. Lily padded halfway down the stairs and leaned over the banister to inquire through the big parlor's open door, "Petal? Where is Julie's dress, please?"

"I'll get it for you," Petal called back. She had been steam pressing the seams at the kitchen ironing board, and the dress was swinging from the back of the pantry door.

"Oh my, yes, very nice," Penny said when Petal unzipped the garment from a protective plastic bag and presented it with a flourish. Smooth ivory white satin rippled and then resolved into a fitted bodice and a long and flowing skirt.

"Very pretty," said Alden, gaining a general impression of pale fabric and delicate lace.

"I can't wait for this wedding to come off. I simply can't wait to see Julie as a bride," Ginger declared, lifting her head. Petal carried the gown over and arranged it over a bedside chair.

"I know. Me too. I'm so excited," she said. "I mean, I don't understand how they can all keep saying Julie's not really going to get married this Saturday."

"What?" asked Betsy. She had started and almost slipped from the windowsill. She regained her balance and asked, very disapprovingly, "Who's saying that?"

"What?" asked Petal. She bit her two lips together. "I didn't mean to say anything. I didn't mean to say that. Just ignore me. It's just been a sort of running joke this summer, you know, about Julie and Nicholas Davenant."

"What sort of running joke?" asked Lily. "What has Nicholas done? What's gone wrong?" She had retrieved her knitting but now she set it down again.

"Nothing. He hasn't done anything, nothing at all," Petal said. "Which I guess is sort of the problem. Because we're not entirely convinced that Nicholas Davenant really exists. Like how nobody's ever seen him, or even a picture, and no one's talked to him because the phone always goes dead when anyone asks if they can say hello; plus, Julie hasn't said that much about him either, and oh, a lot of stuff. Like, who even goes to Siberia? Like, why is Julie acting like she doesn't even care about her own wedding? Like, how Brooks says—"

"Brooks says," Penny interrupted. "Since when does anyone go by anything Brooks says. Well, not unless it's about a computer. *That* you can take to the bank."

"And it's what Rollins and Glover and Ginevra are saying too," Petal said.

"Ginevra's in on this?" asked Betsy. "I can't believe Ginevra would play along." She stared out the window, onto the illuminated nighttime scene where green bled into black.

"Ginevra too," mused Ginger, and Louis shot her a look of concern, for her hand had tensed within his tender clasp.

"When I asked Julie whether Nicholas prefers tea or coffee so I could stock Alden's pantry accordingly, she said she didn't know," Lily spoke up. "Which puzzled me at the time." She remembered the incident and she remembered the unbidden doubt that had visited her, which she could not characterize at the time.

"Perhaps she felt you were fussing at her and she was just being ornery," Penny said. "I think all of this is just Julie being, you know, sort of reticent and private and delicate about her true feelings for the young man." Her eyes pricked a bit with tears, as she reflected how lovely love could be.

"Perhaps Nicholas likes both tea and coffee equally well and that was not the right question to ask in that regard," Louis said. "Since he has not demonstrated a preference, one way or the other, Julie could not immediately say. You asked her the wrong question, Lily."

"Or else she hadn't anticipated the question and already prepared an answer, so you caught her off guard," Andy said. He had left off his planing activities and was standing in the doorway, prodding a splinter lodged in his palm.

"You see," Petal said. "You can just go round and round on this. It's what we've been doing all summer."

"But why would Julie make up such a story?" Ginger wondered. "What would she have to gain? What is she trying to accomplish? Well, of course she must have wanted to lure Becky back home, but that didn't work out very well for her, did it, poor child."

"Maybe she was trying to cheer you up, Mummy," Betsy said. "Look at how she's made Nicholas Davenant everything you'd approve of, a dashing British scientist-explorer-adventurer. And look at how much you've enjoyed yourself over this, how you got to figure out the best Mixmaster for Julie to buy, and what china and silver and crystal and linen patterns she should have. Not to mention all the little things, like how you and she got to be rude, choosing inappropriate wedding hymns. Don't look so innocent, I heard the two of you in here, cracking up over the hymnal."

"I hope she didn't feel she had to do anything so drastic on my behalf," Ginger said. "I was happy just to have her here. I get such a kick out of Julie."

"But she had to have figured out that the day of reckoning would come," Betsy said. "She had to have realized that, and besides, Julie wouldn't want to disappoint you, Mummy, of all people. She couldn't be so cruel. Oh, I have no idea what's going on."

Lily began to bundle the dress back into the garment bag. She was not being as careful as she could have been and then she didn't seem to know what to do with the bag until Petal took it from her and left the room. Petal hesitated at the top of the stairs, having every wish to turn around and bolt to the attic, where she hoped no one would think to look for her, but above all she wanted to let Rollins know the worst of what she had just done. She believed he would understand that she had not meant to cause trouble.

"Unless Julie has some further plan," Ginger said. She had been thinking. "Perhaps if she can't produce Nicholas Davenant tonight, she'll just announce the wedding is to be postponed."

"But where is he then?" asked Penny. She looked ready to organize a search party until Louis shook his head at her.

"Detained in London with a broken leg? He's been hit by a bus and now he can't fly over here because he might throw a blood clot," Ginger suggested. "Yes, I can see how one could easily get away with something like this. I can do it off the top of my head."

"My dear," Louis said. Ginger was not supposed to become overwrought. She was not supposed to be awake at such a late hour. She was not supposed to be sitting upright in her bed turning a fascinating problem over and over in her mind, one which worried her, of course, but she relished the challenge.

"Then Julie will ask us all to give her a late-fall wedding," Ginger said. "We can have chrysanthemums and fallen leaves and muted tones in the big parlor. Maybe she means for all of us to stick around until October to learn how all of this is going to turn out. And then maybe we'll have to plan a Christmas wedding, when the October wedding fizzles. After which, it will be agreed, let's wait until spring, to try again."

"Stop it," said Alden. "My poor Julie." He thought back over the past weeks and realized that he had attempted to play no part in his daughter's story, which was the true pity; he could not begin to say whose claim was true and whose was not. He had not been paying attention.

"Well, we'll find out one way or another soon enough," Penny predicted, which was a sensible if quelling observation.

Lily retrieved her knitting. Alden sat and Tommy yawned and Ginger may even have dozed off for a spell, although she did not let go of Louis's hand. Betsy watched, with even more intensity, from her perch on the windowsill. Andy asked her if she wanted anything, and she shook her head, no. A burst of hilarity (it sounded like) issued through the big parlor French doors; Petal had been forgiven (most likely) for spilling the beans. Tommy must have been dreaming, for his paws twitched and his tail fluttered from time to time, lifting and falling, happy, not happy, and happy again.

It was nearly midnight when Betsy spoke up. "Here comes the car," she reported. "I can see headlights through the trees. It's slowing down. It's turned into the driveway. It's coming up the drive, up the drive. It's coming. I think she's going to park in front of the barn. Yes, that's what she's going to do. She's heading round that way." Betsy peered beyond the screen. A web of headlights crisscrossed the night to tell of the turning and angling and reversing car's progress. The lights blinked out. The car had stopped, must have stopped. Betsy raised the screen and leaned outside to look; a corner of the house stood between her and any clear sight line to the car. She leaned further forward. No, she could not catch even a glimpse. The car, the house, the corner, all contrived—as if by design, as if by chance, as if by mischief—to create a single blind spot. Betsy turned to her mother with a helpless shrug.

"Can you see them?" asked Ginger. She had raised herself on her elbows. "What do you see? Is he with her? Are they together? Tell me." She sat upright and pushed back the blanket as if she meant to get up. "Keep looking, Betsy. What do you see?" Ginger said. "Please tell me she isn't alone."

February 2001

Winds of Summer Fields
Recollect the way—
Instinct picking up the Key
Dropped by memory.

EMILY DICKINSON
from "After a Hundred Years"

BETSY SPOKE UP, UNNECESSARILY ADVISING that they were nearly there. Sally, forsaking her VeeCube's attractions to receive the passing scene, knew perfectly well where they were despite the masking of Towne's colors and contours beneath the mantle of winter. Indeed, she was not surprised that the sky had tarnished and the trees grown bare and the farm stand languished, closed and shuttered, in her absence. Everyone had been so sad saying their last good-byes on her final day here that she herself had forgotten how happy she was to be going home and at the very end she had had to be fetched from the attic to which she had retreated in some confusion, not really intending not to be found but choosing to buy herself just a little more time suspended between going and not going away as everyone called her name and tried to think where she could be. Had anyone stood back and glanced up at the house, they would have seen her face pressed against a dormer window watching the not very urgent search and the not very emphatic demonstrations of impatience to be on their way. Her father had taken a final stroll across the lawn, and her mother had not been able to make up her mind over the best way to load the car. They were leaving with far more than they had come with, but she was determined to make everything fit. Betsy had waved away Harvey's bungee cord, dangled before her, and offered to secure the trunk, which could not be latched even when Penny climbed aboard and sat there straining with all her weight.

Now Sally readied herself for their imminent return. She zipped her parka up to her chin and patted her pockets to make sure of her mittens so she could truthfully answer that she had a pair in her possession even if she failed to wear them. As, rather fussily, she resecured the ribbon that kept her hair from falling across her face, evening out the loops of the bow and tightening the knot, she began to feel that she was making a very nice present of herself and she leaped from the car as soon as Betsy came to a stop in front of the barn even though Betsy hadn't meant to park there directly beneath the glittering rank of icicles which had formed along the eaves, hanging down as long and as thick as tusks. Betsy carefully shifted into reverse (Sally had left the right rear door swinging open) as she wondered what made icicles stay locked in place. As a mother, it was the sort of thing she ought to know; she fielded so many questions about natural phenomena she had once taken on faith. That morning, just after they had left the hotel and were driving off through the narrow streets of bluff and chilly Amherst, Massachusetts, waiting for the rental car's engine to heat up and the vents to expel warmed air, Sally had wondered how such a fierce wind began to blow in the first place. Betsy had told her about the theory which posited that the random flutterings of a faraway butterfly's wings could stir the first faint breaths of an eventual hurricane's fury. Sally, slouched and shivering in the backseat, muttered something dark about butterflies and turned her attention to her VeeCube. She wished her mother had her father to talk to, if Betsy was so keen to go on and on about science and stuff, but they had left Andy behind at the hotel where they had spent the night, reviewing his lecture notes and lingering over coffee. He was there on academic business, and Betsy had said it only made sense for them all to fly east. She meant to spend a day or two visiting Lily while Andy was occupied, after which they would reconnect and head up to New Hampshire for a further few days of family skiing.

Lily, alert to the sound of the car, set aside her library book and waited for them by the front door. Sally bounded up the walk and greeted Lily, so confident of her welcome that Lily, whose anticipation of this particular visit had been tinged with some small measure of reluctance, forgot she had ever been worried. Sally, suddenly feeling hot (the mingled scents of a wood fire and spicy baking told of a blazing hearth and a heated oven elsewhere in the house), unzipped her parka, so lately zipped up. All this zippering; Sally heaved a sigh as she tossed her jacket toward the coat rack, where it was caught by a spindle, and she turned to survey the hallway to satisfy herself that nothing had been permitted to slip or creep out of place since she'd last been there; the same bright lane of carpet was anchored by the feet of the same stiff-backed bench. The same open-fronted desk was crammed with papers and envelopes and loose pens. Objects remembered as having been beautiful had remained beautiful: a bowl, a painting, a vase, another bowl, another painting, another vase, and a gilt-framed mirror which held a confirming vision of Sally herself restored to the changeless scene as she stood there with her hand touching the fluted edge of the small round table that supported the telephone, which would ring (and ring and ring) whenever they called Lily from Santa Barbara to tell her their news.

Agnes, crouching on a stair tread and staring out between the banisters, was noticed and exclaimed at then: "Oh, Agnes." Sally would have lunged lovingly at the cat but for the arrival of Betsy. A fleece-covered bundle filled her arms, and Sally bustled to her mother's side to be in on the excitement. She reached out, attempting to relieve her mother of the bundle, but Betsy checked Sally with a bump of her hip and told her to hush, which made no sense to Sally. She was not being loud; she was being grabby (she admitted to that).

"Well, here he is, Lily," Betsy said, jouncing the bundle with light emphasis.

"Jeffrey," Sally reminded Lily, in the event Lily had forgotten what she'd been told on the telephone a few months earlier about Jeffrey having been born. Sally herself was not entirely used to the idea of him; in all of her calculations, she was used to multiplying or dividing by three and she was thrown off by this fourth person requiring a place at the table and his share of attention.

They moved into the little parlor to sit by the fire, which had been lit with Jeffrey in mind. Lily was concerned about the draftiness of the house, where winter worked its way in through loose windows and unfortified walls, for he was a California baby used to a warmer and sunnier climate and he had yet to be hardened off against the frost. However, Betsy settled him on the rug and began to remove his outer wrappings without any fuss, and Sally flopped down beside them to interfere. She removed a booty, which she was told to restore to him as his foot twitched for it. Lily lowered herself to her knees and her hand hovered helpfully to relieve Betsy of a crocheted cap and a crocheted blanket and a crocheted pullover as they were pulled off. Andy's mother was a relentless crocheter of garments lacily inappropriate for a boy, and Lily tossed them aside without comment.

Sally leaned over Jeffrey, declaring, "He likes it when I make this face." She shriveled her forehead and bared her teeth at him. But Jeffrey only stared at her; he sputtered and began to hiccup. Lily plucked a tissue from her sleeve and swiped an upchucked trace of milky residue from his chin as Sally rolled her eyes and pursed her lips. Jeffrey could not always be counted on to perform as he was supposed to, and she turned to Lily to express her regret at this aspect of her little brother. He was quite stupid, she feared; nevertheless, he was also very cute. She wanted Lily to take to him, which, she acknowledged, was not always an easy thing to do. Lily observed that Jeffrey was very lucky to have such a helpful and understanding older sister, and Sally tried to think of some further way to continue to demonstrate these qualities, which she knew were admirable ones. Jeffrey enjoyed being read to; at any rate, the sound of her voice telling him a story would put him to sleep, and he was obviously fond of being asleep since he devoted so much time to that pursuit, and Sally too was happy when her little brother went down for the count, up in his room. She excused herself to go off in search of suitable reading material (anything with words on a page would do), but she returned immediately, having encountered Tommy hesitating by the little parlor door. He was pining to investigate the newcomers but made too nervous by the glowing orange eyes of a pair of owl andirons which flashed and danced with reflected firelight. He would have to ease past them before he could get to the people and had yet to work out how that could be accomplished.

Sally grabbed Tommy by his collar and hauled him into the little parlor and across the floor. He scrambled onto the sofa, where he pressed himself against the cushions as he submitted to Sally's lavished embraces, and Betsy and Lily moved to place themselves between Jeffrey and the dog should Tommy leap from the sofa to escape Sally's attentions and land upon the baby.

Betsy asked, "Is Uncle Alden here?" She wouldn't mind seeing Alden; she seldom heard from him these days, although she heard of him, what little there was to hear, through the usual channels.

"No," said Lily. "Tommy is staying with me while Alden is visiting Julie and Nicholas in London."

"Nicholas!" Sally exclaimed. She adored Julie's husband. She had danced with him at his wedding; she had danced carefully, narrowly observed by Julie, who'd been sidelined by a pebble in her shoe which had worked its way beneath her stockinged foot, so off had come her stockings in rather a tangle.

Nicholas had been very impressed with her, Sally could tell, because she knew that wolves, reindeer, sable, and nerpa abounded in Siberia. He said he had no idea what a nerpa was, and Sally had confessed neither did she; she only knew *that* they were, not *what* they were. Nicholas, and Sally in Nicholas's arms, had come to a full stop upon the dance-lawn as Ginevra kept on singing "Ten Minutes Ago," and everyone else continued to swirl all around them (or so Sally remembered them, as swirling). Nicholas told Sally he believed she had just said something actually rather deep.

"*Ek*-tually *rah*ther deep," Sally repeated now, those words pleasing her once again. She and Ginger had agreed they were both in heaven over Nicholas's accent and Nicholas had gone out of his way to sit by Ginger's side during the reception, enjoying her conversation as much as she enjoyed his own.

LATER, BETSY HAD AN ERRAND TO RUN. Lily said she was happy to look after Jeffrey; they would be equally content to sit by the fire in the rocking chair. Cam had received written permission to board the River Road route bus after school, and at half past three, Sally and Tommy were to walk down to the end of the driveway to meet her. It was hoped that the girls would pick up where they'd left off and be as friendly as before, if a bit less noisy. They would all have an early supper; Hannah had sent over a frozen salmon potpie, and Harvey and Penny were coming down from the Ridge House. Sally and Cam would set the dining room table when the time came, and Penny was going to bring popovers. Lily had made a batch of hermits for dessert.

These were the subject of the spicy baking aroma, and in fact, she had baked them twice, working on a notion that hermits would become Italian biscotti if she sliced the squat rectangles into slender spears and stuck them back into the oven for an additional half hour after the oven timer first pinged. If her idea worked, she was going to give Hannah the recipe.

So, briefed upon all that she could expect to occur in her absence and apprised of what she would find upon her return, Betsy left them. She had intended to pick up flowers on the way, those roses wrapped in cellophane or perhaps a vine wreath twisted round and round sprays of dried leaves and straw flowers and tough berries. But she'd been mulling over the conventions of cemetery decoration since she and the children had stopped by Emily Dickinson's grave the previous afternoon and she was no longer sure what she thought suitable. She pictured the left-behind roses and that leaning wreath being battered by the wind and weather, and she drove on, past the florist's shop.

Betsy was a conscientious traveler. She ascertained beforehand just what one ought to see in any given location and she hoped to instill that same habit early in Sally. Later on, Jeffrey would be told he'd been there too as an infant wayfarer who had toured the essential Amherst while still in his mother's arms or, more accurately stated, he had made the rounds while cinched within a Polartec sling and near-smothered against her breast, buttoned in beneath her coat. She believed it would be important in the years to come for her children to feel at home wherever they found themselves in the world or whenever the world arrived on their doorsteps, seeking them out.

The walk from the inn had taken longer than Betsy had thought, and halfway there they might have turned back had she known they'd only gone halfway. But the visitors' map was not drawn to scale, and at the end she had had to ask a passerby for directions to steer them what proved to be the last few hundred feet to the entrance of the burial ground. The famous grave was indicated, and hard by the perimeter of the ornate iron fencing that contained a rather cramped company of dead Dickinsons, the poet's tall stone slab bore a line of small pebbles along its flat top. Sally had hoisted herself onto the fretwork of the fence and strained to reach over the palings in an attempt to tidy up for the poor dead lady who had written such nice poetry (they'd read a few of the tamer ones aloud, prior to the outing), but Betsy prevented her, explaining that in some cultures and traditions small stones were placed upon graves as a sign of respect and remembrance and they must not be disturbed. Although, on that score, Betsy wasn't really sure. There had to be someone who tended such a well-attended burial spot (for various paths worn through the snow wandered past the other resting places and converged from every direction upon this very spot). Perhaps, at the end of the day or the end of a week, a sanctioned caretaker swept off and scattered the same small stones, which would be picked up and replaced again and again by pilgrims; otherwise, there would be a mound of them. Betsy had to wonder, as well, whether the occasional goblet of plum wine or slab of black cake wasn't left outside the fence, or a feather or some other trinket or even a private verse written on a page that had been folded and creased into a hard little pellet, with the poem crouched inside like the flower within a seed.

Sally had fruitlessly searched the wintry ground for a stone of her own to leave in remembrance. She was a dedicated little ecumenist; she still maintained her Buddha Shrine, but lately she had also taken up a mild form of Bahaism, which Betsy and Andy were encouraging on the strength of the faith's teaching that one must be kind to one's brother(s). In the end, Betsy had suggested that Sally make a snowball to place atop the gravestone, which would be a graceful offering from the hand of a child. The snowball would melt away on its own, in due course, for a warming trend was forecast to arrive by the end of the week.

Betsy was driving downtown now, passing Peddocks', and she almost stopped there to pick up a *Vogue* and a cappuccino. She came to the green and she glanced at Alden's house as she drove past. Lily had told her he'd made some improvements inside which were not evident on the exterior. Something was going on midweek at the Unitarian Church; there were cars parked in front and the lights were on. Betsy turned onto Bridge Street and rumbled over the bridge and then took the sharp left, through the cemetery gate. She followed a narrow lane sunk deep between steep, plowed banks. Valentine's Day had fallen the week before, and she noted the presence of more than a few red heart balloons tethered to graves, some still floating fully buoyant and others lying crumpled in the snow. They seemed inadequate tokens but were no doubt deeply meant, and she told herself she was no one to judge, having arrived here empty-handed.

The Hill family plot took up the flank of a small rise and there was a further pinnacle of earthen-topped vault entered through a barred iron door that would not easily be opened again because an ash tree had been allowed to grow up in front. Betsy had never spent much time here wandering among the family graves, and winter was not the best time to begin doing so. Snow slopped into the tops of her boots as she climbed up and over an embankment and snow obscured half of the writing on half of the stones. Nevertheless, Betsy saw enough names that she knew and other names which failed to ring a bell; there are those who are renowned within a family, while others remain minor characters for the duration of their own stories, and beyond. It did not occur to Betsy to worry where she would fall in the hierarchy, should she ever end up here, as she thought she might. She understood there was room for her and Andy, or probably would be, unless a bomb dropped on a family reunion, as Harvey had pointed out, or if Lily served them all poison string beans for supper one night.

She and Andy had had to turn around and fly back to Towne for Ginger's funeral only a week after they arrived home in Santa Barbara. (Sally had been left behind with friends, the vehemence of her protest at not being allowed to go with her parents betraying what would have been the passion of her presence had she been permitted to come.) Thus, Betsy had not yet seen the marker which had been carved and set in place later, and at first she looked for it within the wrong fold of the hillside, which disturbed her, to be so wrong about something like that. Adjusting her gaze, she saw what she'd been seeking and she approached, dragging her steps through the snow.

There, she ran an ungloved finger across the incised letters of her mother's name. The lines and angles felt sharp and recent, which was, Betsy decided, reassuring. There was no sense now in translating Ginger into someone whom she had never been. Betsy let her palm settle for a moment upon the strong and polished stone and when she let go she saw that the warmth of her hand had left behind a foggy imprint, which seemed, at once, to be the salute of a loving ghost and the tribute of a living daughter. This shadow failed to fade until some minutes after Betsy turned away and headed back home to Lily.

MERRICK LIBRARY
DISCARD